The Wrecker

Clive Cussler is the author or co-author of a great number of bestselling novels, including the famous Dirk Pitt® adventures, such as *Arctic Drift*; the NUMA® Files adventures, most recently *Medusa*; the *Oregon* Files, such as *Corsair*; and his historical adventures, which began with *The Chase*. He lives in Arizona.

www.clivecussler.co.uk

Justin Scott is the author of twenty-three thrillers and mystery novels, written under his own name and the pen names Paul Garrison, J. S. Blazer and Alexander Cole. He has twice been nominated for the Edgar Allan Poe Awards given by the Mystery Writers of America. He lives in Connecticut.

The Wrecker

CLIVE CUSSLER
and JUSTIN SCOTT

MICHAEL JOSEPH
an imprint of
PENGUIN BOOKS

MICHAEL JOSEPH

Published by the Penguin Group
Penguin Books Ltd, 80 Strand, London WC2R 0RL, England
Penguin Group (USA) Inc., 375 Hudson Street, New York, New York 10014, USA
Penguin Group (Canada), 90 Eglinton Avenue East, Suite 700, Toronto, Ontario, Canada M4P 2Y3
(a division of Pearson Penguin Canada Inc.)
Penguin Ireland, 25 St Stephen's Green, Dublin 2, Ireland (a division of Penguin Books Ltd)
Penguin Group (Australia), 250 Camberwell Road,
Camberwell, Victoria 3124, Australia (a division of Pearson Australia Group Pty Ltd)
Penguin Books India Pvt Ltd, 11 Community Centre,
Panchsheel Park, New Delhi – 110 017, India
Penguin Group (NZ), 67 Apollo Drive, Rosedale, North Shore 0632, New Zealand
(a division of Pearson New Zealand Ltd)
Penguin Books (South Africa) (Pty) Ltd, 24 Sturdee Avenue,
Rosebank, Johannesburg 2196, South Africa

Penguin Books Ltd, Registered Offices: 80 Strand, London WC2R 0RL, England

www.penguin.com

First published in the United States of America by G. P. Putnam's Sons 2009
First published in Great Britain by Michael Joseph 2009

1

Copyright © Sandecker, RLLLP, 2009

Illustrations by Richard Dahlquist

The moral right of the authors has been asserted

Printed in Great Britain by Clays Ltd, St Ives plc

A CIP catalogue record for this book is available from the British Library

HARDBACK ISBN: 978–0–718–15464–6
TRADE PAPERBACK ISBN: 978–0–718–15468–4

www.greenpenguin.co.uk

UNFINISHED BUSINESS

Through the Blizzard

ABOVE THE SNOW LINE, THE GERMAN ALPS TORE AT THE SKY like the jaws of an ancient flesh eater. Storm clouds grazed the windswept peaks, and the jagged rock appeared to move, as if the beast were awakening. Two men, neither young, both strong, watched from the balcony of a ski hotel with quickening anticipation.

Hans Grandzau was a guide whose weathered face was as craggy as the mountaintops. He carried in his head sixty years of traversing the wintery slopes. Last night, he had promised that the wind would shift east. Bitter Siberian cold would whirl wet air from the Mediterranean into blinding snow.

The man to whom Hans had promised snow was a tall American whose blond hair and mustache were edged with silver. He wore a tweed Norfolk suit, a warm fedora on his head, and a Yale University scarf adorned with the shield of Branford College. His dress was typical of a well-to-do tourist who had come to the Alps for winter sport. But his eyes were fastened with a glacial-blue intensity on an isolated stone castle ten miles across the rugged valley.

The castle had dominated its remote glen for a thousand years. It was nearly buried by the winter snows and mostly hidden by the shadow of the peaks that soared above it. Miles below the castle, too long and steep a climb to be undertaken lightly, was a village. The American watched a pillar of smoke creep toward it. He was too far away to see the locomotive venting it, but he knew that it marked the route of the railroad that crossed the border to Innsbruck. Full circle, he thought grimly. Twenty-seven years ago, the crime had started by a railroad in the mountains. Tonight it would end, one way or another, by a railroad in the mountains.

"Are you sure you are up to this?" asked the guide. "The ascents are steep. The wind will cut like a saber."

"I'm fit as you are, old man."

To assure Hans, he explained that he had prepared by bivouacking for a month with Norwegian ski troops, having arranged informal attachment to a United States Army unit dispatched to hone the skills of mountain warfare.

"I was not aware that American troops exercise in Norway," the German said stiffly.

The American's blue eyes turned slightly violet with the hint of a smile. "Just in case we have to come back over here to straighten out another war."

Hans returned an opaque grin. The American knew he was a proud veteran of the Alpenkorps, Germany's elite mountain division formed by Kaiser Wilhelm in the 1914–1918 World War. But he was no friend of the Nazis, who had recently seized control of the German government and threatened to plunge Europe into another war.

The American looked around to be sure they were alone. An elderly chambermaid in a black dress and white apron was rolling a carpet sweeper down the hall behind the balcony doors. He waited until she had moved away, then palmed a leather pouch of Swiss twenty-franc gold coins in his big hand and slipped it to the guide.

"Full payment in advance. The deal is, if I can't keep up, leave me and take yourself home. You get the skis. I'll meet you at the rope tow."

He hurried to his luxurious wood-paneled room, where deep carpets and a crackling fire made the scene beyond the window look even colder. Quickly, he changed into water-repellent gabardine trousers, which he tucked into thick wool socks, laced boots, two light wool sweaters, a windproof leather vest, and a hip-length gabardine jacket, which he left unzipped.

Jeffrey Dennis knocked and entered. He was a smooth young operative from the Berlin office, wearing the Tyrolean hat that tourists bought. Jeffrey was bright, eager, and organized. But he was no outdoorsman.

"Still no snow?"

"Give everyone the go-ahead," the older man told him. "In one hour, you won't see your hand in front of your face."

Dennis handed him a small knapsack. "Papers for you and your, uh, 'luggage.' The train will cross into Austria at midnight. You'll be met at Innsbruck. This passport should be good until tomorrow."

The older man looked out the window at the distant castle. "My wife?"

"Safe in Paris. At the George V."

"What message?"

The young man offered an envelope.

"Read it."

Dennis read in a monotone, " 'Thank you, my darling, for the best twenty-fifth anniversary imaginable.' "

The older man relaxed visibly. That was the code she had chosen with a wink the day before yesterday. She had provided cover, a romantic second honeymoon, in case anyone recognized him and asked whether he was here on business. Now she was safely away. The time for cover was over. The storm was building. He took the envelope and held it to the flames in the fireplace. He inspected the passport, visas, and border permits carefully.

"Sidearm?"

It was compact and light. Dennis said, "It's the new automatic the German cops carry undercover. But I can get you a service revolver if you would be more comfortable with an older gun."

The blue eyes, which had swept again to the castle across the bleak valley, pivoted back at the younger man. Without looking down at his hands, the tall American removed the magazine, checked that the chamber was empty, and proceeded to fieldstrip the Walther PPK by opening the trigger guard and removing the slide and return spring from the barrel. That took twelve seconds. Still looking the courier in the face, he reassembled the pistol in ten.

"This should do the job."

It began to sink into the younger man that he was in the presence of greatness. Before he could stop himself, he asked a boy's question. "How long do you have to practice to do that?"

A surprisingly warm smile creased the stern face, and he said, neither unkindly nor without humor, "Practice at night, Jeff, in the rain, when someone's shooting at you, and you'll pick it up quick enough."

SNOW WAS PELTING HARD when he got to the rope tow, and he could barely see the ridgeline that marked the top of the ski slope. The stony peaks that reared above it were invisible. The other skiers were excited, jostling to grab the moving rope for one more run before the impending storm forced the guides to close the mountain for safety's sake. Hans had brought new skis, the latest design, with steel edges riveted to the wood. "Wind is growing," he said, explaining the edges. "Ice on the tops."

They stepped into their flexible bindings, clamping them around their heels, put on their gloves and picked up their poles, and worked their way through the dwindling crowd to the rope, which was passing around a drum turned by a noisy tractor engine. They grabbed hold of the rope. It jerked their arms, and up the two men glided, providing a typical sight in the posh resort, a wealthy American seeking adventure in late middle age and his private instructor, old enough and wise enough to return him safely to the hotel in time to dress for dinner.

The wind was strong atop the ridge, and shifty. Gusts swirled the snow thick and thin. One moment, there was little to see beyond a clutch of skiers waiting their turns to start down the slope. The next moment, the view opened to reveal the hotel, small as a dollhouse at the bottom of the slope, the high peaks soaring above it. The American and Hans poled along the ridge away from the crowd. And suddenly, when no one saw them, they wheeled off the ridge and plunged down its back side.

Their skis carved fresh tracks through unmarked powder.

Instantly, the calls of the skiers and the drone of the rope-tow engine ceased. The snow fell silently on wool clothing. It was so quiet that they could hear the hiss of the metal-edged wood cutting the powdery surface, their own breath, and their heartbeats. Hans led the way down the slope for a mile, and they swept into a shelter formed by an outcropping of rock. From within it, he pulled out a lightweight improvised sled.

It had been fashioned out of a Robertson stretcher, a litter made of ash and beech and canvas designed to wrap tightly around a wounded sailor to immobilize him so he could be carried through a ship's steep and narrow companionways. The stretcher was lashed to a pair of skis, and Hans pulled it with a rope tied around his waist. That rope was twined around a long ski pole he used as a brake on descent. He led the way another mile across a shallower slope. At the foot of a steep rise, they attached sealskins to their skis. The nap of the fur facing backward gave them traction to climb.

The snow came on thick now. Here was where Hans earned his gold francs. The American could follow a compass as well as the next man. But no compass could guarantee he wouldn't drift off course, pummeled by the wind, disoriented by a crazy hodgepodge of steep angles. But Hans Grandzau, who had skied these mountains since he was a boy, could pinpoint his location by the slant of a particular slope and how that slant shaped the bite of the wind.

They climbed for miles and skied downhill again, and climbed again. Often, they had to stop to rest or clear the sealskins of ice. It was nearly dark when the snow parted suddenly at the top of a ridge. Across one last valley, the American saw a single lighted window in the castle. "Give me the sled," he said. "I'll take it from here."

The German guide heard the steel in his voice. There was no arguing. Hans passed him the sled rope, shook his hand, wished him luck, and cut a curving track into the dark, heading for the village somewhere far below.

The American headed for the light.

THE PROLETARIAT'S ARTILLERY

Gray Wolf Chasing the Train

THE RAILROAD DICK WATCHING THE NIGHT SHIFT TROOP INTO the jagged mouth of the tunnel wondered how much work the Southern Pacific Company would get out of a one-eyed, hard-rock miner limping on a stiff leg. His bib overalls and flannel shirt were threadbare, his boots worn thin as paper. The brim of his battered felt slouch hat drooped low as a circus clown's, and the poor jigger's steel hammer trailed from his glove as if it was too heavy to lift. Something was fishy.

The rail cop was a drinking man, his face so bloated by rotgut that his eyes appeared lost in his cheeks. But they were sharp eyes, miraculously alive with hope and laughter—considering that he had fallen so low he was working for the most despised police force in the country—and still alert. He stepped forward, on the verge of investigating. But just then a powerful young fellow, a fresh-faced galoot straight off the farm, took the old miner's hammer and carried it for him. That act of kindness conspired with the limp and the eye patch to make the first man appear much older than he was, and harmless. Which he was not.

Ahead were two holes in the side of the mountain, the main rail tunnel and, nearby, a smaller "pioneer" tunnel "holed through" first to explore the route, draw fresh air, and drain water. Both were rimmed with timberwork rock sheds to keep the mountainside from falling down on the men and dump cars trundling in and out.

The day shift was staggering out, exhausted men heading for the work train that would take them back to the cookhouse in the camp. A locomotive puffed alongside, hauling cars heaped with crossties. There were freight wagons drawn by ten-mule teams, handcars scuttling along light track, and clouds and clouds of dust. The site was remote, two days of rough, roundabout train travel from San Francisco. But it was not isolated.

Telegraph lines advancing on rickety poles connected Wall Street to the very mouth of the tunnel. They carried grim reports of the financial panic shaking New York three thousand miles away. Eastern bankers, the railroad's paymasters, were frightened. The old man knew that the wires crackled with conflicting demands. Speed up construction of the Cascades Cutoff, a vital express line between San Francisco and the north. Or shut it down.

Just outside the tunnel mouth, the old man stopped to look up at the mountain with his good eye. The ramparts of the Cascade Range glowed red in the setting sun. He gazed at them as if he wanted to remember what the world looked like before the dark tunnel swallowed him deep into the stone. Jostled by the men behind, he rubbed his eye patch, as if uneasily recalling the moment of searing loss. His touch opened a pinhole for his second eye, which was even sharper than the first. The railway detective, who looked a cut above the ordinary slow-witted cinder dick, was still watching him mistrustfully.

The miner was a man with immense reserves of cold nerve. He had the guts to stand his ground, the bloodless effrontery to throw off suspicion by acting unafraid. Ignoring the workmen shoving past him, he peered about as if suddenly spellbound by the rousing spectacle of a new railroad pushing through the mountains.

He did, in fact, marvel at the endeavor. The entire enterprise, which synchronized the labor of thousands, rested on a simple structure at his feet. Two steel rails were spiked four feet eight and a half inches apart to wooden crossties. The ties were firmly fixed in a bed of crushed-stone ballast. The combination formed a strong cradle that could support hundred-ton locomotives thundering along at a mile a minute. Repeated every mile—twenty-seven hundred ties, three hundred fifty-two lengths of rail, sixty kegs of spikes—it made a smooth, near-frictionless road, a steel highway that could run forever. The rails soared over the rugged land, clinging to narrow cuts etched into the sheer sides of near-vertical slopes, jumping ravines on bristling trestles, tunneling in and out of cliffs.

But this miracle of modern engineering and painstaking management was still dwarfed, even mocked, by the mountains. And no one knew better than he how fragile it all was.

He glanced at the cop, who had turned his attention elsewhere.

The night-shift crew vanished into the rough-hewn bore. Water gurgled at their feet as they tramped through endless archways of timber shoring. The limping man held back, accompanied by the big fellow carrying his hammer. They stopped at a side tunnel a hundred yards in and doused their acetylene lamps. Alone in the dark, they watched the others' lamps flicker away into the distance. Then they felt their own way through the side tunnel, through twenty feet of stone, into the parallel pioneer tunnel. It was narrow, cut rougher than the main bore, the ceiling dropping low here and there. They crouched and pressed ahead, deeper into the mountain, relighting their lamps once no one could see.

The old man limped more quickly now, playing his light on the side wall. Suddenly, he stopped and passed his hand over a jagged seam in the stone. The young man watched him and wondered, not for the first time, what kept him fighting for the cause when most men as crippled as he would spend their time in a rocking chair. But a man could get hurt asking too many questions in the hobo jungles, so he kept his wonderings to himself.

"Drill here."

The old man revealed only enough to inspire the confidence of the volunteers he recruited. The farm boy carrying the hammer thought he was helping a shingle weaver down from Puget Sound, where the union had called a general strike that completely tied up the cedar-shingle industry until the bloodsucking manufacturers beat them with scab labor. Just the answer a budding anarchist longed to hear.

His previous recruit had believed he was from Idaho, on the run from the Coeur d'Alene mine wars. To the next he would have fought the good fight organizing for the Wobblies in Chicago. How had he lost an eye? Same place he got the limp, slugging it out with strikebreakers in Colorado City, or bodyguarding for "Big Bill" Haywood of the Western Federation of Miners, or shot when the Governor called up the National Guard. Gilt-edged credentials to those who hungered to make a better world and had the guts to fight for it.

The big fellow produced a three-foot steel chisel and held it in place while the man with the eye patch tapped it until the point was firmly seated in the granite. Then he handed the hammer back.

"Here you go, Kevin. Quickly, now."

"Are you certain smashing this tunnel won't hurt the boys working the main bore?"

"I'd stake my life on it. There are twenty feet of solid granite between us."

Kevin's was a common story in the West. Born to be a farmer before his family lost their land to the bank, he had toiled in the silver mines, until he got fired for speaking up in favor of the union. Riding around the country on freight trains looking for work, he had been beaten by railway police. Rallying for higher wages, he'd been attacked by strikebreakers with ax handles. There were days his

head hurt so bad he couldn't think straight. Worst were the nights
he despaired of ever finding a steady job, or even a regular place to
sleep, much less meeting a girl and raising a family. On one of those
nights, he had been seduced by the anarchists' dream.

Dynamite, "the proletariat's artillery," would make a better world.

Kevin swung the heavy sledge with both hands. He pounded the
chisel a foot in. He stopped to catch his breath and complained about
the tool. "I can't abide these steel hammers. They bounce too much.
Give me old-fashioned cast iron."

"Use the bounce." Surprisingly lithe, the cripple with the eye
patch took the hammer and swung it easily, using his powerful wrists
to whip the steel up on the bounce, flick it back in a one fluid motion,
and bring it hard down on the chisel again. "Make it work for you.
Here, you finish . . . Good. Very good."

They chiseled a hole three feet into the stone.

"Dynamite," said the old man, who had let Kevin carry everything incriminating in case the railway police searched them. Kevin
removed three dull-red sticks from under his shirt. Printed on each in
black ink was the manufacturer's brand, VULCAN. The cripple stuffed
them one after another into the hole.

"Detonator."

"You absolutely certain it won't hurt any workingmen?"

"Guaranteed."

"I guess I wouldn't mind blowing the bosses to hell, but those
men in there, they're on our side."

"Even if they don't know it yet," the old cripple said cynically. He
attached the detonator, which would explode forcefully enough to
make the dynamite itself blow.

"Fuse."

Kevin carefully uncoiled the slow fuse he had hidden in his hat.
A yard of the hemp yarn impregnated with pulverized gunpowder
would burn in ninety seconds—a foot in half a minute. To gain five

minutes to retreat to a safe place, the old man laid eleven feet of fuse. The extra foot was to take into account variations in consistency and dampness.

"Would you like to fire the blast?" he asked casually.

Kevin's eyes were burning like a little boy's on Christmas morning. "Could I?"

"I'll check the coast is clear. Just remember, you've only got five minutes to get out. Don't dawdle. Light it and go—*Wait!* What's that?" Pretending that he had heard someone coming, he whipped around and half drew a blade from his boot.

Kevin fell for the ruse. He cupped his hand to his ear. But all he heard was the distant rumble of the drills in the main bore and the whine of the blowers pulling foul air out of the pioneer tunnel and drawing in fresh. "What? What did you hear?"

"Run down there! See who's coming."

Kevin ran, shadows leaping as his light bounced on the rough walls.

The old man ripped the gunpowder fuse from the detonator and threw it into the darkness. He replaced it with an identical-looking string of hemp yarn soaked in melted trinitrotoluene, which was used to detonate multiple charges simultaneously because it burned so fast.

He was quick and dexterous. By the time he heard Kevin returning from his fool's errand, the treachery was done. But when he looked up, he was stunned to see Kevin holding both hands in the air. Behind him was the railroad dick, the cop who had watched him enter the tunnel. Suspicion had transformed his whiskey-sodden face into a mask of cold vigilance. He was pointing a revolver in a rock-steady grip.

"Elevate!" he commanded. "Hands up!"

Swift eyes took in the fuse and detonator and understood at once.

He tucked his weapon close to his body, clearly a fighting man who knew how to use it.

The old man moved very slowly. But instead of obeying the order to raise his hands, he reached down to his boot and drew his long knife.

The cinder dick smiled. His voice had a musical lilt, and he spoke his words with the self-taught reader's love of the English language.

"Beware, old man. Even though you have brought, in error, a knife to a gunfight, I will be obliged to shoot you dead if it does not fall from your hand in a heartbeat."

The old man flicked his wrist. His knife telescoped open, tripling its length into a rapier-thin sword. Already lunging with fluid grace, he buried the blade in the cop's throat. The cop reached one hand to his throat and tried to aim his gun. The old man thrust deeper, twisting his blade, severing the man's spinal cord as he drove the sword completely through his neck and out the back. The revolver clattered on the tunnel floor. And as the old man withdrew his sword, the cop unfolded onto the stone beside his fallen gun.

Kevin made a gurgling noise in his own throat. His eyes were round with shock and fear, darting from the dead man to the sword that had appeared from nowhere and then back to the dead man. "How—what?"

He touched the spring release and the sword retracted into the blade, which he returned to his boot. "Same principle as the theatrical prop," he explained. "Slightly modified. Got your matches?"

Kevin plunged trembling hands into his pockets, fished blindly, and finally pulled out a padded bottle.

"I'll check the tunnel mouth is clear," the old man told him. "Wait for my signal. Remember, five minutes. Make damned sure it's lit, burning proper, then run like hell! Five minutes."

Five minutes to retreat to a safe place. But not if fast-burning trinitrotoluene, which would leap ten feet in the blink of an eye, had been substituted for slow-burning, pulverized gunpowder.

The old man stepped over the cop's body and hurried to the mouth of the pioneer tunnel. When he saw no one nearby, he tapped loudly with the chisel, two times. Three taps echoed back. The coast was clear.

The old man took out an official Waltham railroad watch, which no hard-rock miner could afford. Every conductor, dispatcher, and locomotive engineer was required by law to carry the seventeen-jewel, lever-set pocket timepiece. It was guaranteed to be accurate within half a minute per week, whether jouncing along in a hot locomotive cab or freezing on the snow-swept platform of a train-order station atop the High Sierra. The white face with Arabic numerals was just visible in the dusk. He watched the interior dial hand sweep seconds instead of the minutes Kevin believed that the slow-burning pulverized gunpowder gave him to hightail it to safety.

Five *seconds* for Kevin to uncork his sulfur matches, remove one, recork the padded bottle, kneel beside the fuse. Three *seconds* for nervous fingers to scrape a sulfur match on the steel sledge. One *second* while it flared full and bright. Touch the flame to the trinitrotoluene fuse.

A puff of air, almost gentle, fanned the old man's face.

Then a burst of wind rushed from the portal, propelled by the hollow thud of the dynamite exploding deep in the rock. An ominous rumble and another burst of wind signaled that the pioneer tunnel had caved in.

The main bore was next.

He hid among the timbers shoring the portal and waited. It was true that there was twenty feet of granite between the pioneer bore and the men digging the main tunnel. But at the point he had set the dynamite, the mountain was far from solid, being riddled with seams of fractured stone.

The ground shook, rolling like an earthquake.

The old man allowed himself a grim smile. That tremor beneath his boots told him more than the frightened yells of the terrorized hard-rock miners and powder men who came pouring out of the main tunnel. More than the frenzied shouts of those converging on the smoke-belching tunnels to see what had happened.

Hundreds of feet under the mountain, the tunnel's ceiling had collapsed. He had timed it to bury the dump train, crushing twenty cars, the locomotive, and its tender. It did not trouble him that men would be crushed, too. They were as unimportant as the railway cop he had just murdered. Nor did he feel sympathy for the injured men trapped in the darkness behind a wall of broken stone. The greater the death, destruction, and confusion, the slower the cleanup, the longer the delay.

He whipped off his eye patch, shoved it in his pocket. Then he removed his drooping slouch hat, folded the brims inside out, and shoved it back on his head in the shape of a miner's flat cap. Quickly untying the scarf under his trousers that immobilized his knee to make him limp, he strode out of the dark on two strong legs, slipped into the scramble of frightened men, and ran with them, stumbling as they did on the crossties, tripping on the rails, fighting to get away. Eventually, the fleeing men slowed, turned by scores of the curious running toward the disaster.

The man notorious as the Wrecker kept going, dropping to the ditch beside the tracks, easily eluding rescue crews and railway police on a well-rehearsed escape route. He skirted a siding where a privately owned special passenger train stretched behind a gleaming black locomotive. The behemoth hissed softly, keeping steam up for electricity and heat. Rows of curtained windows glowed golden in the night. Music drifted on the cold air, and he could see liveried servants setting a table for dinner. Trudging past it to the tunnel bore earlier, young Kevin had railed against the "favored few" who traveled in splendor while hard-rock miners were paid two dollars a day.

The Wrecker smiled. It was the railroad president's personal train. All hell was about to break loose inside the luxurious cars when he learned that the mountain had fallen into his tunnel, and it was a safe bet Kevin's "favored few" would not feel quite so favored tonight.

A mile down the newly laid track, harsh electric light marked the sprawling construction yard of workmen's bunkhouses, materials stores, machine shops, dynamo, scores of sidings thick with materials trains, and a roundhouse for turning and repairing their locomotives. Below that staging area, deep in a hollow, could be seen the oil lamps of an end-of-the-tracks camp, a temporary city of tents and abandoned freight cars housing the makeshift dance halls, saloons, and brothels that followed the ever-moving construction yard.

It would be moving a lot more slowly now.

To clear the rockfall from the tunnel would take days. A week at least to shore the weakened rock and repair the damage before work could resume. He had sabotaged the railroad quite thoroughly this time, his best effort yet. And if they managed to identify what was left of Kevin, the only witness who could connect him to the crime, the young man would prove to be an angry hothead heard spouting radical talk in the hobo jungle before he accidentally blew himself to kingdom come.

By 1907, THE "SPECIAL" TRAIN WAS AN EMBLEM OF WEALTH AND power in America like none other. Ordinary millionaires with a cottage in Newport and a town house on Park Avenue or an estate on the Hudson River shuttled between their palatial abodes in private railcars attached to passenger trains. But the titans—the men who owned the railroads—traveled in their specials, private trains with their own locomotives, able to steam anywhere on the continent at their owners' whim. The fastest and most luxurious special in the United States belonged to the president of the Southern Pacific Railroad, Osgood Hennessy.

Hennessy's train was painted a glossy vermilion red, and hauled by a powerful Baldwin Pacific 4-6-2 locomotive black as the coal in its tender. His private cars, named *Nancy No. 1* and *Nancy No. 2* for his long-dead wife, measured eighty feet long by ten feet wide. They had been built of steel, to his specifications, by the Pullman Company and outfitted by European cabinetmakers.

Nancy No. 1 contained Hennessy's office, parlor, and state rooms, including marble tubs, brass beds, and a telephone that could be connected to the telephone system of any city he rolled into. *Nancy No. 2* carried a modern kitchen, storerooms that could hold a month's provisions, a dining room, and servants' quarters. The baggage car had room reserved for his daughter Lillian's Packard Gray Wolf automobile. A dining car and luxurious Pullman sleepers accommodated the engineers, bankers, and lawyers engaged in building the Cascades Cutoff.

Once on the main line, Hennessy's special could rocket him to San Francisco in half a day, Chicago in three, and New York in four, switching engine types to maximize road conditions. When that wasn't fast enough to serve his lifelong ambition to control every railroad in the country, his special employed "grasshopper telegraphy," an electromagnetic induction system patented by Thomas Edison that jumped telegraphic messages between the speeding train and the telegraph wires running parallel to the tracks.

Hennessy himself was a wisp of an old man, short, bald, and deceptively frail looking. He had a ferret's alert black eyes, a cold gaze that discouraged lying and extinguished false hope, and the heart, his fleeced rivals swore, of a hungry Gila monster. Hours after the tunnel collapse, he was still in shirtsleeves, dictating a mile a minute to a telegrapher, when the first of his dinner guests was ushered in.

The smooth and polished United States senator Charles Kincaid arrived impeccably dressed in evening clothes. He was tall and strikingly handsome. His hair was slick, his mustache trim. No hint of whatever he was thinking—or if he was thinking at all—escaped from his brown eyes. But his sugary smile was at the ready.

Hennessy greeted the politician with barely veiled contempt.

"In case you haven't heard, Kincaid, there's been another accident. And, by God, this one is sabotage."

"Good Lord! Are you sure?"

"So damned sure, I've wired the Van Dorn Detective Agency."

"Excellent choice, sir! Sabotage will be beyond the local sheriffs, if I may say so, even if you could find one up here in the middle of nowhere. Even a bit much for your railway police." Thugs in dirty uniforms, Kincaid could have added, but the senator was a servant of the railroad and careful how he spoke to the man who had made him and could as easily break him. "What's the Van Dorn motto?" he asked ingratiatingly. "'We never give up, never!' Sir, as I am qualified, I feel it's my duty to direct your crews in clearing the tunnel."

Hennessy's face wrinkled with disdain. The popinjay had worked overseas building bridges for the Ottoman Empire's Baghdad Railway until the newspapers started calling him the "Hero Engineer" for supposedly rescuing American Red Cross nurses and missionaries from Turkish capture. Hennessy took the reported heroics with many grains of salt. But Kincaid had somehow parlayed bogus fame into an appointment by a corrupt state legislature to represent "the interests" of the railroads in the "Millionaires' Club" United States Senate. And no one knew better than Hennessy that Kincaid was growing wealthy on railroad-stock bribes.

"Three men dead in a flash," he growled. "Fifteen trapped. I don't need any more engineers. I need an undertaker. And a top-notch detective."

Hennessy whirled back to the telegrapher. "Has Van Dorn replied?"

"Not yet, sir. We've just sent—"

"Joe Van Dorn has agents in every city on the continent. Wire them all!"

Hennessy's daughter Lillian hurried in from their private quarters. Kincaid's eyes widened and his smile grew eager. Though on a dusty siding deep in the Cascade Range, she was dressed to turn heads in the finest dining rooms of New York. Her evening gown of white chiffon was cinched at her narrow waist and dipped low in front, revealing decolletage only partially screened by a silk rose. She wore a pearl choker studded with diamonds around her graceful neck, and her hair high in a golden cloud, with curls draping her high brow. Bright earrings of Peruzzi triple-cut brilliant diamonds drew attention to her face. Plumage, thought Kincaid cynically, showing what she had to offer, which was plenty.

Lillian Hennessy was stunningly beautiful, very young, and very, very wealthy. A match for a king. Or a senator who had his eye on the White House. The trouble was the fierce light in her astonishingly pale blue eyes that announced she was a handful not easily tamed. And now her father, who had never been able to bridle her, had appointed her his confidential secretary, which made her even more independent.

"Father," she said, "I just spoke with the chief engineer by telegraphone. He believes they can enter the pioneer tunnel from the far side and cut their way through to the main shaft. The rescue parties are digging. Your wires are sent. It is time you dressed for dinner."

"I'm not eating dinner while men are trapped."

"Starving yourself won't help them." She turned to Kincaid. "Hello, Charles," she said coolly. "Mrs. Comden's waiting for us in the parlor. We'll have a cocktail while my father gets dressed."

Hennessy had not yet appeared when they had finished their glasses. Mrs. Comden, a voluptuous, dark-haired woman of forty wearing a fitted green silk dress and diamonds cut in the old European style, said, "I'll get him." She went to Hennessy's office. Ignoring the telegrapher, who, like all telegraphers, was sworn never to reveal messages he sent or received, she laid a soft hand on Hennessy's bony shoulder and said, "Everyone is hungry." Her lips parted in a compelling smile. "Let's take them in to supper. Mr. Van Dorn will report soon enough."

As she spoke, the locomotive whistle blew twice, the double *Ahead* signal, and the train slid smoothly into motion.

"Where are we going?" she asked, not surprised they were on the move again.

"Sacramento, Seattle, and Spokane."

FOUR DAYS AFTER THE TUNNEL EXPLOSION, JOSEPH VAN DORN caught up with the fast-moving, far-roaming Osgood Hennessy in the Great Northern rail yard at Hennessyville. The brand-new city on the outskirts of Spokane, Washington, near the Idaho border, reeked of fresh lumber, creosote, and burning coal. But it was already called the "Minneapolis of the Northwest." Van Dorn knew that Hennessy had built here as part of his plan to double the Southern Pacific's trackage by absorbing the northern cross-continent routes.

The founder of the illustrious Van Dorn Detective Agency was a large, balding, well-dressed man in his forties who looked more like a prosperous business traveler than the scourge of the underworld. He appeared convivial, with a strong Roman nose, a ready smile slightly tempered by a hint of Irish melancholy in his eyes, and splendid red burnsides that descended to an even more splendid red beard. As he approached Hennessy's special, the sound of ragtime music playing on a gramophone elicited a nod of heartfelt relief. He recognized the lively, yearning melody of Scott Joplin's brand-new "Search-Light Rag," and the music told him that Hennessy's daughter Lillian was nearby. The cantankerous president of the Southern Pacific Railroad was a mite easier to handle when she was around.

He paused on the platform, sensing a rush from within the car. Here came Hennessy, thrusting the mayor of Spokane out the door. "Get off my train! Hennessyville will never be annexed into your incorporated city. I will not have my rail yard on Spokane's tax rolls!"

To Van Dorn, he snapped, "Took your time getting here."

Van Dorn returned Hennessy's brusqueness with a warm smile. His strong white teeth blazed in his nest of red whiskers as he enveloped the small man's hand in his, booming affably, "I was in Chicago, and you were all over the map. You're looking well, Osgood, if a little splenetic. How is the beauteous Lillian?" he asked, as Hennessy ushered him aboard.

"Still more trouble than a carload of *Eye*-talians."

"Here she is, now! My, my, how you've grown, young lady, I haven't seen you since—"

"Since New York, when father hired you to return me to Miss Porter's School?"

"No," Van Dorn corrected. "I believe the last time was when we bailed you out of jail in Boston following a suffragette parade that got out of hand."

"Lillian!" said Hennessy. "I want notes of this meeting typed up and attached to a contract to hire the Van Dorn Agency."

The mischievous light in her pale blue eyes was extinguished by a steady gaze that was suddenly all business. "The contract is ready to be signed, Father."

"Joe, I assume you know about these attacks."

"I understand," Van Dorn said noncommittally, "that horrific accidents bedevil the Southern Pacific's construction of an express line through the Cascades. You've had workmen killed, as well as several innocent rail passengers. "

"They can't all be accidents." Hennessy retorted sternly. "Someone's doing his damnedest to wreck this railroad. I'm hiring your outfit to hunt down the saboteurs, whether anarchists, foreigners, or strikers. Shoot 'em, hang 'em, do what you have to do, but stop them dead."

"The instant you telegraphed, I assigned my best operative to the case. If the situation appears as you suspect, I will appoint him chief investigator."

"No!" said Hennessy. "I want you in charge, Joe. Personally in charge."

"Isaac Bell is my best man. I only wish I had possessed his talents when I was his age."

Hennessy cut him off. "Get this straight, Joe. My train is parked only three hundred eighty miles north of the sabotaged tunnel, but it took over seven hundred miles to steam here, backtracking, climbing switchbacks. The cutoff line will reduce the run by a full day. The success of the cutoff and the future of this entire railroad is too important to farm out to a hired hand."

Van Dorn knew that Hennessy was used to getting his way. He had, after all, forged continuous transcontinental lines from Atlantic to Pacific by steamrollering his competitors, Commodore Vanderbilt and J. P. Morgan, outfoxing the Interstate Commerce Commission and the United States Congress, and staring down trust-busting President Teddy Roosevelt. Therefore, Van Dorn was glad for a sudden interruption by Hennessy's conductor. The train boss stood in the doorway in his impeccable uniform of deep blue cloth, which was studded with gleaming brass buttons and edged with the Southern Pacific's red piping.

"Sorry to disturb you, sir. They've caught a hobo trying to board your train."

"What are you bothering me for? I'm running a railroad here. Turn him over to the sheriff."

"He claims that Mr. Van Dorn will vouch for him."

A tall man entered Hennessy's private car, guarded by two heavy-set railway police. He wore the rough garb of a hobo who rode the freight trains looking for work. His denim coat and trousers were caked with dust. His boots were scuffed. His hat, a battered cow-poke's J. B. Stetson, had shed a lot of rain.

Lillian Hennessy noticed his eyes first, a violet shade of blue, which raked the parlor with a sharp, searching glance that penetrated every nook and cranny. Swift as his eyes were, they seemed to pause on each face as if to pierce the inner thoughts of her father, Van Dorn, and lastly herself. She stared back boldly, but she found the effect mesmerizing.

He was well over six feet tall and lean as an Arabian thorough-bred. A full mustache covered his upper lip, as golden as his thick hair and the stubble on his unshaven cheeks. His hands hung easily at his sides, his fingers were long and graceful. Lillian took in the determined set to the chin and lips and decided that he was about thirty years old and immensely confident.

His escort stood close by but did not touch him. Only when she had torn her gaze from the tall man's face did she realize that one of the railroad guards was pressing a bloody handkerchief to his nose. The other blinked a swollen, blackened eye.

Joseph Van Dorn allowed himself a smug smile. "Osgood, may I present Isaac Bell, who will be conducting this investigation on my behalf?"

"Good morning," said Isaac Bell. He stepped forward to offer his hand. The guards started to follow after him.

Hennessy dismissed them with a curt "Out!"

The guard dabbing his nose with his handkerchief whispered to the conductor who was herding them toward the door.

"Excuse me, sir," said the conductor. "They want their property back."

Isaac Bell tugged a leather-sheathed sap of lead shot from his pocket. "What's your name?"

"Billy," came the sullen reply. Bell tossed him the sap, and said coldly, with barely contained anger, "Billy, next time a man offers to come quietly, take him at his word."

He turned to the man with the black eye. "And you?"

"Ed."

Bell produced a revolver and passed it to Ed, butt first. Then he dropped five cartridges into the guard's hand, saying, "Never draw a weapon you haven't mastered."

"Thought I had," muttered Ed, and something about his hang-dog expression seemed to touch the tall detective.

"Cowboy before you joined the railroad?" Bell asked.

"Yes, sir, needed the work."

Bell's eyes warmed to a softer blue, and his lips spread in a congenial smile. He slid a gold coin from a pocket concealed inside his belt. "Here you go, Ed. Get a piece of beefsteak for that eye, and buy yourselves a drink."

The guards nodded their heads. "Thank you, Mr. Bell."

Bell turned his attention to the president of the Southern Pacific Company, who was glowering expectantly. "Mr. Hennessy, I will report as soon as I've had a bath and changed my clothes."

"The porter has your bag," Joseph Van Dorn said, smiling.

THE DETECTIVE WAS BACK in thirty minutes, mustache trimmed, hobo garb exchanged for a silver-gray three-piece sack suit tailored from fine, densely woven English wool appropriate to the autumn chill. A pale blue shirt and a dark violet four-in-hand necktie enriched the color of his eyes.

Isaac Bell knew that he had to start the case off on the right foot by establishing that he, *not* the imperious railroad president, would boss the investigation. First, he returned Lillian Hennessy's warm smile. Then he bowed politely to a sensual, dark-eyed woman who entered quietly and sat in a leather armchair. At last, he turned to Osgood Hennessy.

"I am not entirely convinced the accidents are sabotage."

"The hell you say! Labor is striking all over the West. Now we've got a Wall Street panic egging on radicals, inflaming agitators."

"It is true," Bell answered, "that the San Francisco streetcar strike and the Western Union telegraphers' strike embittered labor unionists. And even if the leaders of the Western Federation of Miners standing trial in Boise did conspire to murder Governor Steunenberg—a charge I doubt, as the detective work in that case is slipshod—there was obviously no shortage of vicious radicals to plant the dynamite in the Governor's front gate. Nor was the murderer who assassinated President McKinley the only anarchist in the land. But—"

Isaac Bell paused to turn the full force of his gaze on Hennessy. "Mr. Van Dorn pays me to capture assassins and bank robbers everywhere on the continent. I ride more limited trains, expresses, and crack flyers in a month than most men will in a lifetime."

"What do your travels have to do with these attacks against my railroad?"

"Train wrecks are common. Last year, the Southern Pacific paid out two million dollars for injuries to persons. Before 1907 is over, there'll be *ten thousand* collisions, eight thousand derailments, and over five thousand accidental deaths. As a frequent passenger, I take it personally when railroad cars are rammed inside each other like a telescope."

Osgood Hennessy flushed pink with incipient fury. "I'll tell you what I tell every reformer who thinks the railroad is the root of all evil. The Southern Pacific Railroad employs one hundred thousand men. We work like nailers transporting *one hundred million* passengers and *three hundred million* tons of freight *every year*!"

"I happen to love trains," Bell said, mildly. "But railwaymen don't exaggerate when they say that the tiny steel flange that holds the wheel on the track is 'One inch between here and eternity.'"

Hennessy pounded the table. "These murdering radicals are blinded by hate! Can't they see that railway speed is *God's gift* to every man and woman alive? America is huge! Bigger than squabbling Europe. Wider than divided China. Railroads unite us. How would people get around without our trains? Stagecoaches? Who would carry their crops to market? Oxen? Mules? A single one of my locomotives hauls more freight than all the Conestoga wagons that ever crossed the Great Plains—Mr. Bell, do you know what a Thomas Flyer is?"

"Of course. A Thomas Flyer is a four-cylinder, sixty-horsepower Model 35 Thomas automobile built in Buffalo. It is my hope that the Thomas Company will win the New York to Paris Race next year."

"Why do you think they named an automobile after a railroad train?" Hennessy bellowed. "Speed! A *flyer* is a crack *railroad train* famous for speed! And—"

"Speed is wonderful," Bell interrupted. "Here's why . . ."

That Hennessy used this section of his private car as his office was evinced by the chart pulls suspended from the polished-wood ceiling. The tall, flaxen-haired detective chose from their brass labels and unrolled a railroad map that represented the lines of California, Oregon, Nevada, Idaho, and Washington. He pointed to the mountainous border between northern California and Nevada.

"Sixty years ago, a group of pioneer families calling themselves the Donner Party attempted to cross these mountains by wagon train. They were heading for San Francisco, but early snow blocked the pass they had chosen through the Sierra Nevada. The Donner Party was trapped all winter. They ran out of food. Those who did not starve to death survived by eating the bodies of those who died."

"What the devil do cannibalistic pioneers have to do with my railroad?"

Isaac Bell grinned. "Today, thanks to your railroad, if you get hungry in the Donner Pass it's only a four-hour train ride to San Francisco's excellent restaurants."

Osgood Hennessy's stern face did not allow for much difference between scowls and smiles, but he did concede to Joseph Van Dorn, "You win, Joe. Go ahead, Bell. Speak your piece."

Bell indicated the map. "In the past three weeks, you've had suspicious derailments here at Redding, here at Roseville and at Dunsmuir, and the tunnel collapse, which prompted you to call on Mr. Van Dorn."

"You're not telling me anything I don't already know," Hennessy snapped. "Four track layers and a locomotive engineer dead. Ten off the job with broken limbs. Construction delayed eight days."

"And one railway police detective crushed to death in the pioneer tunnel."

"What? Oh yes. I forgot. One of my cinder dicks."

"His name was Clarke. Aloysius Clarke. His friends called him Wish."

"We knew the man," Joseph Van Dorn explained. "He used to work for my agency. Crackerjack detective. But he had his troubles."

Bell looked each person in the face, and in a clear voice spoke the highest compliment paid in the West. "Wish Clarke was a man to ride the river with."

Then he said to Hennessy, "I stopped in hobo jungles on my way here. Outside Crescent City on the Siskiyou line"—he pointed on the map at the north coast of California—"I caught wind of a radical or an anarchist the hobos call the Wrecker."

"A radical! Just like I said."

"The hobos know little about him, but they fear him. Men who join his cause are not seen again. From what I have gleaned so far, he may have recruited an accomplice for the tunnel job. A young agitator, a miner named Kevin Butler, was seen hopping a freight train south from Crescent City."

"Toward Eureka!" Hennessy broke in. "From Santa Rosa, he cut up to Redding and Weed and onto the Cascades Cutoff. Like I've been saying all along. Labor radicals, foreigners, anarchists. Did this agitator confess his crime?"

"Kevin Butler will be confessing to the devil, sir. His body was found beside Detective Clarke's in the pioneer tunnel. However, nothing in his background indicates the ability to carry out such an attack by himself. The Wrecker, as he is called, is still at large."

A telegraph key rattled in the next room. Lillian Hennessy cocked her ear. When the noise stopped, the telegrapher hurried in with his transcription. Bell noticed that Lillian did not bother to read what was written on the paper, as she said to her father, "From Redding. Collision north of Weed. A workmen's train fouled a signal. A materials train following didn't know the freight was in the section and plowed into the back of it. The caboose telescoped into a freight car. Two train crew killed."

Hennessy leaped to his feet, red faced. "No sabotage? Fouled a signal, my eye. Those trains were bound for the Cascades Cutoff. Which means another delay."

Joseph Van Dorn stepped forward to calm the apoplectic railroad president.

Bell moved closer to Lillian.

"You know the Morse alphabet?" he asked quietly.

"You're observant, Mr. Bell. I've traveled with my father since I was a little girl. He's never far from a telegraph key."

Bell reconsidered the young woman. Perhaps Lillian was more than the spoiled, headstrong only child she appeared to be. She could be a font of valuable information about her father's inner circle. "Who is that lady who just joined us?"

"Emma Comden is a family friend. She tutored me in French and German and tried very hard to improve my behavior"—Lillian blinked long lashes over her pale blue eyes and added—"at the piano."

Emma Comden wore a snug dress with a proper round collar and an elegant brooch at her throat. She was very much Lillian's opposite, rounded where the younger woman was slim, eyes a deep brown, almost black, hair dark, lustrous chestnut with a glint of red, constrained in a French twist.

"Do you mean you were educated at home so you could help your father?"

"I mean that I was kicked out of so many eastern finishing schools that Father hired Mrs. Comden to complete my education."

Bell smiled back. "How can you still have time for French and German and the piano when you're your father's private secretary?"

"I've outgrown my tutor."

"And yet Mrs. Comden remains . . . ?"

Lillian responded coolly. "If you have eyes, Mr. Detective, you might notice that Father is very fond of our 'family friend.'"

Hennessy noticed Isaac and Lillian talking. "What's that?"

"I was just saying that I've heard it said that Mrs. Hennessy was a great beauty."

"Lillian didn't get that face from my side of the family. How much money are you paid to be a detective, Mr. Bell?"

"The top end of the going rate."

"Then I have no doubt you understand that as the father of an innocent young woman, I am obliged to ask who bought you those fancy clothes?"

"My grandfather Isaiah Bell."

Osgood Hennessy stared. He couldn't have been more surprised if Bell had reported he had sprung from the loins of King Midas. "*Isaiah Bell* was your grandfather? That makes your father Ebenezer

Bell, president of the American States Bank of Boston. Good God Almighty, a banker?"

"My father is a banker. I am a detective."

"*My* father never met a banker in his life. He was a section hand, pounding spikes. You're talking to a shirtsleeve railroader, Bell. I started out like he did, spiking rails to ties. I've carried my dinner pail. I've done my ten hours a day up through the grades: brakeman, engineer, conductor, telegrapher, dispatcher—up the line from track to station to general office."

"What my father is trying to say," said Lillian, "is that he rose from pounding iron spikes in the hot sun to driving ceremonial gold spikes under a parasol."

"Don't mock me, young lady." Hennessy yanked another chart down from the ceiling. It was a blueprint, a fine-lined copy on pale blue paper that depicted in exquisite detail the engineering plans for a cantilevered truss bridge that spanned a deep gorge on two tall piers made of stone and steel.

"This is where we're headed, Mr. Bell, the Cascade Canyon Bridge. I hauled a top-hand engineer, Franklin Mowery, out of retirement to build me the finest railroad bridge west of the Mississippi, and Mowery's almost finished. To save time, I built it *ahead* of the expansion by routing work trains on an abandoned timber track that snakes up from the Nevada desert." He pointed at the map. "When we hole through here—Tunnel 13—we'll find the bridge waiting for us. Speed, Mr. Bell. It's all about speed."

"Do you face a deadline?" asked Bell.

Hennessy looked sharply at Joseph Van Dorn. "Joe, can I assume that confidences are as safe with your detectives as they are with my attorneys?"

"Safer," said Van Dorn.

"There is a deadline," Hennessy admitted to Bell.

"Imposed by your bankers?"

"Not those devils. Mother Nature. Old Man Winter is coming, and when he gets to the Cascades that's it for railroad construction 'til Spring. I've got the best credit in the railroad business, but if I don't connect the Cascades Cutoff to the Cascade Canyon Bridge before winter shuts me down even *my* credit will dry up. Between us, Mr. Bell, if this expansion stalls, I will lose any chance of completing the Cascades Cutoff the day after the first snowstorm."

Joseph Van Dorn said, "Rest easy, Osgood. We'll stop him."

Hennessy was not soothed. He shook the blueprint as if to throttle it. "If these saboteurs stop me, it'll take twenty years before anyone can tackle the Cascades Cutoff again. It's the last hurdle impeding progress in the West, and I'm the last man alive with the guts to clear it."

Isaac Bell did not doubt that the old man loved his railroad. Nor did he forget the outrage in his own heart at the prospect of more innocent people killed and injured by the Wrecker. The innocent were sacred. But foremost in Bell's mind at this moment was his memory of Wish Clarke stepping in his casual, offhanded way in front of a knife intended for Bell. He said, "I promise I will stop him."

Hennessy stared at him for a long time, taking his measure. Slowly, he settled into an armchair. "I'm relieved, Mr. Bell, having a top hand of your caliber."

When Hennessy looked to his daughter for agreement, he noticed that she was appraising the wealthy and well-connected detective like a new race car she would ask him to buy for her next birthday. "Son?" he asked. "Is there a Mrs. Bell?"

Bell had already noticed that the lovely young woman was appraising him. Flattering, tempting too, but he did not take it personally. It was an easy guess why. He was surely the first man she had seen whom her father could not bully. But between her fascination and her father's sudden interest in seeing her suitably married off, the moment was overdue for this particular gentleman to make his intentions clear.

"I am engaged to be married," he answered.

"Engaged, eh? Where is she?"

"She lives in San Francisco."

"How did she make out in the earthquake?"

"She lost her home," Bell replied cryptically, the memory still fresh of their first night together ending abruptly when the shock hurled their bed across the room and Marion's piano had fallen through the front wall into the street.

"Marion stayed on, caring for orphans. Now that most are settled, she has taken a position at a newspaper."

"Have you set a wedding date?" Hennessy asked.

"Soon," said Bell.

Lillian Hennessy seemed to take "Soon" as a challenge. "We're so far from San Francisco."

"One thousand miles." said Bell "Much of it slow going on steep grades and endless switchbacks through the Siskiyou Mountains— the reason for your Cascades Cutoff, which will reduce the run by a full day," he added, deftly changing the subject from marriageable daughters to sabotage. "Which reminds me, it would be helpful to have a railway pass."

"I'll do better than that!" said Hennessy, springing to his feet. "You'll have your railway pass—immediate free passage on any train in the country. You will also have a letter written in my own hand authorizing you to charter a special train anywhere you need one. You're working for the railroad now."

"No, sir. I work for Mr. Van Dorn. But I promise to put your specials to good use."

"Mr. Hennessy has equipped you with wings," said Mrs. Comden.

"If only you knew where to fly . . ." The beautiful Lillian smiled. "Or to whom."

When the telegraph key started clattering again, Bell nodded to Van Dorn, and they stepped quietly off the car onto the platform. A cold north wind whipped through the rail yard, swirling smoke and cinders. "I'll need a lot of our men."

"They're yours for the asking. Who do you want?"

Isaac Bell spoke a long list of names. Van Dorn listened, nodding approval. When he had finished, Bell said, "I'd like to base out of Sacramento."

"I would have thought you'd recommend San Francisco."

"For personal reasons, yes. I would prefer the opportunity to be in the same city with my fiancée. But Sacramento has the faster rail connections up the Pacific Coast and inland. Could we assemble at Miss Anne's?"

Van Dorn did not conceal his surprise. "Why do you want to meet in a brothel?"

"If this so-called Wrecker is taking on an entire continental railroad, he is a criminal with a broad reach. I don't want our force seen meeting in a public place until I know what he knows and how he knows it."

"I'm sure Anne Pound will make room for us in her back parlor," Van Dorn said stiffly. "If you think that's the best course. But tell me, have you discovered something else beyond what you just reported to Hennessy?"

"No, sir. But I do have a feeling that the Wrecker is exceptionally alert."

Van Dorn replied with a silent nod. In his experience, when a detective as insightful as Isaac Bell had a "feeling" the feeling took shape from small but telling details that most people wouldn't notice. Then he said, "I'm awfully sorry about Aloysius."

"Came as something of a shock. The man saved my life in Chicago."

"You saved his in New Orleans," Van Dorn retorted. "And again in Cuba."

"He was a crackerjack detective."

"Sober. But he was drinking himself to death. And you couldn't save him from that. Not that you didn't try."

"He was the best," Bell said, stubbornly.

"How was he killed?"

"His body was crushed under the rocks. Clearly, Wish was right there at the precise spot where the dynamite detonated."

Van Dorn shook his head, sadly. "That man's instincts were golden. Even drunk. I hated having to let him go."

Bell kept his voice neutral. "His sidearm was several feet from his body, indicating he had drawn it from his holster before the explosion."

"Could have been blown there by the explosion."

"It was that old single-action Army he loved. In the flap holster. It didn't fall out. He must have had it in his hand."

Van Dorn countered with a cold question to confirm Bell's conjecture that Aloysius Clarke had tried to prevent the attack. "Where was his flask?"

"Still tucked in his clothing."

Van Dorn nodded and started to change the subject, but Isaac Bell was not finished.

"I had to know how he got there in the tunnel. Had he died before or in the explosion? So I put his body on a train and brought it to a doctor in Klamath Falls. Stood by while he examined it. The doctor showed me that before Wish was crushed, he had taken a knife in the throat."

Van Dorn winced. "They slashed his throat?"

"Not slashed. *Pierced*. The knife went in his throat, slid between two cervical vertebrae, severed his spinal cord, and emerged out the back of his neck. The doctor said it was done clean as a surgeon or a butcher."

"Or just lucky."

"If it was, then the killer got lucky twice."

"How do you mean?"

"Getting the drop on Wish Clarke would require considerable luck in the first place, wouldn't you say?"

Van Dorn looked away. "Anything left in the flask?"

Bell gave his boss a thin, sad smile. "Don't worry, Joe, I would have fired him, too. It was dry as a bone."

"Attacked from the front?"

"It looks that way," said Bell.

"But you say Wish had already drawn his gun."

"That's right. So how did the Wrecker get him with a knife?"

"Threw it?" Van Dorn asked dubiously.

Bell's hand flickered toward his boot and came up with his throwing knife. He juggled the sliver of steel in his fingers, weighing it. "He'd need a catapult to drive a throwing knife completely through a big man's neck."

"Of course . . . Watch your step, Isaac. As you say, this Wrecker must be one quick-as-lightning hombre to get the drop on Wish Clarke. Even drunk."

"He will have the opportunity," vowed Isaac Bell, "to show me how quick."

4

THE ELECTRIC LIGHTS OF SANTA MONICA'S VENICE PIER
illuminated the rigging of a three-masted ship docked permanently
alongside it and the rooflines of a large pavilion. A brass band was
playing John Philip Sousa's "Gladiator March" in quick time.

The beachcomber turned his back to the bittersweet music and
walked the hard-packed sand toward the dark. The lights shimmered
across the waves and cast a frothy shadow ahead of him, as the cool
Pacific wind flapped his ragged clothes. It was low tide, and he was
hunting for an anchor he could steal.

He skirted a village of shacks. The Japanese fishermen who lived
there had dragged their boats up on the beach, close to their shacks,
to keep an eye on them. Just past the Japanese he found what he was
looking for, one of the seagoing dories scattered along the beach by
the United States Lifeboat Society to rescue shipwrecked sailors and
drowning tourists. The boats were fully equipped for launching in an
instant by volunteer crews. He pulled open the canvas and pawed in
the dark, feeling oars, floats, tin bailers, and finally the cold metal of
an anchor.

He carried the anchor toward the pier. Before he reached the edge of the light fall, he plodded up the sloping deep sand and into the town. The streets were quiet, the houses dark. He dodged a night watchman on foot patrol and made his way, unchallenged, to a stable, which like most stables in the area was in the process of being converted to accommodate motor vehicles. Trucks and automobiles undergoing repair were parked helter-skelter among the wagons, buggies, and surreys. The scent of gasoline mingled with that of hay and manure.

It was a lively place by day, frequented by hostlers, hackmen, wagoners, and mechanics, smoking and chewing and spinning yarns. But the only one up tonight was the blacksmith, who surprised the beachcomber by giving him a whole dollar for the anchor. He had only promised fifty cents, but he had been drinking and was one of those men who whiskey made generous.

The blacksmith got busy, eager to transform the anchor before anyone noticed it had been stolen. He started by cutting off one of the two cast-iron flukes, battering it repeatedly with hammer and cold chisel until it snapped away. He filed burrs to smooth the ragged break. When he held the anchor up to the light, what was left of it looked like a hook.

Sweating even in the cool of the night, he drank a bottle of beer and swallowed a deep pull from his bottle of Kellogg's Old Bourbon before starting to drill the hole in the shank that the customer had asked for. Drilling cast iron was hard work. Pausing to catch his breath, he drank another beer. He finished at last, vaguely aware that one more swig of Kellogg's and he would drill a hole in his hand instead of the hook.

He wrapped the hook in the blanket the customer had provided and put it in the man's carpetbag. Head reeling, he picked up the fluke he had removed from where it had fallen in the sand beside his anvil. He was wondering what he could make with it when the customer rapped on the door. "Bring it out here."

The man was standing in the dark, and the blacksmith saw even less of his sharp features than he had the night before. But he recognized his strong voice, his precise back east diction, his superior putting-on-airs manner, his height, and his city slicker's knee-length, single-breasted frock coat.

"I said bring it here!"

The blacksmith carried the carpetbag out the door.

"Shut the door!"

He closed it behind him, blocking the light, and his customer took the bag with a brusque, "Thank you, my good man."

"Anytime," mumbled the blacksmith, wondering what in heck a swell in a frock coat was going to do with half an anchor.

A ten-dollar gold piece, a week's work in these hard times, glittered through the shadows. The blacksmith fumbled for it, missed, and had to kneel in the sand to pick it up. He sensed the man looming closer. He looked over, warily, and he saw him reach into a rugged boot that didn't match his fancy duds. Just then, the door behind him flew open, and light caught the man's face. The blacksmith thought he looked familiar. Three grooms and an automobile mechanic staggered out the door, drunk as skunks, whooping with laughter when they saw him kneeling in the sand. "Damn!" shouted the mechanic. "Looks like Jim finished his bottle, too."

The customer whirled away and disappeared down the alley, leaving the blacksmith completely unaware that he had come within one second of being murdered by a man who killed just to be on the safe side.

FOR MOST OF THE forty-seven years that the state capital of California had been in Sacramento, Anne Pound's white mansion had provided congenial hospitality for legislators and lobbyists a short three blocks away. It was large and beautiful, built in the uncluttered early Victorian style. Gleaming white woodwork fringed turrets, gables, porches, and railings. Inside the waxed-walnut front door, an oil painting of the lady of the house in her younger years graced the grand foyer. Her red-carpeted staircase was so renowned in political circles that the level of a man's connections in the state could be gauged by whether he smiled knowingly upon hearing the phrase "The Steps to Heaven."

At eight o'clock this evening, the lady herself, considerably older and noticeably larger, her great mane of blond hair gone white as the woodwork, held court on a burgundy couch in the back drawing room, where she settled in billows of green silk. The room held many such couches, capacious armchairs, polished-brass cuspidors, gilt-framed paintings of nubile women in various states of undress, and a fine bar stacked with crystal. Tonight it was securely closed off from the front room by three-inch-thick mahogany pocket doors. Standing guard was an elegantly top-hatted bouncer, a former prize-fighter believed to have knocked down "Gentleman Jim" Corbett in his heyday and who'd lived to tell the tale.

Isaac Bell had to hide a smile at how much Joseph Van Dorn was thrown off balance by the still-beautiful proprietress. A blush was spreading from beneath his beard, red as the whiskers. For all his oft-proven courage in the face of violent attack, Van Dorn was singularly straitlaced when it came to women in general and intimate behavior in particular. It was clear he would rather be sitting anywhere but in the back parlor of the highest-class sporting house in California.

"Shall we start?" asked Van Dorn.

"Miss Anne," Bell said, courteously extending his hand to help her rise from the couch. "We thank you for your hospitality."

As Bell walked her out the door, she murmured in a soft Virginia drawl how grateful she remained to the Van Dorn Detective Agency for apprehending, in the quietest manner, a vicious killer who had preyed on her hardworking girls. The monster, a twisted fiend whom the Van Dorn operatives had backtracked to one of Sacramento's finest families, was locked forever in an asylum for the criminally insane, and no hint of scandal had ever alarmed her patrons.

Joseph Van Dorn stood up, and said in a low voice that carried, "Let's get to it. Isaac Bell is in charge of this investigation. When he speaks, he speaks with my authority. Isaac, tell them what you have in mind."

Bell looked from face to face before he spoke. He had worked with, or knew of, all the heads of the western cities' agencies: Phoenix, Salt Lake, Boise, Seattle, Spokane, Portland, Sacramento, San Francisco, Los Angeles, Denver, and the other agents Van Dorn had rounded up.

Among the standouts were the immense, powerfully built director of the San Francisco office, Horace Bronson, and short, fat Arthur Curtis, with whom Bell had worked on the Butcher Bandit case, on which they'd lost a mutual friend in Curtis's partner, Glenn Irvine.

"Texas" Walt Hatfield, a barbed-wire-lean former ranger who specialized in stopping railroad express-car robberies, would be of particular value on this case. As would Kansas City's Eddie Edwards, a prematurely white-haired gent who was expert at rousting city gangs out of freight yards, where sidelined trains were particularly vulnerable to robbery and sabotage.

The oldest in the room were ice-eyed Mack Fulton from Boston, who knew every safecracker in the country, and his partner, explosives expert Wally Kisley, dressed in his trademark three-piece drummer's suit with a loud pattern bright as a checkerboard. Mack and Wally had teamed up since the early days in Chicago. Quick with a joke or a prank, they were known in the agency as "Weber and Fields" after the famous vaudeville comedians and producers of burlesque musicals on Broadway.

Last came Bell's particular friend, Archie Abbott from New York, a near-invisible undercover man, sidling through Miss Anne's kitchen door, dressed like a tramp looking for a handout.

Bell said, "If someone detonates a bomb in here, every outlaw on the continent will be buying drinks."

Their laughter was subdued. Texas Walt Hatfield asked the question that was on many minds, "Isaac, you fixing to tell us why we're hunkered down in a sportin' house like we was longhorns canyon-skulking on roundup morning?"

"Because we're up against a saboteur who thinks big, plans smart, and doesn't give a hoot who he kills."

"Well, now that you put it that way—"

"He is a vicious, ruthless murderer. He's done so much damage already and killed so many innocent people that the hobos took notice and nicknamed him 'the Wrecker.' His target appears to be the Southern Pacific Railroad Cascades Cutoff. The railroad is our client. The Wrecker is our target. The Van Dorn Detective Agency has two jobs: protect the client by stopping the Wrecker from doing any more damage and catch him with enough proof to hang him."

Bell nodded briskly. A male secretary in shirtsleeves sprang forward to drape a railroad map over a picture of nymphs in their bath. The map depicted the western railroads from Salt Lake City to San Francisco that served California, Oregon, Washington, Idaho, Utah, Nevada, and Arizona.

"To pinpoint the railroad's most vulnerable locations, I've invited Jethro Watt, superintendent of railway police, to fill you in."

The detectives responded with derisive mutters.

Isaac Bell quieted them with a cold glance. "We all know the shortcomings of the railroad dicks. But Van Dorn hasn't the manpower to cover eight thousand miles of track. Jethro has information we couldn't learn on our own. So if anyone in this room says anything to make Superintendent Watt less than enthusiastically cooperative, he'll answer to me."

At Bell's command, the secretary ushered in Superintendent Watt, who in appearance did not contradict the detectives' low expectations of railway police. From the greasy hair pasted to the forehead above his ill-shaven, bad-tempered face to his grimy collar, wrinkled coat and trousers, to his scuffed boots to the bulges in his clothing that bespoke cannon-caliber sidearms, saps, and billy clubs, Jethro Watt, who was nearly as tall as Isaac Bell and twice as wide, looked like the prototype for every yard bull and cinder dick in the country. Then he opened his mouth and surprised them all.

"There's an old saying: 'Nothing is impossible for the Southern Pacific.'

"What railroad men mean by that is this: We do it all. We grade our own road. We lay our own track. We build our own locomotives and rolling stock. We erect our own bridges—forty in the new expansion, in addition to Cascade Canyon. We bore our own tunnels—they'll be fifty before we're done. We maintain our own machinery. We invent special High Sierra snowplows for winter, fire trains for summer. We are a mighty enterprise."

With neither a softer tone nor the hint of smile, he added, "On San Francisco Bay, our ferry passengers crossing from Oakland Mole to the City claim that our machine shops even bake the doughnuts we sell on our boats. Like 'em or not, they still eat 'em. The Southern Pacific is a mighty enterprise. Like us or not."

Jethro Watt's bloodshot eye fell on the ornate bar heaped high with a pyramid of crystal decanters, and he wet his lips.

"A mighty enterprise makes many enemies. If a fella climbs out of the wrong side of bed in the morning, he'll blame the railroad. If his crop fails, he'll blame the railroad. If he loses his farm, he'll blame the railroad. If his union can't raise his wages, he'll blame the railroad. If he gets laid off in a Panic, he'll blame the railroad. If his bank closes and can't return his money, he'll blame the railroad. Sometimes he gets mad enough to transact a little business with the express car.

Robbing trains. But worse than robbing trains is sabotage. Worse, and harder to stop because a mighty enterprise makes a mammoth target.

"Sabotage by angry fellas is why the company maintains an army of police to protect itself. An enormous army. But like any army, we need so many soldiers we can't pick and choose, and sometimes we must recruit what others more privileged might call the dregs . . ."

He glowered around the room, and half the detectives there expected him to whip out a blackjack. Instead, he concluded, with a cold, derisive smile, "The word has come down from on high that our army is to assist you gentlemen detectives. We are placed at your service, and my boys are instructed to take orders from you gentlemen.

"Mr. Bell and I have already had a long talk with the company's top engineers and superintendents. Mr. Bell knows what we know. Namely, if this so-called Wrecker wants to disrupt our Cascades Cutoff, he can attack us six ways from Sunday:

"He can wreck a train by tampering with the switches that shunt trains around one another. Or he can manipulate the telegraph by which division superintendents control train movements.

"He can burn a bridge. He's already dynamited a tunnel, he can blow another.

"He can attack our shops and foundries that serve the cutoff. Most likely, Sacramento. And Red Bluff, where they fabricate truss rods for the Cascade Canyon Bridge.

"He can set fire to our roundhouses when they're crowded full of locomotives undergoing maintenance.

"He can mine the rails.

"And every time he succeeds and folks get killed, he will panic our workmen.

"At Mr. Bell's request, we have dispatched our 'army' to the places where the railroad is most at risk. Our 'soldiers' are in place and await you gentlemen's requests. Now Mr. Bell will pinpoint those places for you while I go pour me a snort."

Watt plunged across the parlor without apology, heading directly to the crystal-laden bar.

Isaac Bell said, "Listen close. We have our work cut out for us."

BY MIDNIGHT, YOUNG WOMEN'S laughter had replaced the solemn proceedings in Miss Anne's back parlor. The Van Dorn detectives had dispersed, slipping away quietly to their hotels alone or in pairs, leaving only Isaac Bell and Archie Abbott in Miss Anne's library, a windowless room deep in the mansion, where they continued to pore over the railroad maps.

Archie Abbott strained the authenticity of his tramp costume by pouring a twelve-year-old Napoleon brandy into a crystal balloon snifter and inhaling with refined appreciation.

"Weber and Fields made a good point about powder-house burglaries. Missing explosives are a red flag."

"Unless he buys some at the general store."

Archie raised his glass in a toast. "Destruction to the Wrecker! May the wind blow in his face and the hot sun blind him!"

Archie's carefully styled accent sounded as if he hailed from New York City's Hell's Kitchen. But Archie had numerous accents he could fashion to fit his costume. He had become a detective only after his family, blue-blooded but impoverished since the Panic of '93, had forbidden him becoming an actor. The first time they'd met, Isaac Bell was boxing for Yale when the unenviable chore of defending the honor of Princeton had fallen to Archibald Angell Abbott IV.

"All bases covered?"

"Looks that way."

"How come you don't look happier, Isaac?"

"As Watt said, it's a big railroad."

"Oh yes." Abbott took a sip of brandy and leaned over the map again. His high brow knitted. "Who's watching the Redding Yards?"

"Lewis and Minalgo were nearest by," said Bell, not happy with his answer.

"'And the former was a lulu,'" said Archie, quoting the much-loved baseball poem "Casey at the Bat," "'and the latter was a cake.'"

Bell nodded agreement, and, thinking through his roster, said, "I'll move them down to Glendale and put Hatfield in charge of Redding."

"Glendale, hell. I'd move 'em to Mexico."

"So would I, if I could spare the men. But Glendale's mighty far off. I don't think we have to worry too much about Glendale. It's seven hundred miles from the Cascades route . . ." He pulled out his gold watch. "We've done all we can tonight. I've got an extra room in my hotel suite. If I can sneak you past the house dick dressed like that."

Abbott shook his head. "Thanks, but when I came through the kitchen earlier, Miss Anne's cook promised me a midnight supper."

Bell shook his head at his old friend. "Only you, Archie, could spend the night in a whorehouse and sleep with the cook."

"I checked the train schedule," Abbott said. "Give my regards to Miss Marion. You've got time to catch the night flyer to San Francisco."

"I was planning to," said Bell, and strode quickly into the night, heading for the railroad station.

5

AT MIDNIGHT, BENEATH A STARRY SKY, A MAN DRESSED IN A SUIT and a slouch hat like a railroad official worked hand and foot levers to propel a three-wheeled Kalamazoo Velocipede track-inspection vehicle between Burbank and Glendale. The track was smooth on this recently completed section of the San Francisco–to–Los Angeles line. Rowing with his arms and pedaling with his feet, he was making nearly twenty miles per hour in eerie silence broken only by the rhythmic clicking of the wheels passing over the joints between the rails.

The Velocipede was used to watch over the section gangs who replaced worn or rotted crossties, tamped stone ballast between the ties, aligned rails, pounded down loose spikes, and tightened bolts. Its frame, two main wheels, and the outrigger that connected them to its side wheel were made of strong, light ash, its treads of cast iron. The entire vehicle weighed less than one hundred fifty pounds. One man could lift it off the rails and turn it in the opposite direction or get out of the way of a train. The Wrecker, no cripple except when he needed a disguise, would have no trouble tumbling it down an embankment when he was done with it.

Tied to the empty seat beside him were a crowbar, track wrench, spike puller, and a device that no section gang would dare leave on the rails. It was a hook, nearly two feet long, fashioned from a cast-iron boat anchor from which one fluke had been removed.

He had stolen the Velocipede. He had broken into a clapboard building at the edge of Burbank freight depot where the Southern Pacific section inspector stored it and manhandled it onto the rails. In the unlikely event that some cinder dick or village constable saw him and asked what the hell he was doing riding the main line at midnight, his suit and hat would buy him two seconds of hesitation. Ample time to deliver a silent answer with the blade in his boot.

Leaving the lights of Burbank behind, rolling past darkened farmhouses, he quickly adjusted to the starlight. Half an hour later, ten miles north of Los Angeles, he slowed down, recognizing the jagged angles and dense layers of latticework of an iron trestle crossing a dry riverbed. He trundled across the trestle. The rails curved sharply to the right to parallel the riverbed.

He stopped a few yards after he felt the wheels click across a joint where two rails butted together. He unloaded his tools and knelt down on the crushed-stone ballast, cushioning his knees on a wooden crosstie. Feeling the joint between the rails in the dark with his fingers, he located the fishplate, the flat piece of metal fastening the rails to each other. He pried up the spike that anchored the fishplate to the tie with his spike puller. Then he used his track wrench to loosen the nuts on the four bolts that secured the fishplate to the rails and yanked them out. Tossing three of the bolts and nuts and the fishplate down the steep embankment, where even the sharpest-eyed engineer could not see them in his headlight, he threaded the last bolt through a hole in the shank of the hook.

He swore at a sudden stab of sharp pain.

He had cut his finger on a metal burr. Cursing the drunken blacksmith who hadn't bothered to file smooth the edges of the hole he had drilled, he wrapped his finger in a handkerchief to stop the bleeding. Clumsily, he finished screwing the nut on the bolt. With the wrench, he made it tight enough to hold the hook upright. The open end faced west, the direction from which the Coast Line Limited would come.

The Coast Line was a "flyer," one of the fast through passenger trains that sped across long distances between cities. Routed via new tunnels through the Santa Susana Mountains, from Santa Barbara to Oxnard, Burbank, and Glendale, she was bound for Los Angeles.

Suddenly, the Wrecker felt the rail vibrate. He jumped to his feet. The Coast Line Limited was supposed to be running late tonight. If that was she, she had made up a lot of time. If it wasn't, then he had gone to great effort and taken dangerous risks to derail a worthless milk train.

A train whistle moaned. Quickly, he grabbed the spike puller and yanked up spikes that were holding the rail to the wooden ties. He managed to pry eight loose before he saw a glow of a headlight up the line. He threw the spike puller down the steep embankment and jumped onto the Velocipede and pedaled hard. Now he heard the locomotive. The sound was faint in the distance, but he recognized the distinctive clean, sharp *huff* of an Atlantic 4-4-2. It was the Limited, all right, and he could gauge by the rapid beat of the steam exhausted from her smokestack that she was coming fast.

THE ATLANTIC 4-4-2 PULLING the Coast Line Limited was built for speed.

Her engineer, Rufus Patrick, loved her for it. The American Locomotive Company of Schenectady, New York, had fitted her with enormous eighty-inch drive wheels. At sixty miles per hour, the four-wheeled engine truck in front held her on the rails as steady as the Rock of Ages while a two-wheeled truck in back supported a big firebox to generate plenty of superheated steam.

Rufus Patrick would admit that she was not that strong. The new, heavier steel passenger cars coming along soon would demand the more powerful Pacifics. She was no mountain climber, but for blazing speed on a flat, pulling a crack flyer of wooden passenger cars across long distances, she was not to be beat. Her identical sister had been clocked the previous year at 127.1 mph, a speed record unlikely to be bested anytime soon, thought Patrick. At least not by him, not even tonight running late, not when he was hauling ten passenger cars full of folks hoping to get home safe. Sixty was just fine, flying at a mile a minute.

The locomotive's cab was crowded. In addition to Rufus Patrick and his fireman, Zeke Taggert, there were two guests: Bill Wright, an official of the Electrical Workers Union who was a friend of Rufus's, and Bill's nephew, his namesake Billy, whom he was accompanying to Los Angeles, where the boy was to begin an apprenticeship in a laboratory that developed celluloid film for moving pictures. When they had last stopped for water, Rufus had walked back to the baggage car, where they were stealing a free ride, and invited them up to the cab.

Fourteen-year-old Billy couldn't believe his amazing luck to be riding in a locomotive. He'd been mooning over trains rumbling past his house his whole life and been up all night excited about this trip. But he had never dreamed he could actually ride up front in the cab. Mr. Patrick wore a striped cap just like you saw in pictures and was the surest, calmest man Billy had ever seen. He had explained what he was doing every step of the way, as he sounded two long blasts on the whistle and started the train moving again.

"We're off, Billy! I'm dropping the Johnson bar to full forward. All the way forward to go ahead, all the way back for reverse. We can go just as fast backward as forward."

Patrick gripped a long, horizontal bar. "Now I'm opening the throttle, sending steam to the cylinders to turn the drive wheels, and I'm opening the sand valve to get adhesion on the rails. Now I'm pulling back on the throttle so we don't start too fast. You feel her bite and not slipping?"

Billy had nodded eagerly. She had picked up speed smooth as silk as Patrick began notching out the throttle.

Now rolling toward Glendale on the last few miles before Los Angeles, blowing the whistle at grade crossings, Patrick told the awestruck boy, "You'll never drive a finer locomotive. She's a good steamer and rides easy."

The fireman, Zeke Taggert, who had been steadily shoveling coal into the roaring firebox, banged the door shut and sat down to catch his breath. He was a big man, black and greasy, and stunk of sweat. "Billy?" he boomed in a huge voice. "See this here glass?" Taggert tapped a gauge. "It's the most important window on the train. It shows the water level in the boiler. Too low, the crown sheet heats up and melts, and, *BOOM!,* blows us all to kingdom come!"

"Don't pay him no mind, Billy," Patrick said. "It's Zeke's job to be make sure we've got plenty in the boiler. We've got a tender full of water right behind us."

"How come the throttle's in the middle?" asked Billy.

"It sits in the middle when we're rolling. Right now, that's all we need to be steaming at sixty miles an hour. Shove her forward, we'd be doing a hundred twenty."

The engineer winked at Uncle Bill. "The throttle lever also helps us steer her around tight bends. Zeke, do you see any curves coming up?"

"Trestle just ahead, Rufus. Tight bend turning out of it."

"You take her, son."

"*What?*"

"Steer her around the curve. Quick, now! Grab hold. Poke your head out here and look."

Billy took the throttle in his left hand and leaned out the window the same way the engineer had.

The throttle was hot, pulsing in his hand like it was alive. The beam of the locomotive headlight gleamed along the rails. Billy saw the trestle coming up. It looked very narrow.

"Just a light touch," Rufus Patrick cautioned with another wink at the men. "Hardly need to move it at all. Easy. Easy. Yep, you're getting the hang of it. But you gotta get her right down the middle. It's a mighty tight fit."

Zeke and Uncle Bob exchanged grins.

"Look out, now. Yep, you're doing fine. Just ease her—"

"What's that up ahead, Mr. Patrick?"

Rufus Patrick looked where the boy was pointing.

The beam of the locomotive headlight was throwing shadows and reflections from the ironwork in the trestle, which made it hard to see. Probably just a shadow. Suddenly, the headlight glinted on something strange.

"What the—?" In the company of a child, Patrick automatically switched cusswords to "blue blazes."

It was a hooked hunk of metal reaching up from the right rail like a hand from a shallow grave.

"Hit the air!" Patrick yelled to the fireman.

Zeke threw himself on the air-brake lever and yanked it with all this might. The train slowed so violently, it seemed to hit a wall. But only for a moment. An instant later, the weight of ten fully loaded passenger cars and a tender filled with tons of coal and water hurled the locomotive forward.

Patrick clapped his own experienced hand on the air brake. He worked the brakes with the fine touch of a clockmaker and eased the Johnson bar into reverse. The great drive wheels spun, screeching in a blaze of fiery sparks, shaving slivers of steel from the rails. The brakes and the reversing drivers decelerated the speeding Coast

Line Limited. But it was too late. The high-wheeled Atlantic 4-4-2 was already screaming through the trestle, bearing down on the hook, still making forty miles per hour. Patrick could only pray that the wedge-shaped pilot, the so-called cowcatcher that swept along the tracks in front of the locomotive, would sweep it aside before it caught the engine truck's front axle.

Instead, the iron hook that the Wrecker had bolted to the loosened rail latched onto the pilot with a death grip. It tore loose the rail ahead of the front wheels on the right side of the one-hundred-eighty-six-thousand-pound locomotive. Her massive drive wheels crashed onto the ties, bouncing on wood and ballast at forty miles an hour.

The speed, the weight, and the relentless momentum crushed the edge of the bed and ground the ties to splinters. The wheels dropped into air, and, still racing forward, the engine began to careen onto its side, dragging its tender with it. The tender pulled the baggage car over the edge, and the baggage car dragged the first passenger car with it before the coupling to the second passenger car broke free.

Then, almost miraculously, the locomotive seemed to right itself. But it was a brief respite. Shoved by the weight of the tender and cars, it twisted and turned and skidded down the embankment, sliding until it smashed its mangled pilot and headlight into the rock-hard bottom of the dry riverbed.

It stopped at last, tilted at a steep angle, with its nose down and its trailing truck in the air. The water in the tightly sealed boiler, which was superheated to three hundred eighty degrees, spilled forward, off the red-hot crown plate, which was at the back of the boiler.

"Get out!" roared the engineer. "Get out before she blows!"

Bill was sprawled unconscious against the firebox. Little Billy was sitting dazed on the footplate, holding his head. Blood was pouring through his fingers.

Zeke, like Patrick, had braced for the impact and not been hurt badly.

"Grab Bill," Patrick told Zeke, who was a powerful man. "I've got the boy."

Patrick slung Billy under his arm like a gunnysack and jumped for the ground. Zeke draped Bill Wright over his shoulder, leaped from the engine, and hit the steep gravel slope running. Patrick stumbled with the boy. Zeke grabbed Patrick with his free arm and kept him upright. The crashing sounds had ceased abruptly. In the comparative quiet, they could hear injured passengers screaming in the first car, which was crumpled open like Christmas wrapping paper.

"Run!"

The coal fire that Zeke Taggert had shoveled so hard to feed was still raging under the locomotive's crown plate. Burning fiercely to maintain the twenty-two hundred degrees necessary to boil two thousand gallons of water, it continued to heat the steel. But with no water above it to absorb the heat, the temperature of the steel soared from its normal six hundred degrees to the fire's twenty-two hundred. At that temperature, the half-inch-thick plate softened like butter in a skillet.

Two-hundred-pounds-per-square-inch steam pressure inside the boiler was fourteen times ordinary air pressure outside. It took only seconds for the captive steam to exploit the sudden weakness and burst a hole in the crown plate.

Even as the steam escaped, two thousand gallons of water pressure-cooked to three hundred eighty degrees also turned to steam the instant it came in contact with the chill Glendale air. Its volume multiplied by a thousand six hundred times. In a flash, two thousand gallons of water vaporized into three million gallons of steam. Trapped inside the 4-4-2 Atlantic's boiler, it expanded outward with a concussive roar that exploded the steel locomotive into a million small pieces of shrapnel.

Billy and his uncle never knew what hit them. Nor did the Wells Fargo Express messenger in the baggage car, nor three friends who had been playing draw poker in the front of the derailed Pullman. But Zeke Taggert and Rufus Patrick, who understood the cause and nature of the nightmarish forces gathering like a tornado, actually felt the unspeakable pain of scalding steam for a tenth of a second, before the explosion ended all they knew forever.

WITH A CLANG OF cast iron on stone and the crackle of splintering ash, the Kalamazoo Velocipede tumbled down the railroad embankment.

"What the hell is that?"

Jack Douglas, ninety-two, was so old he'd started out as an Indian fighter protecting the first western railroad's right of way. The company kept him on out of rare sentiment and let him act as a sort of night watchman patrolling the quiet Glendale rail yard with a heavy single-action Colt .44 on his hip. He reached for it with a veined and bony hand and began sliding it with practiced ease from its oiled holster.

The Wrecker lunged with shocking swiftness. His thrust was so efficient that it would have caught a man his own age flat-footed. The watchman never had a chance. The telescoping sword was in his throat and out again before he crumpled to the ground.

The Wrecker looked down at the body in disgust. Of all the ridiculous things to go wrong. Jumped by an old geezer who should have been in bed hours ago. He shrugged and said, half aloud, with a smile, "Waste not, want not." Pulling a poster from his coat pocket, he crushed it into a ball. Then he knelt beside the body, forced open the dead hand, and closed the fingers around the crumpled paper.

Dark and empty streets led to where the Southern Pacific rails crossed the narrow tracks of the Los Angeles & Glendale Electric Railway. The big green streetcars of the interurban passenger line did not run after midnight. Instead, taking advantage of inexpensive electricity purchased in bulk at night, the railway carried freight. Keeping a sharp eye for police, the Wrecker hopped aboard a car filled with milk cans and fresh carrots bound for Los Angeles.

It was growing light when he jumped off in the city and made his way across East Second Street. The dome of the Atchison, Topeka and Santa Fe Railway's Moorish-style La Grande Station was silhouetted against a lurid red dawn. He retrieved a suitcase from the luggage room and changed out of his dusty clothes in the men's room. Then he boarded the Santa Fe's flyer to Albuquerque and sat down to a breakfast of steak and eggs and fresh-baked rolls in a dining car set with silver and china.

As the flyer's locomotive gathered way, the imperious conductor of the express passenger train came through, demanding, "Tickets, gents."

Affecting the brusque attitude of a man who traveled regularly for business, the Wrecker did not bother to look up from his *Los Angeles Times,* which allowed him to keep his face down, concealing his features, as he wiped his fingers on a fine linen napkin and fished out his wallet.

"You've cut your finger!" said the conductor, staring at a bright red bloodstain on the napkin.

"Stropping my razor," said the Wrecker, still not looking up from his newspaper while cursing again the drunken blacksmith he wished he had killed.

6

IT WAS STILL THREE IN THE MORNING WHEN ISAAC BELL bounded off the train before it stopped rolling onto the waterfront terminal on Oakland Mole. This was the end of the line for westbound passengers, a mile-long arm of rock that the Southern Pacific Railroad had built into San Francisco Bay. The pier reached another mile into the bay to deliver freight trains to seagoing vessels and boxcar floats to the city, but passengers transferred here to their ferry.

Bell ran for the ferry, scanning the bustling terminal for Lori March, the old farm woman from whom he always bought flowers. Nestled in the bottom of his watch pocket was a small, flat key to Marion Morgan's apartment.

Drowsy newsboys with seeds in their hair from the hay barges where they slept were crying in shrill voices "Extra! Extra!" and waving special editions of every newspaper printed in San Francisco.

The first headline to rivet Isaac Bell's eye stopped him dead.

TRAIN WRECKERS DITCH COAST LINE
LIMITED AT GLENDALE

Bell felt as if he'd taken a bowie knife in the stomach. Glendale was seven hundred miles from the Cascades Cutoff.

"Mr. Bell, sir? Mr. Bell?"

Right behind the newsboy was an operative from Van Dorn's San Francisco office. He didn't look much older than the kid hawking the papers. His brown hair was pillow-flattened against his head, and he had a sleep wrinkle still creasing his cheek. But his bright blue eyes were wide with excitement.

"I'm Dashwood, Mr. Bell. San Francisco office. Mr. Bronson left me in charge when he took everyone to Sacramento. They won't be back until tomorrow."

"What do you know about the Limited?"

"I just spoke with the railway police supervisor here in Oakland. It looks like they dynamited the locomotive, blew it right off the tracks."

"How many killed?"

"Six, so far. Fifty injured. Some missing."

"When's the next train to Los Angeles?"

"There's a flyer leaving in ten minutes."

"I'll be on it. Telephone the Los Angeles office. Tell them I said to get to the wreck and don't let anyone touch anything. Including the police."

Young Dashwood leaned in close, as if to impart information not privy to the newsboys, and whispered, "The police think the train wrecker was killed in the explosion."

"*What?*"

"A union agitator named William Wright. Obviously, a radical."

"Who says?"

"Everybody."

Isaac Bell cast a cold eye on the kaleidoscope of headlines that the newsboys were brandishing.

DEED OF DASTARDS
DEATH LIST SWELLS. TWENTY LIVES LOST
TRAIN WRECKERS DYNAMITE LOCOMOTIVE
EXPRESS PLUNGES INTO RIVERBED

He suspected that the closest to actual fact was EXPRESS PLUNGES INTO RIVERBED. How it happened was speculation. How could they possibly know the death toll of a wreck that happened just hours ago, five hundred miles away? He was not surprised that the lurid headline DEATH LIST SWELLS. TWENTY LIVES LOST was splashed on a newspaper owned by yellow journalist Preston Whiteway, a man who never let facts get in the way of sales. Marion Morgan had just started to work as the assistant to the editor of his *San Francisco Inquirer*.

"Dashwood! What's your given name?"

"Jimmy—James."

"O.K., James. Here's what I want you to do. Find out everything about Mr. William Wright that 'everybody' doesn't know. What union does he belong to? Is he an official of that union? What have the police arrested him for? What are his grievances? Who are his associates?" Staring down at the smaller man, he fixed James Dashwood in a powerful gaze. "Can you do that for me?"

"Yes, sir."

"It's vital that we know whether he worked alone or with a gang. You have my authority to call on every Van Dorn operative you need to help you. Wire your report to me care of the Southern Pacific's Burbank station. I'll read it when I get off the train."

As the Los Angeles flyer steamed from the piers, the fog was thick, and Isaac Bell looked in vain for the electric lights of San Francisco twinkling across the bay. He checked his watch that the train had departed on time. When he returned the watch to its pocket, he felt the brass key that shared the same space. He had planned to surprise Marion with a middle-of-the-night visit. Instead, he was the one surprised. Badly surprised. The Wrecker's reach extended much further than he had presumed. And more innocent people had died.

THE SHARP SOUTHERN CALIFORNIA noonday sun illuminated wreckage unlike any Isaac Bell had ever seen. The front of the Coast Line Limited's locomotive stood pitched forward, intact, at a steep angle in a dry riverbed at the bottom of the railroad embankment. The cowcatcher in the ground and the headlight and smokestack were readily identifiable. Behind them, where the rest of locomotive should be, all that remained was a crazy spiderweb of boiler tubes, scores of pipes twisted at every angle imaginable. Some ninety tons of steel boiler, brick firebox, cab, pistons, and drive wheels had disappeared.

"Close shave for the passengers," said the director of maintenance and operations for Southern Pacific, who was showing Bell around. He was a portly, potbellied man in a sober three-piece suit, and he seemed genuinely surprised that the death toll had not been much higher than the now-confirmed seven. The passengers had already been taken to Los Angeles on a relief train. The Southern Pacific's special hospital car stood unused on the main line, its doctor and nurse with little to do but bandage the occasional cut suffered by the track crews repairing the damage to reopen the line.

"Nine of the cars held to the rails," the director explained. "The tender and baggage car shielded them from the full force of the explosion."

Bell could see how they had deflected the shock wave and the flying debris. The tender, with its cargo spilled from its demolished sides, looked more like a coal pile than rolling stock. The baggage car was riddled as if it had been shelled by artillery. But he saw none of the singeing associated with an explosion of dynamite.

"Dynamite never blew a locomotive like that."

"Of course not. You're looking at the effects of a boiler explosion. Water sloshed forward when she tipped and the crown sheet failed."

"So she derailed first?"

"Appears she did."

Bell fixed him with a cold stare. "A passenger reported she was running very fast and hitting the curves hard."

"Nonsense."

"Are you sure? She was running late."

"I knew Rufus Patrick. Safest engineer on the line."

"Then why'd she leave the tracks?"

"She had help from that son of a bitch unionist."

Bell said, "Show me where she left the tracks."

The director led Bell to the point where the track stopped on one side. Past the missing rail was a line of splintered ties and a deep rut through the ballast where the drive wheels had scattered the crushed stone.

"The sidewinder knew his business, I'll give him that."

"What do you mean 'knew his business'?"

The portly official stuck his thumbs in his vest, and explained. "There are numerous ways to derail a train, and I've seen them all. I was a locomotive engineer back in the eighties during the big strikes, which got bloody, you may recall—no, you're too young. Take it from me, there was plenty of sabotage in those days. And it was hard on fellows like me that sided with the company, driving a train never knowing when strikers were conspiring to knock the rails out from under you."

"What are the ways to derail a train?" Bell asked.

"You can mine the track with dynamite. Trouble is, you have to stick around to light the fuse. You might make a timing device out of an alarm clock, giving you time to get away, but if the train is delayed it'll blow at the wrong time. Or you set up a trigger so the weight of the engine detonates the powder, but triggers are not reliable, and some poor track inspector comes along on a handcar and blows himself to eternity. Another way is, you pry up some tie spikes and unscrew the bolts out of the fisheye that holds two rails together, reeve a long cable through those bolt-holes, and yank on it when the train comes. Trouble is, you need a whole bunch of fellows strong enough to move the rail. And you're standing there in plain sight, holding the cable, when she hits the ground. But this sidewinder used a hook, which is damned-near foolproof."

The director showed Bell marks on the crosstie where a spike puller had dented the wood. Then he showed him scratches on the last rail made by a track wrench. "Pried up spikes and unbolted the fisheye, like I told you. We found his tools thrown down the embankment. On a curve, it's possible the loose rail might move. But to be sure, he bolted a hook onto the loose rail. The locomotive caught the hook and ripped her own rail right out from under her. Diabolical."

"What sort of man would know how to do something so effective?"

"Effective?" The director bridled.

"You just said he knows his business."

"Yes, I get your point. Well, he could have been a railroad man. Or even a civil engineer. And from what I heard of that cutoff tunnel explosion, he must have known a thing or two about geology to collapse both bores with one charge."

"But the dead unionist you found was an electrician."

"Then his radical unionist associates showed him the ropes."

"Where did you find the unionist's body?"

The director pointed at a tall tree two hundred feet away. The boiler explosion had blown all its leaves off, and bare branches clawed at the sky like a skeletal hand. "Found him and the poor fireman top of that sycamore."

Isaac Bell barely glanced at the tree. In his pocket was James Dashwood's report on William Wright. It was so remarkably detailed that young Dashwood would get a "slap on the shoulder" promotion next time he saw him. Inside of eight hours, Dashwood had discovered that William Wright had been treasurer of the Electrical Workers Union. He was credited with averting strikes by employing negotiating tactics that elicited the admiration of both labor and owners. He had also served as a deacon of the Trinity Episcopal Church in Santa Barbara. According to his grieving sister, Wright had been accompanying her son to a job in Los Angeles with a film laboratory. The office manager of the laboratory had confirmed they were expecting the boy to arrive that morning and had reported to Dashwood that the apprenticeship had been offered because he and William Wright belonged to the same Shriners lodge. So much for the Wrecker killed in the crash. The murderous saboteur was still alive, and God alone knew where he would attack next.

"Where's the hook?"

"Your men over there are guarding it. Now, if you'll excuse me, Mr. Bell, I've got a railroad to put back together."

Bell walked along the torn roadbed to where Larry Sanders from Van Dorn's Los Angeles office was crouched down inspecting a tie. Two of his heavyset musclemen were holding the railway police at bay. Bell introduced himself, and Sanders stood up, brushing dust from his knees.

Larry Sanders was a slim man with stylishly short hair and a mustache so thin it looked like he had applied it with a pencil. He was dressed similarly to Bell in a white linen suit appropriate to the warm climate, but his hat was a city man's derby and, oddly, was as white as his suit. Unlike Bell's boots, his shoes were shiny dancing pumps, and he looked like he would be happier guarding the lobby of an expensive hotel than standing in the coal dust that coated the busily trafficked roadbed. Bell, who was used to sartorial eccentrics in Los Angeles, paid Sander's odd head and footwear little mind at first, and started on the assumption that the Van Dorn man was competent.

"Heard about you," Sanders said, offering a soft, manicured hand. "My boss wired from Sacramento, said you were coming down. I always wanted to meet you."

"Where's the hook?"

"The cinder dicks had already found it by the time we got here."

Sanders led Bell to a length of rail that had been bent like a pretzel. On one end was bolted a hook that looked like it had been fashioned from an anchor. "Is that blood or rust?"

"Didn't notice that." Sanders opened a pearl-handled pocketknife and scratched at it. "Blood. Dried blood. Looks like he cut his hand on a burr of metal. Keen eyes, Mr. Bell."

Isaac ignored the flattery. "Find out who drilled this hole."

"What's that, Mr. Bell?"

"We can't haul in every man in California with a cut on his hand, but you can find out who drilled that hole in this peculiar piece of metal. Canvas every machine shop and blacksmith in the county. Immediately. On the jump!"

Isaac Bell turned on his heel and went to talk to the railroad dicks, who were watching sullenly. "Ever seen a hook like that before?"

"Hunk of boat anchor."

"That's what I thought." He opened a gold cigarette case and passed it around. When the cinder dicks had smokes going and Bell had established their names, Tom Griggs and Ed Bottomley, he asked, "If that fellow in the tree happened *not* to wreck the Limited, how do you think the real wrecker got away after he ditched the train?"

The railway cops exchanged glances.

Ed said, "That hook bought him plenty of time."

Then Tom said, "We found a track-inspection vehicle tipped over the side in Glendale. Got a report someone stole it from the freight depot at Burbank."

"O.K. But if he got to Glendale by handcar, it must have been three or four in the morning," Bell mused. "How do you suppose he got away from Glendale? Streetcars don't run that late."

"Could have had a automobile waiting for him."

"Think so?"

"Well, you could ask Jack Douglas, except he's dead. He was watching Glendale. Someone killed him last night. Ran him straight through like a stuck pig."

"First I heard," said Bell.

"Well, maybe you ain't been talking to the right people," replied the cinder dick, with a scornful glance at the dandified Sanders waiting nearby.

Isaac Bell returned a thin smile. "What did you mean by 'ran through'? Stabbed?"

"Stabbed?" asked Ed. "When's the last time you saw a stabbing dust both sides of a fellow's coat? The man who killed him was either one strong son of a bitch or used a sword."

"A sword?" Bell repeated. "Why do you say a sword?"

"Even if he were strong enough to stick him in one side and out the other with a bowie knife, he'd have a heck of a time trying to pull it out. That's why folks leave knives in bodies. Damned things get stuck. So I'm thinking a long, thin blade, like a sword."

"That is very interesting," said Bell. "A very interesting idea . . . Anything else I should know?"

The cinder dicks thought on that for a long moment. Bell waited patiently, looking both in the eye. Superintendent Jethro Watt's "orders from on high" to cooperate did not automatically percolate down to the cops in the field, particularly when they ran up against a supercilious Van Dorn agent like Larry Sanders. Abruptly, Tom Griggs came to a decision. "Found this in Jack's hand." He pulled out a crumpled sheet of paper and smoothed it with his grimy fingers. Black lettering stood starkly in the sun.

ARISE!
FAN THE FLAMES OF DISCONTENT
DESTROY THE FAVORED FEW
SO WORKINGMEN MAY LIVE!

"I don't suppose it was Jack's," said Tom. "That old man weren't the sort to turn radical."

"Looks like," explained Ed, "Jack grabbed hold of it in their struggle."

Tom said, "Would have done better to grab his gun."

"So it would appear," said Isaac Bell.

"Strange thing is why he didn't."

"What do you mean?" asked Bell.

Tom said, "I mean you could make a mistake thinking that because Jack Douglas was ninety-two years old that he was asleep at the switch. Just last year, a couple of city boys came out to Glendale looking for easy pickings. Drew guns on Jack. He drilled one through the shoulder with that old hogleg of his and the other in the backside."

Ed chuckled. "Jack told me he was getting soft. In the old days, he would have killed them both and scalped them. I said, 'You didn't miss by much, Jack. You plugged one in the shoulder and the other in the rear.' But Jack said, 'I said *soft*, not *afflicted*. I didn't *miss*. I hit 'em right where I aimed. Shows I'm turning kindly in my old age.' So whoever got the drop on Jack last night knew how to handle himself."

"Particularly," Tom added, "if all he had on him was a sword. Jack would have seen that coming a mile away. I mean, how does a man with a sword get the jump on a man with a gun?"

"I've been wondering the same thing," said Bell. "Thank you, gentlemen. Thank you very much." He took out two of his cards and gave one to each. "If you ever need anything from the Van Dorn Agency, get in touch with me."

● ● ●

"I WAS RIGHT," BELL told Joseph Van Dorn when Van Dorn summoned him to San Francisco. "But not right enough. He's thinking even bigger than I imagined."

"Sounds like he knows his business," said Van Dorn, grimly echoing the Southern Pacific maintenance director. "At least, enough to run circles around us. But how does he get around? Freight trains?"

Bell answered, "I've sent operatives to question the hobos in every jungle in the West. And we're asking every stationmaster and ticket clerk in every station he might have been near who bought a ticket on a long-distance flyer."

Van Dorn groaned. "The ticket clerks are even a longer shot than the hobos. How many passengers did Hennessy say the Southern Pacific carries per year?"

"One hundred million," Bell admitted.

7

WHEN ISAAC BELL TELEPHONED MARION MORGAN TO TELL
her he had one hour free in San Francisco before he caught his train
to Sacramento and could she possibly get off work early, Marion
replied, "Meet me at the clock!"

The Great Magneta Clock, the first master clock west of the Mississippi, which had come around the Horn by steamship, was famous
already, even though it had been installed in the St. Francis Hotel
only the week before. Dominating the Powell Street lobby of the
St. Francis, the ornately carved Viennese timepiece resembled a very
large grandfather clock and looked somewhat old-fashioned in the
European mode. But it was, in fact, electrically powered, and it automatically controlled all the clocks in the vast hotel that towered over
Union Square.

The lobby was furnished with suites of chairs and couches arranged
on oriental carpets. Parchment- and glass-shaded electric lamps cast
a warm glow, which was reflected and multiplied in gilt mirrors. The
air smelled sweetly of sawn wood and fresh paint. Eighteen months
after the fires ignited by the Great Earthquake had gutted its interior, San Francisco's newest and grandest hotel was open for business

with four hundred eighty rooms, and a new wing planned for the following spring. It had instantly become the most popular hotel in the city. Most of the chairs and couches were occupied by paying guests reading newspapers. The headlines blared the latest rumors about the labor agitators and foreign radicals who had ditched the Coast Line Limited.

Marion swept into the lobby first, so excited to see Isaac that she was oblivious to the open stares of admiration she drew from various gentlemen as they watched her pace before the clock. She wore her straw-blond hair high on her head, a fashionable style that drew attention to her long, graceful neck and the beauty of her face. Her waist was narrow, her hands delicate, and, judging how she seemed to flow across the carpet, the legs beneath her full skirt were long.

Her coral-sea green eyes flashed toward the clock as the minute hand inched upright and the Great Magneta struck three mighty *gongs* that resounded so much like the bells of a cathedral that they seemed to shake the walls.

One minute later, Isaac strode into the lobby, tall and ruggedly handsome in a cream-colored woolen sack suit, crisp blue fold-collar shirt, and the gold-striped necktie she had given him that matched his flaxen hair and mustache. She was so delighted by the sight of him that all she could think to say was, "I've never seen you late before."

Isaac smiled back as he opened his gold pocket watch. "The Great Magneta is sixty seconds fast." He let his eyes roam over her, saying, "And I've never seen you prettier." Then he swept her into his arms and kissed her.

He guided her to a pair of chairs where he could watch the entire lobby with the aid of several mirrors, and they ordered tea with lemon cake from a waiter in a tailcoat.

"What are you looking at?" Bell asked. She was staring at him with a soft smile on her beautiful face.

"You turned my life upside down."

"That was the earthquake," he teased her.

"Before the earthquake. The earthquake was only an interruption."

Ladies Marion Morgan's age were supposed to have married years before, but she was a levelheaded woman who enjoyed her independence. At thirty, with years of experience supporting herself working as a senior secretary in the banking business, she had lived on her own since graduating with her law degree from Stanford University. The handsome, wealthy suitors who had begged for her hand in marriage had all been disappointed. Perhaps it was the air of San Francisco, so filled with endless possibilities, that gave her courage. Perhaps it was her education by handpicked tutors and her loving father after her mother died. Perhaps it was living in modern times, the excitement of being alive in the bold first years of the new century. But something had filled her with confidence and a rare ability to take real pleasure in the circumstance of being alone.

That is, until Isaac Bell walked into her life and made her heart quicken as if she were seventeen years old and on her first date.

I am so lucky, she thought.

Isaac took Marion's hand.

For a long moment, he found it difficult to speak. Her beauty, her poise, and her grace never failed to move him. Staring into her green eyes, he finally said, "I am the happiest man in San Francisco. And if we were in New York right now, I would be the happiest man in New York."

She smiled and looked away. When she looked back to meet his eyes, she saw that his gaze had shifted to a newspaper headline: DITCHED!

Train wrecks were a part of daily life in 1907, but to have a Los Angeles flyer crash and knowing that Isaac rode trains all the time was terrifying. Oddly, she worried less about the dangers in his work. They were real, and she had seen his scars. But to worry about Isaac encountering gunmen and knife fighters would be as irrational as fretting about a tiger's safety in the jungle.

He was staring at the paper, his face dark with anger. She touched his hand. "Isaac, is that train wreck about your case?"

"Yes. It's at least the fifth attack."

"But there is something in your face, something fierce, that tells me it is very personal."

"Do you remember when I told you about Wish Clarke?"

"Of course. He saved your life. I hope to meet him one day to thank him personally."

"The man who wrecked that train killed Wish," Bell said coldly.

"Oh, Isaac. I'm so sorry."

With that, Bell filled her in, as was his custom with her, detailing all he knew of the Wrecker's attacks on Osgood Hennessy's Southern Pacific Cascades Cutoff and how he was trying to stop them. Marion had a keen, analytical mind. She could focus on pertinent facts and see patterns early in their development. Above all, she raised critical questions that honed his own thinking.

"Motive is still an open question," he concluded. "What ulterior motive is driving him to such destruction?"

"Do you believe the theory that the Wrecker is a radical?" Marion asked.

"The evidence is there. His accomplices. The radical poster. Even the target—the railroad is a prime villain to radicals."

"You sound dubious, Isaac."

"I am," he admitted. "I've tried to put myself in his shoes, tried to think like an angry agitator—but I still can't imagine the wholesale slaughter of innocent people. In the heat of a riot or in a strike, they might attack the police. While I will not condone such violence, I can *understand* how a man's thinking gets twisted. But this relentless attack on ordinary people . . . such viciousness makes no sense."

"Could he be a madman? A lunatic?"

"He could. Except that he is remarkably ambitious and methodical for a lunatic. These are not impulsive attacks. He plans them meticulously. And he plans his escape just as carefully. If it's madness, it's under fine control."

"He may be an anarchist."

"I know. But why kill so many people? In fact," he mused, "it's almost as if he is trying to sow terror. But what does he gain by sowing terror?"

Marion answered, "The public humiliation of the Southern Pacific Railroad Company."

"He is certainly achieving that," said Bell.

"Maybe instead of thinking like a radical or an anarchist or a madman, you should think like a banker."

"What do you mean?" He looked at her, uncomprehending.

Marion answered in a clear, steady voice. "Imagine what it is costing Osgood Hennessy."

Bell nodded thoughtfully. The irony of "thinking like a banker" was not lost on a man who had turned his back on an obligatory career in his own family's powerful bank. He touched her cheek. "Thank you," he said. "You've given me a lot to ponder."

"I'm relieved," said Marion, and teasingly added, "I'd rather you ponder than get into gunfights."

"I like gunfights," Bell bantered back. "They focus the mind. Though in this case we may be talking about sword fights."

"Sword fights?"

"It's very strange. He killed Wish and another man with what appears to be some kind of sword. The question is: how does he get the drop on a man with a gun? You can't hide a sword."

"What about a sword cane? Plenty of men in San Francisco carry sword canes for protection."

"But just unsheathing it, drawing the blade out of the cane, would give a man with a gun all the time he needed to shoot first."

"Well, if he comes after *you* with a sword, he'll be sorry. You fenced for Yale."

Bell shook his head with a smile. "Fenced, not dueled. There's a big difference between sport and combat. I recall my coach, who had been a duelist, explaining that the fencing mask hides your opponent's eyes. As he put it, the first time you fight a duel, you are shocked to meet the cold gaze of a man who intends to kill you."

"Were you?"

"Was I what?"

"Shocked." She smiled. "Don't pretend to me you've never fought a duel."

Bell smiled back. "Only once. We were both very young. And the sight of spurting red blood soon convinced us that we didn't really want to kill each other. In fact, we're still friends."

"If you're looking for a duelist, there can't be too many of them left in this day and age."

"Likely, a European," mused Bell. "Italian or French."

"Or German. With one of those horrible Heidelberg scars on his cheek. Didn't Mark Twain write that they pulled the surgeon's stitches apart and poured wine in their wounds to make the scars even uglier?"

"Probably not a German," said Bell. "They're known for the plunging blow. The thrust that killed Wish and the other fellow was more in the style of an Italian or a Frenchman."

"Or the student of?" Marion suggested. "An American who went to school in Europe. There are plenty of anarchists in France and Italy. Maybe that's where he became one."

"I still don't know how he takes a man with a gun by surprise." He demonstrated with a gesture. "In the time it takes to draw a sword, you can step in and punch him in the nose."

Marion reached across the teacups and took Bell's hand. "To tell the truth, I would be delighted if a bloody nose is the most I have to worry about."

"At this point, I would love a bloody nose, or even a flesh wound or two."

"Whatever for?"

"You remember Weber and Fields?"

"The funny old gents." Wally Kisley and Mack Fulton had taken her to dinner while passing through San Francisco recently and kept her laughing all evening.

"Wally and Mack always say, 'Bloody noses are a sure sign of progress. You know you're close when your quarry pokes you in the snoot.' Right now, I could use a good poke in the snoot." The comment brought a smile to their faces.

Two women, fashionably dressed in the latest hats and gowns, entered the hotel lobby and crossed it in a flourish of feathers and silk. The younger was so striking that many of the lowered newspapers remained on their owners' laps.

Marion said, "What a beautiful girl!"

Bell had already seen her in a mirror.

"The girl wearing pale blue," said Marion.

"She is Osgood Hennessy's daughter, Lillian," said Bell, wondering if it was coincidence that had brought Lillian to the St. Francis while he was here, and suspecting it was not.

"Do you know her?"

"I met her last week aboard Hennessy's special. She's his private secretary."

"What is she like?"

Bell smiled. "She has pretensions to being a seductress. Flashes her eyes like that French actress."

"Anna Held."

"She is intelligent, though, and savvy about business. She's very young, spoiled by her adoring father, and, I suspect, very innocent when it comes to matters of the heart. The dark-haired woman with her used to be her tutor. Now she's Hennessy's mistress."

"Do you want to go over and say hello?"

"Not when I have only minutes left to spend with you."

Marion returned a pleased grin. "I am flattered. She is young, unspeakably beautiful, and presumably very rich."

"You are unspeakably beautiful, and when you marry me you will be very rich, too."

"But I'm not an heiress."

"I've known my fill of heiresses, thank you very much, since we were taught the Boston Waltz in dancing school," he said, grinning back. "It's a slow waltz with a long glide. We can dance it at our wedding, if you like."

"Oh, Isaac, are you sure you want to marry me?"

"I am sure."

"Most people would call me an old maid. And they would say that a man your age should marry a girl her age."

"I've never done what I 'should' do. Why should I start now when I've finally met the girl of my dreams? *And* made a friend for life?"

"But what will your family think of me? I have no money. They'll think I'm a gold digger."

"They will think I am the luckiest man in America." Isaac smiled. But then he added, soberly, "Any who don't can go straight to hell. Shall we set a date?"

"Isaac . . . I have to talk to you."

"What is it? Is something the matter?"

"I am deeply in love with you. I hope you know that."

"You show me in every way."

"And I want ever so much to marry you. But I wonder if we could wait a little while."

"Why?"

"I've been offered an exciting job, and it is something I would like to try very much."

"What sort of job?"

"Well . . . you know who Preston Whiteway is, of course?"

"Of course. Preston Whiteway is a yellow journalist who inherited three of California's leading newspapers, including the *San Francisco Inquirer*." He gave her a curious smile. "The newspaper you happen to work for . . . He's said to be quite handsome and a celebrated 'man-about-town,' and he flaunts his wealth, which he earns publishing sensationalist headlines. He's also sunk his hooks into national politics by using the power of his newspapers to get his friends appointed to the United States Senate—first among them Osgood Hennessy's lapdog legislator, Senator Charles Kincaid. In fact, I believe that it was your Mr. Whiteway who gave Kincaid the moniker 'Hero Engineer.'"

"He's not *my* Mr. Whiteway, but— Oh, Isaac, he has a wonderful new idea. He came up with it while the paper was reporting on the earthquake—a moving-picture newsreel. He's calling it *Picture World*. They'll take moving pictures of actual events and play them in theaters and nickelodeons. And, Isaac!"—she gripped his arm in her excitement—"Preston asked me to help get it started."

"For how long?"

"I'm not sure. Six months or a year. Isaac, I know I can do this. And this man will give me a chance to try. You know that I took my degree in law in Stanford's first graduating class, but a woman can't get a job in law, which is why I've worked nine years in banking. I've learned so much. It's not that I want to work my whole life. But I want to *make* something, and this is my chance to make something."

Bell was not surprised by Marion's desire to work at an exciting job. Nor did he doubt their love. They were both too well aware of their great good fortune at having discovered each other to ever let someone come between them. Some sort of a compromise was in order. And he could not deny that he had his own hands full trying to stop the Wrecker.

"What if we were to promise that in six months we would set a date to marry? When things have settled down? You can still work and be married."

"Oh, Isaac, that would be wonderful. I so much want to be in at the beginning of *Picture World*."

The bells of the Magneta Clock began to strike four o'clock.

"I wish we had more time," she said sadly.

It seemed to Bell like only minutes since they had sat down. "I'll drive you to your office."

He noticed that Lillian Hennessy was looking pointedly the other way as they left the lobby. But Mrs. Comden parted her lips in a discreet smile as their eyes met. He returned a polite nod, struck again, forcibly, by the woman's sensuality, and gripped Marion's arm a little tighter.

A fire-engine-red, gasoline-powered Locomobile racer was parked directly in front of the St. Francis. It was modified for street traffic with fenders and searchlight headlamps. The hotel doormen were guarding the car from gawking small boys, threatening dire punishment to the first who dared lay dirty fingers on the gleaming brass eagle atop its radiator, much less breathe near its red leather seats.

"You got your race car back! It's beautiful," said Marion, showing her delight.

Bell's beloved Locomobile had been beaten half to death by a five-hundred-mile race against a locomotive from San Francisco to San Diego, with the locomotive steaming on smooth rails and the Locomobile pounding over California's rock-strewn dirt roads. A race, Bell remembered with a grim smile, that he had won. His trophy had been the arrest of the Butcher Bandit at gunpoint.

"As soon as the factory rebuilt it, I had it shipped out here from Bridgeport, Connecticut. Hop in."

Bell leaned past the big steering wheel to turn the ignition switch on the wooden dashboard. He set the throttle and spark levers. Then he pumped the pressure tank. The doorman offered to crank the motor. Still warm from the drive from the freight depot where Bell had taken delivery, the four-cylinder engine thundered to life on the first heave. Bell advanced the spark and eased the throttle. As he reached to release the brake, he beckoned the smallest of the boys who were watching big-eyed.

"Can you give me a hand? She can't roll without blowing her horn!"

The boy squeezed the big rubber horn bulb with both hands. The Locomobile bellowed like a Rocky Mountain bighorn. Boys scattered. The car lurched ahead. Marion laughed and leaned across the gas tank to hold Bell's arm. Soon they were racing toward Market Street, weaving around straining horse carts and streetcars and thundering past slower automobiles.

As they pulled up in front of the twelve-story, steel-frame building that housed the *San Francisco Inquirer*, Bell spotted the last parking space left by the curb. A fair-haired gent in an open Rolls-Royce veered toward it, blowing his horn.

"Oh, there's Preston! You can meet him."

"Can't wait," said Bell, stomping his accelerator and brake in quick succession to skid the big Locomobile into the last spot, a half second ahead of Preston Whiteway's Rolls.

"Hey! That's my spot."

Bell noticed that Whiteway was as handsome as rumored, a bluff, broad-shouldered, clean-shaven man with extravagant waves of blond hair. As tall as Bell, though considerably bulkier in the middle, he looked like he had played football in college and could not recall the last time he had not had his way.

"I got here first," said Bell.

"I own this building!"

"You can have it back after I say good-bye to my girl."

Now Preston Whiteway craned his neck to look past Bell, and bawled, "Marion? Is that you?"

"Yes! This is Isaac. I want you to meet him."

"Pleased to meet you!" said Preston Whiteway, looking anything but. "Marion, we better get upstairs. We've got work to do."

"You go ahead," she said coolly. "I want to say good-bye to Isaac."

Whiteway leaped from his car, bellowing for the doorman to park it. As he charged past, he asked Bell, "How fast is your Locomobile?"

"Faster than that," said Bell, nodding at the Rolls-Royce.

Marion covered her mouth to keep from laughing, and when Whiteway had moved out of earshot she said to Bell, "You two sounded like boys in a school yard. How could you be jealous of Preston? He's really very nice. You'll like him when you get to know him."

"I'm sure," said Bell. He took her beautiful face gently in his hands and kissed her lips. "Now, you take care of yourself."

"Me? You take care of yourself. Please, take care of yourself." She forced a smile. "Maybe you should bone up on your sword fighting."

"I intend to."

"Oh, Isaac, I wish we had more time."

"I'll get back as soon as I can."

"I love you, my darling."

HIGH ABOVE THE CASCADES Cutoff construction yard, a single gondola car had been left behind on a siding. It sat a short distance above the switch that, when closed, would connect the siding to the steep grade of a supply spur that connected the railroad's newly built lumber mill in the forest miles up the mountain to the construction yard below. The car was heavily laden, heaped higher than its sides with a crown of freshly sawn mountain hemlock crossties bound for the cut-off's creosoting plant to be impregnated with coal tar preservative.

The Wrecker saw an opportunity to strike again, sooner than he had planned, killing two birds with one stone. This attack would rattle not only the Southern Pacific Railroad. If he could pull it off, it would announce how immune he was from the protective efforts of the Van Dorn Detective Agency.

He was a coldly methodical man. He had planned the tunnel attack meticulously, allotting time to every stage, from recruiting an accomplice with the ideal mix of zeal and naïveté to pinpointing the geologically propitious location for the dynamite to planning his escape route. The Coast Line Limited attack had taken similar efforts, including using a hook to make it obvious that the destruction was sabotage, not a mere accident. He had similar schemes for wreckage lined up, in various stages of readiness, although some of them had to be scrapped now that the Van Dorn detectives were guarding key rail yards and maintenance shops.

But not every sabotage job had to be planned. The railroad system that crisscrossed the nation was immensely complex. Opportunities for destruction abounded, so long as he employed his superior knowledge to be ever alert to mistakes and negligence.

So long as he moved quickly and did the unexpected.

The gondola would remain only briefly on the siding. With twenty-seven hundred ties required per mile of track, it could not be more than a day or two before a hard-pressed materials superintendent down in the yard roared "Where the hell are the rest of my ties?" and terrified clerks began desperately combing through invoices and dispatches for the missing car.

The nearest hobo jungle big enough that he would not be noticed, in the crush of men cooking meals, hunting a space to sleep, and coming and going on their endless quest for work, was outside the rail yards in Dunsmuir, California. But Dunsmuir was a hundred fifty miles down the line. That left no time to recruit a believer. He would have to do the gondola job himself. There was risk in attacking alone and risk in attacking quickly. But the destruction he could wreak with that single car was almost incalculable.

WITH MARION'S GOOD-BYE KISS STILL SWEET ON HIS LIPS, Isaac Bell settled into his seat on the flyer to Sacramento and waited for the train to pull out of Oakland Terminal. She knew him well, better than he knew himself. On the other hand, there were things she might never know. *How could you be jealous of Preston?* Let me count the ways, thought Bell. Starting with, Whiteway is there with you and I'm not, because I'm falling behind in my race to stop the Wrecker.

He closed his eyes. He hadn't slept in a bed for days, but sleep eluded him. His mind was racing. From the state capital, he would take a series of trains north toward distant Oregon. He needed a fresh look at the Cascades Cutoff tunnel collapse, with an eye toward reckoning whether the Wrecker intended another attack at the front end of the tunnel. On the way, he would meet with Archie Abbott, who'd wired him that he might be hitting pay dirt with the hobo jungle outside Dunsmuir.

"Mr. Bell?"

The conductor interrupted Isaac's thoughts. The man touched a knuckle to his polished visor in a respectful salute, and said with a sly wink, "Mr. Bell, there's a lady asking if you would be more comfortable sitting with her."

Suspecting he would find the enterprising young Miss Hennessy in the next Pullman, Bell followed the conductor up the aisle. The conductor led him off the train and directed him across the platform toward a private car coupled to a baggage car hauled by a sleek Atlantic 4-4-2 so shiny it looked like it had just come from the shop.

Bell stepped aboard the car and through a door into a plush red parlor that would not have looked out of place in Anne Pound's brothel. Lillian Hennessy, who had changed out of the pale blue that matched her eyes into a scarlet tea gown that matched the parlor, greeted him with a glass of champagne and a triumphant smile. "You're not the only one who can charter a special."

Bell replied coolly, "It is inappropriate for us to be traveling alone."

"We're not alone. Unfortunately."

As Bell was saying "Besides, may I remind you that I am committed to Marion Morgan," a jazz band struck up in a room at the rear of the car. Bell peered through the door. Six black musicians playing clarinet, bass fiddle, guitar, trombone, and cornet were gathered around an upright piano improvising on Adaline Shepherd's brisk hit rag, "Pickles and Peppers."

Lillian Hennessy pressed close to look past Bell's shoulder. She was tucked into a swan-bill underbust corset, and Bell felt her breasts soft against his back. He had to raise his voice to be heard over the music. "I've never met a jazz musician qualified to act as a chaperone."

"Not *them*." She made a face. "*Her.* Father caught wind of my scheme to ambush you in San Francisco. She sent her to keep an eye on me."

The cornet player wheeled his horn in the air, as if to spear the ceiling. In the gap he opened in the circle of musicians, Bell saw that the piano player arched over the keys, with fingers flying, eyes bright, and full lips parted in a gleeful smile, was none other than Mrs. Comden.

Lillian said, "I don't know how he found out. But thanks to Father and Mrs. Comden, your honor will be safe, Mr. Bell. Please stay. All I ask is that we become friends. We'll have a fast ride. We're cleared straight through to the Cascades Cutoff."

Bell was tempted. The line north of Sacramento was congested with materials and work trains heading to and from the cutoff. He had been considering ordering up one of Hennessy's specials. Lillian's was ready to roll. Steaming northward on cleared tracks, the railroad president's daughter's special would save him a day of travel time.

Lillian said, "There's a telegraph in the baggage car, if you need to send messages."

That tipped it. "Thank you," Bell said with a smile. "I accept your 'ambush,' though I may have to hop off at Dunsmuir."

"Have a glass of champagne, and tell me all about your Miss Morgan."

The train lurched into motion as she handed him the glass. She licked a spilled drop from an exquisitely delicate knuckle and flashed her eyes in French-actress mode. "She was very pretty."

"Marion thought you were, too."

She made another face. "'Pretty' is rosy cheeks and gingham dresses. I am usually called more than pretty."

"Actually, she said you were unspeakably beautiful."

"Is that why you didn't introduce me?"

"I preferred to remind her that she is unspeakably beautiful, too."

Lillian's pale blue eyes flashed. "You don't pull your punches, do you?"

Bell returned a disarming smile. "Never in love, young lady—a habit I recommend you cultivate when you grow up. Now, tell me about your father's troubles with his bankers."

"He has no trouble with his bankers," Lillian shot back. She answered so quickly and so vehemently, Bell knew what to say next.

"He said he would by winter."

"Only if you don't catch the Wrecker," she said pointedly.

"But what of this Panic brewing in New York? It started last March. It doesn't appear to be going away."

Lillian answered with sober deliberateness. "The Panic, if it remains one much longer, will bring boom times in the railroad business to a crashing halt. We're in the midst of wonderful expansion, but even Father admits it can't go on forever."

Bell was again reminded that Lillian Hennessy was more complicated than a coddled heiress.

"Does the Panic threaten your father's control of his lines?"

"No," she said quickly. Then she explained to Bell, "My father learned early on that the way to pay for his second railroad was to manage his first so well that it was solvent and creditworthy and then borrow against it. The bankers would dance to *his* tune. No railroad man in the country would fare better. If the others collapsed, he'd snap up the pieces and come out of it smelling like a rose."

Bell touched his glass to hers. "To roses." He smiled. But he was not sure whether the young woman was boasting truthfully or whistling past the graveyard. And he was even less sure of why the Wrecker was so determined to uproot the tangled garden of railroads.

"Ask any banker in the country," she said, proudly. "He will tell you that Osgood Hennessy is impregnable."

"Let me send a wire telling people where to find me."

Lillian grabbed the champagne bottle and walked him to the baggage car, where the conductor, who doubled as the train's telegrapher, sent Bell's message reporting his whereabouts to Van Dorn. As they were starting to head back to the parlor car, the telegraph key started clattering. Lillian listened for a few seconds, then rolled her eyes and called over her shoulder to the conductor, "Do not answer that."

Bell asked, "Who is that transmitting, your father?"

"No. The Senator."

"Which Senator?"

"Kincaid. Charles Kincaid. He's courting me."

"Do I gather that you are not interested?"

"Senator Charles Kincaid is too poor, too old, and too annoying."

"But very handsome," called Mrs. Comden, with a smile for Bell.

"Very handsome," Lillian agreed. "But still too poor, too old, and too annoying."

"How old?" Bell asked.

"At least forty."

"He's forty-two and extremely vigorous," said Mrs. Comden. "Most girls would call him quite a catch."

"I'd rather catch mumps."

Lillian refilled her glass and Bell's. Then she said, "Emma, is there any chance that you might hop off the train in Sacramento and disappear while Mr. Bell and I steam our way north?"

"Not in this life, dear. You are too young—and far too innocent—to travel without a chaperone. And Mr. Bell is too . . ."

"Too what?"

Emma Comden smiled.

"Interesting."

THE WRECKER HURRIED UP the lumber-mill spur after dark, walking on the crossties so as not make noise crunching the ballast.

He carried a four-foot-long crowbar that weighed thirty pounds.

On his back was a Spanish-American War soldier's knapsack of eighteen-ounce cotton duck with a rubberized flap. Its straps tugged hard on his shoulders. In it were a heavy two-gallon tin of coal oil and a horseshoe he had lifted from one of the many blacksmiths busy shoeing the hundreds of mules that pulled the freight wagons.

The chill mountain air smelled of pine pitch, and something else that took him a moment to recognize. There was actually a hint of snow on the wind. Although it was a clear night, he could feel winter coming early to the mountains. He increased his pace, as his eyes adjusted to the starlight. The rails shone in front of him, and trees took shape along the cut.

A tall, long-legged, fit man, he climbed the steep slope with swift efficiency. He was racing the clock. He had less than two hours until moonrise. When the moon cleared the mountains, lancing the darkness with its full light, he would be a sitting duck for the railway police patrolling on horseback.

After a mile, he came to a Y junction where the spur split. The left-hand spur, which he had been climbing, descended to the construction yard. The spur to the right veered to join the newly completed main line to the south. He checked the switch that controlled which spur was connected.

The switch was positioned so that a train descending from the lumber mill would be routed toward the construction yard. He was tempted to send the heavy car on to the main line. Properly timed, it would collide head-on with a northbound locomotive. But such a collision would block the tracks so the dispatchers would have to stop all trains, which would block his only way out from this end of the line.

The grade continued, a little lighter, and he increased his pace. After another mile, he saw the dark gondola looming. It was still there!

Suddenly, he heard something. He stopped walking. He froze in place. He cupped his hands to his ears. He heard it again, an incongruous sound. Laughter. Drunken men laughing, farther up the mountain. Way in the distance, he could see the orange glow of a campfire. Lumberjacks, he realized, sharing a bottle of Squirrel whiskey. They were too far away to hear him or see him, blinded by the blaze of their fire. Even if they heard the car roll through the switch, by then there would be no stopping it.

He stepped from the spur across a ditch to the siding on which sat the laden gondola. He found the switch handle and threw it, closing the point where the two sets of tracks met, joining the siding to the lumber spur. Then he went to the gondola, kicked wooden chocks from under the front truck, found the cold rim of the brake and turned it until the brake shoes lifted from the car's massive iron wheels.

Now she could roll, and he waited for her to start moving of her own weight since the siding was on an incline. But she sat fast, locked by gravity or the natural minute flattening of her wheels as she sat heavily on the rails. He would have to improvise a car mover.

He went to the back of the gondola, placed his horseshoe a few inches behind the rearmost wheel, propped his crowbar under the wheel where it met the rail, and lowered the bar to the horseshoe, which would serve as his fulcrum. He threw his weight down on the bar and rocked on it.

The bar slipped with a loud screech of metal on metal. He shoved it under the wheel again and resumed rocking. The wheel moved an inch. He jammed the crowbar in deeper, kicked the horseshoe to meet it, and again threw his weight on his makeshift car mover.

A voice spoke, directly overhead, almost in his ear.

"What you doing there?"

He fell back, astonished. Leaning down from the heap of crossties was a lumberjack, waking from a drunken sleep, breath reeking as he slurred, "Partner, you start her rolling, she won't stop 'til she hits bottom. Let me hop down before she sets off."

The Wrecker swung the crowbar in a lightning blur.

The heavy steel crunched against the drunk's skull and knocked him back on the ties like a rag doll. The Wrecker watched for movement, and, when there was none, calmly resumed rocking on the crowbar as if nothing had happened.

He felt the space between the wheel and fulcrum open. The gondola was rolling. He dropped the crowbar and jumped on the car with the tin of coal oil. The car rolled slowly toward the switch and rumbled through it and onto the spur, where it gathered speed. He scrambled past the body of the drunk and turned the brake, tightening it until he felt the shoes rub the wheels, slowing the gondola to about ten miles an hour. Then he opened the tin and splashed the oil on the ties.

The gondola rolled on for a mile to the Y junction, where the grade began to steepen.

He lit a match and, shielding it from the wind of passage, touched it to the coal oil. As the flames spread, he released the brakes. The gondola lunged ahead. He hung down behind the back wheels. The moon chose that moment to clear a mountain and cast light on the tracks brightly enough to illuminate a safe place for him to jump. The Wrecker took it as his just due. He had always been a lucky man. Things always broke his way. Just as they were breaking his way now. He jumped, landed easily. He could hear the gondola turning to the left, rumbling heavily through the Y junction and toward the construction yard.

He turned to the right, down the spur to the main line, away from the yard. The wheels made a humming sound as the gondola sped down the steep grade. The last thing he saw was orange flames moving rapidly down the mountain. In three minutes, every cinder dick on the mountain would be running hell-bent toward the construction yard while he was running the other way.

• • •

SWAYING AS IT ACCELERATED to thirty, forty, then fifty miles an hour, trailing flames behind it, the runaway gondola began to shake its cargo, causing the massive crossties to creak against one another like the timbers of a ship in a heavy sea. The lumberjack, whose name was Don Albert, rolled one way and then the other, arms and legs flopping. His hand slipped into a slot between two ties. When the squared timbers shifted back against each other again and slammed shut on his fingers, he awoke with a howl of pain.

Albert stuck his fingers in his mouth and sucked hard, and began to wonder why everything seemed to be moving. His head, which hurt like hell, was spinning. The cloying taste of red-eye whiskey in his craw explained both familiar sensations. But why did the stars overhead keep shifting position? And why did the splintery wood he was sprawled against seem to vibrate? He reached under his thick knit cap with the hand that didn't hurt and felt a sharp pain in his skull and the stickiness of blood. Must have fallen on his head. Good thing he has a skull like a cannonball.

No, he hadn't fallen. He'd gotten into a fight. He vaguely remembered talking to a tall, rangy jigger right before the lights went out. The damnedest thing was, he felt like he was on a train. Where he had found a train in a remote lumber camp halfway up a mountain in the Cascades was a mystery to him. Still sprawled on his back, he looked around. There was a fire behind him. The wind was blowing the flames away from him, but it was too close for comfort. He could feel the heat.

A whistle screamed so close he could touch it.

Don Albert sat up and was nearly blinded by a locomotive headlight right in his face. He was riding a train all right, rolling fast, a mile a minute, with flames behind him and another train in front of him coming straight at him. A hundred lights whirled around him like lights inside a nickelodeon: the flames behind him, the locomotive's headlamp flanked by green signal lights in front of him, the electric lights on poles glaring down at the freight yard, the lights in the yard's buildings, the lights in the tents, the lantern lights bouncing up and down as men ran for their lives, trying to get out of the way of the runaway train on which he was riding.

The locomotive blowing its whistle was not coming straight at him after all but was on a track next to the one he was rolling on. That was a huge relief, until he saw the switch dead ahead.

At sixty miles an hour, the heavy gondola blasted through the closed switch as if it were made of straw instead of steel and sideswiped the locomotive, which was a switch engine shuttling a string of empty boxcars. The gondola slammed past the locomotive in a thunderstorm of sparks, screeched against the locomotive's tender and into the empties, which tumbled off the tracks as if a child had swept a checkerboard with an angry fist.

The impact barely slowed the burning gondola. Upon jumping the tracks, it crashed into a wooden roundhouse filled with mechanics repairing locomotives. Before Don Albert could even think of leaping for his life, the lights went out again.

THREE MILES TO THE south, the right spur joined the main line where it began rising in a steep grade. The Wrecker climbed the incline for a half mile and retrieved a canvas gripsack he had stashed in a thick stand of lodgepole pine. He extracted wire cutters, climbing spurs, and gloves from the grip, strapped the spurs to his boots, and waited beside a telegraph pole for the first freight train of empties that regularly headed south for fresh loads. The northern sky began to glow red. He watched with satisfaction as the redness grew brighter and brighter, blotting out the starlight. As planned, the runaway had started a fire in the construction camp and rail yard.

No train came. He feared that he had been too successful and wreaked so much havoc that no freights could leave the yard. If so, he was trapped near the end of the line with no way out. But at last he saw the white glow of a headlight approaching. He donned his gloves, climbed the telegraph pole, and snipped all four wires.

Back on the ground, having severed the head of the cutoff from the rest of the world, he could hear the freight train's 2-8-0 Consolidation huffing up the grade. The grade slowed it enough for him to jump aboard an open car.

He bundled up in a canvas coat he took from the gripbag and slept until the train stopped for water. Carefully watching for the brakemen, he climbed a telegraph pole and cut the wires. He slept again, scrambling awake to cut more wires at the next water stop. At dawn, he found himself still trundling slowly south on the main line in what was a bright green cattle car that stank of mules. It was so cold, he could see his breath.

He stood, cautiously, for a look around when the freight rounded a curve and ascertained that his green car was in a string of some fifty empties, midway between a slow but powerful locomotive in front and a faded red caboose in back. He ducked down before the brakeman looked out from the caboose's raised cupola for his periodic inspection of the train. In just a few more hours, the Wrecker would jump off at Dunsmuir.

9

ISAAC BELL AWOKE BETWEEN FINE LINEN SHEETS TO FIND THAT Lillian's special had been sidelined on a siding to allow an empty materials train to trundle through. From his stateroom window, it looked like the middle of nowhere. The only sign of civilization was a rutted buggy path beside the rails. A cold wind whipped through the clearing in the trees, scattering a gray mix of powder-dry soil and coal dust.

He dressed quickly. This was the fourth sidelining since Sacramento, despite Lillian's boast about cleared tracks. The only time Bell had ridden on a special that had been stopped this often had been after the Great Earthquake, to let relief trains steaming to the aid of the stricken city pass. That passenger trains and the usually sacrosanct specials would bow to freight was a stark reminder of how critical the Cascades Cutoff was to the future of the Southern Pacific.

He headed for the baggage car, where he had spent half the night, to see whether the telegrapher had any new transmissions from Archie Abbott. In his last message, Archie had told him not to bother stopping at Dunsmuir, as his undercover investigations among the hobos had not panned out. The special had steamed through the busy yards and the hobo camp beyond, stopping only for coal and water.

James, the special's steward, who was dressed in a snowy-white uniform, saw Bell rush past the galley and hurried after him with a cup of coffee and a stern lecture about the value of breakfast for a man who had been up all night working. Breakfast sounded good. But before Bell could accept, Barrett, the special's conductor and telegrapher, stood up from his key with a message he had written out in clear copperplate script. His expression was grim.

"Just come in, Mr. Bell."

It was not from Archie but from Osgood Hennessy himself:

SABOTEURS SET RUNAWAY TRAIN AND CUT TELEGRAPH. STOP.

HEAD-OF-LINE YARD A SHAMBLES. STOP.

EXPANSION YARD IN FLAMES. STOP.

LABOR TERRORIZED.

Isaac Bell gripped Barrett's shoulder so hard it made him wince.

"How long would a freight train take to get from the cutoff railhead to here?"

"Eight to ten hours."

"The empty freight that just came through. Did it leave the railhead after the runaway?"

Barrett looked at his pocket watch. "No, sir. He must have been well out of there."

"So any train that left after the attack is still between us and them."

"Nowhere else for him to go. It's single track all the way."

"Then he's trapped!"

The Wrecker had made a fatal mistake. He had boxed himself in at the end of a single-tracked line through rugged country with only one line out. All Bell had to do was intercept him. But he had to take him by surprise, ambush him, before he could jump off his train and run off into the woods.

"Get your train moving. We'll block him."

"Can't move. We're sidelined. We could run head-on into a south-bound freight."

Bell pointed at the telegraph key. "Find out how many trains are between us and the railhead."

Barrett sat at his key and began sending slowly. "My hand's a little muddy," he apologized. "It's been a while since I did this for a living."

Bell paced the confines of the baggage car while the key clattered out Morse code. The bulk of the open space was around the telegraph desk. Beyond was a narrow aisle between stacked trunks and boxes of provisions, cut short by Lillian's Packard Gray Wolf, which was tied down under canvas. She had shown the car to Bell the previous night, proudly reminding him of what a man like him who loved speed already knew: the splendid racer kept setting new records at Daytona Beach.

Barrett looked up from his key warily. The cold resolve on Bell's face was as harsh as the icebound light in his blue eyes. "Sir, the dispatcher at Weed says he knows of one freight highballing down the line. Left the railhead after the accident."

"What does he mean 'knows of'? Are there more trains on the road?"

"Wires to the north were down in a couple of places through the night. The dispatcher can't know for sure what moved there while the wires were out. We've got no protection, no way of knowing what's coming from the north, until the wires are fixed. So we have no authority to be on the main line."

Of course, Bell raged inwardly. Each time the empty freight had stopped for water, the Wrecker had climbed the nearest pole and cut the telegraph wires, throwing the entire system into disarray to smooth his escape.

"Mr. Bell, I'd like to help you, but I can't put the lives of men in danger because I don't know what's coming around the next bend in the road."

Isaac Bell thought quickly. The Wrecker would see the smoke from the special's locomotive miles before he would see the train itself. Even if Bell stopped their train to block the main line, the Wrecker would smell a rat when his train stopped. Plenty of time to jump off. The terrain was gentler here south of the Cascade Range, less mountainous than up the line, and a man could disappear in the woods and hike his way out.

"How soon will that freight come through?"

"Less than an hour."

Bell leveled an imperious hand at Lillian's automobile.

"Unload that."

"But Miss Lillian—"

"Now!"

The train crew slid open the barn doors in the side of the baggage car, laid a ramp, and rolled the Packard down it and onto the buggy road beside the track. It was a tiny machine compared to Bell's Locomobile. Standing lightly on wide-spread airy wire wheels, the open car scarcely came up to his waist. A snug gray sheet-metal cowling over its motor formed a pointed snout. Behind the cowling was a steering wheel and a leather-backed bench seat, and little else. The cockpit was open. Below it, on either side of the chassis, bright copper tubes, arranged in seven horizontal rows, served as a radiator to cool the powerful four-cylinder motor.

"Strap a couple of gasoline cans on the back," Bell ordered, "and that spare wheel."

They quickly complied while Bell ran to his stateroom. He returned armed with a knife in his boot and his over-under two-shot derringer in the low crown of his wide-brimmed hat. Under his coat was a new pistol he had taken a shine to, a Belgian-made Browning No. 2 semiautomatic that an American gunsmith had modified to fire a .380 caliber cartridge. It was light, and quick to reload. What it lacked in stopping power it made up for with deadly accuracy.

Lillian Hennessy came running from her private car, tugging a silk robe over her nightdress, and Bell thought fleetingly that even the consequences of passing out from three bottles of champagne looked beautiful on her.

"What are you doing?"

"The Wrecker's up the line. I am going to intercept him."

"I'll drive you!" Eagerly, she jumped behind the steering wheel and called for the trainmen to crank her engine. Wide awake in an instant, eyes alight, she was ready for anything. But as the motor fired, Bell leashed all the power of his voice to shout, *"Mrs. Comden!"*

Emma Comden came running in a dressing gown, her dark hair in a long braid and her face pale at the urgency in his voice.

"Hold this!" he said.

Bell circled Lillian's slender waist in his long hands and lifted her out of the car.

"What are you doing?" she shouted. "Put me down!"

He thrust Lillian, kicking and shouting, into Mrs. Comden's arms. Both women went down in a flashing tangle of bare legs.

"I can help you!" Lillian shouted. "Aren't we friends?"

"I don't bring friends to gunfights."

Bell leaped behind the steering wheel and sent the Gray Wolf flying up the buggy track in a cloud of dust

"That's my car! You're stealing my race car!"

"I just bought it!" he fired over his shoulder. "Send the bill to Van Dorn." Although, strictly speaking, he thought with a last grim smile as he wrestled the low-slung car over the ruts gouged by freight wagons, once Van Dorn's expense sheets were submitted Osgood Hennessy would end up buying his daughter's Gray Wolf twice.

The look over his shoulder revealed that he was trailing a dust cloud as tall and dark as a locomotive's smoke. The Wrecker would see him coming miles away, a sight that would put the murderer on high alert.

Bell twisted the steering wheel. The Wolf sprang off the buggy track, up the railroad embankment, and onto the rail bed. He wrenched the wheel again to force the tires over the nearest rail. Straddling it, the Wolf pounded on the crossties and ballast. It was a bone-jarring ride, though the banging and bouncing was far more predictable than the ruts in the road. And unless he punctured a tire on a loose spike, his chances of keeping the car intact at such speed were better than on rocks and ruts. He glanced back, confirming that the chief benefit of riding on the rail bed was he was no longer trailing a dust cloud like a flag.

He raced northward on the line for a quarter of an hour.

Suddenly, he saw a column of smoke spurting upward into the hard-blue sky. The train itself was invisible, hidden around a bend in the track that appeared to pass through a wooded valley between two hills. It was much closer than he had expected on first glimpsing the smoke. He instantly steered off the track, down the embankment, and bounced into a thicket of bare shrubs. Turning the car around in the thin cover, he watched the smoke draw nearer.

The wet huffing of the locomotive grew audible over the insistent rumble of the Gray Wolf's idling motor. Soon it became a loud, smacking sound, louder and louder. Then the big black engine rounded the bend, spewing smoke and hauling a long coal tender and a string of empty gondolas and boxcars. Lightly burdened and rolling easily on the slope of a downgrade, the train was moving fast for a freight.

Bell counted fifty cars, scrutinizing each. The flatbeds looked empty. He could not tell about a couple of cattle cars. Most of the boxcars had open doors. He saw no one peering out. The last car was a faded red caboose with a windowed cupola on the roof.

The second the caboose passed by, Bell gunned the Wolf's motor and drove it out of the thicket, up the gravel embankment and onto the tracks. He fought his right-side tires over the nearest rail and opened the throttle. The Wolf tore after the train, bouncing hard on its ties. At nearly forty miles an hour, it bucked violently and swayed from side to side. Rubber squealed against steel, as the tires slammed against the rails. Bell halved the distance between him and the train. Halved it again, until he was only ten feet behind the train. Now he saw that he could not jump onto the caboose without pulling along-side the train. He slewed the car back over the rail and steered on the edge of the embankment, which was steep and narrow and studded with telegraph poles.

He had to pull alongside the caboose, grab one of its side ladders, and jump before the race car lost speed and fell back. He overtook the train, steered alongside it. A car length ahead, he saw a telegraph pole that was set closer than the others to the rail. There was no room to squeeze between it and the train.

10

BELL GUNNED THE ENGINE, SEIZED THE CABOOSE'S LADDER IN his right hand, and jumped.

His fingers slipped on the cold steel rung. He heard the Packard Wolf crash into the telegraph pole behind him. Swinging wildly from one arm, he glimpsed the Wolf tumbling down the embankment and fought with all his strength to avoid the same fate. But his arm felt as if it had been ripped out of his shoulder. The pain tore down his arm like fire. Hard as he tried to hold on, he could not stop his fingers from splaying open.

He fell. As his boots hit the ballast, he caught the bottom rung of the ladder with his left hand. His boots dragged on the stones, threatening his precarious grip. Then he got both hands on the ladder, tucked his legs up in a tight ball, and hauled himself up, climbing hand over hand, until he could plant a boot on the rung and swing onto the rear platform of the caboose.

He threw open the back door and took in the interior of the caboose in a swift glance. He saw a brakeman stirring a vile-smelling stewpot on a potbellied woodstove. There were tool lockers, trunks on either side with hinged tops doubling as benches and bunk beds, a toilet, a desk stuffed with waybills. A ladder led up to the cupola, the train's crow's nest, where the crew could observe the string of boxcars they were trailing and communicate by flag and lantern with the locomotive.

The brakeman jumped as the door banged against the wall. He whirled around from the stove, wild-eyed. "Where the heck did you come from?"

"Bell. Van Dorn investigator. Where's your conductor?"

"He went up to the locomotive when we took on water. Van Dorn, you say? The detectives?"

Bell was already climbing the ladder into the cupola from where he could see the train cars stretching ahead. "Bring your flag! Signal the engineer to stop the train. A saboteur is riding in one of the freight cars."

Bell leaned his arms on the shelf in front of the windows and watched intently. Fifty cars stretched between him and the smoke-belching locomotive. He saw no one on the roofs of the boxcars, which blocked his view of the low-slung gondolas.

The brakeman climbed up beside Bell with a flag. The stew smell was worse in the raised cupola. Or the brakeman hadn't bathed recently. "Did you see anyone stealing a ride?" Bell asked.

"Just one old hobo. Too crippled to walk. I didn't have the heart to roust the poor devil."

"Where is he?"

"About the middle of the train. See that green cattle car? The old man was riding in the box right ahead of it."

"Stop the train."

The brakeman stuck his flag out a side window and waved frantically. After several minutes, a head bobbed up from the locomotive cab.

"That's the conductor. He sees us."

"Wave your flag."

The locomotive's chugging slowed down. Bell felt the brake shoes grind. The cars banged into one another as they filled the slack caused by the train slowed to a stop. He watched the roofs of the boxcars.

"Soon as the train stops, I want you to run ahead and check each car. *Do not engage.* Just give a shout if you see anyone, then get out of the way. He'll kill you soon as look at you."

"Can't."

"Why not?"

"We have to send a flagman back when we stop. I'm it. In case a train's following us, I have to wave it down. Wires are screwy today."

"Not before you check each car," said Bell, drawing the Browning from his coat.

The brakeman climbed down from the cupola. He jumped from the rear platform to the tracks and jogged alongside the train, pausing to look into each car. The engineer blew his whistle, demanding an explanation. Bell watched the rooftops and moved to either side of the cupola, to see alongside the train.

THE WRECKER LAY ON his back in a bench locker less than ten feet from the cupola ladder, gripping a knife in one hand and a pistol in the other. All night, he had worried that by setting loose the runaway gondola he had put himself in danger by trapping himself so far up the line. Fearing that railway police, goaded by Van Dorn detectives, would mob the train before it reached Weed or Dunsmuir and search it thoroughly, he had taken decisive action. During the last water stop, he had run back to the caboose and slipped inside while the crew were busy tending the locomotive and checking the journal boxes under the railcars.

He had chosen a locker that held lanterns, reasoning that no one would open it in the daytime. If someone did, he would kill him with whichever weapon suited the moment, then spring out and kill any-one else he came across.

He smiled grimly in the cramped, dark space. He had guessed right. And who had boarded the train but none other than Van Dorn's chief investigator himself, the famous Isaac Bell? At worst, the Wrecker would make a complete fool out of Bell. At best, he'd shoot him between the eyes.

THE BRAKEMAN CHECKED EVERY car, and when he reached the loco-motive Bell saw him confer with the conductor, the engineer, and the fireman, who had gathered on the ground. Then the conductor and the brakeman hurried back, checking each of the fifty boxcars, cattle cars, and gondolas again. When they got to the caboose, the conduc-tor, an older man with sharp brown eyes and a put-out expression on his lined face, said, "No saboteurs. No hobos. Nobody. The train is empty. We've wasted enough time here."

He raised his flag to signal the engineer.

"Wait," said Bell.

He jumped down from the caboose and ran alongside the train, peering inside each car and each chassis underneath. Midway to the locomotive, he paused at a green cattle car that stank of mules.

Bell whirled around and ran full tilt back toward the caboose.

He knew that smell. It wasn't stew. And it wasn't an unwashed brakeman. A man who had ridden in the green cattle car that stank of mules was now hiding somewhere in the caboose.

Bell bounded up onto the caboose's platform, shoved through the door, flung the nearest mattress off a bench, and pulled up the hinged top. The locker held boots and yellow rain slickers. He flung open the next. It was filled with flags and light repair tools. There were two more. The conductor and the brakeman were watching curiously from the far door.

"Get back," Bell told them. And he opened the third bench. It contained tins of lubricating oil and kerosene for lamps. Gun in hand, he leaned in to open the last.

"Nothing in there but lanterns," said the brakeman.

Bell opened it.

The brakeman was right. The locker contained red, green, and yellow lanterns.

Angry, baffled, wondering if the man had somehow managed to run for the trees from one side while he was watching the other, Bell stalked to the locomotive and told the engineer, "Move your train!"

Gradually, he calmed down. And finally he smiled, remembering something Wish Clarke had taught him: "You can't think when you're mad. And that goes double when you're mad at yourself."

He had no doubt that the Wrecker was a capable man, even a brilliant one, but now it seemed he had something else going for him too: luck, the intangible element that could throw an investigation into chaos and prolong capture. Bell believed it was only a matter of time before they caught up with the Wrecker, but time was short—terribly short—because the Wrecker was so active. This was no ordinary bank robber. He wasn't going to hole up in a brothel and spend his ill-gotten gains on wine and women. Even now, he would be planning his next attack. Bell was painfully aware that he still had no idea what motivated the man. But he did know that the Wrecker was not the sort of criminal who wasted time celebrating his victories.

Twenty minutes later, Bell ordered the train stopped beside Lillian Hennessy's special, which was still on the siding. The crew moved the freight ahead to the water tank.

THE WRECKER WAITED UNTIL the train crew was busy taking on water. Then he dropped down from the cupola's shelf and slipped back into his first hiding place, the lanterns locker. The next water stop, he slipped out of the caboose and back into a boxcar, as the crew would be reaching for lanterns when the sun went down.

Ten hours later, in the dead of the night, he jumped off at a staging area at Redding. Seeing many detectives and railroad police searching trains ahead, he hid in a culvert and watched their lights bobbing in the dark.

While he waited them out, he used the time to think about Isaac Bell's investigation. He was tempted to mail him a letter: "Sorry we didn't meet on the freight train." But it wasn't worth the joke. Don't gloat. Let Bell think he wasn't on that train. That he got away by some other means. He would find some better way to sow confusion.

An empty freight rumbled out of the yard, heading south, just before first light. The Wrecker ran alongside, grabbed a ladder on the back of a boxcar, and worked his way under the car and wedged himself into the supporting framework.

In Sacramento, he climbed out when the train halted for permission to enter the yards. He walked a mile through factories and workers' housing to a cheap rooming house, eight blocks from the capitol building. He paid the landlady four dollars for holding his suitcase and carried it to another rooming house that he chose at random ten blocks away. He rented a room, paying in advance for a week. Midmorning, the house was empty, the lodgers away at work. He locked himself in the shared bathroom at the end of the hall, stuffed his filthy clothes in the gripsack, shaved and bathed. In his room, he pulled a top-quality blond wig over his hair and applied a similarly colored groomed beard and mustache with spirit gum. Then he dressed in a clean shirt, a four-in-hand necktie, and an expensive sack suit. He packed his bags, transferring his climbing spurs to the suitcase, and polished his boots.

He left the rooming house by the back door so no one would see him in his new persona and walked a roundabout route to the railroad station, checking repeatedly that he was not followed. He threw the gripsack behind a board fence but kept the suitcase.

Hundreds of travelers were streaming into the Southern Pacific station. He blended in as he joined them, another well-dressed businessman embarking for a distant city. But suddenly, before he could stop himself, he laughed out loud. He laughed so hard he covered his mouth to make sure the beard didn't shift.

The latest *Harper's Weekly* magazine was displayed on a newsstand. The cover cartoon depicted none other than Osgood Hennessy. The railroad president was rendered as a fearsome octopus extending train tracks like tentacles into New York City. Smiling broadly, the Wrecker bought the magazine for ten cents.

The newsie was staring at him, so he went to another stand outside the station to ask, "Do you have pencils? A thick one. And an envelope and stamp, if you please."

In the privacy of a toilet in the nearest hotel, he tore off the magazine cover, wrote on it, and sealed it in the envelope. He addressed the envelope to Chief Investigator Isaac Bell, Van Dorn Detective Agency, San Francisco.

He attached the stamp, hurried back to the station, and dropped the envelope in a mailbox. Then he boarded the flyer to Ogden, Utah, six hundred miles to the east, a junction city near Great Salt Lake where nine railroads converged.

The conductor came through. "Tickets, gents."

The Wrecker had bought a ticket. But as he reached to pull it from his vest pocket, he sensed danger. He did not question whatever had sparked the premonition. It could have been anything. He had seen extra railway police at the Sacramento yards. The ticket clerk had eyed him closely. A hanger-on he had noticed in the passenger station could have been a Van Dorn operative. Trusting his instincts, he left his ticket in his pocket and flashed a railway pass instead.

11

Bell battled his way through forty-eight hours of maddening delays to reach the Cascades construction site at the head of the cutoff line. The Southern Pacific dispatchers were beset by downed telegraph wires, making train scheduling haphazard. Lillian had given up and taken her special back to Sacramento. Bell had hitched rides on material trains and finally arrived on a trainload of canvas and dynamite.

The Southern Pacific Company had used the time better than he had. The fire-ravaged locomotive roundhouse had been demolished and the debris carted away, and a hundred carpenters were hammering a new structure together with green wood hauled down from the lumber mill. "Winter," a burly foreman explained the speed of repairs. "You don't want to be fixing locomotives in the snow."

Heaps of twisted rail had been loaded on flatcars and new track laid where the runaway gondola had torn up the switches. Cranes were hoisting fallen boxcars onto the fresh rails. Roustabouts were raising giant circus tents to replace the cookhouse that burning embers from the roundhouse had set on fire. The workmen eating lunch standing up were in a sullen mood, and Bell overheard talk of refusing to return to the job. It wasn't the inconvenience of having no tables and benches but fear that upset them. "If the railroad can't protect us, who will?" he heard asked. And the answer came hot and heavy from several quarters. "Save ourselves. Pull out, come payday."

Bell saw Osgood Hennessy's vermilion red private train gliding into the yards and he hurried after it, though he was not looking forward to the meeting. Joseph Van Dorn, who had joined Hennessy in San Francisco, met him at the door, looking grave. "The Old Man's fit to be tied," he said. "You and I are going to hunker down and listen to him roar."

And roar Hennessy did. Although not at first. At first, he sounded like a beaten man. "I was not exaggerating, boys. If I don't connect to the Cascade Canyon Bridge before it snows, the cutoff is dead. And those sons of bitches bankers will cart me off with it." He looked at Bell with mournful eyes. "I saw your face when I told you I started out driving spikes like my father. You wondered, how could that scrawny, fossilized rooster swing a sledgehammer? I wasn't always skin and bones. I could have pounded circles around you in those days. But I got a bum heart, and it's shrunk me down to what you see."

"Well, now," soothed Van Dorn.

Hennessy cut him off. "You asked about a deadline. I'm the one on a deadline. And no railroad man still alive can finish the Cascades Cutoff but me. The new fellows just don't have it in them. They'll run the trains on time, but only on track I laid."

"Bookkeepers," Mrs. Comden said, "do not build empires."

Something about her attempt to comfort him made Hennessy roar. He yanked the blueprint of the Cascade Canyon Bridge down from the ceiling. "The finest bridge in the West is almost complete," he shouted. "But it goes nowhere until my cutoff line connects. But what do I find when I get back here, having left highly paid detectives on guard? Another god-awful week lost rebuilding what I've already built. My hands are spooked, afraid to work. Two brakemen and a master roundhouse mechanic dead. Four rock miners burned. Yard foreman laid up with a split skull. And a lumberjack in a coma."

Bell exchanged a quick glance with Van Dorn.

"What was a lumberjack doing in the railroad-construction yard? Your mill is high up the mountain."

"Who the hell knows?" Hennessy exploded. "And I doubt he'll wake up to tell us."

"Where is he?"

"I don't know. Ask Lillian . . . No, you can't, dammit. I sent her to New York to sweet-talk those lowdown bankers."

Bell turned on his heel and hurried off the private car to the field hospital the company had set up in a Pullman. He found the burned miners swathed in white dressings, and a bandaged yard foreman yelling he was cured, dammit to hell, just turn him loose, he had a railroad to fix. But no lumberjack.

"His friends carried him off," said the doctor.

"Why?"

"No one asked my permission. I was eating supper."

"Was he awake?"

"Sometimes."

Bell ran to the yard superintendent's office, where he had made friends with the dispatcher and the chief clerk, who kept enormous amounts of information at his fingertips. The chief clerk said, "I heard they moved him down to the town somewhere."

"What's his name?"

"Don Albert."

Bell borrowed a horse from the railway police stable and urged the animal at a quick clip to the boomtown that had sprung up behind the railhead. It was down in a hollow, a temporary city of tents, shacks, and abandoned freight cars outfitted to house the saloons, dance halls, and whorehouses that served the construction crews.

Midweek, midafternoon, the narrow dirt streets were deserted, as if the occupants were catching their breath before the next payday Saturday night.

Bell poked his head into a dingy saloon. The barkeep, presiding over planks resting on whiskey barrels, looked up morosely from a week-old Sacramento newspaper. "Where," Bell asked him, "do the lumberjacks hang out?"

"The Double Eagle, just down the street. But you won't find any there now. They're sawing crossties up the mountain. Working double shifts to get 'em down before it snows."

Bell thanked him and headed for the Double Eagle, a battered boxcar off the trucks. A painted sign on the roof depicted a red eagle with wings spread and they had found a set of swinging doors somewhere. As in the previous saloon, the only occupant was a barkeep, as morose as the last. He brightened when Bell tossed a coin on his plank.

"What'll you have, mister?"

"I'm looking for the lumberjack who got hurt in the accident. Don Albert."

"I heard he's in a coma."

"I heard he wakes up now and then," said Bell. "Where can I find him?"

"Are you a cinder dick?"

"Do I look like a cinder dick?"

"I don't know, mister. They've been swarming around here like flies on a carcass." He sized Bell up again and came to a decision. "There's an old lady in a shack tending him down by the creek. Follow the ruts down to the water, you can't miss it."

Leaving his horse where he had tied it, Bell descended to the creek, which by the smell wafting up the slope served as the town's sewer. He passed an ancient Central Pacific boxcar that had once been painted yellow. From one of the holes cut in the side that served as windows, a young woman with a runny nose called, "You found it, handsome. This is the spot you're looking for."

"Thank you, no," Bell answered politely.

"Honey, you'll find nothing down there better than this."

"I'm looking for the lady taking care of the lumberjack who got hurt?"

"Mister, she's retired."

Bell kept walking until he came to a row of rickety shacks hammered out of wood from packing crates. Here and there were stenciled their original contents. SPIKES. COTTON WOOL. PICK HANDLES. OVERALLS.

Outside of one marked PIANO ROLLS, he saw an old woman sitting on an overturned bucket, holding her head in her hands. Her hair was white. Her clothing, a cotton dress with a shawl around her shoulders, was too thin for the cold damp rising from the fetid creek. She saw him coming and jumped up with an expression of terror.

"He's not here!" she cried.

"Who? Take it easy, ma'am. I won't hurt you."

"Donny!" she yelled. "The law's come."

Bell said, "I'm not the law. I—"

"Donny! Run!"

Out of the shack stormed a six-foot-five lumberjack. He had an enormous walrus mustache that drooped below his grizzled chin, long greasy hair, and a bowie knife in his fist.

"Are you Don Albert?" asked Bell.

"Donny's my cousin," said the lumberjack. "You better run while you can, mister. This is family."

Concerned that Don Albert was belting out the back door, Bell reached for his hat and brought his hand down filled with his .44 derringer. "I enjoy a knife fight as much as the next man, but right now I haven't the time. Drop it!"

The lumberjack did not blink. Instead, he backed up four fast steps and pulled a second, shorter knife that had no handle. "Want to bet I can throw this more accurate than you can shoot that snub nose?" he asked.

"I'm not a gambler," said Bell, whipped his new Browning from his coat, and shot the bowie knife out of the lumberjack's hand. The lumberjack gave a howl of pain and stared in disbelief at his shiny knife spinning through the sunlight. Bell said, "I can always hit a bowie, but that short one you're holding I'm not sure. So, just to be on the safe side, I'm going plug your hand instead."

The lumberjack dropped his throwing knife.

"Where is Don Albert?" Bell asked.

"Don't bother him, mister. He's hurt bad."

"If he's hurt bad, he should be in the hospital."

"Cain't be in the hospital."

"Why?"

"The cinder dicks'll blame him for the runaway."

"Why?"

"He was on it."

"On it?" Bell echoed. "Do you expect me to believe he survived a mile-a-minute crash?"

"Yes, sir. 'Cause he did."

"Donny's got a head like a cannonball," said the old woman.

Bell pried the story, step-by-step, out of the lumberjack and the old woman, who turned out to be Don Albert's mother. Albert had been sleeping off an innocent drunk on the gondola when he interrupted the man who set the gondola rolling. The man had bashed him in the head with a crowbar.

"Skull like pig iron," the lumberjack assured Bell, and Don's mother agreed. Tearfully, she explained that every time Don had opened his eyes in the hospital, a railroad dick would shout at him. "Donny was afraid to tell them about the man who bashed him."

"Why?" Bell asked.

"He reckoned they wouldn't believe him, so he pretended to be hurt worse than he was. I told Cousin John here. And he rounded up his friends to carry Donny off when the doctor was eating his supper."

Bell assured her that he would make sure the railroad police didn't bother her son. "I'm a Van Dorn investigator, ma'am. They're under my command. I'll tell them to leave you be." At last, he persuaded her to take him into the shack.

"Donny? There's a man to see you."

Bell sat on a crate beside the plank bed where the bandage-swathed Don Albert was sleeping on a straw mattress. He was a big man, bigger than his cousin, with a large moon of a face, a mustache like his cousin's, and enormous, work-splintered hands. His mother rubbed the back of his hand and he began to stir.

"Donny? There's a man to see you."

He regarded Bell through murky eyes, which cleared up as they came into focus. When he was fully awake, they were an intense stony blue, which spoke of fierce intelligence. Bell's interest quickened. Not only was the man not in a state of coma, he seemed the sort who might have made a sharp observer. And he was the only man Bell knew of who had been within just a few feet of the Wrecker and was still alive.

"How are you feeling?" Bell asked.

"Head hurts."

"I'm not surprised."

Don Albert laughed, then winced at the pain it caused him.

"I understand a fellow bashed you one."

Albert nodded slowly. "With a crowbar, I believe. Least, that's what it felt like. Iron, not wood. Sure didn't feel like an ax handle."

Bell nodded. Don Albert spoke as a man who had been slugged by at least one ax handle in his life, which would not be that unusual for a lumberjack. "Did you happen to see his face?"

Albert glanced at his cousin and then his mother.

She said, "Mr. Bell says he'll tell the cinder dicks to lay off."

"He's a straight shooter," said John.

Don Albert nodded, wincing again as movement resonated through his head. "Yeah, I saw his face."

"It was night," said Bell.

"Stars on the hill are like searchlights. I had no campfire down there on the car, nothing to blind my eyes. Yeah, I could see him. Also, I was looking down at him—I was up on top of the ties—and he looked up into the starlight when I spoke, so I seen his face clear."

"Do you remember what he looked like?"

"Surprised as hell. Plumb ready to jump out of his skin. He wasn't expecting company."

This was almost too good to be true, thought Bell, excitement rising. "Can you describe him?"

"Clean-shaven fellow, no beard, miner's cap on his head. Hair was probably black. Big ears. Sharp nose. Eyes wide-set. Couldn't see their color. It wasn't that bright. Narrow cheeks—I mean, a little sunken. Wide mouth, sort of like yours, excepting the mustache."

Bell was not accustomed to witnesses itemizing specifics so readily. Ordinarily, it took listening closely and asking many subtle questions to elicit such detail. But the lumberjack had the memory of a newspaper reporter. Or an artist. Which gave Bell an idea. "If I could bring you a sketch artist, could you tell him what you saw while he draws it on paper?"

"I'll draw him for you."

"Beg pardon?"

"Donny's a good drawer," said his mother.

Bell looked dubiously at Albert's rough hands. His fingers were as thick as sausages and ribbed with calluses. But being an artist would explain the lumberjack's recollection for detail. Again Bell thought, What an astonishing break. Too good to be true.

"Get me pencil and paper," said Don Albert. "I know how to draw."

Bell gave him his pocket notebook and a pencil. With astonishingly quick, deft strokes, the powerful hands sketched a handsome face with chiseled features. Bell studied it carefully, hopes sinking. Too good to be true indeed.

Concealing his disappointment, he patted the injured giant lightly on the shoulder. "Thank you, partner. That's a big help. Now do one of me."

"You?"

"Could you draw my picture?" Bell asked. It was a simple test of the giant's powers of observation

"Well, sure." Again the thick fingers flew. A few minutes later, Bell held it to the light. "It's almost like looking in the mirror. You really draw what you see, don't you?"

"Why the hell else do it?"

"Thank you very much, Donny. You rest easy, now." He pressed several gold pieces into the old woman's hand, two hundred dollars, enough to carry them through the winter, hurried back to where he had tied his horse, and rode uphill to the construction yard. He found Joseph Van Dorn pacing outside Hennessy's railcar, smoking a cigar.

"Well?"

"The lumberjack is an artist," said Bell. "He saw the Wrecker. He drew me a face." He opened his notebook and showed Van Dorn the first drawing. "Do you recognize this man?"

"Of course." growled Van Dorn. "Don't you?"

"Broncho Billy Anderson."

"The actor."

"That poor devil must have seen him in *The Great Train Robbery.*"

The Great Train Robbery was a gripping motion picture of several years back. After shooting up the train, the outlaws made their getaway on the locomotive, which they uncoupled and rode to their horses waiting up the line, pursued by a posse. There were few people in America who had not seen it at least once.

"I will never forget the first time I saw that motion picture," said Van Dorn. "I was in New York City in the Hammerstein's Vaudeville at Forty-second and Broadway. It was the kind of theater where they ran a picture between the acts. When the picture started, we all got up as usual to walk out for a smoke or a drink. But then a few turned back to look at it, and then slowly everyone took his seat again as the picture went on. Mesmerizing . . . I'd seen the play back in the nineties. But the picture was better."

"As I recall," Bell said, "Broncho Billy played several different parts."

"I heard that he's traveling the West on his own train now, making pictures."

"Yes," said Bell. "Broncho Billy has started up his own picture studio."

"Don't suppose that leaves him much time to wreck railroads," Van Dorn said drily. "Which leaves us nowhere."

"Not quite nowhere," said Bell.

Van Dorn looked incredulous. "Our lumberjack recalls a famous actor whose image in a moving picture stuck in what's left of his head."

"Look at this. I tested him to see how accurate he is." He showed Van Dorn the sketch of himself.

"Son of a gun. That's pretty good. He drew this?"

"While I was sitting there. He can really draw faces as they are."

"Not entirely. He's got your ears all wrong. And he gave you a cleft in your chin just like Broncho Billy's. Yours is a scar, not a cleft."

"He's not perfect, but he's pretty close. Besides, Marion says it looks like a cleft."

"Marion is prejudiced, you lucky devil. The point is, our lumberjack could have seen any one of Broncho Billy's pictures. Or he might have seen him on the stage somewhere."

"But, either way, we know what the Wrecker looks like."

"Are you suggesting that he actually looks like Broncho Billy's twin?"

"More like a cousin." Detail by detail, Bell pointed out the features of the lumberjack's sketch. "Not his twin. But if the Wrecker's face jogged the lumberjack's memory of Broncho Billy, then we are looking for a man who has a similar broad high brow, a cleft chin, a penetrating gaze, an intelligent face with strong features, and big ears. Not Broncho Billy's twin, exactly. But I would say that the Wrecker looks more in general like a matinee idol."

Van Dorn puffed angrily on his cigar. "Am I to instruct my detectives not to arrest ugly mugs?"

Isaac Bell pushed back, demanding his boss see the possibilities. The more he thought about it, the more he felt they were on to something. "How old do you suppose this fellow is?"

Van Dorn scowled at the drawing. "Anywhere from his late twenties to early forties."

"We are looking for a handsome man somewhere in his late twenties, thirties, or early forties. We'll print copies of this. Take it around, show it to the hobos. Show it to stationmasters and ticket clerks wherever he might have fled on a train. Anyone who might have seen him."

"So far that's no one. No one alive anyway. Except for your Michelangelo lumberjack."

Bell said, "I'm still betting on the machinist or the blacksmith who drilled that hole in the Glendale hook."

"Sanders's boys might hit it lucky," Van Dorn agreed. "It's been in the newspapers enough, and, God knows, I've made it clear to him that his soft berth in Los Angeles is at risk of a transfer to Missoula,

Montana. Failing that, maybe someone will see the Wrecker next time and survive the experience. And we do know there will be a next time."

"There will be a next time," Bell agreed grimly. "Unless we stop him first."

·12·

THE HOBO JUNGLE OUTSIDE OGDEN FILLED A THINLY WOODED spot between the railroad tracks and a stream that provided clean water for drinking and washing. It was one of the largest jungles in the country—nine rail lines converging in one place offered a steady flow of freight trains steaming night and day in every direction—and growing larger every day. As the Panic put factories out of business, more and more men rode the rails to find work. Their hats marked them as newcomers. City men's derbies outnumbered miners' caps and range riders' J.B.s these days. There was even a sprinkling of trilbies and homburgs worn by former men of means who had never dreamed they would be down-and-out.

A thousand hobos were hurrying to finish cleanup before dark. They scrubbed laundry and cookpots in cans of boiling water, hung laundered clothes on ropes and tree limbs and set pots upside down on rocks to dry. When night fell, they kicked dirt on their fires and sat back to eat meager meals in the dark.

Campfires would have been welcomed. Northern Utah was cold in November, and snow flurries had blown repeatedly over the camp.

Five thousand feet above sea level, it was exposed to westerly gales off nearby Great Salt Lake and easterly gusts tumbling down from the Wasatch Mountains. But the railroad bulls from the Ogden yards had raided the jungle with pistols and billy clubs three nights in a row to convince the burgeoning population to move on. No one wanted them back for the fourth, so it was no night for campfires. They ate in silence, worrying about the bulls and fearing winter.

A hobo jungle, like any town or city, had neighborhoods whose boundaries were clear in the residents' minds. Some areas were friendly, some safer than others. Downstream, farthest from the tracks, where the creek veered to join the Weber River, was a section best visited armed. There, the rules of live and let live gave way to take or be taken.

The Wrecker headed there fearlessly. He was at home in outlaw land. Yet even he loosened the knife in his boot and moved his pistol from a deep pocket of his canvas coat to his waistband, where he could draw it quickly. Despite the absence of campfires, it was not entirely dark. The trains huffing constantly by pierced the night with their headlights, and the thin snow cover reflected the golden glow from the windows of passenger cars. A string of bright Pullmans started past, slowing for the nearby town, and by its light the Wrecker saw a hunched shadow shivering beside a tree, both hands in pockets.

"Sharpton," he called in a harsh voice, and Sharpton answered, "Right here, mister."

"Put your hands where I can see them," commanded the Wrecker.

Sharpton obeyed, partly because the Wrecker was paying money for service and partly out of fear. A bank and train robber who had served time in the penitentiary, Pete Sharpton knew a dangerous hombre when he met one. He had never seen his face. They had only met once before, when the Wrecker had tracked Sharpton down and braced him in the alley behind the livery stable where he rented a room. But he had been on the wrong side of the law his entire life and knew they did not come more deadly than this one.

"Did you find your man?" the Wrecker asked.

"He'll do the job for a thousand dollars," Sharpton answered.

"Give him five hundred down. Make him come back for the second half after he has done the job."

"What's to keep him from running off with the first five hundred? Found money, no risk."

"What will prevent him will be his clear understanding that you will hunt him down and kill him. Can you make that clear to him?"

Sharpton chuckled in the dark. "Oh yes. Besides, he's not that tough anymore. He'll do as he's told."

"Take this," said the Wrecker.

Sharpton felt the package with his fingers. "This isn't money."

"You'll have the money in a minute. This is the fuse I want him to use."

"You mind me asking why?"

"Not at all," the Wrecker said easily. "This looks exactly like a fast fuse. It would fool even an experienced safecracker. Do I assume correctly that yours is experienced?"

"Blowing safes and express cars his whole life."

"As I asked for. Despite its appearance, this is actually a slow fuse. When he lights it, it will take longer to detonate the dynamite than he's calculated."

"If it takes too long, it will blow up the train instead of just blocking the tracks."

"Does that pose difficulties for you, Sharpton?"

"I'm just saying what'll happen," Sharpton said hastily. "If you want to blow up the train instead of just rob it, well I guess that's none of my business. You're paying the bill."

The Wrecker pressed a second package into Sharpton's hand. "Here is three thousand dollars. Two thousand for you, a thousand for your man. You can't count it in the dark. You'll have to trust me."

13

THE LUMBERJACK'S DRAWING OF THE WRECKER PAID OFF IN five days.

A sharp-eyed Southern Pacific ticket clerk in Sacramento recalled selling an Ogden, Utah, ticket to a man who looked like the man that Don Albert had drawn. Even though his customer had a beard, and his hair was almost as blond as Isaac Bell's, there was something similar in the face, the clerk insisted.

Bell interviewed him personally to ascertain that the clerk was not another fan of *The Great Train Robbery,* and was impressed enough to order operatives to canvass the train crews on the Ogden flyer.

They hit pay dirt in Reno, Nevada. One of the flyer's conductors, a resident of Reno, recalled the passenger too and agreed it could have been the man in the drawing, though he pointed out the difference in hair color.

Bell raced to Nevada, ran him down at his home, and asked casually, as if only making conversation, whether the conductor had seen the *The Great Train Robbery.* He planned to, the conductor answered, the next time it showed at the vaudeville house. His missus had been pestering him to take her for a year.

From Reno, Bell caught an overnight express to Ogden, and had dinner as the train climbed through the Trinity Mountains. He sent telegrams when it stopped at Lovelock and received several replies when it stopped at Imlay, and he finally fell asleep in a comfortable Pullman as it steamed across Nevada. The wires awaiting him at Montello, just before they crossed the Utah border, had nothing new to report.

Nearing Ogden, midday, the train sped across Great Salt Lake on the long redwood trestles of the Lucin Cutoff. Osgood Hennessy had spent eight million dollars and clear-cut miles of Oregon forest to build the new, level route between Lucin and Ogden. It shortened the Sacramento–Ogden trip by two hours and dismayed Commodore Vanderbilt and J. P. Morgan, his rivals on the southern and northern routes. At the point where Bell was so close to the rail-junction city that he could see the snowcapped peaks of the Wasatch Mountains to Ogden's east, his train ground to a halt.

The tracks were blocked six miles ahead, the conductor told him.

An explosion had derailed the westbound Sacramento Limited.

BELL JUMPED TO THE ground and ran alongside the train to the front end. The engineer and fireman had dismounted from their locomotive and were standing on the ballast, rolling cigarettes. Bell showed them his Van Dorn identification, and ordered, "Get me as close to the wreck as you can."

"Sorry, Mr. Detective, I take my orders from the dispatcher."

Bell's derringer appeared in his hand suddenly. Two dark muzzles yawned at the engineer. "This is a matter of life and death, starting with yours," said Bell. He pointed at the cowcatcher on the front of the locomotive, and said, "Move this train to the wreck and don't stop until you hit debris!"

"You wouldn't shoot a man in cold blood," said the fireman.

"The hell he wouldn't," said the engineer, shifting his gaze nervously from the derringer to the expression on Isaac Bell's face. "Get up there and shovel coal."

The locomotive, a big 4-6-2, steamed six miles before a brakeman with a red flag stopped them where the tracks disappeared in a large hole in the ballast. Just beyond the hole, six Pullmans, a baggage car, and a tender lay on their sides. Bell dismounted from the locomotive and strode through the wreckage. "How many hurt?" he asked the railroad official who was pointed out to him as the wreck master.

"Thirty-five. Four seriously."

"Dead?"

"None. They were lucky. The bastard blew the rail a minute early. The engineer had time to reduce his speed."

"Strange," said Bell. "His attacks have always been so precisely timed."

"Well, this'll be his last. We got him."

"What? Where is he?"

"Sheriff caught him in Ogden. Lucky for him. Passengers tried to lynch him. He got away, but then one of them spotted him later, hiding in a stable."

Bell found a locomotive on the other side of the wreck to run him into Union Depot.

The jailhouse was situated in Ogden's mansard-roofed City Hall a block from the railroad station. Two top Van Dorn agents were there ahead of him, the older Weber-and-Fields duo of Mack Fulton and Wally Kisley. Neither was cracking jokes. In fact, both men looked glum.

"Where is he?" Bell demanded.

"It's not him," said Fulton wearily. He seemed exhausted, Bell thought, and for the first time he wondered if Mack should be considering retirement. Always lean, his face was shrunken as a cadaver's.

"Not who blew the train?"

"Oh, he blew the train all right," said Kisley, whose trademark three-piece checkerboard suit was caked with dust. Wally looked as tired as Mack but not ill. "Only he's not the Wrecker. Go ahead, you take a crack at him."

"You'll have a better chance of getting him to talk. He sure as hell won't admit a word to us."

"Why would he talk to me?"

"Old friend of yours," Fulton explained cryptically. He and Kisley were both twenty years older than Bell, celebrated veterans and friends, who were free to say whatever popped in their heads even though Bell was boss of the Wrecker investigation.

"I'd knock it out of him," said the sheriff. "But your boys said to wait for you, and the railroad company tells me Van Dorn calls the tune. Damned foolishness, in my opinion. But no one's asking my opinion."

Bell strode into the room where they had the prisoner manacled to a table affixed solidly to the stone floor. An "old friend," to be sure, the prisoner was Jake Dunn, a safecracker. On the end of the table was a neat, banded stack of crisp five-dollar bills, five hundred dollars' worth, according to the sheriff, clearly payment for services rendered. Bell's first grim thought was that now the Wrecker was hiring accomplices to do his murderous work for him. Which means he could strike anywhere and be long gone before the strike happened.

"Jake, what in blazes have you gotten mixed up in this time?"

"Hello, Mr. Bell. Haven't seen you since you sent me to San Quentin."

Bell sat quietly and looked him over. San Quentin had not been kind to the safecracker. He looked twenty years older, a hollow shell of the hard case he had been. His hands were shaking so hard it was difficult to imagine him setting a charge without detonating it accidentally. Relieved at first to see a familiar face, Dunn shriveled now under Bell's gaze.

"Blowing Wells Fargo safes is robbery, Jake. Wrecking passenger trains is murder. The man who paid you that money has killed innocent people by the dozen."

"I didn't know we were wrecking the train."

"You didn't know that blowing the rails out from under a speeding train would cause a wreck?" Bell said in disbelief, his face dark with disgust. "What did you think would happen?"

The prisoner hung his head.

"Jake! What did you think would happen?"

"You gotta believe me, Mr. Bell. He told me to blow the rail so the train would stop so they could hit the express car. I didn't know he was gonna put her on the ground."

"What do you mean? You're the one who lit the fuse."

"He switched fuses on me. I thought I was lighting a fast fuse that would detonate the charge in time for the train to stop. Instead, it burned slow. I couldn't believe my eyes, Mr. Bell. It was burning so slow the train was going to run right over the charge. I tried to stop it."

Bell stared at him coldly.

"That's how they caught me, Mr. Bell. I ran after it, trying to stomp it out. Too late. They saw me, and after she hit the ground they lit out after me like I was the guy who shot McKinley."

"Jake, you've got the hangman's rope around your neck and one way to get it loose. Take me to the man who paid you this money."

Jake Dunn shook his head violently. He looked, Bell thought, frantic as a wolf with a leg caught in a trap. But no, not a wolf. There was no raw power in him, no nobility. Truth be told, Dunn looked like a mongrel dog that had fallen for bait left for bigger game.

"Where is he, Jake?"

"I don't know."

"Why are you lying to me, Jake?"

"I didn't kill nobody."

"You wrecked a train, Jake. You're damned lucky you didn't kill anybody. If they don't hang you, they'll put you in the penitentiary for the rest of your life."

"I didn't kill nobody."

Bell changed tactics abruptly.

"How'd you happen to get out of prison so soon, Jake? What did you serve, three years? Why'd they let you go?"

Jake regarded Bell with eyes that were suddenly wide open and guileless. "I got the cancer."

Bell was taken aback. He had no truck with lawbreakers, but a killing disease reduced a criminal to just an ordinary man. Jake Dunn was no innocent, but he was quite suddenly a victim who would suffer pain and fear and despair. "I'm sorry, Jake. I didn't realize."

"I guess they figured to set me loose to die on my own. I needed the money. That's how I took this job."

"Jake, you were always a craftsman, never a killer. Why are you covering for a killer?" Bell pressed.

Jake answered in a hoarse whisper. "He's in the livery stable on Twenty-fourth, across the tracks."

Bell snapped his fingers. Wally Kisley and Mack Fulton rushed to his side. "Twenty-fourth Street," said Bell. "Livery stable. Cover it, station the sheriff's deputies on the outer perimeter, and wait for me."

Jake looked up. "He's not going anywhere, Mr. Bell."

"What do you mean?"

"When I went back to get my second half of the money, I found him upstairs, in one of the rooms they rent out."

"Found him? What do you mean, dead?"

"Slit his throat. I was afraid to tell—they'd pin that on me, too."

"*Slit his throat?*" Bell demanded. "Or *stabbed?*"

Jake ran a hand through his thinning hair. "Stabbed, I guess."

"Did you see a knife?"

"No."

"Was he run through? Did the wound exit the back of his neck?"

"I didn't stick around to examine him close, Mr. Bell. Like I said, I knew they'd blame me."

"Get over there," Bell told Kisley and Fulton. "Sheriff, would you send a doctor? See if he can reckon what killed him and how long he's been dead."

"Where will you be, Isaac?"

Another dead end, thought Bell. The Wrecker wasn't just lucky, he made his own luck. "Railroad station," he answered without a lot of hope. "See if any ticket clerks recall selling him a ticket out of here."

He took copies of the lumberjack's drawing to Union Depot, a multigabled, two-story building with a tall clock tower, and queried the clerks. Then, driven in a Ford by a railway police official through tree-lined neighborhoods of cottages with jigsaw woodwork, he visited the homes of clerks and supervisors who were off work that day. Bell showed the drawing to each man, and when the man did not recognize the face, Bell showed him an altered version with a beard. No one recognized either face.

How did the Wrecker get out of Ogden? Bell wondered.

The answer was easy. The city was served by nine different railroads. Hundreds, if not thousands, of passengers passed through it every day. By now, the Wrecker had to know that the Van Dorn Agency was hunting him. Which meant he would choose his targets more carefully when it came to preparing his escapes.

Bell enlisted Van Dorn agents from the Ogden office to canvass hotels, on the odd chance that the Wrecker had stayed in the junction city. No front-desk clerk recognized either drawing. At the Broom, an expensive, three-story brick hotel, the proprietor of the cigar store thought he might have served a customer who looked like the picture with the beard. A waitress in the ice-cream parlor remembered a man who looked like the clean-shaven version. He had stuck in her mind because he was so handsome. But she had seen him only once, and that was three days ago.

Kisley and Fulton caught up with Bell in the spartan Van Dorn office, one large room on the wrong side of Twenty-fifth Street, which was a wide boulevard divided by electric-streetcar tracks. The side of the street that served the legitimate needs of railroad passengers using the station was lined with restaurants, tailors, barbers, soda fountains, ice-cream parlors, and a Chinese laundry, each shaded by a colorful awning. Van Dorn's side housed saloons, rooming houses, gambling casinos, and hotels fronting for brothels.

The office had a bare floor, ancient furniture, and a single window. Decoration consisted of wanted posters, the newest being the two freshly printed versions of the lumberjack's drawing of the Wrecker, with and without the beard, noted by the sharp-eyed Southern Pacific ticket clerk in Sacramento.

Kisley and Fulton had regained their spirits, though Fulton appeared exhausted.

"Clearly," Wally remarked, "the boss doesn't waste money on office space in Ogden."

"Or furnishings," Mack added. "That desk looks like it arrived by wagon train."

"Perhaps it's the neighborhood that appeals, located within spitting distance of Union Depot."

"And spitting they are, on our sidewalk."

Continuing in Weber-and-Fields mode, they went to the window and pointed down at the crowded sidewalk. "Perceive Mr. Van Dorn's genius. The view from this window can be used to instruct apprentice detectives in the nature of crime in all its varieties."

"Come here, young Isaac, gaze down upon our neighboring saloons, brothels, and opium dens. Observe potential customers down on their luck earning the price of a drink or a woman by panhandling. Or, failing to kindle charity, sticking up citizens in that alley."

"Note there, a mustachioed fop luring the gullible with shell games on a folding table."

"And look at those out-of-work hard-rock miners dressed in rags, pretending to sleep on the pavement outside that saloon while actually laying in wait for drunks to roll."

"How long was the man dead?" Bell asked.

"Better part of a day, Doc thinks. You were right about the stabbing. A narrow blade straight through his neck. Just like Wish and the Glendale yard bull."

"So if the Wrecker killed him, he could not have left Ogden before last night. But no one saw him buy a ticket."

"Plenty of freights in and out," ventured Wally.

"He is covering mighty long distances in a short time to rely on stealing rides on freights," said Mack.

"Probably using both, depending on his situation," said Wally.

Bell asked, "Who was the murdered man?"

"Local owlhoot, according to the sheriff. Sort of a real-life Broncho Billy—our chief suspect . . . Sorry, Isaac, couldn't resist." Fulton nodded at the wanted poster.

"Keep it up and I won't resist asking Mr. Van Dorn to post Weber and Fields to Alaska."

". . . Suspected of knocking over a stagecoach up in the mountains last August. The cinder dicks caught him robbing a copper-mine payroll off the Utah and Northern ten years ago. Turned in his partners for a lighter sentence. Looks like he knew Jake Dunn from prison."

Bell shook his head in disgust. "The Wrecker is not only hiring hands to help but hiring criminals to hire help. He can hit anywhere on the continent."

There was a tentative knock at the door. The detectives looked up, gazes narrowing at the sight of a nervous-looking youth in a wrinkled sack suit. He had a cheap suitcase in one hand and his hat in the other. "Mr. Bell, sir?"

Isaac Bell recognized young James Dashwood from the San Francisco office, the apprentice detective who had done such a thorough
job establishing the innocence of the union man killed in the Coast
Line Limited wreck.

"Come on in, James. Meet Weber and Fields, the oldest detectives
in America."

"Hello, Mr. Weber. Hello, Mr. Fields."

"I'm Weber," said Mack. "He's Fields."

"Sorry, sir."

Bell asked, "What are you doing here, James?"

"Mr. Bronson sent me with this, sir. He told me to ride expresses
to beat the mail."

The apprentice handed Bell a brown paper envelope. Inside was
a second envelope addressed to him in penciled block letters, care of
the San Francisco office. Bronson had clipped a note to it: "Opened
this rather than wait. Glad I did. Looks like he made you."

Bell opened the envelope addressed to him. From it, he withdrew
the front cover of a recent *Harper's Weekly* magazine. A cartoon by
William Allen Rogers depicted Osgood Hennessy in a tycoon's silk
top hat astride a locomotive marked SOUTHERN PACIFIC RAILROAD.
Hennessy was pulling a train labeled CENTRAL RAILROAD OF NEW JER-
SEY into New York City. The train was drawn to look like a writhing
octopus. Hand-lettered in black pencil across the cartoon was the
question CAN THE LONG ARM OF THE WRECKER REACH FARTHER THAN
OSGOOD'S TENTACLE?

"What the heck is that?" asked Wally.

"A gauntlet," answered Bell. "He's challenging us."

"And rubbing our noses in it," said Mack.

"Mack's right," said Wally. "I wouldn't cloud my head taking it
personal, Isaac."

"The magazine is in there, too," said Dashwood. "Mr. Bronson
thought you'd want to read it, Mr. Bell."

Seething inwardly, Bell quickly scanned the essence of the first page. *Harper's,* dubbing itself "A Journal of Civilization," was reporting avidly the depredations of the railroad monopolies. This issue devoted an article to Osgood Hennessy's ambitions. Hennessy, it seemed, had secretly acquired a "near-dominating interest" in the Baltimore & Ohio Railroad. The B&O already held, jointly with the Illinois Central—in which Hennessy had a large interest—a dominating interest in the Reading Railroad Company. The Reading controlled the Central Railroad of New Jersey, which gave Hennessy entry into the coveted New York district.

"What does it mean?" asked James.

"It means," explained a grim Isaac Bell, "that the Wrecker can attack Hennessy's interests directly in New York City."

"Any train wreck he causes in New York," said Mack Fulton, "will hit the Southern Pacific even harder than an attack in California."

"New York," said Wally Kisley, "being the biggest city in the country."

Bell looked at his watch. "I've got time to catch the Overland Limited. Send my bags after me to the Yale Club of New York City."

He headed for the door, firing orders. "Wire Archie Abbott! Tell him to meet me in New York. And wire Irv Arlen and tell him to cover the rail yards in Jersey City. And Eddie Edwards, too. He knows those yards. He broke up the Lava Bed gang that was doing express-car jobs on the piers. You two finish up here, make sure he's not still in Ogden—which I doubt—and find which way he went."

"New York is, according to this," Wally said, holding up the *Harper's Weekly* and quoting from the article, "'the Holy Land to which all railroaders long to make a pilgrimage.'"

"Which means," said his partner, "he's on his way already and will be waiting for you when you get there."

Halfway out the door, Bell looked back at Dashwood, who was watching eagerly.

"James, do something for me."

"Yes, sir."

"You've read the reports on the wreck of the Coast Line Limited?"

"Yes, sir."

"Tell Mr. Bronson I'm sending you to Los Angeles. I want you to find the blacksmith or machinist who drilled a hole in that hook that derailed the Limited. Can you do that for me—what's the matter?"

"But Mr. Sanders is in charge of Los Angeles, and he might—"

"Stay out of Sanders's way. You're on your own. Catch the next flyer west. On the jump!"

Dashwood ran past Bell and thundered down the wooden stairs like a boy let out of school.

"What's a kid going do on his own?" asked Wally.

"He's a crackerjack," said Bell. "And he can't do worse than Sanders has so far, O.K. I'm on my way. Mack, get some rest. You look beat."

"You'd look beat too if you'd been sleeping sitting up on trains for the last week."

"Let me remind you geezers to watch your step. The Wrecker is poison."

"Thank you for your wise advice, sonny," answered Wally.

"We'll try real hard to remember it," said Mack. "But, like I said, even money he's already on his way to New York."

Wally Kisley went to the window and watched Isaac Bell run to catch the Overland Limited.

"Oh, this'll be fun. Our hard-rock miners ran out of drunks."

He motioned for Mack to join him at the window. Springing suddenly from the sidewalk, the hard-rock miners swooped from both sides to ambush the well-groomed dude running for his train in an expensive suit. Neither stopping or even slowing, Bell cut through them like a one-man flying wedge and the miners returned to the sidewalk facedown.

"Did you see that?" Kisley asked.

"Nope. And neither did they."

They stayed at the window, observing closely the citizens swarming about the sidewalk.

"That kid Dashwood?" Fulton asked. "Remind you of anybody?"

"Who? Isaac?"

"No. Fifteen—what am I saying?—twenty years ago, Isaac was still chasing lacrosse balls at that fancy prep school his old man sent him to. You and me, we was in Chicago. You were investigating certain parties engineering the corner in grain. I was up to my ears in the Haymarket bombing, when we figured out the cops did most of the killing. Remember, this slum kid showed up looking for work? Mr. Van Dorn took a shine to him, had you and me show him the ropes. He was a natural. Sharp, quick, ice water in his veins."

"Son of a gun," said Mack. "Wish Clarke."

"Let's hope Dashwood teetotals."

"Look!" Mack leaned close to the glass.

"I see him!" said Wally. He ripped the lumberjack's drawing off the wall, the picture with the beard added, and brought it to the window.

A tall, bearded workman dressed in overalls and derby who had been striding toward the railroad station carrying a large tool sack over his shoulder had been forced onto stop in front of a saloon to allow two bartenders to throw four drunks to the sidewalk. Hemmed in by the cheering crowd, the tall man was glancing around impatiently, raising his face out of the shadow of his derby.

The detectives looked at the drawing.

"Is that him?"

"Could be. But it looks like he's had that beard awhile."

"Unless it's rented."

"If it is, it's a good one," said Mack. "I don't like the ears either. They're nowhere near this big."

"If it's not him," Wally insisted, "it could be his brother."

"Why don't we ask him if he has a brother?"

14

"I'M FIRST, YOU WATCH."

Wally Kisley ran for the stairs.

The tall workman with the sack slung over his shoulder shoved through the crowd, stepped over one drunk and around another, and resumed his quick pace toward Union Depot. From the window, Mack Fulton traced the path he drove relentlessly through the pedestrians who were hurrying to and from the station.

Wally bounded down the stairs and out the building. When he got to the sidewalk, he looked up. Mack pointed him in the right direction. Wally sprinted ahead. A quick wave said he found their quarry, and Mack tore down the stairs after him, his heart pounding. He'd been feeling lousy for days, and now he was having trouble snatching a breath.

He caught up with Wally, who said, "You're white as a sheet. You O.K.?"

"Tip-top. Where'd he go?"

"Down that alley. I think he saw me."

"If he did and he ran, he's our man. Come on!"

Mack led the way, sucking air. The alley was muddy underfoot and stank. Instead of cutting through to Twenty-fourth Street, as the detectives assumed it would, it hooked left where the way was blocked by a steel-shuttered warehouse. There were barrels in front big enough to hide behind.

"We got him trapped," said Wally.

Mack gasped. Wally looked at him. His face was rigid with pain. He doubled over, clutching his chest, and fell hard in the mud. Wally knelt beside him. "Jesus, Mack!"

Mack's face was deathly pale, his eyes wide. He raised his head, staring over Wally's shoulder. "Behind you!" he muttered.

Wally whirled toward the rush of footfalls.

The man they had been chasing, the man who looked like the sketch, the man who was definitely the Wrecker, was running straight at him with a knife. Wally shielded his old friend's body with his own, and smoothly whipped a gun from under his checkerboard coat. He cocked the single-action revolver with a practiced thumb on the gnarled hammer and brought the barrel to bear. Coolly, he aimed so as to smash the bones in the Wrecker's shoulder rather than kill him so they could question the saboteur about future attacks already set in motion.

Before Wally could fire, he heard a metallic *click,* and was stunned to see a glint of light on steel as the knife blade suddenly jumped at his face. The Wrecker was still five feet from him, but the tip was already entering his eye.

He's made a sword that telescopes out of a spring-loaded knife, was Wally Kisley's last thought as the Wrecker's blade plunged through his brain. *And I thought I had seen it all.*

THE WRECKER JERKED HIS blade out of the detective's skull and rammed it through the neck of his fallen partner. The man looked like he was dead already, but this was no time to take chances. He withdrew the blade and glanced around coldly. When he saw that no one had followed the detectives into the alley, he wiped the blade on the checkerboard coat, clicked the release to shorten it, and returned it to the sheath in his boot.

It had been a close call, the sort of near disaster you couldn't plan for, other than to be always primed to be fast and deadly, and he was exhilarated by his escape. *Keep moving!.* he thought. The Overland Limited would not wait while he celebrated.

He hurried from the alley, pushed through the mob on the sidewalk, and cut across Twenty-fifth Street. Darting in front of an electric trolley, he turned right on Wall Street, and walked for a block parallel to the long Union Depot train station. When he was sure he was not followed, he crossed Wall and entered the station by a door at the north end.

He found the men's room and locked himself in a stall. Racing against the clock, he stripped off the overalls that had concealed his elegant traveling clothes and took an expensive leather Gladstone bag with brass fittings from his tool sack. He removed polished black laced dress boots from the Gladstone, a gray Homburg from its own protective hatbox, and a derringer and packed in it the rough boots that held his sword. He laced up the dress boots and dropped the derringer into his coat pocket. He removed his beard, which he also put in the Gladstone, and rubbed traces of spirit gum off his skin. Then he stuffed the overalls in the sack and shoved the sack behind the toilet. There was nothing in the overalls or the sack that could be traced to him. He checked the time on his railroad watch and waited exactly two minutes, rubbing his boots against the back of his trouser legs to polish them and running an ivory comb through his hair.

He stepped out of the stall. He inspected himself carefully in the mirror over the sink. He flicked a speck of spirit gum off his chin and placed his gray Homburg on his head.

Smiling, he sauntered from the men's room and across the bustling lobby, which was suddenly swarming with railroad detectives. With only seconds to spare, he brushed past station attendants who were closing the gates to the smoky train platforms. A locomotive shrieked the double *Ahead* signal, and the Overland Limited, a luxury flyer made up of eight first-class Pullmans, dining car, and an observation-lounge car, began to roll east for Cheyenne, Omaha, and Chicago.

The Wrecker strode alongside the last car, the observation-lounge, matching its pace, his eyes everywhere.

Far ahead, just behind the baggage car, he saw a man leaning from the steps of the first Pullman, holding on to a handrail so he could swing out to get a clear look at whoever was catching the Limited at the last minute. It was six hundred feet from there to where the Wrecker was reaching for a handrail to pull himself aboard the last car of the moving train, but there was no mistaking the sharp silhouette of a hunter.

The head of the train moved out of the shadow cast by the station, and he saw that the man leaning out to watch the platform had a full head of flaxen hair that gleamed like gold in the light of the setting sun. Which meant, as he had suspected, that the hunter was none other than Detective Isaac Bell.

Without hesitation, the Wrecker gripped the handrail and stepped onto the train's end platform. From this open vestibule, he entered the observation-lounge car. He closed the door behind him, shutting out the smoke and noise, and luxuriated in the peace and quiet of a first-class transcontinental flyer decorated with heavy moldings, polished-wood panels, mirrors, and a thick carpet on the floor. Stewards were carrying drinks on silver trays to passengers lounging on comfortable couches. Those who looked up from newspapers and conversation acknowledged the well-dressed late arrival with the sociable nods of brother clubmen.

The conductor broke the mood. Flinty of eye, hard of mouth, and impeccably uniformed, from his gleaming visor to his gleaming shoes, he was imperious, brusque, and suspicious like conductors everywhere. "Tickets, gents! Ogden tickets."

The Wrecker flourished his railway pass.

The conductor's eyes widened at the name on the pass, and he greeted his new passenger with great deference.

"Welcome aboard, sir."

THE FAVORED FEW

Explosion of the Lillian I

"TAKE ME TO MY STATEROOM IMMEDIATELY!"

Isaac Bell would be racing to the back of the train to see who had boarded last minute, and the Wrecker intended to confront the detective at a time of his own choosing.

The conductor, obsequious as a palace courtier serving a prince robed in ermine, led the Wrecker down a window aisle to a large suite in the middle of a car where the train was smoothest riding.

"Come in! Shut the door!"

The private suite, reserved for the railroad's special guests, was palatially fitted with hand-carved cabinetry and an embossed-leather ceiling. It included a sitting room, a sleeping compartment, and its own bathroom with a marble tub and fixtures of pure silver. He tossed his Gladstone bag on the bed.

"Any 'interests' on your train?" he asked the conductor, meaning were there other important personages aboard. He made the inquiry with a confidential smile and slipped the conductor a gold piece.

No guest of the Southern Pacific Railroad Company had to tip to ensure lavish treatment and fawning service. But the conductor of a transcontinental train, like the purser of an Atlantic liner, could be a useful confederate and a source of inside information about the powerful passengers traveling across the country. The combination of pretended intimacy and cold cash was an investment that would pay off in spades. And indeed it did, as the conductor answered freely.

"Mr. Jack Thomas, president of First National Bank, got on at Oakland, along with Mr. Bruce Payne, Esquire."

"The oil attorney?"

"Yes, sir. Mr. Payne and Mr. Thomas are very close, as you can imagine."

"Money and petroleum law make fast bedfellows," the Wrecker smiled, encouraging the conductor to keep talking.

"Judge Congdon and Colonel Bloom, the gentleman in coal, have been on the train since Sacramento."

The Wrecker nodded. Judge James Congdon had joined with J. P. Morgan to buy Andrew Carnegie's steel trust. Kenneth Bloom owned coal in partnership with the Pennsylvania Railroad.

"And Mr. Moser of Providence, the mill owner, whose son sits in the Senate, sir."

"Capital fellow," said the Wrecker. "His father's textile interests are in good hands."

The conductor beamed, basking in the proximity of such celebrated plutocrats. "I am certain that they would be honored if you would join them for dinner."

"I'll see how I feel," he answered casually, adding with an almost imperceptible wink, "Any talk of a little game of draw?"

"Yes, sir. Poker after dinner in Judge Congdon's stateroom."

"And who else is aboard?"

The conductor rattled off the names of cattle barons, western mining magnates, and the usual complement of railroad attorneys. Then he lowered his voice to confide, "There's a Van Dorn detective got on at Ogden just before you, sir."

"A detective? Sounds exciting. Did you catch his name?"

"Isaac Bell."

"Bell . . . Hmm. I don't suppose he is sleuthing 'undercover' if he told you his name."

"I recognized him. He travels often."

"Is he on a case?"

"I don't know about that. But he's riding on a pass signed by President Hennessy himself. And the orders came down that we are supposed to give Van Dorn agents anything they ask for."

The Wrecker's smile hardened as a wintery light filled his eyes. "What has Isaac Bell asked of you?"

"Nothing yet, sir. I presume he is investigating all those Southern Pacific wrecks. "

"Perhaps we can make things expensive for Mr. Bell in our friendly game of draw." The conductor looked surprised. "Would a detective have the blood in him for your gentlemen's game?"

"I suspect that Mr. Bell can afford it," said the Wrecker. "If he's the same Isaac Bell who I've heard rumored is a wealthy man. I've never played poker with a detective. It could be interesting. Why don't you ask him if he would care to join us?" It was not a question but an order, and the conductor promised to invite the detective to join the high-stakes poker game after dinner in Judge Congdon's stateroom.

The way a man played poker revealed all there was to know of him. The Wrecker would use the opportunity to size Bell up and decide how to kill him.

ISAAC BELL'S STATEROOM WAS in a Pullman car that had a gentleman's washroom at the front end with beveled mirrors, nickel fixtures, and massive marble sinks. There was room for two easy chairs. A potted palm in the room swayed in rhythm with the train, which was speeding along the Weber River, drawn by its powerful locomotive, up the one percent grade into the Wasatch Range.

Bell shaved there before dressing for dinner. While he could afford a lavish suite with its own facilities, he preferred shared facilities when he traveled. In such lounges, just as in the changing rooms of gymnasiums and private clubs, something about the combination of marble, tile, running water, and comfortable chairs in the absence of women made men boastful. Boastful men talked openly to strangers, and there was always some tidbit of information to glean from overheard conversations. And indeed, as he slid his Wootz steel straight razor across his face, a rotund and cheerful slaughterhouse owner from Chicago put down his cigar to remark, "Porter told me that Senator Charles Kincaid boarded the train in Ogden."

"The 'Hero Engineer'?" replied a well-dressed drummer stretched out comfortably in the other leather armchair. "I'd like to shake his hand."

"All you gotta do is corral him in the dining car."

"You can never tell with those senators," said the salesman. "Congressmen and governors will shake any hand that still has blood flowing in it, but United States senators can be a stuck-up lot."

"That's what comes from being appointed instead of elected."

"Was he the tall fellow who jumped aboard at the last second?" Bell asked from the shaving mirror.

The Chicago meatpacker said he'd been reading the newspaper as the train pulled out and hadn't noticed.

The drummer had. "Hopped on quick as a hobo."

"A mighty well-dressed hobo," said Bell, and the meatpacker and the drummer laughed.

"That's a good one," the meatpacker chortled. "Well-dressed hobo. What line are you in, son?"

"Insurance," said Bell. He caught the drummer's eye in the mirror. "Was the fellow you saw jump on last minute Senator Kincaid?"

"Could have been," said the drummer. "I didn't look close. I was

talking to a gent at the front of the car and the conductor was blocking my view. But wouldn't they hold the train for a senator?"

"Reckon so," said the meatpacker. He heaved his heavy body out
of the chair, stubbed out his cigar and said, "So long, boys. I'm heading for the observation car. Anyone use a drink, I'm buying."

Bell went back to his stateroom.

Whoever had jumped on at the last minute had disappeared by the
time Bell reached the observation car at the rear of the train, which
was not surprising since this Overland Limited was an all-stateroom
train, the only public spaces being the dining car and the observation
car. The dining car had been empty except for the stewards setting
tables for the evening meal, and none of the smokers in the observation car resembled the well-dressed man Bell had seen at a distance. Nor did any of them resemble the lumberjack's sketch of the
Wrecker.

Bell rang for the porter. The black man was in late middle age, old
enough to have not only been born into slavery but to have endured
it as an adult. "What is your name?" Bell asked. He could not abide
the custom of calling Pullman porters "George" after their employer
George Pullman.

"Jonathan, sir."

Bell pressed a ten-dollar gold piece into his soft palm. "Jonathan,
would you look at this picture? Have you see this man on the train?"

Jonathan studied the drawing.

Suddenly, a westbound express flashed by the windows with a roar
of wind and steam as the two trains passed each other at a combined
speed of one hundred twenty miles an hour. Osgood Hennessy had
double-tracked much of the route to Omaha, which meant that limit-
eds wasted little time on sidings waiting for trains to pass.

"No, sir," said the porter, shaking his head. "I've not seen no gentleman who looks like this."

"How about this one?" Bell showed the porter the sketch with the beard, but the answer was the same. He was disappointed but not surprised. The eastbound Overland Limited was only one of a hundred fifty trains that had left Ogden since the outlaw in the stable had been stabbed. Though fewer, of course, would connect to New York City, where the Wrecker's baiting note had virtually promised he was going.

"Thank you, Jonathan." He gave the porter his card. "Please ask the conductor to call on me at his earliest convenience."

Less than five minutes later, the conductor knocked. Bell let him in, established that his name was Bill Kux, and showed him the two sketches, one with beard, one without.

"Did anyone board your train at Ogden who looked like either of these men?"

The conductor studied them carefully, holding the first one in his hand, then the other, turning then to the light cast by the lamp since night had blackened the window. Bell watched Kux's stern face for a reaction. Charged with the safety of the train and responsible for making every passenger pay his fare, conductors were sharp observers with good memories. "No, sir. I don't think so . . . Though this one looks familiar."

"Have you seen this man?"

"Well, I don't know . . . But I know this face." He stroked his chin and suddenly snapped his fingers. "That's how I know that face. I just saw him at the picture show."

Bell took back the sketches. "But no one who looks at all like either of these got on at Ogden?"

"No, sir." He chuckled. "You had me on the go there, for a minute, 'til I remembered the moving picture. You know who that looks like? Actor fella. Broncho Bill Anderson. Doesn't it?"

"Who was the man who boarded the train at the last minute?"

The conductor smiled. "Now, there's a coincidence."

"What do you mean?"

"I was already heading to your stateroom when the porter gave me your card. That gentleman you're inquiring after asked me to invite you to a game of draw after dinner in Judge Congdon's stateroom."

"Who is he?"

"Why, that's Senator Charles Kincaid!"

16

"THAT WAS KINCAID?"

Bell knew it had been a long shot. But there was something purposeful about the way the last man had come aboard, as if he had made a special effort to leave the Ogden depot undetected. A very long shot, he had to admit. Aside from the number of trains the Wrecker could have taken, men routinely ran to catch trains. He himself did it often. Sometimes deliberately, either to dupe someone already on the train or give the slip to someone following him in the station.

"The last I heard," Bell mused, "the Senator was in New York."

"Oh, he gets around, sir. You know those officeholders, always on the go. Can I tell him you will play draw?"

Bell fixed Bill Kux with a cold stare. "How is it that Senator Kincaid happened to know my name and that I am on this train?"

It was unusual to see a conductor of a limited flustered by anything less than jumping the tracks. Kux began to stammer. "Well, he, I . . . Well, you know, sir, the way it is."

"The way it is, the wise traveler befriends his conductor," Bell said, softening his expression to take the man into his trust. "The wise conductor endeavors to make everyone on his train happy. But especially those passengers most deserving of happiness. Do I have to remind you, Mr. Kux, that you have orders straight from the president of the line that Van Dorn detectives are your *first* friends?"

"No, sir."

"Is that clear?"

"Yes, sir, Mr. Bell. I'm sorry if I caused you any trouble."

"Don't worry yourself." Bell smiled. "It's not as if you betrayed a confidence to a train robber."

"Very big of you, sir, thank you . . . May I inform Senator Kincaid that you'll join his game?"

"Who else will be gaming?"

"Well, Judge Congdon, of course, and Colonel Bloom."

"*Kenneth* Bloom?"

"Yes, sir, the coal magnate."

"Last time I saw Kenny Bloom, he was behind the elephants with a shovel."

"I beg your pardon, sir. I don't understand."

"We were in the circus together briefly as boys. Until our fathers caught up with us. Who else?"

"Mr. Thomas, the banker, and Mr. Payne, the attorney, and Mr. Moser of Providence. His son sits with Mr. Kincaid in the Senate."

Two more slavish champions of the corporations would be harder to imagine, thought Bell, but all he said was, "Tell the Senator that I will be honored to play."

Conductor Kux reached for the door. "I should warn you, Mr. Bell . . ."

"The stakes are high?"

"That, too. But if a Van Dorn agent is my first friend, it is my duty to advise you that one of the gentlemen playing tonight has been known to make his own luck."

Isaac Bell showed his teeth in a smile. "Don't tell me which one cheats. It will more interesting to find out for myself."

• • •

JUDGE JAMES CONGDON, the host of the evening's game of draw poker, was a lean and craggy old man with an aristocratic bearing and a manner as hard and unbending as the purified metal on which he had made his fortune. "The ten-hour workday," he proclaimed in a voice like a coal chute, "will be the ruination of the steel industry."

The warning elicited solemn nods from the plutocrats gathered around the green-felt-topped card table, and a hearty "Hear! Hear!" from Senator Charles Kincaid. The Senator had opened the subject with an ingratiating promise to vote for stricter laws in Washington to make it easier for the judiciary to issue injunctions against strikers.

If anyone on an Overland Limited steaming through the Wyoming night doubted the gravity of the conflict between labor unions and factory owners, Ken Bloom, who had inherited half of the anthracite coal in Pennsylvania, set them straight. "The rights and interests of the laboring men will be looked after and cared for not by agitators but by Christian men to whom God in His infinite wisdom has given control of the property interests of the country."

"How many cards, Judge?" said Isaac Bell, whose turn it was to deal. They were in the middle of a hand, and it was the dealer's responsibility to keep the game moving. Which was not always easy, since, despite the enormous stakes, it was a friendly game. Most of the men knew one another and played together often. Table talk ranged from gossip to good-natured ribbing, sometimes intended to smoke out a rival's intention and the strength or weakness of his hand.

Senator Kincaid, Bell had already noticed, seemed intimidated by Judge Congdon, who occasionally called him Charlie even though the Senator was the sort who would demand to be called Charles if not "Senator, sir."

"Cards?" Bell asked again.

Suddenly, the railroad car shook hard.

The wheels were pounding over a rough patch of track. The car lurched. Brandy and whiskey sloshed from glasses onto green felt. Everyone in the luxurious stateroom fell quiet, reminded that they, along with the crystal, the card table, the brass lamps affixed to the walls, the playing cards, and the gold coins, were hurtling through the night at seventy miles an hour.

"Are we are on the ties?" someone asked. The question met nervous laughter from all but the cold Judge Congdon, who snatched up his glass before it could spill any more and remarked, as the car shook even harder, "This reminds me, Senator Kincaid, what is your opinion about the flood of accidents plaguing the Southern Pacific Railroad?"

Kincaid, who had apparently had too much to drink at dinner, answered loudly, "Speaking as an engineer, the rumors of Southern Pacific mismanagement are scandalous lies. Railroading is dangerous business. Always has been. Always will be."

As suddenly as the shuddering had begun, it stopped, and the ride smoothed out. The train sped on, safe on its rails. Its passengers exhaled sighs of relief that the morning newspapers would not be listing their names among the dead in a train wreck.

"How many cards, Judge?"

But Judge Congdon was not done talking. "I made no reference to mismanagement, Charlie. If you could speak as a close associate of Osgood Hennessy rather than as an engineer, sir, how are things going with Hennessy's Cascades Cutoff where these accidents seem to be concentrated?"

Kincaid delivered an impassioned speech more suited to a joint session of Congress than a high-stakes game of poker. "I assure you gentlemen that gossip about reckless expansion of the Cascades Line is poppycock. Our great nation was built by bold men like Southern Pacific president Hennessy who took enormous risks in the face of adversity and pressed on even when cooler heads pleaded to go easy, even when braving bankruptcy and financial ruin."

Bell noticed that Jack Thomas, the banker, looked less than assured. Kincaid was certainly doing Hennessy's reputation no favors tonight.

"How many cards would you like, Judge Congdon?" he asked again.

Congdon's reply was more alarming than the Overland Limited's sudden rough ride. "No cards, thank you. I don't need any. I'll stand pat."

The other players stared. Bruce Payne, the oil attorney, said out loud what they were all thinking. "Standing pat in five-card draw is like galloping into town at the head of marauding cavalry."

The hand was in its second round. Isaac Bell had already dealt each player five cards facedown. Congdon, "under the gun" to Bell's immediate left in a position that ordinarily passes, had opened the first round of betting. All of the men playing in the palatial stateroom except for Payne had called the steel baron's first-round bet. Charles Kincaid, seated to Bell's immediate right, had impetuously raised that bet, forcing the players who had stayed in to throw more money in the pot. Gold coins had rung mutedly on the felt tabletop as all the players, including Bell, had called the raise, largely because Kincaid had been playing with a noticeable lack of good sense.

With the first round of betting complete, the players were permitted to discard one, two, or three cards and draw replacements to improve their hands. Judge Congdon's announcement that he already had all the cards he needed, thank you, and would stand pat, made no one happy. By claiming that he needed no improvement, he was suggesting that he held a winning hand already, a hand that utilized all five of his cards and would beat hands as strong as two pairs or three of a kind. That meant he held at least a straight (five cards in numerical sequence) or a straight-beating flush (five cards in the same suit) or even a full house (three of a kind plus two of a kind), a potent combination that beat a straight or a flush.

"If Mr. Bell would please deal the other gentlemen the number of cards they ask for," gloated Congdon, who had suddenly lost interest in the subjects of labor strife and train wrecks, "I am anxious to open the next round of betting."

Bell asked, "Cards, Kenny?" And Bloom, who was nowhere near as rich in coal as Congdon was in steel, asked for three cards with little hope.

Jack Thomas took two cards, hinting that he might already hold three of a kind. But it was more likely, Bell decided, that he held a moderate pair and had kept an ace kicker in the desperate hope of drawing two more aces. If he really had trips, he would have raised on the first round.

The next man, Douglas Moser, the patrician New England textile-mill owner, said he would draw one card, which might be two pair but was a probably a hopeful straight or flush. Bell had seen enough of his play to judge him as too wealthy to care enough to play to win. That left Senator Kincaid, to Bell's immediate right.

Kincaid said, "I'll stand pat, too."

Judge Congdon's eyebrows, which were rough as strands of wire rope, rose a full inch. And several men exclaimed out loud. Two pat hands in the same round of draw poker was unheard of.

Bell was as surprised as the rest of the men. He had established already that Senator Kincaid cheated when he could by skillfully dealing from the bottom of the deck. But Kincaid hadn't dealt this hand, Bell had. As unusual as a pat hand was, if Kincaid had one it was due to genuine luck, not double-dealing.

"The last time I saw two pat hands," said Jack Thomas, "it ended in gunfire."

"Fortunately," said Moser, "no one at this table is armed."

Which was not true, Bell had noticed. The double-dealing Senator had a derringer tugging the cloth of his side pocket. A sensible precaution, Bell supposed, for men in public life since McKinley was shot.

Bell said, "Dealer takes two," discarded two cards, dealt himself two replacements, and put down the deck. "Opener bets," he said. "I believe that was you, Judge Congdon."

Old James Congdon, showing more yellow teeth than a timber wolf, smiled past Bell at Senator Kincaid. "I will bet the pot."

They were playing pot limit, which meant that the only restriction on any one bet was the amount on the table at that moment. Congdon's bet said that while he was surprised by Kincaid's pat hand, he did not fear it, suggesting he had a very powerful hand, more likely a full house rather than a straight or a flush. Bruce Payne, who looked extremely happy to be out of the hand, helpfully counted the pot, and announced, in his thin, reedy voice, "In round numbers, your pot bet will be three thousand six hundred dollars."

Joseph Van Dorn had taught Isaac Bell to gauge fortunes in terms of what a workingman earned in a day. He had taken him to the toughest saloon in Chicago and watched approvingly as his well-dressed apprentice won a couple of fistfights. Then he steered Bell's attention to the customers lining up for the free lunch. Clearly, the scion of a Boston banking family and a graduate of Yale had insights into the thinking apparatus of the privileged, the boss had noted with a smile. But a detective had to understand the other ninety-eight percent of the population, too. How did a man think when he had no money in his pocket? What did a man do who had nothing to lose but his fear?

The thirty-six hundred dollars in the pot for just this hand was more money than Judge Congdon's steelworkers made in six years.

"I bet three thousand six hundred," said Congdon, shoving all the coins in front of him to the center of the table and tossing in a red baize sack with more gold coins in it that thunked heavily on the felt.

Ken Bloom, Jack Thomas, and Douglas Moser folded their cards hurriedly.

"I call your three thousand six hundred," said Senator Kincaid. "And I raise the pot. Ten thousand eight hundred dollars." Eighteen years' wages.

"The line must be very grateful to you," said Congdon, needling the Senator about the railroad stock with which legislators notoriously were bribed.

"The line gets its money's worth," Kincaid replied with a smile.

"Or you would have us believe that your pat hand is very pat indeed."

"Pat enough to raise. What are you going to do, Judge? The bet is ten thousand eight hundred dollars to you."

Isaac Bell interrupted. "I believe the bet is to me."

"OH, I AM TERRIBLY sorry, Mr. Bell. We skipped your turn to fold your cards."

"That's all right, Senator. I saw you just barely catch the train at Ogden. You're probably still in a rush."

"I thought I saw a detective hanging off the side. Dangerous work, Mr. Bell."

"Not until a criminal hammers on one's fingers."

"The bet," growled Judge Congdon impatiently, "is my three thousand six hundred dollars plus Senator Kincaid's ten thousand eight hundred dollars, which makes the bet to Mr. Bell fourteen thousand four hundred dollars."

Payne interrupted to intone, "The pot, which includes Senator Kincaid's call, is now twenty-one thousand six hundred dollars."

Payne's calculations were hardly necessary. Even the richest, most carefree men at the table were aware that twenty-one thousand six hundred dollars was enough money to purchase the locomotive hauling their train and maybe one of the Pullmans.

"Mr. Bell," said Judge Congdon. "We await your response."

"I call your bet, Judge, and Senator Kincaid's ten-thousand-eight-hundred-dollar raise," said Bell, "making the pot thirty-six thousand dollars, which I raise."

"You *raise*?"

"Thirty-six thousand dollars."

Bell's reward was the pleasure of seeing the jaws of a United States senator and the richest steel baron in America drop in unison.

"The pot is now seventy-two thousand dollars," calculated Mr. Payne.

A deep silence pervaded the stateroom. All that could be heard was the muffled clatter of the wheels. Judge Congdon's wrinkled hand crept into his breast pocket and emerged with a bank check. He took a gold fountain pen from another pocket, uncapped it, and slowly wrote a number on his check. Then he signed his name, blew on the paper to dry the ink, and smiled.

"I call your thirty-six-thousand-dollar raise, Mr. Bell, and the Senator's ten thousand eight hundred, which by now seems a paltry sum, and I raise one hundred eighteen thousand eight hundred dollars . . . Senator Kincaid, it's to you. My raise and Mr. Bell's raise means it will cost you one hundred fifty-four thousand eight hundred dollars to stay in the hand."

"Good God," said Payne.

"Whatcha gonna do, Charlie?" asked Congdon. "One hundred fifty-four thousand eight hundred dollars if you want to play."

"Call," Kincaid said stiffly, scribbling the number on his calling card and tossing it on the heap of gold.

"No raise?" Congdon mocked.

"You heard me."

Congdon turned his dry smile on Bell. "Mr. Bell, my raise was one hundred eighteen thousand eight hundred dollars."

Bell smiled back, concealing the thought that merely to call would put a deep dent in his personal fortune. To raise would deepen it dangerously.

Judge James Congdon was one of the richest men in America. If Bell did raise, there was nothing to stop the man from raising him back and wiping him out.

17

"Mr. Payne," asked Isaac Bell. "how much money is in the pot?"

"Well, let me see . . . The pot now contains two hundred thirty-seven thousand six hundred dollars."

Bell mentally counted steelworkers. Four hundred men together could earn that pot in a good year. Ten men, if they were fortunate enough to survive long working lives uninterrupted by injury and lay-off, might together earn that amount between boyhood and old age.

Congdon asked innocently, "Mr. Payne, what will the pot contain if Mr. Bell continues to believe that his two-card draw improved him sufficiently to call?"

"Umm, the pot would contain four hundred seventy-five thousand two hundred dollars."

"Nearly half a million dollars," said the judge. "This is turning into real money."

Bell decided that Congdon was talking too much. The hard old steel baron actually sounded nervous. Like a man holding a straight, which, in pat-hand terms, was at the bottom of the barrel. "May I presume, sir, that you will accept my check on the American States Bank of Boston?"

"Of course, son. We're all gentlemen here."

"I call, and I raise four hundred seventy-five thousand two hundred dollars."

"I'm skunked," said Congdon, throwing his cards on the table.

Kincaid smiled, obviously relieved that Congdon was out of the hand.

"How many cards did you take, Mr. Bell?"

"Two."

Kincaid stared for a long time at the cards Bell cupped in his hand. When Bell looked up, he let his mind stray, which made it easier to appear unconcerned whether Kincaid called or folded.

The Pullman car was swaying due to an increase in speed. The muffling effect of the rugs and furniture in the palatial stateroom tended to mask the fact that they had accelerated to eighty miles an hour on the flats of Wyoming's Great Divide Basin. Bell knew this arid, windblown high country well, having spent months on horseback tracking the Wild Bunch.

Kincaid's fingers strayed toward the vest pocket where he kept his calling cards. The man had large hands, Bell noticed. And powerful wrists.

"That is a lot of money," the Senator said.

"A lot for a public servant," Congdon agreed. Annoyed that he had been forced out of the hand, he added another unpleasant reference to the Senator's railroad stocks. "Even one with 'interests' on the side."

Payne repeated Congdon's estimate. "Nearly half a million dollars."

"Serious money in these days of panic, with the markets falling," Congdon added.

"Mr. Bell," asked Kincaid, "what *does* a detective hanging off the side of a train do when a criminal starts hammering on his fingers?"

"Depends," said Bell.

"On what?"

"On whether he's been trained to fly."

Kenny Bloom laughed.

Kincaid's eyes never left Bell's face. "Have you been trained to fly?"

"Not yet."

"So what do you do?"

"I hammer back," said Bell.

"I believe you do," said Kincaid. "I fold."

Still expressionless, Bell laid his cards facedown on the table and raked in nine hundred fifty thousand four hundred dollars in gold, markers, and checks, including his own. Kincaid reached for Bell's cards. Bell placed his hand firmly on top of them.

"Curious what you had under there," said Kincaid.

"So am I," said Congdon. "Surely you weren't bluffing against two pat hands."

"It crossed my mind that the pat hands were bluffing, Judge."

"*Both?* I don't think so."

"I sure as hell wasn't bluffing," said Kincaid. "I had a very pretty heart flush."

He turned his cards over and spread them faceup so all could see.

"God Almighty, Senator!" said Payne, "Eight, nine, ten, jack, king. Just one short of a straight flush. You'd sure as hell have raised back with that."

"*Short* being the key word," observed Bloom. "And a reminder that straight flushes are scarcer than hens' teeth."

"I would very much like to see your cards, Mr. Bell," said Kincaid.

"You didn't pay to see them," said Bell.

Congdon said, "I'll pay."

"I beg your pardon, sir?"

"It's worth one hundred thousand dollars to me to prove that you had a high three of a kind and then drew a pair to make a full house. Which would beat the Senator's flush and my miserable straight."

"No bet," said Bell. "An old friend of mine used to say a bluff should keep them guessing."

"Just as I thought," said Congdon. "You won't take the bet because I'm right. You got lucky and caught another pair."

"If that is what you would like to believe, Judge, we'll both go home happy."

"Dammit!" said the steel magnate. "I'll make it two hundred thousand. Just show me your hand."

Bell turned them over. "That fellow also said to show them now and then to make them wonder. You were right about the high three of a kind."

The steel magnate stared. "I'll be damned. Three lonely ladies. You *were* bluffing. You only had trips. I'd have beat you with my straight. Though your flush would have beaten me, Charlie. If Mr. Bell hadn't forced us both out."

Charles Kincaid exploded, "You bet half a million dollars on three lousy queens?"

"I'm partial to the ladies," said Isaac Bell. "Always have been."

KINCAID REACHED ACROSS AND touched the queens as if not quite believing his eyes. "I will have to arrange to transfer funds when I get to Washington," he said stiffly.

"No rush," Bell said graciously. "I'd have had to ask the same."

"Where should I mail my check?"

"I'll be at the Yale Club of New York City."

"Son," said Congdon, writing a check for which he did *not* have to transfer funds to cover, "you sure paid for your train ticket."

"Train ticket, hell," said Bloom. "He could buy the train."

"Sold!" Bell laughed. "Come back to my observation car and drinks are on me, and maybe a bite of late supper. All this bluffing makes me hungry."

As Bell led them to the rear of the train, he wondered why Senator Kincaid had folded. It had been a strictly correct move, he supposed, but after Congdon had folded it was a lot more cautious than Kincaid had been all night, which was puzzling. It was almost if Kincaid had been acting a bit more the fool earlier than he really was. And what was all that blather about Osgood Hennessy taking enormous risks? He certainly hadn't improved his benefactor's standing with the bankers.

Bell ordered champagne for all in the observation car and asked the stewards to serve up a late-night supper. Kincaid said he could stay for only one quick glass. He was tired, he said. But he let Bell pour him a second glass of champagne and then ate some steak and eggs and seemed to get over his disappointment at the card table. The players mingled with one another and some other travelers who were passing the night drinking. Groups formed fluidly, broke up, and formed again. The tale of the three queens was told over and over. As the crowd thinned, Isaac Bell found himself alone with Ken Bloom, Judge Congdon, and Senator Kincaid, who remarked, "I understand you've been showing the train crew a wanted poster."

"A sketch of a man we're investigating," Bell answered.

"Show us!" said Bloom. "Maybe we've seen him."

Bell took one from his coat, pushed plates aside, and spread it on the table.

Bloom took one look. "That's the actor! In *The Great Train Robbery.*"

"Is it really the actor?" asked Kincaid.

"No. But there is a similarity to Broncho Billy Anderson."

Kincaid trailed his fingers across the sketch. "I think he looks like me."

"Arrest this man!" laughed Ken Bloom.

"He does," said Congdon. "Sort of. This fellow has chiseled features. So does the Senator. Look at the cleft in the chin. You've got one of those too, Charles. I heard a bunch of damned fool women in Washington squawking like hens that you look like a matinee idol."

"My ears aren't that big, are they?"

"No."

"That's a relief," said Kincaid. "I can't be a matinee idol with big ears."

Bell laughed. "My boss warned us, 'Don't arrest any ugly mugs.'"

Curiously, he looked from the sketch to the Senator and back to the sketch. There was a similarity in the high brow. The ears were definitely different. Both the suspect in the sketch and the Senator had intelligent faces with strong features. So did a lot of men, as Joseph Van Dorn had pointed out. Where the Senator and the suspect diverged, in addition to ear size, was the penetrating gaze. The man who had struck the lumberjack with a crowbar looked harder and filled with purpose. It was hardly surprising that he had looked intense to the man he was attacking. But Kincaid did not seem driven by purpose. Even at the height of their betting duel, Kincaid had struck him as essentially self-satisfied and self-indulgent, more the servant of the powerful than powerful himself. Although, Bell reminded himself, he had wondered earlier whether Kincaid playing the fool was an act.

"Well," said Kincaid, "if we see this fellow, we'll nab him for you."

"If you do, stay out of his way and call for reinforcements," Bell said soberly. "He is poison."

"All right, I'm off to bed. Long day. Good night, Mr. Bell," Kincaid said cordially. "Interesting playing cards with you."

"Expensive, too," said Judge Congdon. "What are you going to do with all those winnings, Mr. Bell?"

"I'm going to buy my fiancée a mansion."

"Where?"

"San Francisco. Up on Nob Hill."

"How many survived the earthquake?"

"The one I'm thinking of was built to stand for a thousand years. The only trouble is, it might hold ghosts for my fiancée. It belonged to her former employer, who turned out to be a depraved bank robber and murderer."

"In my experience," Congdon chuckled, "the best way to make a woman comfortable in a previous woman's house is to hand her a stick of dynamite and instruct her to enjoy the process of redecorating. I've done it repeatedly. Works like a charm. That might apply to former employers, too."

Charles Kincaid rose and said good night all around. Then he asked, casually, almost mockingly, "Whatever happened to the depraved bank robber and murderer?"

Isaac Bell looked the Senator in the eye until the Senator dropped his gaze. Only then did the tall detective say, "I ran him to ground, Senator. He won't hurt anyone ever again."

Kincaid responded with a hearty laugh. "The famous Van Dorn motto: 'We never give up.'"

"Never," said Bell.

Senator Kincaid, Judge Congdon, and the others drifted off to bed, leaving Bell and Kenny Bloom alone in the observation car. Half an hour later, the train began to slow. Here and there, a light shone in the black night. The outskirts of the town of Rawlins took shape. The Overland Limited trundled through dimly lit streets.

THE WRECKER GAUGED THE train's speed from the platform at the end of the Pullman car that housed his stateroom. Bell's sketch had shaken him far more than his enormous losses at poker. The money meant nothing in the long run, because he would soon be richer than Congdon, Bloom, and Moser combined. But the sketch represented a rare piece of bad luck. Someone had seen his face and described him to an artist. Fortunately, they'd got his ears wrong. And thank God for the resemblance to the movie star. But he could not count on those lucky breaks confusing Isaac Bell for much longer.

He jumped from the slowing train, and set out to explore the dark streets. He had to work fast. The stop was scheduled for only thirty minutes, and he didn't know Rawlins. But there was a pattern to railroad towns, and he believed the flow of luck that had moved against him tonight was shifting his way. For one thing, Isaac Bell's guard was down. The detective was exhilarated by his great fortune at the card table. And it was likely that among the telegraph messages waiting at the depot would be tragic news from Ogden that would throw him for a loop.

He found what he was looking for within minutes, tracing the sound of a piano to a saloon, which was still going strong even though it was well past midnight. He didn't push through the swinging doors but instead filled his hand with a fat wad of money and circled the saloon by plunging fearlessly down side and back alleys. Bright lights from the second story revealed the dance hall and gambling casino, duller lights the cribs of the attached brothel. The sheriff, bribed to ignore the illegal operations, wouldn't venture near their doors. Bouncers were hired, therefore, to keep the peace and discourage robbers. And there they were.

Two broken-nosed, bare-knuckle boxers of the type that competed at rodeos and Elk halls were smoking cigarettes on the plank steps that led upstairs. They eyed him with increasing interest as he approached unsteadily. Twenty feet from the steps, he stumbled and reached out to the wall to catch his balance. His hand touched the rough wood precisely where a shaft of light spilled down from above and illuminated the cash he was holding. The two stood up, exchanged glances, and flicked out their cigarettes.

The Wrecker reeled drunkenly away, lurching into the dark toward the open door of a livery stable. He saw another gleam of exchanged glances, as the bouncers' luck seemed to get better and better. The drunk with the roll of *dinero* was making it easy for them to relieve him of it in private.

He got inside the stable ahead of them and swiftly chose a spot where light from next door spilled through a window. They came after him, the lead bouncer pulling a sap from his pocket. The Wrecker kicked his feet out from under him. The surprise was complete, and he fell to the hoof-beaten straw. His partner, comprehending that the Wrecker was not as drunk as they had supposed, raised his powerful fists.

The Wrecker went down on one knee, drew his knife from his boot, flicked his wrist. The blade leaped to its full length, the tip touching the bouncer's throat. With his other hand, the Wrecker pressed his derringer to the temple of the man fallen in the straw. For a moment, the only sound was the piano in the distance and the bouncers' hard, startled breath.

"Relax, gentlemen," said the Wrecker. "It's a business proposition. I will pay you ten thousand dollars to kill a passenger on the Overland Limited. You have twenty minutes before it leaves the station."

The bouncers had no objection to killing a man for ten thousand dollars. The Wrecker could have bought them for five. But they were practical men.

"How do we get him off the train?"

"He is a protector of the innocent," said the Wrecker. "He will come to the rescue of someone in danger—a damsel in distress, for example. Would such be available?"

They looked across the alley. A red brakeman's lantern hung in a window. "For two dollars, she'll be available."

•   •   •

THE OVERLAND LIMITED had come to a stop with a metallic shriek of brake shoes and the clank of couplings in the narrow pool of electric light beside the low brick Rawlins Depot. Most of her passengers were asleep in their beds. The few who were not stepped onto the platform to stretch their legs only to retreat from the stink of alkali springs mingled with coal smoke. The train crew changed engines while provisions, newspapers, and telegrams came aboard.

The porter, the former slave Jonathan, approached Isaac Bell in the deserted observation car, where the detective was contentedly sprawled on a couch reminiscing with Kenneth Bloom about their days in the circus.

"Telegram from Ogden, Mr. Bell."

Bell tipped the old man a thousand dollars.

"That's all right, Jonathan," he said, laughing. "I got lucky tonight. The least I can do is share the wealth. Excuse me a moment, Ken." He turned away to read the wire.

His face turned cold even as hot tears burned his eyes.

"You all right, Isaac?" asked Ken.

"No," he choked out, and stepped onto the rear platform to try to fill his lungs with the acrid-smelling air. Though it was the middle of the night, a shunt engine was moving freight cars about the yards. Bloom followed him out.

"What happened?"

"Weber and Fields . . ."

"Vaudeville? What are you talking about?"

All Isaac Bell could say was, "My old friends." He crumpled the telegram in his fist, and whispered to himself, "Last thing I told them was to watch their step. I told them the Wrecker is poison."

"Who?" asked Bloom.

Bell turned terrible eyes on him, and Bloom retreated hastily into the observation car.

Bell smoothed the telegraph flat and read it again. Their bodies had been found in an alley, two blocks from the office. They must have spotted the Wrecker and tailed him. It was hard to believe that a single man could have taken both veteran detectives down. But Wally had not been well. Maybe it had slowed him. As chief investigator, as the man responsible for the safety of his operatives, he should have replaced him—should have taken a vulnerable man out of danger.

Bell's head felt like it would explode, it was so filled with pain and fury. For what felt like a very long time, he could not think. Then, gradually, it struck him that Wally and Mack had left him a dying legacy. The man they had tailed must have looked enough like the man in the lumberjack's sketch to raise their suspicions. Otherwise, why would they have followed him into an alley? That he had turned on them and killed them proved that the sketch of the Wrecker was accurate, no matter how much it reminded people of a matinee idol.

The fresh locomotive hooted the go-ahead signal. Bell, gripping the platform handrail, tears streaming down his face, was so lost in his heartsick thoughts that he barely heard the whistle. When the train started moving, he grew vaguely aware that the crossties appeared to slide behind the observation car as it rolled out of the station and passed under the last electric light in the station yard.

A woman screamed.

Bell looked up. He saw her running down the tracks like she was trying to catch the accelerating train. Her white dress seemed to glow in the night, backlit as it was by the distance light. A man was lumbering after her, a hulking shape, who caught her in his arms and cut off her scream with a hand clapped over her mouth and forced her to the roadbed under the weight of his body.

Bell exploded into motion. He leaped over the railing and hit the ties running, pumping his legs as fast as he could. But the train was moving too fast, and he lost his balance. He tucked into a tight ball, shielded his face with his hands, hit the ties, and rolled between the rails as the train raced away at thirty miles an hour.

Bell rolled over a switch and stopped suddenly against a signal post. He jumped to his feet and ran to help the woman. The man had one hand around her throat and was ramming at her dress with the other.

"Let her go!" Bell shouted.

The man sprang to his feet.

"Get lost," he told the woman.

"Pay me!" she demanded, thrusting out her hand. He slapped money in it. She cast Bell a blank look and walked back toward the distant depot. The man pretending to attack her turned on Bell, hurling punches like a prizefighter.

Staring in disbelief at the red light on the back of the Overland Limited disappearing into the night, Bell automatically ducked the man's heavy blows and they passed harmlessly over his shoulder. Then a rock-hard fist slammed into the back of his head.

THE WRECKER WATCHED FROM the rear platform of the Overland Limited as the train picked up speed. The red light on the back of the observation car shone on the rails. Three stick figures growing smaller by the moment were silhouetted against the glow of the Rawlins rail yards. Two appeared stationary. The third bounced back and forth between them.

"Good-bye, Mr. Bell. Don't forget to 'hammer back.'"

THERE WERE TWO OF THEM.

The punch from behind flung Bell reeling at the first boxer, who gave him a shot to the jaw. The blow spun him like a top. The second boxer was waiting with a fist that knocked the detective clean off his feet.

Bell hit the ballast with his shoulder and rolled across splintery ties and banged into one of the rails. The cold steel made a pillow for his head, as he looked up, trying to focus on what was happening to him. Seconds ago, he had been standing on the rear platform of a first-class, all-stateroom train. Then he'd run to rescue a woman not needing rescuing. Now two bare-knuckle prizefighters were hurling punches at him.

They circled, blocking any thought of escape.

A quarter mile down the tracks, the busy depot switch engine stopped on a siding and cast the long glow of its headlamp down the rails, illuminating Bell and his attackers enough so that they could see one another but not enough, Bell knew, to be seen by anyone who might intervene.

In the light of the distant headlamp, he saw that they were big men, not as tall as him but each outweighing him handily. He could tell by their stance that they were professionals. Light on their feet, they knew how to throw a punch, knew where to hit the body to inflict the most damage, knew every dirty trick in the book. He could tell by their cold expressions to expect no mercy.

"On your feet, boyo. Stand up and take it like a man."

They backed up to allow him room, so confident were they of their skills and the fact that they outnumbered him two to one.

Bell shook his head to clear it and gathered his legs under him. He was a trained boxer. He knew how to take a punch. He knew how to slip a punch. He knew how to throw punches in lightning combinations. But they outnumbered him, and they knew their business, too.

The first man poised to charge, eyes gleaming, fists held low in the brawling stance of bare-knuckle champion John L. Sullivan. The second man held his hands higher in the style of "Gentleman Jim" Corbett, the only man who had ever knocked Sullivan out. He would be the one to look out for, Corbett being a scientific boxer as opposed to a fighter. This man's left hand and shoulder were protecting his jaw, just like Corbett would. His right, guarding his stomach, was a sledgehammer held in reserve.

Bell stood up.

Corbett stepped back.

Sullivan charged.

Their strategy, Bell saw, was simple and would be brutally effective. While Sullivan attacked from the front, Corbett would stand by to slam Bell back whenever Bell staggered out of range. If Bell lasted long enough to tire out Sullivan, Corbett would take his place and start fresh.

Bell's two-shot derringer was in his hat, which was hanging in his stateroom. His pistol was on the train too, steaming toward Cheyenne. He was dressed in the evening attire in which he had dined and played poker: tuxedo jacket, pleated dress shirt with diamond studs, silk bow tie. Only his footwear, polished black boots, largely concealed by his trouser legs, instead of patent leather dancing pumps, might have caused a discerning maître d' not to seat him at the best table in a restaurant.

Sullivan threw a roundhouse right. Bell ducked. The fist whizzed over his head, and Sullivan, thrown off balance, stumbled past. As he did, Bell hit him twice, once in his rock-hard stomach, which had absolutely no effect, then on the side of his face, which made him shout in anger.

Corbett laughed, harshly. "A *scientific* fighter," he mocked. "Where'd you learn to box, sonny? Harvard?"

"Yale," said Bell.

"Well, here's one for Boola Boola." Corbett feinted with his right and delivered a sharp left to Bell's ribs. Even though Bell had managed to move away, it was like getting hit by a locomotive. He tumbled to the ground with a searing pain in his side. Sullivan ran over to kick him in the head. Bell twisted frantically, and the hobnailed boot aimed at his face ripped the shoulder of his dinner jacket.

Two on one was no time for Marquess of Queensberry rules. He scooped a heavy piece of ballast from the rail bed as he rolled to his feet.

"Did I mention I also studied in Chicago?" he asked, "On the West Side."

He threw the stone with all his strength into Corbett's face.

Corbett cried out in pain and clutched his eye. Bell had expected to stagger him, if not take him right out of the fight. But Corbett was very fast. He had ducked quickly enough to dodge the stone's full force. He lowered his hand from his eye, wiped the blood on the front of his shirt, and closed his hand into a fist again.

"That'll cost you, college. There's quick ways to die and slow ways to die, and you just earned a slow way."

Corbett circled, one fist high, the other low, one eye dark, the other glaring malevolently. He threw several jabs—four, five, six—contrived to calculate, by Bell's reactions, just how good he was and where his weaknesses lay. Suddenly, he came at Bell with a quick one-two, a left and a right, designed to soften him for a heavier blow.

Bell slipped both punches. But Sullivan charged from the side and landed a hard fist across Bell's mouth that knocked him down again.

Bell tasted salt in his mouth. He sat up, shaking his head. Blood ran down his face, over his lips. The switch engine light gleamed on his teeth.

"He's smiling," Sullivan said to Corbett. "Is he loco?"

"Punch-drunk. I hit him harder than I thought."

"Hey, college, what's the joke?"

"Get in there, finish him off."

"Then what?"

"Leave him on the track. It'll look like a train killed him."

Bell's smile grew wider.

A bloody nose at last, he thought. *Wally and Mack, old friends, I must be closer to catching the Wrecker than I know.*

The Wrecker had gotten on at Ogden after all. He had laid low, waiting for his chance, while Bell ate dinner, played cards, and hosted a victory party in the observation car. Then the Wrecker had jumped off at Rawlins to hire these two to kill him.

"I'll give him something to smile about," said Sullivan.

"Got a match?" Bell asked him.

Sullivan lowered his hands and stared. "What?"

"A match. A lucifer. I need more light to show you this picture I have in my pocket."

"*What?*"

"You asked, what's the joke. I'm hunting a killer. The same killer who hired you hydrophobic skunks to kill me. Here's the joke: you hydrophobic skunks are going to tell me what he looks like."

Sullivan rushed at Bell, throwing a vicious right at his face. Bell moved quickly. The fist whizzed over his head like a boulder, and he brought his left down on the Sullivan's head as he stumbled from the force of missing Bell. It drove Sullivan to the ground like a pile driver. This time when Corbett rushed in from the side, Bell was ready, and he backhanded Corbett with the same left, smashing his nose with a sharp crack.

Corbett grunted, wheeling gracefully out of a predicament that would have seen an ordinary mortal fall. He whipped his left high to protect his chin from Bell's right cross and kept his right low to block Bell's left to the stomach. Conversationally, he said, "Here's one they didn't teach you in college," and hit Bell with a one-two that nearly tore his head off.

Sullivan slugged Bell as he hurtled past. The full force of the blow struck just above his temple and knocked him flat. The pain was sharp as a needle in his brain. But the fact that he felt pain at all meant he was still alive, and conscious that Sullivan and Corbett were moving in for the kill. His head was spinning, and he had to push with his hands to regain his feet.

"Gentlemen, this is your last chance. Is this the man who paid you to kill me?"

Sullivan's powerful jab knocked the paper from Bell's hand.

Bell straightened up as much as he could, given the searing pain in his ribs, and managed to elude the combination Sullivan threw next. "I'll take you next," he taunted Sullivan. "Soon as I teach your partner something I learned in college." Then he turned his scorn on Corbett. "If you were half as good as you think you are, you wouldn't be hiring yourself out to beat people up in a godforsaken railroad town."

It worked. As table talk could smoke out intentions in poker, fight talk provoked recklessness. Corbett shoved Sullivan aside.

"Get out of my way! I'm going to make this son of a bitch weep before he dies."

He charged in a rage, throwing punches like cannon fire.

Bell knew he had taken too much punishment to count on speed. He had one last chance to gather all his strength into one killing blow. Too tired to slip the punches, he absorbed two, stepped inside the next, and hit Corbett hard on the jaw, which snapped Corbett's head back. Then Bell unleashed a right with every ounce of his strength and plunged it into Corbett's body. The breath exploded out of the man, and he collapsed as if his knees had turned to water. Fighting to the last, he lunged for Bell's throat as he went down but fell short.

Bell lurched at Sullivan. He was gasping at the exertion, but his face was a mask of grim purpose: *Who hired you to kill me?*

Sullivan dropped to his knees beside Corbett, reached inside his fallen partner's coat, yanked out a flick knife. Leaping to his feet, he charged Bell.

Bell knew that the heavily built brawler was stronger than he was. In his own half-dead state, attempting to take the knife away was too risky. He slipped his own blade from his boot and pitched it over-hand, dragging his index finger on the smooth handle to prevent it from rotating. Flickering like a lizard's tongue, it flew flat and true into Corbett's throat. The brawler fell, spewing blood through hands desperately trying to close the wound.

He would not be answering Bell's questions.

The detective knelt beside Corbett. His eyes were staring wide open. Blood was trickling from his mouth. If he wasn't dying from internal ruptures from Bell's blow to his stomach, he was close to it, and would not be answering questions tonight either. Without wasting another moment, Isaac Bell staggered along the rails to the Rawlins Depot and burst through the dispatcher's door.

The dispatcher stared at the man in ripped evening clothes with blood pouring down his face.

"What the hell happened to you, mister?"

Bell said, "The president of the line has authorized me to charter a special."

"You bet. And the Pope just gave me a pass for the Pearly Gates."

Bell pulled Osgood Hennessy's letter from his wallet and thrust it in the dispatcher's face.

"I want your fastest locomotive."

The dispatcher read it twice, stood up, and said, "Yes, sir! But I've only got one engine, and she's scheduled to hitch onto the westbound limited, which is due in twenty minutes."

"Turn her around, we're going east."

"Where to?"

"After the Overland Limited."

"You'll never catch her."

"If I don't, you'll be hearing from Mr. Hennessy. Get on that telegraph and clear the tracks."

The Overland Limited had a fifty-minute head start, but Bell's locomotive had the advantage of hauling only the weight of her own coal and water while the Limited's engine was towing eight Pullmans and baggage, dining, and observation cars. Hundred-dollar tips to the fireman and engineer didn't hurt her speed either. They climbed through the night, encountering snow in the Medicine Bow Mountains, a harbinger of the winter that Osgood Hennessy's railroad builders were striving to beat even as the Wrecker sowed death and destruction to stop them.

They left the snow behind as they descended into the Laramie Valley, stormed through it and the town, stopping only for water, and climbed again. They finally caught up with the Overland Limited east of Laramie at Buford Station, where the rising sun was illuminating the pink granite on the crest of Sherman Hill. The Limited was sidetracked on the water siding, her fireman wrestling the spigot down from the tall wooden tank and jerking the chain that caused the water to flow into the locomotive's tender.

"Do you have sufficient water to make it to Cheyenne without stopping?" Bell asked his fireman.

"I believe so, Mr. Bell."

"Pass him!" Bell told the engineer. "Take me straight to the Cheyenne Depot. Fast as you can."

From Buford Station to Cheyenne, the road descended two thousand feet in thirty miles. With nothing on the eastbound track in front of Bell's special, they headed for Cheyenne at ninety miles an hour.

THE WRECKER HAD AWAKENED THE INSTANT THE TRAIN HAD stopped. He parted the shade a crack and saw the sun shining on pink Sherman granite, which the railroad quarried for track ballast. They would be in Cheyenne for breakfast. He closed his eyes, glad for another hour of sleep.

A locomotive thundered past the sidetracked Limited.

The Wrecker opened his eyes. He rang for the porter.

"George," he said to Jonathan. "Why have we stopped?"

"Stopped for water, suh."

"Why did a train overtake us?"

"Don't know, suh."

"We are the Limited."

"Yes, suh."

"What train would be faster than this one, *damn you?*"

The porter flinched. Senator Kincaid's face was suddenly wracked with rage, his eyes hot, his mouth twisted with hate. Jonathan was terrified. The Senator could order him fired in a breath. They'd throw him off the train at the next stop. Or right here on top of the Rocky

Mountains. "It weren't no train passing us, suh. It was just a locomotive all by hisself."

"A single locomotive?"

"Yes, suh! Just him and his tender."

"So it must have been a chartered special."

"Must have been, suh. Just like you say, suh. Going lickety-split, suh."

The Wrecker lay back on the bed, clasped his hands behind his head, and thought hard.

"Will there be anything else, suh?" Jonathan asked warily.

"Coffee."

BELL'S CHARTERED LOCOMOTIVE RACED through Cheyenne's stockyards and into Union Depot shortly after nine in the morning. He ran directly to the Inter-Ocean Hotel, the best among the three-story establishments he could see from the station. The house detective took one look at the tall man in ripped and torn evening clothes and blood-soaked shirt and crossed the lobby at a dead run to intercept him.

"You can't come in here looking like that."

"Bell. Van Dorn Agency. Take me to the tailor. And round up a haberdasher, a shoe-shine boy, and a barber."

"Right this way, sir . . . Shall I get you a doctor, too?"

"No time."

The Overland Limited glided into Union Depot forty minutes later.

Isaac Bell was waiting on the platform at the middle of the train, looking far better than he felt. His entire body ached and his ribs hurt with every breath. But he was groomed, shaved, and dressed as well as he had been at the poker game the night before, in crisp black evening clothes, snow-white shirt, silk bow tie and cummerbund, and boots shined like mirrors.

A smile played across his swollen lips. Someone on this train was in for a big surprise. The question was would the Wrecker be so shocked that he gave himself away?

Before the train stopped rolling, Bell stepped aboard the Pullman just ahead of the dining car, pulled himself painfully up the steps, crossed to the dining car, and sauntered in. Forcing himself to stand and walk normally for the benefit of all watching, he asked the steward for a table in the middle, which allowed him to see who entered from either end.

Last night's thousand-dollar tip in the observation car had not gone unnoticed by the train crew. He was seated immediately and brought hot coffee, steaming breakfast rolls, and a warm recommendation to order the freshly caught Wyoming cutthroat trout.

Bell had watched every man's face as he had come into the dining car to gauge reactions to his presence. Several, noting his evening attire, remarked with a clubby smile, "Long night?" The Chicago meatpacker gave him a friendly wave, as did the well-dressed drummer he had spoken with in the washroom.

Judge Congdon wandered in, and said, "Forgive me if I don't join you, Mr. Bell. With the obvious exception of a young lady's company, I prefer my own in the morning."

Kenny Bloom staggered into the diner with a hangover clouding his eyes and sat beside Bell.

"Good morning," said Bell.

"What the hell is good about it . . . Say, what happened to your face?"

"Cut myself shaving."

"George! George! Coffee over here before a man dies."

Bruce Payne, the oil lawyer, hurried up to their table, talking a blue streak about what he had read in the Cheyenne newspapers.

Kenny Bloom covered his eyes. Jack Thomas sat down at the last empty chair, and said, "That's a heck of a shiner."

"Cut myself shaving."

"There's the Senator! Hell, we don't have room for him. George! George! Rustle up another chair for Senator Kincaid. A man who loses as much money as he did shouldn't have to eat alone."

Bell watched Kincaid approach slowly, nodding to acquaintances as he passed through the dining car. Suddenly, he recoiled, his expression startled. The well-dressed drummer had leaped up from his breakfast, reaching out to shake hands. Kincaid gave the salesman a cold stare, brushed past, and proceeded to Bell's table.

"Good morning, gentlemen. Feeling satisfied, Mr. Bell?"

"Satisfied about what, Senator?"

"About what? About winning nearly a million dollars last night. A fair piece of which was mine."

"*That's* what I was doing last night," said Bell, still watching the doors. "I was trying to remember. I knew it was something that caught my attention."

"It looks like something caught your attention full in the face. What happened? Did you fall off a moving train?"

"Close shave," said Isaac Bell, still watching the doors. But though he lingered over breakfast until the last table was cleared, he saw no one react as if his presence were a shock. He was not particularly surprised and only mildly disappointed. It had been a long shot. But even if he hadn't spooked the Wrecker into revealing his identity, from now on the Wrecker would be watching a bit anxiously over his shoulder. Who said a Van Dorn detective couldn't fly?

WONG LEE, OF JERSEY CITY, NEW JERSEY, WAS A TINY MAN WITH a lopsided face and a blinded eye. Twenty years ago, an Irish hod carrier, thick-armed from lugging bricks, knocked Wong's hat to the sidewalk, and when Wong asked why he had insulted him, the hod carrier and two companions beat Wong so badly that his friends didn't recognize him when they came to the hospital. He had been twenty-eight years old when he was attacked and full of hope, improving his English and working in a laundry to save enough money to bring his wife to America from their village in Kowloon.

Now he was nearly fifty. At one point, he had saved enough to buy his own laundry across the Hudson River on Manhattan Island in New York City in hopes of earning her passage faster. His good English drew customers until the Panic of 1893 had put a sudden end to that dream, and Wong Lee's Fine Hand Wash Laundering joined the tens of thousands of businesses that were bankrupt in the nineties. When prosperity finally returned, the long hard years had left Wong too weary to start a new business. Though ever hopeful, he now was saving money by sleeping on the floor of the laundry where he worked in Jersey City. Much of that money went to get a certificate of residence, which was a new provision included in the Chinese Exclusion Act when it was renewed in 1902. It seems that he had neglected to defend himself from assault charges, the lawyer explained, filed all those years ago while he was still in the hospital. So bribes would have to be paid. Or so the lawyer claimed.

Then that past February, with winter still lingering, a stranger approached Wong when he was alone in his employer's laundry. He was a white American, so muffled against the river wind that only his eyes showed above the collar of his inverness coat and below the brim of his fedora.

"Wong Lee," he said. "Our mutual friend, Peter Boa, sends greetings."

Wong Lee hadn't see Peter Boa in twenty-five years, not since they'd worked together as immigrant dynamiters blowing cuts in the mountains for the Central Pacific Railroad. Young and daring and hopeful of returning to their villages rich men, they'd scrambled down cliff faces setting charges, competing to blast the most foot-holds for the trains.

Wong said that he was happy to hear that Boa was alive and well. When last Wong had seen him, in the Sierra Nevada, Peter had lost a hand to a sooner-than-expected explosion. Gangrene was creep-ing up his arm, and he had been too sick to flee California from the mobs attacking Chinese immigrants.

"Peter Boa told me to look you up in Jersey City. He said you could help me, as he was unable."

"By your clothes," Wong observed, "I can see that you are too rich to need help from a poor man."

"Rich indeed," said the stranger, sliding a wad of banknotes across the wooden counter. "An advance," he called it, "until I return," add-ing, "Rich enough to pay you whatever you need."

"What do *you* need?" Wong countered.

"Peter Boa told me that you had a special gift for demolition. He said that you used one stick of dynamite when most men needed five. They called you Dragon Wong. And when you protested that only emperors could be dragons, they proclaimed you Emperor of Dynamite."

Flattered, Wong Lee knew it was true. He had had an intuitive understanding of dynamite back when no one knew that much about the new explosive. He still had the gift. He had kept up with all the modern advances in demolition, including how electricity made explosives safer and more powerful, in the unlikely hope that one day quarries and construction contractors would deign to hire the Chinese they used to hire but now shunned.

Wong immediately used the money to buy a half interest in his boss's business. But one month later, that past March, a Panic swept Wall Street again. Jersey City factories closed, as did factories all over the nation. The trains had less freight to carry, so the car floats had fewer boxcars to ferry across the river. Jobs grew scarce on the piers, and fewer people could afford to have their clothing laundered. All spring and summer, the Panic deepened. By autumn, Wong had little hope of ever seeing his wife again.

Now it was November, bitterly cold today, with another winter looming.

And the stranger came back to Jersey City, muffled against the Hudson wind.

He reminded Wong that accepting an advance was a promise to deliver.

Wong reminded the stranger that he had promised to pay whatever he needed.

"Five thousand dollars when the job is done. Will that do you?"

"Very good, sir." Then, feeling unusually bold because the stranger truly needed him, Wong asked, "Are you an anarchist?"

"Why do you ask?" the stranger asked coldly.

"Anarchists like dynamite," Wong answered.

"So do labor strikers," the stranger answered patiently, proving that he truly needed Wong Lee and only Wong Lee. "You know the expression 'the proletariat's artillery'?"

"But you do not wear workman's clothes."

The Wrecker studied the Chinaman's battered face for a long minute, as if memorizing every scar.

Even though the laundry counter separated them, Wong suddenly felt they were standing too close.

"I don't care," he tried to explain. "Just curious," he added nervously.

"Ask me again," said the stranger, "and I will remove your other eye."

Wong Lee backed up a step. The stranger asked a question, watching Wong's battered face as if testing his skills.

"What will you need to make the biggest bang possible out of twenty-five tons?"

"Twenty-five *tons* of dynamite? Twenty-five tons is a lot of dynamite."

"A full boxcar load. What will you need to make the biggest explosion?"

Wong told him precisely what he needed, and the stranger said, "You will have it."

On the ferry back to Manhattan Island, Charles Kincaid stood out on the open deck, still muffled against the cold wind that scattered the coal smoke normally hanging over the harbor. He could not help but smile.

Striker or anarchist?

In fact, he was neither, despite the fear-mongering "evidence" he had taken pains to leave behind. Radical talk, rabble-rousing posters, diabolical foreigners, the Yellow Peril that Wong Lee's body would soon furnish, even the name Wrecker, were all smoke in his enemies' eyes. He was no radical. He was no destroyer. He was a builder.

His smile broadened even as his eyes grew colder.

He had nothing against the "favored few." Before he was finished, he would be first among them, the most favored of all.

21

ISAAC BELL AND ARCHIE ABBOTT CLIMBED ON TOP OF A BOX-
car filled with dynamite to survey the intercontinental freight terminal that carpeted Jersey City's Communipaw District. This was
the end of the line for every railroad from the West and the South.
Freight cars that had traveled two and three thousand miles across
America stopped at the New Jersey piers one mile short of their des-
tination, their way blocked by a stretch of water known to mariners
as the North River and called by everyone else the Hudson.

The boxcar stood on the powder pier, a single-tracked wharf
reserved for unloading explosives. But they were close enough
to see the main terminal that thrust into the Hudson River on
six-hundred-foot finger piers. Four freight trains were strung out on
each pier waiting to be rolled onto sturdy wooden barges and floated
across the river. They carried every commodity consumed by the
city: cement, lumber, steel, sulfur, wheat, corn, coal, kerosene, and
refrigerated fruits, vegetables, beef, and pork.

A mile across the water, Manhattan Island rose out of the smoky
harbor, bristling with church steeples and ships' masts. Above the
steeples and masts soared the mighty towers of the Brooklyn Bridge

and dozens of skyscrapers, many newly finished since Bell's last visit only a year earlier. The twenty-two-story Flatiron Building had been surpassed by the Times Building, and both were dwarfed by a six-hundred-foot steel frame being built for the Singer Sewing Machine Company's new headquarters.

"Only in New York," boasted Archie Abbott.

Abbott was as proud as a Chamber of Commerce promoter, but he knew the city inside out, which made him Bell's invaluable guide.

"Look at that boat flying the flag of the Southern Pacific Railroad even though she is three thousand miles from home plate. Everyone has to come to New York. We have become the center of the world."

"You've become a target," said Bell. "The Wrecker got you in his sights the instant Osgood Hennessy sealed his deal to take control of the Jersey Central, which gained him access to the city."

The harbor vessel that had sparked Abbott's civic pride was a long, low-in-the-water steam lighter, a materials and work vessel considerably bigger than a tugboat. She belonged to the newly formed Eastern Marine Division of the Southern Pacific Railroad and flew her colors more boldly than the local work vessels plying the Port of New York. A brand-new vermilion flag snapped in the breeze, and four red rings, bright as sealing wax, circled her soot-smeared smokestack.

Even her old name, *Oxford,* had been painted over. *Lillian I* now circled her cruiser stern. Hennessy had renamed every lighter and tugboat in the Eastern Marine Division fleet, *Lillian I* through *Lillian XII,* and had ordered SOUTHERN PACIFIC RAILROAD painted on their transoms and wheelhouses in bright-white letters.

"Just in case," Archie remarked, "the Wrecker doesn't know he's here."

"He knows," Bell said grimly.

His restlessly probing blue eyes were dark with concern. New York City *was* the Holy Land, as *Harper's Weekly* had put it, to which all railroaders longed make a pilgrimage. Osgood Hennessy had achieved that goal, and Isaac Bell knew in his heart that the Wrecker's taunting note on the magazine's cartoon of the railroad president was no bluff. The murderous saboteur was bent on a public attack. The next battle would be fought here.

Stone-faced, Bell watched one of the countless tugboats shunting a rail barge, or car float, past the pier. Deckhands cut the barge loose, and it continued under its own momentum to glide smoothly and accurately as a billiard ball in for a gentle landing. In the short time it took longshoremen to secure the barge's lines, the tug had seized another barge filled with a dozen freight cars and shoved it into the strong current, urging it toward Manhattan. Similar maneuvers were being repeated everywhere Bell looked, like the moving parts in a colossal, well-oiled machine. But despite every precaution he had taken, the rail yards, the piers, and the car floats looked to him like the Wrecker's playground.

He had put a score of Van Dorn operatives in charge of the terminal. Superintendent Jethro Watt had furnished one hundred handpicked Southern Pacific special railway police, and for a week nothing had moved in or out that they did not approve. No cargo went unchecked. Dynamite trains especially were searched car by car, box by box. They had discovered an astonishingly casual approach to the handling of high explosives in Jersey City, which was the largest city in the state and as densely peopled as Manhattan and Brooklyn across the harbor.

Under Bell's regime, armed guards boarded the dynamite trains miles before even entering the yards. After allowing the trains to enter, the guards oversaw every step of the off-loading, as boxcars bearing twenty-five tons of dynamite dispensed their deadly cargo into steam lighters and barges and into smaller two-ton loads for wagons drawn by draft horses. Van Dorn detectives intercepted all but that which would be immediately shipped out to contractors.

Still, Bell knew that the Wrecker would find no shortage of high explosives. Dynamite was in such demand that trainloads arrived on the powder pier day and night. New Yorkers were blowing up the city's bedrock of mica schist to dig subways and cellars in Manhattan, Brooklyn, Queens, and the Bronx. New Jerseyites were blasting traprock from hilltops to make concrete. Quarrymen were carving building stone out of the Hudson River cliffs, from New Jersey's Palisades all the way up to West Point. Railroad builders were blasting approaches to the Hudson tunnels being bored under the river.

"When the rail tunnels connecting New Jersey and New York are finished next year," Archie bragged, "Osgood Hennessy can park his special eight blocks from Times Square."

"Thank the Lord the tunnels are *not* finished," said Bell. "If they were, the Wrecker would try to blow them with a Southern Pacific Limited trapped under the river."

Archie Abbott flaunted the New Yorker's disdain for districts west of the Hudson in general, and the state of New Jersey in particular, by reminding Isaac Bell that over the years entire sections of Jersey City and nearby Hoboken had been periodically leveled by dynamite accidents, most recently in 1904.

Bell did not need any reminding. The word about the new police presence had gotten around, and tips had poured in from a fearful public. Just yesterday, they had they caught some fool in a wagon carting a half ton of dynamite for the New York and New Jersey Trap Rock Company up Newark Avenue. Failure to dodge a trolley would have resulted in a deadly explosion on the busiest street in Jersey City. The company was protesting mightily about the expense of being forced to take dynamite up the Hackensack River to their Secaucus mine. But the Jersey City fire commissioner, not at all pleased by all the public attention, had stood untypically firm.

"These Jersey harebrains won't need any help from the Wrecker to blow themselves sky-high one of these days," Archie Abbott predicted, "purely through negligence."

"Not on my watch," said Isaac Bell.

"In fact," Abbott persisted. "If there were an explosion, how would we know it was the Wrecker and *not* a Jersey harebrain?"

"We'll know. If he manages to get around us, it will be the biggest explosion New York has ever seen."

Accordingly, Bell had stationed railway police on every train and boat and freight wagon owned by the Southern Pacific. He backed them up with Van Dorn operatives and inspectors borrowed from the Bureau of Explosives, newly founded by the railroads to promote safe transportation of dynamite, gunpowder, and TNT.

Every man carried the lumberjack's sketch. Bell's hopes for it had been bolstered by a report on the Ogden disaster from Nicolas Alexander, the self-important head of the Denver office, who, despite his flaws, happened to be an able detective. Some had wondered if the Wrecker had sought Wally Kisley and Mack Fulton out deliberately to attack Van Dorn agents. But Alexander had confirmed Bell's initial conclusion that Wally and Mack had pursued the Wrecker down an alley. Which meant they had recognized him from the sketch. And the by-now-familiar sword-puncture wounds left no doubt the Wrecker had killed them with his own hand.

"My friend," said Archie, "you're worrying too much. We have every base covered. We've been at it a week. Not a peep out of the Wrecker. The boss is tickled pink."

Bell knew that Joseph Van Dorn would not be tickled entirely pink until they arrested the Wrecker or shot him dead. But it was true that the powerful Van Dorn presence had already had the wonderful side effect of apprehending various criminals and fugitives. They had arrested a Jersey City gangster masquerading as a Jersey Central railroad detective, a trio of bank robbers, and a corrupt Fire Commission inspector who had taken bribes to overlook the dangerous practice of storing dynamite on steam radiators to keep it from freezing in the winter cold.

The powder pier worried Bell the most, even though it swarmed with railroad police. Isolated as far as possible from the main piers, it was still too close in Bell's opinion. And as many as six cars at a time were off-loading dynamite onto the lighters that nuzzled around it. Taking no chances, Bell had put in command of the railway police the seasoned Van Dorn agent Eddie Edwards, who knew well the rail yards, the docks, and the local gangs.

WONG LEE WALKED TO the Communipaw piers, his tiny frame bent nearly in half under the weight of a huge laundry sack. A railroad detective loomed over him, demanding where the hell chink boy thought he was going.

"Chop-chop, laundry for captain," Wong answered in the pidgin English that he knew the detective expected of him.

"What ship?"

Deliberately mispronouncing the *l*s and *r*s, he named the *Julia Reidhead,* a steel three-masted barque carrying bones for fertilizer, and the cop let him pass.

But when he got to the barque where Polish day laborers were unloading the reeking cargo, he plodded past and climbed the gangplank to a battered two-masted schooner in the lumber trade.

"Hey, chink?" shouted the mate. "Where the hell are you going?"

"Captain Yatkowski, chop-chop, clothes."

"In his cabin."

The captain was a hard-bitten waterman from Yonkers who smuggled bootleg whiskey, Chinese opium, and fugitives seeking friendlier jurisdictions across the river. Criminals who refused to pay up for passage to safer shores were found facedown in the Lower Bay, and word had gotten around the underworld never to cheat Captain Paul Yatkowski and his mate "Big Ben" Weitzman.

"What do you got, Chinaman?"

Wong Lee put down his sack and gently tugged open the drawstring. Then he felt carefully among the clean shirts and sheets and removed a round cookie tin. He was done speaking pidgin.

"I have everything I need," he replied. Inside the tin was a rack made of a metal plate drilled with holes into which fit copper capsules so that they could be stored and carried without touching one another. There were thirty holes, each filled with a copper capsule as big around as a pencil and half as long. From the sulfur plug in the top of each extended two insulated "leg wires." They were No. 6 high-grade mercury-fulminate detonators, the most powerful.

The secret to "Dragon Wong" Lee's success in his earlier life blowing rock for the western railroads had been a combination of instinct and bravery. Working seven days a week on the cliffs, and being unusually observant, he had come to understand that any one stick of dynamite contained within its greasy wrapping more power than was supposed. It all depended upon how quickly it exploded. He had developed an innate understanding that multiple detonators fired simultaneously sped up the rate of detonation.

The faster a charge exploded, the greater the power, the more Wong could increase its shattering effect. Few civil engineers had understood that thirty years ago when dynamite was relatively new, still fewer illiterate Chinese peasants. Fewest of all had been brave enough, before electrically fired blasting caps reduced the danger, to take the chances that had to be taken when the only means of detonation was an unreliable burning fuse. So the real secret to big bangs was bravery.

"Do you have the electrical batteries?" Wong asked.

"I got 'em," said the schooner's captain.

"And the wires?"

"All here. Now what?"

Wong savored the moment. The captain, a hard, brutal man who would knock his hat off in the street, was awed by Wong's dark skills.

"Now what?" Wong repeated. "Now I get busy. You sail boat."

A DOZEN RIFLE-TOTING RAILROAD police guarded a string of six boxcars on the powder pier. Three kept a sharp eye on the gang of day laborers hired to remove from one of the boxcars eight hundred fifty sixty-pound boxes of six-inch sticks that had been manufactured by the Du Pont de Nemours Powder Works in Wilmington, Delaware. Four more watched the *Lillian I*'s crew stow the dynamite in the lighter's capacious hold. One, a bank auditor by training, harassed the lighter's captain by poring repeatedly through his invoices and dispatches.

Lillian I's master, Captain Whit Petrie, was in a foul mood. He had already missed a rising tide that would have sped his run upriver. Any more delay, he would be butting against the current the entire sixty miles to the traprock quarry at Sutton Point. On top of that, his new Southern Pacific bosses were even cheaper than his old New Jersey Central bosses, and even less inclined to spend money for necessary repairs on his beloved *Oxford*. Which they had renamed *Lillian,* against all tradition, when anyone with half a brain knew it was bad luck to change a vessel's name, tempting the fates, and, even worse, reducing her to a number, *Lillian I,* as if she were not a finer steam lighter than *Lillian*s *II* through *XII.*

"Say, here's an idea," said the exasperated captain. "I'll go home and have supper with the wife. You boys run the boat."

Not one cop cracked a smile. Only when they were absolutely sure that he was delivering a legitimate cargo of twenty-five tons of dynamite to a legitimate contractor blasting traprock out of the Hudson

Valley cliffs—a run up the river, he pointed out repeatedly, that he had been doing for eight years—did they finally let him go.

Not so fast!

Just as they were casting off lines, a tall, grim-faced, yellow-haired dude in an expensive topcoat came marching up the powder pier, accompanied by a sidekick who looked like a Fifth Avenue swell except for the fine white lines of boxing scars creasing his brow. They jumped aboard, light on their feet as acrobats, and the yellow-haired man flashed a Van Dorn detective badge. He said he was Chief Investigator Isaac Bell, and this was Detective Archibald Abbott, and he demanded to see Petrie's papers. The ice in Bell's eyes told Petrie not to joke about going home for supper, and he waited patiently while his dispatches were read line by line for the tenth time that afternoon.

It was the sidekick, Abbott, who finally said, in a voice straight out of New York's Hell's Kitchen, "All right, Cap, shove off. Sorry to hold you up, but we're not taking any chances." He beckoned a Southern Pacific Railroad bull with arms like a gorilla. "McColleen, you ride with Captain Petrie. He's headed for the Upper Hudson Pulverized Slate Company at Sutton Point. He's got twenty-five tons of dynamite in his hold. Anyone tries to change course, shoot the bastard!"

Then Abbott threw an arm around Isaac Bell's shoulders and tried to steer him up the gangplank, and speaking in an entirely different voice that sounded like he truly was a Fifth Avenue swell, said, "That's it, my friend. You've been at it full bore for a straight week. You've left good chaps in charge. We're taking a night off."

"No," growled Bell, casting an anxious eye on the five remaining boxcars of the powder train. Dusk was gathering. Three railroad guards were aiming a water-cooled, tripod-mounted, belt-fed Vickers automatic machine gun at the gate that blocked the rails from the main freight yards.

"Mr. Van Dorn's orders," said Abbott. "He says if you won't take the night off, you're off the case and so am I. He's not fooling, Isaac. He said he wants clear heads all around. He even bought us tickets to the Follies."

"I thought it closed."

"The show's reopened for a special run while they're getting it ready to take on tour. My friend the newspaper critic called it, quote, 'The best melange of mirth, music, and pretty girls that has been seen here in many a year.' Everyone in town is beating down doors to get tickets. We've got 'em! Come. We'll get dressed, and have a bite at my club first."

"First," Bell said grimly, "I want three fully loaded coal tenders parked, brake wheels locked, on the other side of that gate, in case some brain gets a bright idea to ram it with a locomotive."

22

ARCHIE ABBOTT, WHOSE BLUE-BLOODED FAMILY HAD FORBADE him to become an actor, belonged to a club in Gramercy Park called The Players. The Players had been founded nineteen years earlier by the stage actor Edwin Booth, the finest Hamlet of the previous century and the brother of the man who had shot President Lincoln. Mark Twain and General William Tecumseh Sherman, whose famously destructive march through Georgia had hastened the end of the Civil War, had joined the effort. Booth had deeded over his own home, and celebrated architect Stanford White had transformed it into a clubhouse before he was shot to death in Madison Square Garden by steel heir Harry Thaw.

Bell and Abbott met for a quick supper downstairs in the Grill. It was their first meal since a breakfast gulped at dawn in a Jersey City saloon. They climbed a grand staircase for coffee before they headed uptown to Forty-fourth Street and Broadway to see the *Follies of 1907*.

Bell paused in the Reading Room to admire a full-length portrait of Edwin Booth. The artist's unmistakable style, a powerful mix of clear-eyed realism and romantic impressionism raised a tide of emotion in his heart.

"That was painted by a brother Player," Abbott remarked. "Rather good, isn't it?"

"John Singer Sargent," said Bell.

"Oh, of course you recognize his work," said Abbott. "Sargent painted that portrait of your mother that hangs in your father's drawing room in Boston."

"Just before she died," said Bell. "Though you would never know it looking at such a beautiful young woman." He smiled at the memory. "Sometimes I'd sit on the stair and talk to it. She looked impatient and I could tell she was saying to Sargent, 'Finish up, already, I'm getting bored holding this flower.'"

"Frankly," Abbott joked, "I'd rather answer to a painting than *my* mother."

"Let's get going! I have to stop at the office and tell them where to find me." Like all Van Dorn offices in large cities, their headquarters in Times Square was open twenty-four hours a day.

Dressed in white tie and tails, opera capes and top hats, they hurried to Park Avenue, which they found jammed with hansom cabs, automobile taxicabs, and town cars creeping uptown. "We'll beat this mess on the subway."

The underground station at Twenty-third was ablaze in electric light and gleaming white tile. Passengers crowding the train platform ran the gamut from men and women out for the night to tradesmen, laborers, and housemaids traveling home. A speeding express train flickered through the station, windows packed with humanity, and Abbott boasted, "Our subways will make it possible for millions of New Yorkers to go to work in skyscrapers."

"Your subway," Bell observed drily, "will make it possible for criminals to rob a bank downtown and celebrate uptown before the cops arrive on the scene."

The subway whisked them in moments uptown to Forty-second and Broadway. They climbed the steps into a world where night had been banished. Times Square was lit bright as noon by "spectaculars," electric billboards on which thousands of white lights advertised theaters, hotels, and lobster palaces. Motorcars, taxicabs, and buses roared in the streets. Crowds rushed eagerly on wide sidewalks.

Bell cut into the Knickerbocker Hotel, a first-class hostelry with a mural of Old King Cole painted by Maxfield Parrish decorating the lobby. The Van Dorn office was on the second floor, set back a discreet distance from the grand stairway. A competent-looking youth with slicked-back hair and a sliver of a bow tie greeted clients in a tastefully decorated front room. His tailored coat concealed a sidearm he knew how to use. A short-barreled scatter gun was close at hand in a bottom drawer of his desk. He controlled the lock to the back room by an electric switch beside his knee.

The back room looked like an advertising manager's office, with typewriters, green-glass lamps, steel filing cabinets, a calendar on the wall, a telegraph key, and a row of candlestick telephones on the duty officer's desk. Instead of women in white blouses typing at the desks, a half dozen detectives were filling out paperwork, discussing tactics, or lounging on a break from house-dick lobby duty in the Times Square hotels. It had separate entrances for visitors whose appearance might not pass muster in the Knickerbocker's fine lobby or were more comfortable entering and leaving a detective agency by the alley.

Catcalls greeted Bell's and Abbott's costumes.

"Gangway! Opera swells comin' through!"

"You bums never seen a gentleman before?" asked Abbott.

"Where you headed dressed like penguins?"

"The Jardin de Paris on the roof of the Hammerstein Theater," said Abbott, tipping his silk hat and flourishing his cane. "To the *Follies of 1907.*"

"What? You have tickets to the *Follies*?" they blurted in amazement. "How did you get your mitts on them?"

"Courtesy of the boss," said Abbott. "The producer, Mr. Ziegfeld, owes Mr. Van Dorn a favor. Something about a wife that wasn't his. Come on, Isaac. Curtain's going up!"

But Isaac Bell stood stock-still, staring at the telephones, which were lined up like soldiers. Something was nagging at him. Something forgotten. Something overlooked. Or a memory of something wrong.

The Jersey City powder pier leaped into his mind's eye. He had a photographic memory, and he traced the pier's reach from the land into the water, foot by foot, yard by yard. He saw the Vickers machine gun pointed at the gate that isolated it from the main yards. He saw the coal tenders he had ordered moved to protect the gate. He saw the string of loaded boxcars, the smoke, the tide-roiled water, the redbrick Communipaw passenger terminal with its ferry dock at the water's edge in the distance . . .

What was missing?

A telephone rang. The duty officer snapped up the middle one, which someone had marked as foremost with an urgent slash of showgirl's lip rouge. "Yes, sir, Mr. Van Dorn! . . . Yes, sir! He's here . . . Yes, sir! I'll tell him. Good-bye, Mr. Van Dorn."

The duty officer, cradling the earpiece, said to Isaac Bell, "Mr. Van Dorn says if you don't leave the office this minute, you're fired."

They fled the Knickerbocker.

Archie Abbott, ever the proud tour guide, pointed out the two-story yellow façade of Rector's Restaurant as they headed up Broadway. He took particular note of a huge statue out front. "See that griffin?"

"Hard to miss."

"It's guarding the greatest lobster palace in the whole city!"

LILLIAN HENNESSY LOVED MAKING her entrance at Rector's. Sweeping past the griffin on the sidewalk, ushered into an enormous green-and-yellow wonderland of crystal and gold brilliantly lit by giant chandeliers, she felt what it must be like to be a great and beloved actress. The best part was the floor-to-ceiling mirrors that let everyone in the restaurant see who was entering the revolving door.

Tonight, people had stared at her beautiful golden gown, gaped at the diamonds nestled about her breasts, and whispered about her astonishingly handsome escort. Or, to use Marion Morgan's term, her *unspeakably* handsome escort. Too bad it was only Senator Kincaid, still tirelessly courting her, still hoping to get his hands on her fortune. How much more exciting it would be to walk in here with a man like Isaac Bell, handsome but not pretty, strong but not brutish, rugged but not rough.

"A penny for your thoughts," said Kincaid.

"I think we should finish our lobsters and get to the show . . . Oh, hear the band . . . Anna Held's coming!"

The restaurant's band always played a Broadway actress's new hit when she entered. The song was "I Just Can't Make My Eyes Behave."

Lillian sang along in a sweet voice in perfect pitch,

In the northeast corner of my face,
and the northeast corner of the self-same place . . .

There she was, the French actress Anna Held, with her tiny waist shown off by a magnificent green gown much longer than she wore on stage, wreathed in smiles and flashing her eyes.

"Oh, Charles, this is so exciting. I'm glad we came."

Charles Kincaid smiled at the astonishingly rich girl leaning across the tablecloth and suddenly realized how truly young and innocent she was. He would bet money that she'd learned the tricks she played with her beautiful eyes by studying Held's every gesture. Very effectively too, he had to admit, as she gave him a well-practiced up-from-under blaze of pale blue.

He said, "I'm so glad you telephoned."

"The *Follies* are back," she answered blithely. "I had to come. Who wants to go to a show alone?"

That pretty much summed up her attitude toward him. He hated that she spurned him. But when he got done with her father, the old man wouldn't have two bits to leave in his will while he would be rich enough to own Lillian, lock, stock, and barrel. In the meantime, pretending to court her gave him the excuse he needed to spend more time around her father than he would have been permitted in his role of tame senator casting votes on issues dear to the railroad corporations. Let Lillian Hennessy spurn her too old, vaguely comic, gold-digging suitor, a hopeless lover as unremarkable and unnoticed as the furniture. He would own her in the end—not as a wife but an object, like a beautiful piece of sculpture, to be enjoyed when he felt the urge.

"I had to come, too," Kincaid answered her, silently cursing the Rawlins prizefighters who'd failed to murder Isaac Bell.

This night of all nights, he had to be seen in public. If Bell was not growing suspicious, he would soon. By now, an early sense of something wrong must have begun percolating in the detective's mind. How long before Bell's wanted poster jogged the memory of someone who had seen him preparing destruction? The oversize ears in the sketch would not protect him forever.

What better alibis than the *Follies of 1907* in Hammerstein's Jardin de Paris?

Hundreds of people would remember Senator Charles Kincaid dining at Rector's with the most sought-after heiress in New York. A thousand would see the Hero Engineer arrive at the biggest show on Broadway with an unforgettable girl on his arm—a full mile and half away from a "show" that would outshine even the *Follies*.

"What are you smiling about, Charles?" Lillian asked him.

"I'm looking forward to the entertainment."

23

PIRACY WAS RARE ON THE HUDSON RIVER IN THE EARLY YEARS of the twentieth century. When Captain Whit Petrie saw a raked bow loom out of the rain, his only reaction was to blow *Lillian I*'s whistle to warn the other boat not to get too close. The sonorous blast of steam woke McColleen, the railroad dick who was snoozing on the bench in the back of the wheelhouse as *Lillian I* churned north past Yonkers, fighting an ebb tide and a powerful river current.

"What's that?"

"Vessel under sail . . . Damned fool must be deaf."

The looming bow was still bearing down on him, close enough to reveal that the sails silhouetted against the dark sky were schooner-rigged. Whit Petrie lowered a wheelhouse window to see better and heard the thump of her auxiliary gasoline engine driving hard. He yanked his whistle pull again and put the wheel over to veer away before they collided. The other boat veered with him.

"What the hell?"

By now, McColleen was on his feet, all business, yanking a revolver from his coat.

A shotgun bellowed, blowing out the windows and blinding

McColleen with flying glass. The railway dick fell back, crying out in pain and clutching his face and firing blindly. Captain Petrie drew on bred-in-the-bone Jersey City street-fighter instincts. He whirled his wheel hard over to ram the attacker.

It was the right tactic. The heavily laden steam lighter would be certain to cut the wooden schooner in half. But *Lillian I*'s worn rudder linkage, long neglected by the New Jersey Central Railroad and now the Southern Pacific, failed under the wrenching maneuver. Steering gear carried away, rudder gone, the dynamite boat stalled partway into the sharp turn and wallowed helplessly. The schooner slammed alongside, and a gang of men stormed aboard, howling like banshees and firing guns at anyone who moved.

THE JARDIN DE PARIS was a makeshift theater on the roof of Hammerstein's Olympia. This cold, rainy night, canvas curtains were lowered to keep out the wind but did little to muffle the noise of the gasoline buses on Broadway below. But no one holding a ticket looked anything but happy to be there.

Tables and chairs were arranged on a flat floor more like a dance hall than an auditorium. But the management had added elaborate boxes to attract what Archie Abbott called "a better class of audience." The boxes were newly built on a sweeping horseshoe-shaped platform on top of a pagoda that spanned the elevator entrance. Florenz Ziegfeld, the producer of the *Follies,* had given the Van Dorn detectives the best of those seats. They offered a clear, close view of the stage and a sweeping panorama of the rest of the boxes, which were filling with men wearing white tie and tails and women in gowns fit for a ball.

Scanning the arriving audience, Bell suddenly locked eyes with Lillian Hennessy as she took a seat across the way. She looked more beautiful than ever in a gold gown and with her blond hair piled high upon her head. He smiled at her, and her face lit up with genuine pleasure, forgiving him apparently for wrecking her Packard automobile. In fact, he reflected worriedly, she was smiling at him like a girl on the brink of total infatuation—which was the last thing either of them needed.

"Look at that girl!" blurted Abbott.

"Archie, if you lean out any farther, you'll fall into the cheap seats."

"Worth it if she'll weep over my body—you'll tell her how I died. Wait a minute, she's smiling at *you*."

"Her name is Lillian," said Bell. "That Southern Pacific steam lighter you were gawking at this afternoon is named after her. As is everything that floats that's owned by the railroad. She's old Hennessy's daughter."

"Rich, too? God in heaven. Who's the stuffed shirt with her? He looks familiar."

"Senator Charles Kincaid."

"Oh yes. The Hero Engineer."

Bell returned Kincaid's nod coolly. He was not surprised that Kincaid's check for poker losses had still not arrived at the Yale Club. Men who dealt from the bottom of the deck tended not to pay their debts when they thought they could get away with it.

"The Senator certainly got lucky."

"I don't think so," said Bell. "She's too rich and independent to fall for his line."

"What makes you say that?"

"She told me."

"Why would she confide in you, Isaac?"

"She was polishing off her third bottle of Mumm."

"So *you* got lucky."

"I got lucky with Marion, and I'm going to stay lucky with Marion."

"Love," Archie mock mourned in a doleful voice as the house-lights began to dim, "stalks us like death and taxes."

A grand dowager, wrapped in yards of silk, behatted in feathers, and dripping diamonds, leaned from the next box to rap Abbott's shoulder imperiously with her lorgnette.

"Quiet down, young man. The show is starting . . . Oh, Archie, it's you. How is your mother?"

"Very well, thank you, Mrs. Vanderbilt. I'll tell her you asked."

"Please do. And Archie? I could not help but overhear. The gentleman with you is correct. The young lady has little regard for that *loathsome* legislator. And, I must say, she could handily repair your family's tattered fortunes."

"Mother would be delighted," Abbott agreed, adding in a mutter for only Bell to hear, "As Mother regards the Vanderbilts as unculti-vated 'new money,' you can imagine her horror were I to bring home the daughter of a 'shirtsleeve railroader.'"

"You should be so lucky," said Bell.

"I know. But Mother's made it clear, no one below an Astor."

Bell shot a look across the boxes at Lillian, and a brilliant scheme leaped full blown into his mind. A scheme to derail Miss Lillian's growing infatuation with him and simultaneously get poor Archie's mother off Archie's back. But it would require the restraint of a dip-lomat and the light touch of a jeweler. So all he said was, "Pipe down! The show is starting."

IN THE MIDDLE OF the Hudson River, a mile west of Broadway, the pirated Southern Pacific steam lighter *Lillian I* dashed downstream. The outflowing tide doubled the speed of the current, making up for the time they had lost repairing her steering gear. She steamed in company with the wooden sailing schooner that had captured her.

The wind was southeast, thick with rain. The schooner's sails were close-hauled, her gasoline engine churning its hardest to keep up with *Lillian I.*

The schooner's captain, the smuggler from Yonkers, felt a twinge of sentiment for the old girl who was about to be blown to smithereens. A minor twinge, Yatkowski thought, smiling, having been paid twice the value of the schooner to drown the steam lighter's crew in the river and stand by to rescue the Chinaman when they sent her on her last voyage. The boss paying the bills had made it clear: look out for the Chinaman until the job was done. Bring him back in one piece. The boss had use for the explosives expert.

THE ANNA HELD GIRLS, acclaimed by the producer to be "the most beautiful women ever gathered in one theater," were dancing up a storm, in short white dresses, wide hats, and red sashes, as they sang "I Just Can't Make My Eyes Behave."

"Some of those women are imported straight from Paris," Abbott whispered.

"I don't see Anna Held," Bell muttered back, familiar as any man in the nation under the age of ninety with the French actress's expressive eyes, eighteen-inch waist, and resultantly curvaceous hips. Her skin, it was claimed, was conditioned by daily baths in milk. Bell glanced across at Lillian Hennessy, who was watching with rapt attention, and he suddenly realized that her tutor, Mrs. Comden, was shaped very much like Anna Held. Did President Hennessy pour her milk baths?

Abbott applauded loudly, and the audience followed suit. "For some reason, known best to Mr. Ziegfeld," he told Bell over the roar, "Anna Held is not one of the Anna Held Girls. Even though she's his common-law wife."

"I doubt the entire Van Dorn Detective Agency can get him out of that fix."

The *Follies of 1907* raced on. Burlesque comedians argued about a bar bill in German accents like Weber and Fields and a suddenly sobered Bell fixed on Mack and Wally. When Annabelle Whitford came on stage in a black bathing costume as the Gibson Bathing Girl, Abbott nudged Bell and whispered, "Remember the nickelodeon when we were kids? She did the butterfly dance."

Bell was listening with half attention, pondering the Wrecker's plan. Where would he attack now that they had all bases covered? And what, Bell wondered, had he himself missed? The grim answer was that whatever he missed, the Wrecker would see.

The orchestra had struck up a raucous "I've Been Working on the Railroad," and Abbott nudged Bell again.

"Look. They put our client in the act."

The burlesque comedians were posing in front of a painted backdrop of a Southern Pacific locomotive steaming up behind them as if about to run them over. Even paying half attention, it was clear that the comedian in colonial dress cavorting on a hobby horse was supposed to be Paul Revere. His costar in engineer's striped cap and overalls represented Southern Pacific Railroad president Osgood Hennessy.

Paul Revere galloped up, waving a telegram.

"Telegram from the United States Senate, President Hennessy."

"Hand it over, Paul Revere!" Hennessy snatched it from the horseman and read aloud, "'Please, sir, telegraph instructions. You forgot to tell us how to vote.'"

"What are your instructions to the senators, President Hennessy?"

"The railroad is coming. The railroad is coming."

"How should they vote?"

"One if by land."

"Shine one lantern in the steeple if the railroad comes by land?"

"Bribes, dummkopf! Not lanterns. Bribes!"

"How many bribes by sea?"

"Two if by—"

Isaac Bell leaped from his seat.

IN THE DARK HOLD OF THE STEAM LIGHTER *LILLIAN I,* WONG
Lee was finishing his intricate wiring by the light of an Eveready
wooden bicycle lantern powered by three dry cell "D" batteries.
Wong Lee was grateful for it, recalling with no nostalgia the old days
of connecting dynamite fuses by the light of an open flame. Thank
the gods for electricity, which provided light to work by and power
to ignite detonators with uncanny precision.

ISAAC BELL EXITED THE Jardin de Paris through the canvas rain
curtains and pounded down a steel stairway attached to the outside
of the Hammerstein Theater. He landed in an alley and ran to Broadway. It was two blocks to the Knickerbocker Hotel. The sidewalks
were jammed with people. He darted into the street, dodging traffic,
raced downtown, tore through the lobby of the Knickerbocker, and
bounded up the stairs to the Van Dorn Agency, reached under the
startled front man's desk for the secret door-lock switch, and burst
into the back room.

"I want Eddie Edwards on the powder pier. Which is the telephone line to Jersey City?"

"Number one, sir. Like you ordered."

Bell picked up the telephone and clicked repeatedly.

"Get me Eddie Edwards."

"That you, Isaac? Are you bringing us home a *Follies* girl?"

"Listen to me, Eddie. Move the Vickers machine gun so you can cover the water as well as the main gate."

"Can't."

"Why not?"

"Those five powder cars block the field of fire. I can cover one or the other, but not the gate and the water both."

"Then get another machine gun. In case he attacks from the water."

"I'm trying to borrow one from the Army, but it ain't gonna happen tonight. Sorry, Isaac. What if I put a couple of riflemen on the end of the pier?"

"You say the powder cars block the field of fire? Put your machine gun on *top* of them."

"On *top* of them?"

"You heard me. Position your machine gun on top of the dynamite cars so they can swivel the gun in either direction. That way, they can cover the gate and the water. On the jump, Eddie. Do it now!"

Bell cradled the earpiece with great relief. That was what he had forgotten. The water. An attack by boat. He grinned at the other detectives, who had been listening avidly.

"Manning an automatic machine gun on top of a dynamite train ought to be plenty incentive to stay awake," he said.

He sauntered back to the theater, feeling much less worried, and slipped into his seat just as the curtain came down on the *Follies'* first act.

"What was that all about?" Abbott asked.

"If the Wrecker decides to attack from the water, he's going to run head-on into a Vickers automatic machine gun."

"Good thinking, Isaac. So now you can relax by introducing me to your friend."

"Senator Kincaid?" Bell asked innocently. "I wouldn't call him a friend. We played a little draw, but . . ."

"You know who I mean, you son of a gun. I am referring to the Southern Pacific Helen of Troy whose gorgeous face launched twelve steamboats."

"She strikes me as much too intelligent to fall for a Princeton man."

"She's getting into the elevator! Come on, Isaac!"

Crowds of people were waiting for the elevators. Bell led Abbott through the canvas rain curtains, down the outside stairway, and into the cavernous lobby on the ground floor that served all three theaters in the building.

"There she is!"

Lillian Hennessy and Senator Kincaid were surrounded by admirers. Women were vying to shake his hand while their husbands elbowed one another trying to make Lillian's acquaintance. It was doubtful that their wives noticed or even cared. Bell saw two of them slip their calling cards surreptitiously into Kincaid's pocket.

Taller than most, and experienced in barroom brawls and riot control, the Van Dorn detectives parted the crush like a squadron of battleships. Lillian smiled at Bell.

Bell focused his gaze on Kincaid and Kincaid looked his way with a friendly wave.

"Isn't the show wonderful?" the Senator called over heads as Bell drew near. "I love the theater. You know, I heard you talking with Kenny Bloom about running off to the circus. For me, it was the stage instead of the circus. I always wanted to be an actor. I even ran off with a touring company, before sanity prevailed."

"Like my good friend Archie Abbott here. Archie, meet Senator Charles Kincaid, a fellow thwarted thespian."

"Good evening, Senator," Abbott said, extending his hand politely but missing Kincaid's hand entirely as he gaped at Lillian.

"Oh, hello, Lillian," said Bell casually. "May I present my old friend Archibald Angel Abbott?"

Lillian started to bat her eyes in the style of Anna Held. But it seemed as if something she saw in Abbott's face made her look again. He had compelling gray eyes, and Bell saw them working full steam to keep her attention. Her gaze traversed the scars on Abbott's brow and took in his red hair and sparkling smile. Kincaid said something to her, but she did not seem to hear as she looked Abbott squarely in the face and said, "Pleased to meet you, Mr. Abbott. Isaac has told me all about you."

"Not all, Miss Hennessy, or you would have fled the room."

Lillian laughed, Archie preened, and the Senator looked very displeased.

Bell used the excuse of the poker debt to nudge Kincaid away from Archie and Lillian. "I did enjoy our game of draw. And it was a pleasure to receive your calling card, but a check for the amount written on it would stir even better memories."

"My check will be here tomorrow," Kincaid replied affably. "You're still at the Yale Club?"

"Until further notice. And you, Senator? Will you be in New York a while or are you off to Washington?"

"Actually, I'm leaving for San Francisco in the morning."

"Isn't the Senate in session?"

"I am chairman of a subcommittee conducting a hearing in San Francisco about the Chinese problem." He looked around at the mobs of theatergoers trying to catch his attention, took Bell's elbow, and lowered his voice. "Between us poker players, Mr. Bell, the hearing will mask my true purpose for traveling to San Francisco."

"And what is that?"

"I've been persuaded by a select group of California businessmen to listen to them implore me to run for president." He winked conspiratorially. "They offered to take me on a camping trip in the redwoods. You can imagine what little pleasure a former bridge builder takes in sleeping out of doors. I told them I would prefer one of their fabled western resort lodges. Antlers, stuffed grizzly bears, pine logs . . . and indoor plumbing."

"Are you persuadable?" asked Bell.

"Between you and me, I'm playing hard to get. But of course I would be deeply honored to run for president," said Kincaid. "Who wouldn't? It is the dream of every politician who serves the public."

"Would Preston Whiteway be one of those California businessmen?"

Kincaid looked at him sharply.

"Shrewd question, Mr. Bell."

For a moment, locked eye to eye, the two men could have been standing alone on a cliff in Oregon instead of in a crowded theater lobby on the Great White Way.

"And your answer?" asked Bell.

"I am not at liberty to say. But so much depends upon what President Roosevelt decides to do next year. I can't see any room for me if he wants a third term. At any rate, I prefer if you would keep that under your hat."

Bell said he would. He wondered why a United States senator would confide in a man he had only met once. "Have you confided in Mr. Hennessy?"

"I will confide in Osgood Hennessy at the proper time, which is to say after such an arrangement is consummated."

"Why wait? Wouldn't a railroad president be helpful to your cause?"

"I would not want to raise his hopes of having a friend in the White House at this early stage only to dash them."

The lobby lights flashed on and off, signaling an end to the intermission. They returned to their seats in the rooftop theater.

Abbott said to Bell, "What a wonderful girl."

"What do you think of the Senator?"

"What senator?" asked Abbott, waving across the boxes to Lillian.

"Do you still think he's a stuffed shirt?"

Abbott looked at Bell, perceived that he was not asking idly, and answered in all seriousness, "Certainly acts like one. Why do you ask, Isaac?"

"Because I have a feeling that there is more to Kincaid than meets the eye."

"From the look he gave me when he saw me talking to her, he would kill to get his mitts on Miss Lillian and her fortune."

"He wants to be president, too."

"Of the railroad?" asked Archie. "Or the United States?"

"The United States. He told me he's having a secret meeting with California businessmen who want him to run if Teddy Roosevelt doesn't stand again next year."

"If it's secret, why did he tell you?" asked Archie.

"That's what I was wondering. Only a complete fool would blab that about."

"Do you believe him?"

"Good question, Archie. Funny thing is, he said nothing about William Howard Taft."

"That's like not mentioning the elephant in the drawing room. If Roosevelt doesn't choose to run for a third term, then Secretary of War Taft will be the good friend he designates to replace him. No wonder Kincaid wants it secret. He'll be challenging his own party."

"Yet another reason not to confide in me," said Isaac Bell. "What is he up to?"

Across the boxes, Lillian Hennessy asked, "What did you think of Mr. Abbott, Charles?"

"The Abbotts are among the oldest families in New York, except for the Dutch, and they've got plenty of Dutch roots under their family tree. Too bad they lost all their money in the Panic of '93," Kincaid added with a big smile.

"He told me that straight off," said Lillian. "It doesn't seem to trouble him."

"It would certainly trouble the father of any young woman he proposed to," Kincaid needled her.

"And what do you think of Isaac Bell?" Lillian needled back. "Archie told me you and Isaac played cards. I noticed you two deep in conversation in the lobby."

Kincaid kept smiling, deeply pleased by his conversation with Bell. If the detective was getting suspicious, then pretending that he was one of the many senators who dreamed of becoming president of the United States had to be a convincing demonstration that he was not a train wrecker. If Bell investigated further, he would discover that there *were* California businessmen, Preston Whiteway first among them, who were shopping for their own candidate for president. And Senator Charles Kincaid topped their list, having encouraged and manipulated the mercurial San Francisco newspaper magnate to believe that the Hero Engineer he had helped make a senator would serve him in the White House.

"What were you talking about?" Lillian persisted.

Kincaid's smile turned cruel.

"Bell is engaged to be married. He told me he was buying a mansion for his intended . . . the lucky girl."

Was there sadness in her face or was it merely the houselights dimming for Act Two?

• • •

"JERSEY CITY DEAD AHEAD, chink boy!" yelled the mate "Big Ben" Weitzman, whom Captain Yatkowski had put aboard *Lillian I* to steer after they threw the steam lighter's crew in the river. "Shake a leg down there."

Wong Lee kept working at his own pace, treating twenty-five tons of dynamite with the respect it deserved. Decades of pressing shirts with heavy irons had thickened his hands. His fingers were not so nimble anymore.

He had one detonator left over when he was done and he slipped it in his pocket, maintaining old habits of frugality. Then he reached for the double electric wire that he had strung from the bow of the boat into the hold where the boxes of dynamite were stacked. He had already exposed two inches of its copper core by stripping off the insulation. He connected one wire to one leg of the first detonator. He reached for the second wire and stopped.

"Weitzman! Are you up there?"

"What?"

"Check that the switch at the bow is still open."

"It's open. I already checked."

"If it is not open, we will explode when I touch these wires."

"Wait! Hold on. I'll check again."

Weitzman slipped a loop of rope around the wheel spoke to hold the lighter on course and hurried to the bow, cursing the cold rain. Yatkowski had given him a cylinder flashlight and in its flickering beam he saw that the jaws of the switch the Chinaman had rigged to the tip of the bow were open and would stay open until the bow crashed into the powder pier. The impact would close the jaws, completing the electric connection between the battery and the detonators, and blow up twenty-five tons of dynamite. That, in turn, would set off a hundred tons more on the powder pier, which would make it the biggest explosion New York had ever heard.

Weitzman hurried back to the wheel and shouted down the hatch. "It's open. Like I told you."

Wong took a breath and attached the positive wire to the detonator's second leg. Nothing happened. Of course, he thought wryly, if it had gone wrong he wouldn't know it, being suddenly dead. He scrambled up the ladder, emerged from the hatch, and told the man steering to signal the schooner. It came alongside, sails flapping wetly, and banged hard against the lighter.

"Take it easy!" yelled Weitzman. "You want to kill us?"

"Chinaman!" yelled Captain Yatkowski. "Get up here."

Wong Lee launched his creaky middle-aged limbs up a rope ladder. He had climbed much worse in the mountains, but he had been thirty years younger.

"Weitzman!" the captain yelled. "Do you see the pier?"

"How could I miss it?"

Electric lights blazed a quarter mile ahead. The railroad cops had it lit up like the Great White Way so no one could sneak up on them from the yards, but it had never occurred to them that somebody would sneak up from the water.

"Aim her at it and get off quick."

Weitzman turned the wheel until he had lined *Lillian I*'s bow with the lights on the powder pier. They were coming in from the side, and the pier was six hundred feet long, so even if she went off course a bit she would still hit close enough to the five boxcars of dynamite.

"Quick, I say!" roared the captain.

Weitzman didn't need any urging. He scrambled onto the wooden deck of the schooner.

"Go fast!" shouted Wong. "Get us away."

No one was better qualified than Wong to understand the forces about to be unleashed on the rail yards, the harbor, and the cities around it.

When Wong and the schooner's crew looked back to check that the steam lighter was on course, they saw a New Jersey Central Railroad ferryboat cast off lines to steam out of the Communipaw Passenger Terminal. A train must have just pulled in from somewhere, and the ferry was taking the passengers on the last leg.

"Welcome to New York!" the captain muttered. When twenty-five tons on the lighter detonated one hundred tons on the powder pier, that ferryboat would vanish in a ball of fire.

MARION MORGAN STOOD OUTSIDE ON THE OPEN DECK OF THE
Jersey Central Ferry. She pressed against the railing, ignoring the
rain. Her heart was pounding with joy and excitement. She had not
seen New York City since her father had taken her on a trip back East
when she was a little girl. Now dozens of skyscrapers with lighted
windows soared just across the river. And somewhere on that fabled
island was her beloved Isaac Bell.

She had debated whether to wire ahead or surprise him. She had
settled on surprise. Her trip had been on again and off again and
on again as Preston Whiteway juggled his busy schedule. He had
decided at the last minute to stay in California and send her to meet
with his bankers in New York to present his proposal for financing
the *Picture World* moving picture newsreels. The brash young newspaper publisher must have been impressed enough by her banking
experience to give her such an important assignment. But the real
reason he would send a woman, she suspected, was that he hoped
to woo her and thought that the way to her heart was to respect her
independence. She had invented a phrase to emphasize to the persis-
tent Whiteway her commitment to Isaac.

My heart is spoken for.

She had already had to use it twice. But it said it all, and she would use it ten times if she had to.

The rain was thinning and the city lights were bright. As soon as she got to her hotel, she would telephone Isaac at the Yale Club. Respectable hotels like the Astor frowned upon unmarried women receiving gentleman visitors. But there wasn't a house dick in the country who would not turn a blind eye to a Van Dorn operative. Professional courtesy, Isaac would smile.

The ferry tooted its whistle. She felt the propellers shudder beneath her feet. As they pulled away from the New Jersey shore, she saw the sails of an old-fashioned schooner silhouetted by a brightly lighted pier.

IT HAD TAKEN FOUR men a full ten minutes to lift the heavy automatic machine gun atop the boxcar. And as Isaac Bell had predicted, the railroad police manning the water-cooled, tripod-mounted, belt-fed Vickers on top of the dynamite train stayed wide awake. But Eddie Edwards, the forty-year-old Van Dorn investigator with a startling shock of prematurely white hair, kept climbing up the boxcar's ladder to check on them anyway.

Their weapon was equally reliable, adapted from the Maxim gun which had proved itself mowing down African armies. One of the rail bulls was a transplanted Englishman who told tales of slaughtering "natives" with a Maxim in the previous decade's colonial wars. Edwards had instructed him to leave the natives of Jersey City alone. Unless they tried something. The old gangs there weren't as tough as they had been when Edwards had led the Van Dorn fight to clear the rail yards, but they were still ornery.

Standing on top of the railcar, turning slowly on his heel and surveying the machine gun's field of fire, which now encompassed a full circle, Edwards was reminded of the old days guarding bullion ship-ments. Of course the Lava Bed Gang's weapons in those days were mostly lead pipes, brass knuckles, and the occasional sawed-off shot-gun. He watched a brightly lit ferry leaving Communipaw Terminal. He turned back toward the gate, blocked by three coal tenders and manned by cinder dicks with rifles, and saw that the freight yards looked as calm as a freight yard ever looked. Switch engines were scuttling about making up trains. But in each cab rode an armed detective. He looked back at the river. The rain was lifting. He could see the lights of New York City clearly now.

"Is that schooner going to run into that steam lighter?"

"No. They were close, but they're moving apart. See? He's sailing off, and the lighter's turning this way."

"I see," said Edwards, his jaw tightening. "Where the hell is he going?"

"Coming our way."

Edwards watched, liking the situation less and less.

"How far is that red buoy?" he asked.

"The red light? I'd say a quarter mile."

"If he passes that buoy, give him four rounds ahead of his bow."

"You mean that?" the rail cop asked dubiously.

"Dammit, yes, I mean it. Get set to fire."

"He's passing it, Mr. Edwards."

"Shoot! Now!"

The water-cooled Vickers made an oddly muffled *pop-pop-pop-pop* noise. Where the bullets hit was too far off in the dark to see. The steam lighter kept coming straight at the powder pier.

"Give him ten rounds across the roof of his wheelhouse."

"That'll be a wake-up call," said the Englishman. "Those slugs sound like thunder overhead."

"Just make sure you're clear behind him. I don't want to rake some poor tugboat."

"Clear."

"Fire! Now! Don't wait!"

The canvas cartridge belt twitched. Ten rounds spit from the barrel. A wisp of steam rose from the water cooler.

The boat kept coming.

Eddie Edwards wet his lips. God knew who was on it. A drunk? A frightened boy at the helm while his captain slept? A terrified old man who had no clue where the shooting was coming from?

"Get up there in the light. Wave them off . . . Not you! You stay on the gun."

The belt feeder and the water bearer jumped up and down on the roof of the boxcar, frantically waving their arms. The boat kept coming.

"Get out of the way!" Edwards told them. "Shoot the wheel-house." He grabbed the belt and began feeding as the gun opened up in a continuous roar.

Two hundred rounds spewed from its barrel, crossed a quarter mile of water, and tore through the steam lighter's wheelhouse, scattering wood and glass. Two rounds smashed the top spoke of the helm. Another cut the rope looped around the helm and it was suddenly free to turn. But water passing over the rudder held it steady on course to the powder pier. Then the frame of the wheelhouse collapsed. The roof fell on the helm, pushing the spokes down, turning the wheel and the rudder to which it was attached.

THE SECOND ACT OF the *Follies* started off big and got bigger. The "Ju-Jitsu Waltz," featuring Prince Tokio "straight from Japan," was followed by a comic song "I Think I Oughtn't Auto Any More":

> . . . *happened to be smoking when I got beneath her car,*
> *gasoline was leaking and fell on my cigar,*
> *blew that chorus girl so high I thought she was a star . . .*

When the song was over, a solitary snare drum began to rattle. A single chorus girl in a blue blouse, a short white skirt, and red tights marched across the empty stage. A second snare drum joined in. A second chorus girl fell in with the first. Then another drum and another girl. Then six drums were rattling and six chorus girls marching to and fro. Then another and another. Bass drums took up the beat with a thumping that shook the seats. Suddenly, all fifty of the most beautiful chorus girls on Broadway broke off their dance on stage, snatched up fifty drums from stacks beside the wings, ran down the stairs on either side, and stormed the aisles pounding their drums and kicking their red-clad legs.

"Aren't you glad we came?" shouted Abbott.

Bell looked up. A flash through the skylight caught his eye, as if the theater were training lights down from the roof in addition to those already blazing on the stage. It looked as if the night sky were on fire. He felt a harsh thump shake the building and thought for a moment it was the rolling shock wave of an earthquake. Then he heard a thunderous explosion.

THE *FOLLIES* ORCHESTRA STOPPED PLAYING ABRUPTLY. AN eerie silence gripped the theater. Then debris clattered on the tin roof like a thousand snare drums. Glass flew out of the skylight, and everyone in the theater—audience, stagehands, and chorus girls—began screaming.

Isaac Bell and Archie Abbott moved as one, up the aisle, through the canvas rain curtains and across the roof to the outside staircase. They saw a red glow in the southwest sky in the direction of Jersey City.

"The powder pier," said Bell with a sinking heart. "We better get over there."

"Look," said Archie as they started down the stairs. "Broken windows everywhere."

Every building on the block had lost a window. Forty-fourth Street was littered with broken glass. They turned their backs on the crowds surging in panic on Broadway and ran west on Forty-fourth toward the river. They crossed Eighth Avenue, then Ninth, and ran through the slums of Hell's Kitchen, dodging the residents spilling out of saloons and tenements. Everyone was shouting "What happened?"

The Van Dorn detectives raced across Tenth Avenue, over the New York Central Railroad tracks, across Eleventh, dodging fire engines and panicked horses. The closer they got to the water, the more broken windows they saw. A cop tried to stop them from running onto the piers. They showed their badges and brushed past him.

"Fireboat!" Bell shouted.

Bristling with fire monitors and belching smoke, a New York City fireboat was pulling away from Pier 84. Bell ran after it, jumped. Abbott landed beside him.

"Van Dorn," they told the startled deckhand. "We have to get to Jersey City."

"Wrong boat. We're dispatched downtown to spray the piers."

The reason for the fireboat's orders was soon apparent. Across the river, flames were shooting into the sky from the Jersey City piers. With the end of the rain, the wind had shifted west, and it was blowing sparks across the river onto Manhattan's piers. So instead of helping fight the fire in Jersey City, the fireboat was wetting down Manhattan's piers to keep the sparks from igniting their roofs and wooden ships moored alongside.

"He's a mastermind," said Bell. "I've got to hand him that."

"A Napoleon of crime," Archie agreed. "As if Conan Doyle sicced Professor Moriarty on us instead of Sherlock Holmes."

Bell spotted a New York Police Department Marine Division launch at the Twenty-third Street Lackawanna Ferry Terminal. "Drop us there!"

The New York cops agreed to run them across the river. They passed damaged boats with sails in tatters or smokestacks toppled by the blast. Some were adrift. On others, crewmen were jury-rigging repairs sufficient to get them to shore. A Jersey Central Railroad ferry limped toward Manhattan, its windows shattered and its super-structure blackened.

"There's Eddie Edwards!"

Edwards's white hair had been singed black, and his eyes were gleaming in a face of soot, but he was otherwise unhurt.

"Thank God you telephoned, Isaac. We got the gun in place in time to stop the bastards."

"Stop them? What are you talking about?"

"They didn't blow the powder pier." He pointed through the thick smoke. "The dynamite train is O.K."

Bell peered through the smoke and saw the string of cars. The five that been sitting there when he left Jersey City last evening to take the night off at the *Follies* were still there.

"What did they blow up? We felt it in Manhattan. It broke every window in the city."

"Themselves. Thanks to the Vickers."

Eddie described how they had driven off the Southern Pacific steam lighter with machine-gun fire.

"She turned around and took off after a schooner. We saw them in company earlier. I would guess that the schooner probably took their crew off. After the murdering scum locked the helm and aimed her at the pier."

"Did your gunfire detonate the dynamite?"

"I don't think so. We shot her wheelhouse to pieces, but she didn't explode. She bore off, turned a full hundred eighty degrees, and steamed away. Must have been three, four minutes before the dyna-mite exploded. One of the boys on the Vickers thought he saw her hit the schooner. And we all saw her sails in the flash."

"It's almost impossible to detonate dynamite by impact," Bell mused. "They must have devised a trigger of some sort . . . How do you see it, Eddie? How did they get their hands on the Southern Pacific steam lighter?"

"The way I see it," said Edwards, "they ambushed the lighter up-river, shot McColleen, and threw the crew overboard."

"We must find their bodies," Bell ordered in a voice heavy with sorrow. "Archie, tell the cops on both sides of the river. Jersey City, Hoboken, Weehawken, New York, Brooklyn, Staten Island. The Van Dorn Agency wants every body that washes up. I will pay for decent burials for our man and the innocent crew of the lighter. We must identify the criminals who were working for the Wrecker."

Dawn broke on a scene of devastation that stretched to both sides of the harbor. Where six Communipaw piers had pushed into the river now there were only five. The sixth had burned to the water-line. All that remained of it were blackened pilings and a heap of ruined boxcars poking out of the tide. Every window on the river side of the Jersey Central passenger terminal was broken, and half its roof was blown off. A ferry that had been moored there listed drunkenly, struck by an out-of-control tugboat that had holed her hull and was still pressed into her like a nursing lamb. The masts of ships beside the piers were splintered, tin roofs and the corrugated sides of pier shacks were scattered, the sides of boxcars split open with cargo spilling out. Bandaged railroad workers, injured by flying glass and falling debris, were poking through the ruins of the rail yards, and the frightened residents of the nearby slums could be seen trudging away with their possessions on their backs.

The most incongruous sight Bell saw in the dull morning light was that of the stern of a wooden sailing schooner that had been blown out of the water and landed on a triple-tracked car float. From across the Hudson, there were reports of thousands of broken windows in lower Manhattan and the streets littered with glass.

Abbott nudged Bell.

"Here comes the boss."

A trim New York Police launch with a low cabin and a short stack was approaching. Joseph Van Dorn stood on the foredeck in a topcoat with a newspaper tucked under his arm.

Bell walked directly to him.

"It is time for me to submit my resignation."

27

"Request denied!" Van Dorn shot back.

"It is not a request, sir," Isaac Bell said coldly. "It is my intention. I will hunt the Wrecker on my own, if it takes the rest of my life. While I promise you I will not impede the Van Dorn investigation led by a better-qualified investigator."

A small smile parted Van Dorn's red whiskers. "Better-qualified? Perhaps you've been too busy to read the morning papers."

He seized Bell's hand and practically crushed it in his powerful grip. "We've won a round at last, Isaac. Well done!"

"Won a round? What are you talking about, sir? People killed on the ferry. Half the windows in Manhattan blown out. These piers a shambles. All due to the sabotage of a Southern Pacific Railroad vessel that I was hired to protect."

"A partial victory, I'll admit. But a victory nonetheless. You stopped the Wrecker from blowing the powder train, which was his target. He would have killed hundreds had you allowed him to. Look here." Van Dorn opened the newspaper. Three headlines of immense type covered the front page.

EXPLOSION DAMAGE EQUAL OF MAY 1904 PIER FIRE

WORSE LOSS OF LIFE ON FERRY, 3 DEAD,

COUNTLESS INJURED

COULD HAVE BEEN FAR WORSE,

SAYS FIRE COMMISSIONER

"And look at this one! Even better . . ."

THE WRECKER RAGED.

Manhattan's streets were strewn with broken glass. From the railway ferry, he saw black smoke still billowing over the Jersey shore. The harbor was littered with damaged ships and barges. And the dynamite explosion was all the talk in saloons and chophouses on both sides of the river. It even invaded the plush sanctuary of the observation-lounge car as the Chicago-bound Pennsylvania Special steamed from its battered Jersey City Terminal.

But, maddeningly, every newsboy in the city was shouting the headlines on the extra editions and every newsstand was plastered with the lies:

SABOTEURS FOILED

RAILWAY POLICE AND VAN DORN AGENTS

SAVED DYNAMITE TRAIN

MAYOR CREDITS SOUND SOUTHERN PACIFIC MANAGEMENT

If Isaac Bell were on this train, he would choke him to death with his bare hands. Or run him through. That moment would come, he reminded himself. He had lost only a battle, not the war. The war was his to win, Bell's to lose. And that deserved a celebration!

Imperiously, he beckoned a steward.

"George!"

"Yes, Senator, suh."

"Champagne!"

A steward rushed him a bottle of Renaudin Bollinger in an ice bucket.

"Not that swill! The company knows goddamned well I will only drink Mumm."

The steward bowed low.

"I'm terribly sorry, Senator. But as Renaudin Bollinger was the favorite champagne of Queen Victoria, and now of King Edward, we hoped it would make a worthy substitute."

"Substitute? What the devil are you talking about? Bring me Mumm champagne or I'll have your job!"

"But, sir, the Pennsylvania Railroad's entire store of Mumm was destroyed in the explosion."

"A VICTORY AT LAST," repeated Joseph Van Dorn. "And if you're right that the Wrecker is trying to discredit the Southern Pacific Railroad, then he cannot be happy with these results. 'Sound Southern Pacific Management' indeed. Exactly the opposite of what he had hoped to achieve with this attack."

"It doesn't feel like a victory to me," said Isaac Bell.

"Savor it, Isaac. Then get busy finding out how he set this up."

"The Wrecker isn't done."

"This attack," Van Dorn said sternly, "wasn't planned overnight. There'll be clues in his method as to what he is scheming next."

A search of the section of the schooner's stern that had been hurled onto the railroad float revealed the body of a man the Marine Division police knew well. "A water rat named Weitzman" was how a grizzled patrol-launch captain put it. "Hung out with that schooner's captain, a son of a crocodile named Yatkowski. Smuggler when he wasn't up to something worse. From Yonkers."

The Yonkers police searched the old river city to no avail. But the next morning, the captain's remains drifted ashore at Weehawken. By then, Van Dorn operatives had traced ownership of the schooner to a lumber dealer who was related to Yatkowski by marriage. The dealer admitted to no crimes, however, claiming that he had sold the ship to his brother-in-law the previous year. Asked whether the captain had ever used her to smuggle fugitives across the river, the dealer replied that when it came to his brother-in-law, anything was possible.

As Bell had surmised in Ogden, the Wrecker was changing tactics. Instead of relying on zealous radicals, he was proving adept at hiring cold-blooded criminals to do his dirty work for cash.

"Did either of these men ever use explosives in their crimes?" he asked the launch captain.

"Looks like this was the first time," the water cop replied with a grim chuckle, "and they weren't all that good at it. Seeing as how they blew themselves to smithereens."

"BEAUTIFUL GIRL TO SEE you, Mr. Bell."

Bell did not look up from his desk in the Van Dorn offices at the Knickerbocker Hotel. Three candlestick telephones were ringing constantly. Messengers were racing in and out. Operatives were standing by to make their reports and awaiting new orders.

"I'm busy. Pass her on to Archie."

"Archie's at the morgue."

"Then send her away."

It was forty hours since the explosion had shaken the Port of New York. Experts from the railroad-backed Bureau of Explosives combing through the wreckage had discovered a dry cell battery that led them to conclude that the dynamite had been skillfully detonated using electricity. But Bell still hadn't a clue as to whether the dead schooner crew had set off the dynamite or had expert help. He was wondering if the Wrecker himself had wired it to explode. Had he been on the schooner? Was he dead? Or was he preparing his next attack?

"I'd see this one if I were you," the front-desk man persisted.

"I've seen her. She's beautiful. She's rich. I don't have time."

"But she's got a gang of fellows with a moving-picture camera."

"What?" Bell glanced through the door. *"Marion!"*

Bell pushed through the door, picked her up in his arms, and kissed her on the mouth. His fiancée was wearing a hat anchored with a scarf that covered the side of her face, and Bell noticed that she had combed her straw-blond hair, which she ordinarily wore piled high upon her head, so that it draped one cheek.

"What are you doing here?"

"Attempting to take pictures of the hero, if you'll put me down. Come outside in the light."

"Hero? I'm the hero of the glassmakers' union." He pressed his lips to her ear, and added in a whisper, "And the only place I'm putting you down is on a bed."

"Not before we take pictures of the famous detective who saved New York."

"Showing my face in nickelodeons won't help me sneak up on criminals."

"We'll take your picture from behind, just the back of your head, very mysterious. Come quickly or we'll lose the light."

They trooped down the Knickerbocker's grand stair, trailed by Bell's assistants muttering reports and whispering questions, and Marion's cameraman and assistants carrying a compact Lumière camera, a wooden tripod, and accessory cases. Outside on the sidewalk, workmen were replacing windows in the Knickerbocker.

"Put him there!" said the cameraman pointing to a shaft of sunlight illuminating a patch of sidewalk.

"Here," said Marion. "So we see the broken glass behind him."

"Yes, ma'am."

She gripped Bell's shoulders.

"Turn this way."

"I feel like a package being delivered."

"You are—a wonderful package called 'The Detective in the White Suit.' Now, point at the broken window . . ."

Bell heard gears and flywheels whirring behind him, a mechanism clicking like a sewing machine, and a flapping of film.

"What are your questions?" he called over his shoulder.

"I know you're busy. I've already written your answers for the title cards."

"What did I say?"

"The Van Dorn Detective Agency will pursue the criminal who attacked New York City to the ends of the earth. We will never give up. Never!"

"Couldn't have put it better myself."

"Now, wait a moment while we attach the telescopic lens . . . O.K., point at that crane lifting the window . . . Thank you. That was wonderful."

As Bell turned to face her smile, a gust of wind lifted her hair, and he suddenly realized that she had arranged her hair, hat, and scarf to conceal a bandage.

"What happened to your face?"

"Flying glass. I was on the ferry when the bomb exploded."

"*What?*"

"It's nothing."

"Have you seen a doctor?"

"Of course. There won't even be much of a scar. And, if there is, I can wear my hair on that side."

Bell was stunned and almost paralyzed with rage. The Wrecker had come within inches of killing her. At that moment of almost losing control, a Van Dorn operative ran from the hotel, waving to get Bell's attention.

"Isaac! Archie telephoned from the Manhattan morgue. He thinks we've got something."

THE CORONER'S PHYSICIAN IN the Borough of Manhattan commanded a salary of thirty-six hundred dollars a year, which allowed him to enjoy the luxuries of middle-class life. These included summers abroad. Recently, he had installed a modern photographic-identification device that he had discovered in Paris.

A camera hung overhead beneath a large skylight. Its lens was aimed at the floor, where marks had been painted indicating height in feet and inches. A dead body lay on the floor, brightly illuminated by the skylight. Bell saw it was a man, though the face had been obliterated by fire and blunt force. His clothes were wet. From the mark where they had placed his feet to the mark at the top of his head, he measured five feet three inches.

"It's only a Chinaman," said the coroner's physician. "At least, I think it's a Chinaman, judging by his hands, feet, skin tone. But they said you wanted to see every drowned body."

"I found this in his pocket," said Abbott, holding up a pencil-sized cylinder with wires extending from it like two short legs.

"Mercury-fulminate detonator," said Bell. "Where was the man found?"

"Floating past the Battery."

"Could he have drifted across the river from Jersey City to the tip of Manhattan?"

"The currents are unpredictable," said the coroner's physician.

"Between ocean tide and river flux, bodies go every which way, depending upon ebb and flow. Do you think he set off the explosion?"

"He looks like he was near it," Abbott said noncommitally with an inquiring glance at Bell.

"Thank you for calling us, Doctor," said Bell, and walked out.

Abbott caught up with him on the sidewalk.

"How did the Wrecker recruit a Chinese to his cause?"

Bell said, "We can't know that until we find out who the man was."

"That's going to be hard without a face."

"We must find out who he was. What are the principal sources of employment for Chinese in New York?"

"The Chinese work mostly at cigarmaking, running grocery stores, and hand-wash laundries, of course."

"This man's fingers and palms were heavily callused," said Bell, "which makes it likely he was a laundryman working with a hot, heavy iron."

"That's a lot of laundries," said Archie. "One in every block of the working districts."

"Start in Jersey City. The schooner was tied up there. And that's where the Southern Pacific lighter loaded her dynamite."

SUDDENLY, THINGS MOVED QUICKLY. One of Jethro Watt's railroad detectives recalled allowing a Chinese with a huge sack of laundry on a pier. "Said he was heading for the *Julia Reidhead,* a steel barque unloading bones."

The *Julia Reidhead* was still moored at the pier, her masts shattered by the explosion. No, said her captain. He had not had his laundry done ashore. He had a wife on board who did it herself. Then the harbormaster's log revealed that Yatkowski's wooden schooner had been tied near the *Julia* that afternoon.

The Van Dorn detectives found missionary students who were studying Chinese at a seminary in Chelsea. They hired the students to translate for them and then intensified the search for the laundry that had employed the dead man. Archie Abbott returned to the Knickerbocker Hotel triumphant.

"His name was Wong Lee. People who knew him said he used to work for the railroad. In the West."

"Dynamiting cuts in the mountains," said Bell. "Of course. That's where he learned his trade."

"Probably came here twenty, twenty-five years ago," said Abbott. "A lot of the Chinese fled California to escape mob attacks."

"Did his employer confirm this just to make him sound good? To make the white detective go away?"

"Wong Lee wasn't really an employee. At least, not anymore. He bought a half interest from his boss."

"So the Wrecker paid him well." Bell said.

"Very well. Up front, no less, and enough to buy himself a business. Have to admire his enterprise. How many workingmen would resist the temptation to spend it on wine and women? . . . Isaac, why are you staring at me?"

"*When?*"

"When what?"

"When did Wong Lee buy a half interest in his laundry?"

"Last February."

"*February?* Where did he get the money?"

"The Wrecker, of course. When he hired him. Where else would a poor Chinese laundryman get that much money?"

"You're sure it was February?"

"Absolutely. The boss told me it was right after the Chinese New Year. That fits the Wrecker's pattern, doesn't it? Plans far ahead."

Isaac Bell could barely contain his excitement.

"Wong Lee bought his share of the laundry last February. But Osgood Hennessy concluded his secret deal only this *November.* How did the Wrecker know back in February that the Southern Pacific Railroad was going to gain entry to New York in November?"

28

"Somehow the Wrecker caught wind of the deal," Abbott answered.

"No!" Bell shot back. "Osgood Hennessy knew he had to acquire a dominating interest in the Jersey Central in the deepest secrecy or his rivals would have stopped him. No one 'catches wind' of that old pirate's intentions until he wants them to."

Bell snatched up the nearest telephone.

"Book two adjoining staterooms on the Twentieth Century Limited, with through connections to San Francisco!"

"Are you saying the Wrecker has inside knowledge of the Southern Pacific?" asked Archie.

"Somehow, he does," said Bell, grabbing his coat and hat. "Either some fool spilled the beans. Or a spy deliberately passed on the information about Hennessy's plans. Either way, he's no stranger to Hennessy's circle."

"Or in it," said Abbott, trotting alongside as Bell strode from the office.

"He's certainly close to the top," Bell agreed. "You're in charge of shutting down the Jersey City operation. Move every man you can to the Cascades Cutoff. Now that he lost out in New York, I'm betting the Wrecker will hit there next. Catch up with me as soon as you can."

"Who's in Hennessy's circle?" asked Archie.

"He's got bankers on his board of directors. He's got lawyers. And his special train tows Pullman sleepers packed with engineers and superintendents managing the cutoff."

"It will take forever to investigate them all."

"We don't have forever," said Bell. "I'll start with Hennessy himself. Tell him what we know and see who comes to mind."

"I would not telegraph such a question," said Archie.

"That's why I'm heading west. For all we know, the Wrecker's spy could be a telegrapher. I have to speak with Hennessy face-to-face."

"Why don't you charter a special train?"

"Because the Wrecker's spy might take notice and figure something's up. Not worth the day I'd save."

Abbott grinned. *"That's* why you booked two adjoining staterooms. Very clever, Isaac. It'll look like Mr. Van Dorn took you off the Wrecker case and assigned you to another job."

"What are you talking about?"

"Personal protection service?" Archie answered innocently. "For a certain lady in the moving-picture-news line returning home to California?"

THE SAN FRANCISCO TELEGRAPHERS' strike had ended disastrously for their union. The majority had returned to work. But some telegraphers and linemen made bitter by highhanded company tactics had turned to sabotage, cutting wires and burning telegraph offices. Among these renegades, one band found a new paymaster in the Wrecker, a mysterious figure who communicated with messages and money left in railroad-station luggage rooms. On his orders, they rehearsed a nationwide disruption of the telegraph system. At a crucial moment, he would isolate Osgood Hennessy from his bankers.

The Wrecker's linemen practiced the old Civil War tactic of cutting key telegraph wires and reconnecting the ends with bypass wires so that the splices could not be detected by eye from the ground. It would take many days to restore communication. Since northern California and Oregon were not yet connected to the eastern states by telephone, the telegraph was still the only method of instantaneous intracontinental communication. When the Wrecker was ready, he could launch a coordinated attack that would hurl the Cascades Cutoff fifty years back in time to the days when the fastest means of communication was mail sent by stagecoach and Pony Express.

In the meantime, he had other uses for disgruntled telegraphers.

His attack on the Southern Pacific in New York had been a disaster. Isaac Bell and his detectives and the railroad police had turned what would have been the final stake in the heart of the Southern Pacific Railroad into near victory. His effort to discredit the Southern Pacific had failed. And after his attack, the Van Dorn Agency had moved swiftly, conspiring with the newspapers to paint the railroad president as a hero.

A bloody accident would turn things around.

The railroads maintained their own telegraph systems to keep the trains moving swiftly and safely. Single-tracked lines, which were still in the majority, were divided into blocks maintained by strict rules of entry. A train given permission to be in a block possessed the right-of-way. Only after it passed through the block, or was sidetracked onto a siding, was another train permitted in the block. Observations that a train had left a block were communicated by telegraph. Orders to pull off onto a siding were sent by telegraph. Acknowledgment of those orders was made by telegraph. That a train was stopped safely on the siding had to be confirmed by telegraph.

But the Wrecker's telegraphers could intercept orders, stop them, and change them. He had already caused a collision by this method, a rear ender on the Cascades Cutoff that had telescoped a materials train into a work train's caboose, killing two crewmen.

A bloodier accident would erase Isaac Bell's "victory."

And what could be bloodier than two locomotives hauling work trains packed with laborers colliding head-on? When his train to San Francisco stopped in Sacramento, he checked a satchel in the luggage room containing orders and a generous envelope of cash and mailed the ticket to an embittered former union official named Ross Parker.

"GOOD NIGHT, MISS MORGAN."

"Good night, Mr. Bell. That was a delicious dinner, thank you."

"Need help with your door?"

"I have it."

Five hours after her passengers walked the famous red carpet to board at Grand Central Terminal, the 20th Century Limited was racing across the flatlands of western New York State at eighty miles an hour. A Pullman porter, gaze discreetly averted, shuffled along the narrow corridor outside the staterooms, gathering shoes that the sleeping passengers had left out to be shined.

"Well, good night, then."

Bell waited for Marion to step into her stateroom and lock the door. Then he opened the door to his stateroom, changed into a silk robe, removed his throwing knife from his boots and put them outside in the corridor. The speed of the train caused ice to tremble musically in a silver bucket. In it was chilling a bottle of Mumm. Bell wrapped the dripping bottle in a linen napkin and held it behind his back.

He heard a soft knock on the interior door and threw it open.

"Yes, Miss Morgan?"

Marion was standing there in a dressing gown, her lustrous

hair cascading over her shoulders, her eyes mischievous, her smile radiant.

"Could I possibly borrow a cup of champagne?"

LATER, WHISPERING SIDE BY SIDE as the 20th Century rocketed through the night, Marion asked, "Did you really win a million dollars at poker?"

"Almost. But half of it was my money. "

"That's still a half million. What are you going to do with it?"

"I was thinking of buying the Cromwell Mansion."

"Whatever for?"

"For you."

Marion stared at him, puzzled and intrigued and wanting to know more.

"I know what you're thinking," said Isaac. "And you may be right. It might be filled with ghosts. But an old coot I played cards with told me that he always gave his new wife a stick of dynamite to redecorate the house."

"Dynamite?" She smiled. "Something to consider. I loved the house from the outside. It was the inside I couldn't stand. It was so cold, like him . . . Isaac, I felt you flinch before. Are you hurt?"

"No."

"What's this?"

She touched a wide yellow bruise on his torso, and Bell recoiled despite himself.

"Just a couple of ribs."

"Broken?"

"No, no, no . . . Just cracked."

"What happened?"

"Bumped into a couple of prizefighters in Wyoming."

"How do you have time to pick fights when you're hunting the Wrecker?"

"He paid them."

"Oh," she said quietly. Then she smiled. "A bloody nose? Doesn't that mean you're getting close?"

"You remember. Yes, it was the best news I'd had in a week . . . Mr. Van Dorn thinks we've got him on the run."

"But *you* don't?"

"We've got Hennessy's lines heavily guarded. We've got that sketch. We've got good men on the case. Something's bound to break our way. Question is, does it break before he strikes again."

"Have you been practicing your dueling?" she asked only half jesting.

"I got a session in every day in New York," Bell told her. "My old fencing master hooked me up with a naval officer who was very good. Brilliant fencer. Trained in France."

"Did you beat him?"

Bell smiled and poured more champagne into her glass. "Let's just say that Lieutenant Ash brought out the best in me."

JAMES DASHWOOD FILLED HIS notebook with a list of the blacksmiths, stables, auto garages, and machine shops he visited with the lumberjack sketch. The list had just topped a hundred. Discouraged, and weary of hearing about Broncho Billy Anderson, he telegraphed Mr. Bell to report that he had canvassed every town, village, and hamlet in Los Angeles County, from Glendale in the north to Montebello in the east to Huntington Park in the south. No blacksmith, mechanic, or machinist had recognized the picture, much less admitted to fashioning a hook out of an anchor.

"Go west, young man," Isaac Bell wired back. "Don't stop 'til your hat floats."

Which brought him late the next afternoon by Red Train trolley to Santa Monica on the shore of the Pacific Ocean. He wasted a few minutes, uncharacteristically, walking out on the Venice Pier to smell the salt water and watch girls bathing in the low surf. Two in bright costumes had their legs bared almost to their knees. They ran to a blanket they had spread next to a lifeboat that was on the beach ready to be rolled from the sand to the water. Dashwood noticed another lifeboat a half mile down the beach poised in the distant haze. Each surely had an anchor under its canvas. He berated himself for not thinking of Santa Monica sooner, squared his scrawny shoulders, and hurried into town.

The first place he walked into was typical of the many livery stables he had visited. It was a sprawling wooden structure big enough to shelter a variety of buggies and wagons for rent, with stalls for numerous horses, and a new mechanic's section with wrenches, grease guns, and a chain hoist for motor repairs. A bunch of men were sitting around jawing: stablemen, grooms, auto mechanics, and a brawny blacksmith. By now, he had seen enough to know all these types and was no longer intimidated.

"Horse or car, kid?" one of them yelled.

"Horseshoes," said James.

"There's the blacksmith. You're up, Jim."

"Good afternoon, sir," said James, thinking that the blacksmith looked morose. Big as the man was, his cheeks were hollow. His eyes were red, as if he didn't sleep well.

"What can I do for you, young fella?"

By now, Dashwood had learned to ask his questions privately. Later, he would show the sketch to the whole group. But if he started off in front of all of them, it would turn into a debate that resembled a saloon brawl.

"Can we step outside? I want to show you something."

The blacksmith shrugged his sloping shoulders, got up from the milk crate he was sitting on, and followed James Dashwood outside next to a newly installed gasoline pump.

"Where's your horse?" the blacksmith asked.

Dashwood offered his hand. "I'm a Jim, too. James. James Dashwood."

"I thought you wanted horseshoes."

"Do you recognize this man?" Dashwood asked, holding up the sketch with the mustache. He watched the blacksmith's face and, to his astonished delight, he saw him recoil. The man's unhappy face flushed darkly.

Dashwood's heart soared. This was the blacksmith who had fashioned the hook that had derailed the Coast Line Limited. This man had seen the Wrecker.

"Who are you?" asked the blacksmith.

"Van Dorn investigator," James answered proudly. The next thing he knew, he was flat on his back, and the blacksmith was running full tilt down an alley.

"Stop!" Dashwood yelled, jumped to his feet, and gave chase. The blacksmith ran fast for a big man and was surprisingly agile, whipping around corners as if he were on rails, losing no speed in his mad turns and jinks, up and down alleys, through backyards, tearing through laundry hung from clotheslines, around woodsheds, toolsheds, and gardens and onto a street. But he hadn't the stamina of a man just out of boyhood who neither smoked nor drank. Once they were out in the open, Dashwood gained on him for several blocks. "Stop!" he kept shouting, but no one on the sidewalks was inclined to get in the path of such a big man. Nor was there a constable or watchman in sight.

He caught up in front of a Presbyterian church on a tree-lined street. Grouped on the sidewalk were three middle-aged men in suits, the minister in a dog collar, the choirmaster gripping a sheaf of music, and the deacon holding the congregation's account books under his arm. The blacksmith barreled past them, with James hot on his tail.

"Stop!"

Only a yard behind, James Dashwood launched himself into a flying tackle. As he flew, he took a heel on the chin, but he still managed to close his skinny arms around the blacksmith's ankles. They crashed to the sidewalk, rolled onto a lawn, and scrambled to their feet. James clung to the blacksmith's arm, which was as thick as the young detective's thigh.

"Now that you caught him," called the deacon, "what are you going to do with him?"

The answer came from the blacksmith himself in the form of a wide fist ribbed with thick knuckles. When James Dashwood came to, he was lying on the grass, with the three men in suits peering down curiously at him.

"Where'd he go?" said James.

"He ran off."

"Where to?"

"Anywhere he wanted to, I'd reckon. Are you all right, sonny?"

James Dashwood rose swaying to his feet and wiped the blood off his face with a handkerchief his mother had given him when he moved to San Francisco to work for the Van Dorn Detective Agency.

"Did any of you recognize that man?"

"I believe he's a blacksmith," said the choirmaster.

"Where does he live?"

"Don't know," he answered, and the minister said, "Why don't you let be whatever got between you, son? Before you get hurt."

Dashwood staggered back to the livery stable. The blacksmith was not there.

"Why'd Jim run off?" a mechanic asked.

"I don't know. You tell me."

"He's been acting strange, lately," said a stable hand.

"Stopped drinking," said another.

"That'll do it," said a groom, laughing.

"The church ladies claim another victim. Poor Jim. Getting so a man's not safe on the streets when the Women's Christian Temperance Union holds a meeting."

With that, grooms, stable hands, and mechanics broke into a song that James had never heard but they all seemed to know:

Here's to a temperance supper,
With water in glasses tall,
And coffee and tea to end with—
And me not there at all!

James took out another copy of the sketch. "Do you recognize this man?"

He received a chorus of nos. He braced for a "Broncho Billy" or two, but apparently none of them went to the pictures.

"Where does Jim live?" he asked.

No one would tell him.

He went to the Santa Monica Police Department, where an elderly patrolman led him to the chief of the department. The chief was a fifty-year-old, well-groomed gentleman in a dark suit, with his hair cut close on the sides in the modern way. Dashwood introduced himself. The chief acted cordially and said he was happy to help a Van Dorn operative. The blacksmith's last name was Higgins, he told Dashwood. Jim Higgins lived in a rented room above the stable. Where would he go to hide out? The chief had no idea.

Dashwood stopped at the Western Union office to telegraph a report to the Sacramento office to be forwarded to wherever Isaac Bell was. Then he walked the streets, as darkness fell, hoping to catch a glimpse of the man. At eleven, when the last streetcar left for Los Angeles, he decided to rent a room in a tourist hotel instead of riding back to town so he could start hunting early in the morning.

A LONE HORSEMAN ON a glossy bay rode a ridge that overlooked the remote single-tracked Southern Pacific line just south of the Oregon border. Three men, who were grouped around a telegraph pole squeezed between the track and an abandoned tin-roofed barn, spotted him silhouetted against the sharp-blue sky. Their leader removed his broad-brimmed Stetson and swept it in a slow full circle over his head.

"Hey, what are you doing, Ross? Don't wave hello like you're inviting him down here."

"I'm not waving hello," said Ross Parker. "I'm waving him off."

"How the hell is he going know the difference?"

"He forks his horse like a cowhand. A cowhand knows damned well the cattle rustlers signal for *Mind your own damned business and sift sand away from us.*"

"We ain't rustling cattle. We ain't even seen any cattle."

"The principle is the same. Unless the man is a total fool, he'll leave us alone."

"What if he doesn't?"

"We'll blow his head off."

Even as Ross explained waving off to Andy, who was a city slicker from San Francisco, the horseman turned his animal away and dropped from sight behind the ridge. The three went back to work. Ross ordered Lowell, the lineman, to climb the pole with two long wires connected to Andy's telegraph key.

Had the cowboy on the ridge ridden closer, he would have seen that they were unusually heavily armed for a telegraph crew working in 1907. Decades after the last Indian attack, Ross Parker packed a

.45 holster on his hip and a Winchester rifle behind his saddle. Lowell had a coach gun, a sawed-off shotgun, slung over his back within
easy reach. Even the city boy, the telegrapher Andy, had a .38 revolver
tucked in his belt. Their horses were tied in the shade of a clump of
trees, as they had come in cross-country instead of along the tracks
on a handcar.

"Stay up there!" Ross ordered Lowell. "This won't take long." He
and Andy settled down beside the old barn.

In fact, it was nearly an hour before Andy's key started clattering, having intercepted a train dispatcher's orders to the operator at
Weed, north of their position. By then, all three had backed against
the barn, dozing in the sun out of the cool wind.

"What's he saying?" asked Ross.

"The dispatcher is sending train orders to the Weed operator.
He's telling him to signal the southbound freight to take the siding
at Azalea."

Ross checked his copy of the schedule.

"O.K. The northbound work train is passing Azalea siding in half
an hour. Change the orders to give the southbound freight authority
clear to Dunsmuir."

Andy did as directed, altering the train orders to tell the southbound freight that the track was clear when in fact a work train was
racing north with carloads of laborers. An experienced telegrapher,
he mimicked the "fist" of the Dunsmuir dispatcher so the Weed
operator would not realize a different man was operating the key.

"Uh-oh. They want to know what happened to the scheduled
northbound?" Scheduled trains had authority over extras.

Ross was prepared for this. He didn't bother opening his eyes.

"Tell them the scheduled northbound just reported by telegraphone that it's on the siding at Shasta Springs with a burned-up journal box."

This false message suggested that the northbound had broken

down and its crew had switched it off the main line onto a siding. Then they had reached up to the telegraph wires with the eighteen-foot sectional "fishpole" carried in the caboose to hook a portable telegraphone on the wires. The telegraphone permitted rudimentary voice communication. The Weed operator accepted the explanation and passed on the false orders that would place the two trains on a collision course.

"Get up there, Lowell," Ross ordered, still not opening his eyes. "Pull your wires down. We're done."

"Lowell's behind the barn," said Andy. "Went to take a leak."

"Delicate of him."

Things were going exactly as planned until a rifle barrel poked around the side of the barn and pressed hard against the telegrapher's head.

A MUSICAL VOICE DRAWLED, "UNSEND THAT MESSAGE YOU just sent."

The telegrapher looked up in disbelief into the grim, hawklike features of Van Dorn investigator "Texas" Walt Hatfield. Behind him stood a glossy bay horse, silent as a statue. "And in case you're wondering, yes, I do know the Morse alphabet. Change a word and I'll blow your head off and send it myself. As for you, mister," Hatfield told Ross Parker, whose hand was creeping toward his holster, "don't make any mistakes or you won't have time to make another."

"Yes, sir," said Ross, raising his hands high. In addition to the Winchester pointed at Andy's head, the tall Texan carried two six-guns in oiled holsters worn low on his hips. If he wasn't a gunfighter, he sure dressed like one.

Andy decided to believe him, too. He clattered out a cancellation of the false order.

"Now, pass along the original order you sidewinders intercepted."

Andy sent along the original orders to tell the southbound extra to wait on the Azalea siding as the northbound work train was coming through.

"Much better," drawled Hatfield. "We can't have locomotives butting heads, can we?"

His smile was as pleasant as his musical drawl. His eyes, however, were dark as a grave.

"And now, gents, you all are gonna tell me who paid you to attempt such a dastardly deed."

"Drop it."

Lowell the lineman had come around the back of the barn with his wide-barreled coach gun.

Walt Hatfield did not doubt that the gent with the coach gun would have blasted him to pieces if he weren't concerned about accidentally killing his partners with the same swath of buckshot. Cussing his own stupidity—there was no other word for it because even though he hadn't seen him, he should have reckoned there would be a third man to climb the pole—he did as he was told.

He dropped his rifle. All eyes shifted momentarily to the clatter of steel on stone.

Hatfield drove sideways and drew his six-guns with blinding speed. He sent a well-aimed slug at Lowell that drilled through the lineman's heart. But even as Lowell died, he jerked the triggers of the coach gun. Both barrels roared, and heavy double-aught lead shot tore into Andy, nearly cutting the telegrapher in half.

Ross was already running for his horse. Andy had fallen on Hatfield's rifle, and in the time it took to retrieve it from under his body Ross had mounted and galloped away. Hatfield whipped up the weapon, which was slippery with blood, and fired once. He thought he winged him. Ross reeled in the saddle. But by then, he was in the trees.

"Tarnation," muttered Hatfield. A glance at their bodies told him that neither man would ever talk about the Wrecker. He jumped on his bay, roared, "Trail!," and the big horse sprang to a gallop.

• • •

MARION MORGAN KISSED ISAAC BELL good-bye at Sacramento. She was traveling on to San Francisco. He would change trains north to the head of the Cascades Cutoff. Her parting words were, "I can't recall a train ride I enjoyed more."

Half a day later, trundling through the Dunsmuir yards, Bell counted reassuring numbers of railway police guarding key switches, the roundhouse, and dispatch offices. At the station, he spoke with a pair of Van Dorn operatives in dark suits and derbies who took him on a brisk tour of the various checkpoints they had established. Satisfied, he asked where he could find Texas Walt Hatfield.

Dunsmuir's main street, Sacramento Avenue, was a mud thoroughfare rutted by buggy wheels. On one side were frame houses and shops separated from the mud by a narrow plank sidewalk. The Southern Pacific tracks, rows of telegraph and electric poles, and scattered sheds and warehouses bordered the other side. The hotel was a two-story affair with porches overhanging the sidewalk. Bell found Hatfield in the lobby, drinking whiskey in a teacup. He had a bandage plastered across his brow and his right arm in a sling.

"I'm sorry, Isaac. I let you down."

He told Bell how while riding the rounds of the watch points he had established along that vulnerable line, he had spotted what looked from a distance to be an attempt to sabotage the telegraph lines. "Thought at first they were cutting the lines. But when I got close, I saw they had wired up a key and I realized they were intercepting train orders. With a view to causing collisions."

He shifted uncomfortably in his chair, clearly sore from head to toe, and admitted, "I also thought at first there were only two of them. Forgot they'd have a lineman to go up the pole, and he got the drop on me. I managed to wriggle out of that mess, but unfortunately two of them died in the process. The third lit out. I reckoned he was the boss, so I lit out after him, thinking he could tell us plenty about the Wrecker. I winged him with my rifle, but not enough to spoil his aim. The dry-gulching hellion shot my horse out from under me."

"Maybe he was aiming at you and hit your horse instead."

"I'm real sorry, Isaac. I feel plumb stupid."

"I would, too," said Bell. Then he smiled. "But let's not forget you stopped a head-on collision of two trains, one of them full of workmen."

"The sidewinder is still fanging," Hatfield retorted morosely. "Stopping the Wrecker ain't catching him."

This was the truth, Bell knew. But the next day, when he caught up with Osgood Hennessy at the cutoff railhead, the Southern Pacific president was looking at the bright side too, partly because construction was roaring ahead of schedule again. The last long tunnel on the route to the Cascade Canyon Bridge—Tunnel 13—was almost holed through.

"We're beating him at every turn," Hennessy exulted. "New York was bad, but, bad as it was, everyone knows it could have been so much worse. The Southern Pacific comes out smelling like a rose. Now your boys averted a catastrophic collision. And you say you're closing in on the blacksmith who made that hook that derailed the Coast Line Limited."

Bell had passed on the essence of Dashwood's report, that the blacksmith who had fled must know something about the hook and therefore about the Wrecker, too. Bell had ordered Larry Sanders to give Dashwood the full support of the Los Angeles office in running down the blacksmith, who had disappeared without a trace. With Van Dorn's entire Los Angeles force hunting him, he should turn up soon.

"That blacksmith could lead you straight to the Wrecker," said Hennessy.

"That is my hope," said Bell.

"It strikes me that you've got the murdering radical on the run. He won't have time to make trouble if he's running to stay ahead of you."

"I hope you are right, sir. But we mustn't forget that the Wrecker is resourceful. And he plans ahead, far ahead. We know now that he hired his accomplice in the New York attack as long as a year ago. That's why I crossed the continent to ask you one question face-to-face."

"What's that?"

"I assure you we speak in confidence. In return, I must ask you to be entirely candid."

"That was understood from the beginning," Hennessy growled. "What the hell are you asking?"

"Who might have known of your plan to acquire a controlling interest in the New Jersey Central Railroad?"

"No one."

"No one? No lawyer? No banker?"

"I had to play it close to the vest."

"But surely a complex endeavor demands the help of various experts."

"I'd sic one lawyer on one portion of the arrangement and another on another. Same with bankers. I put different devils on different aspects. If the word got out, J. P. Morgan and Vanderbilt would fall on me like landslides. The longer I kept it quiet, the better my shot at roping in the Jersey Central."

"So no one attorney or banker understood the entire picture?"

"Correct . . . Of course," Hennessy reflected, "a really sharp devil might put two and two together."

Bell took out his notebook.

"Please name those bankers and attorneys who might have known enough to surmise your intention."

Hennessy fired off four names, taking care to point out that, of them, only two were actually likely to have understood the broader picture. Bell wrote them down.

"Would you have shared knowledge of the impending arrangement with your engineers and superintendents who would take charge of the new line?"

Hennessy hesitated. "To a certain extent. But, again, I gave them only as much information as was necessary to keep them on track."

"Would you give me the names of those who might have parlayed the information to understand your intention?"

Hennessy mentioned two engineers. Bell wrote them down and put away his book.

"Did Lillian know?"

"Lillian? Of course. But she wasn't about to blab it."

"Mrs. Comden?"

"Same as Lillian."

"Did you share your plans with Senator Kincaid?"

"Kincaid? Are you joking. Of course not, why would I?"

"To procure his help in the Senate."

"He helps me when I tell him to help me. I don't have to prime him."

"Why did you say 'Of course not'?"

"The man's a fool. He thinks I don't know that he's hanging around me to court my daughter."

Bell wired for a Van Dorn courier, and when he arrived handed him a sealed letter for the Sacramento office, ordering immediate investigations of the Southern Pacific's head engineer, Lillian Hennessy, Mrs. Comden, two bankers, two attorneys, and Senator Charles Kincaid.

A SOUTHBOUND WORK TRAIN, RETURNING HUNDREDS OF exhausted men for three days' recuperation after four straight weeks of work, was sidelined to let a northbound materials train through. They were waiting to climb the Diamond Canyon Loop, a sweeping switchback curve fifty miles south of Tunnel 13. The siding had been gouged out of the canyon wall at the foot of a steep slope, and the sweep of the switchback allowed a clear view of the tracks running parallel high above them. What the men saw next would haunt them for the rest of their lives.

The locomotive hauling the long string of boxcars and gondolas was a heavy 2-8-0 Consolidation. She was a mountain-climbing workhorse with eight drive wheels. On this light grade, etched from the side of the canyon, the coupling rods that linked her drivers were a blur of swift motion as she entered the curve at nearly forty miles an hour. Few of the weary slumped on the hard benches of the sidelined work train below took much notice, but those who did look up saw her smoke flatten behind her as she raced high above them. One even remarked to a dozing friend, "She's highballing like Old Man Hennessy's got his hand on the throttle."

The 2-8-0's engine truck, the short, stabilizing front wheels that prevented swaying at such speed, screeched as they pressed against the curve. Her engineer knew the run to the cutoff like the back of his hand, and this particular bend on the lip of Diamond Canyon was one spot he did not want to hear the screech of a loose rail. "Don't like that noise one bit," he started to say to his fireman. In the next millisecond, long before he could finish the sentence, much less throttle back, the one-hundred-twenty-ton locomotives's lead drive wheel hit the loose rail. The rail parted from the ties with a loud bang.

Free of the wooden ties that held them a hard-and-fast four feet eight and a half inches apart, the tracks spread. All four drive wheels on the outside of the curve dropped off the steel, and the locomotive charged straight ahead at forty miles an hour, spraying crushed stone, splintered wood, and broken spikes.

To the men watching from the work train sidelined at the bottom of the canyon, it looked as if the freight hurtling overhead had developed a mind of its own and decided to fly. Years later, survivors would swear that it soared for an amazingly long way before gravity took charge. Several found religion, convinced that God had intervened to help the freight train fly just far enough that most of it overshot the work train when it tumbled down the mountain. At the time, however, what most saw when they looked up at the terrible thunder was a 2-8-0 Consolidation locomotive toppling off the edge of a cliff and rolling at them with fifty boxcars and gondolas that swept trees and boulders from the slope like a long black whip.

Most remembered the noise. It started as thunder, swelled to the roar of an avalanche, and ended, hours later it seemed, in the sharp, rending clatter of steel and wood raining down on the stationary work train. None forgot the fear.

Isaac Bell was on the scene within hours.

He wired Hennessy that the wreck was very possibly an accident.

There was no evidence that the Wrecker had tampered with the rails. Admittedly, the heavy Consolidation had so battered the point where she jumped the track that it was impossible to distinguish for sure between deliberate removal of spikes or an accidental loose rail. But meticulously filed Southern Pacific Railway police reports indicated that patrols on horseback and handcar had blanketed the area. It was unlikely, Bell concluded, that the saboteur could have gotten close enough to strike at the Diamond Canyon Loop.

Livid because the wreck had unsettled his workforce, Hennessy sent Franklin Mowery, the civil engineer he had hauled out of retirement to build the Cascade Canyon Bridge, to inspect the wreck. Mowery limped along the ruined bed, leaning heavily on his bespectacled assistant's arm. He was a talkative old man—born, he told Bell, in 1837, when Andrew Jackson was still president. He said he had been present when the first continental railroad linked east and west lines at Promontory Point, Utah, in 1869. "Nearly forty years ago. Time flies. Hard to believe I was even younger that day than this rascal helping me walk."

He gave his assistant an affectionate slap on the shoulder. Eric Soares, whose wire-rimmed glasses, wavy dark hair, expressive eyes, broad brow, narrow chin, and thin, waxed handlebar mustache made him look more like a poet or a painter than a civil engineer, returned a sly smile.

"What do you think, Mr. Mowery?" asked Bell. "Was it an accident?"

"Hard to say, son. Ties smashed like kindling, no piece large enough to register tool marks. Spikes bent or snapped in two. Reminds me of a derailment I saw back in '83. String of passenger cars descending the High Sierra, the rear cars telescoping into one another like that caboose over there rammed inside that boxcar."

The tall detective and the two engineers cast sober eyes on the caboose stuffed into the boxcar like a hastily packed suitcase.

"What will you report to Mr. Hennessy?" Bell asked.

Mowery nudged Eric Soares. "What should we tell him, Eric?"

Soares removed his glasses, glanced about myopically, then dropped to his knees and closely examined a crosstie severed by a locomotive drive wheel.

"As you say, Mr. Mowery," he said, "if they did pull spikes, no tool marks survived."

"But," Mowery said, "I'd venture the old man is not going to want to hear that slack maintenance was the culprit, is he, Eric?"

"No, Mr. Mowery," Eric answered with another of his sly smiles. Their friendship, Bell noticed, seemed based on Mowery acting like an uncle and Soares the favorite nephew.

"Nor will he welcome speculation that hasty construction could have resulted in a weakness exploited by the fast-moving heavy locomotive, will he, Eric?"

"No, Mr. Mowery."

"Compromise, Mr. Bell, is the essence of engineering. We surrender one thing to get another. Build too fast, we get shabby construction. Build too scrupulously, we never get the job done."

Eric stood up, hooked his glasses around his ears again, and took up the older's chant.

"Build it so strong that it will never fail, we risk building too heavy. Build it light, we might build it too weak."

"Eric's a metallurgist," Mowery said, chuckling. "Speaking of essence. He knows forty types of steel that didn't even exist in my day."

Bell was still studying the telescoped wreckage of the caboose stuffed inside the boxcar when an intriguing idea struck him. These men were engineers. They understood how things were made.

"Could you make a sword that starts short and gets longer?" he asked.

"Beg your pardon?"

"You were talking about telescoping and steel, and I was wondering whether the blade of a sword could be hidden inside itself then extended to make it long."

"Like a collapsible stage sword?" asked Mowery. "Where the actor appears to be run through but the blade actually retracts into itself?"

"Only this one would not retract. It would run you through."

"What do you say, Eric? You studied metallurgy at Cornell. Could you make such a sword?"

"You can make anything, if you've got the money," Eric answered. "But it would be difficult to make it strong."

"Strong enough to run a man through?"

"Easily strong enough to *thrust*. Strong enough to pierce flesh. But it could not endure lateral impact."

"Lateral impact?"

Mowery explained. "Eric means that it would not stand up to whacking it sideways in a real sword fight against a real sword."

"The beat," said Bell. "A sharp blow to push your opponent's blade aside."

"You compromise strength in the interest of compactness. Two or three short lengths of steel joined cannot be as strong as one. Why do you ask, Mr. Bell?"

"I was curious what it would be like to make a knife turn into a sword," said Bell.

"Surprising," Mowery said drily, "to the fellow on the business end."

The bridge builder took a final look around and steadied himself on Eric's arm.

"Let's go, Eric. No putting it off any longer. I've got to report to the old man exactly what Mr. Bell reported, which is exactly what the old man doesn't want to hear. Who the heck knows what happened. But we found no evidence of sabotage."

When Mowery did make his report, an angry Osgood Hennessy asked in a low, dangerous voice, "Was the engineer killed?"

"Barely a scratch. He must be the luckiest locomotive driver alive."

"Fire him! If it wasn't radical sabotage, then excessive speed caused that wreck. That'll show the hands I don't tolerate reckless engineers risking their lives."

But firing the engineer did nothing to calm the terrified workmen employed to finish the Cascades Cutoff. Whether the wreck had been an accident or the work of a saboteur, they didn't care. Although they were inclined to believe that the Wrecker had struck again. Police spies reported that there was talk in the camp of a strike.

"Strike!" echoed the apoplectic Hennessy. "I'm paying them top dollar. What the hell else do they want?"

"They want to go home," Isaac Bell explained. He was keeping close track of the men's mood by polling his covert operatives in the cookhouses and saloons and visiting personally to gauge the effect of the Wrecker's attacks on the Southern Pacific labor force. "They're afraid to ride the work train."

"That's insane. I'm about to hole through the last tunnel to the bridge."

"They say that the cutoff has become the most dangerous line in the West."

Ironically, Bell admitted, the Wrecker had won this round, whether he intended to or not.

The old man dropped his head in his hands. "God in Heaven, where am I going to get a thousand men with winter coming?" He looked up angrily. "Round up their ringleaders. Clap a bunch in jail. The rest'll come around."

"May I suggest," said Bell, "a more productive course?"

"No! I know how to crush a strike." He turned to Lillian, who was watching him intently. "Get me Jethro Watt. And wire the Governor. I want troops here by morning."

"Sir," said Bell. "I've just come back from the camp. It's gripped with fear. Watt's police will, at best, provoke a riot and, at worst, cause vast numbers to drift away. Troops will make it even worse. You can't force decent work out of frightened men. But you can attempt to alleviate their fright."

"What do you mean?"

"Bring in Jethro Watt. Bring five hundred officers with him. But put them to work patrolling the line. Blanket it until it is apparent that *you,* not the Wrecker, control every inch of track between here and Tunnel 13."

"That'll never work," said Hennessy. "Those agitators won't buy it. They just want to strike."

Lillian spoke up at last.

"Try it, Father."

And so the old man did.

Within a day, every mile of track was guarded and every mile scoured for loose rails and buried explosives. Just as had happened in Jersey City, where Van Dorn operatives had arrested various criminals swept up in the search for the Wrecker's accomplices, here, in the course of hunting for signs of sabotage, track crews discovered several weaknesses in the track and repaired them.

Bell mounted a horse and rode the twenty-mile line. He returned by locomotive, satisfied that this newest stretch of the cutoff had been transformed from the most dangerous in the West to the best maintained. And the best guarded.

THE WRECKER DROVE A trader's wagon pulled by two strong mules. It had a patched and faded canvas top stretched over seven hoops.

Under the canvas were pots and pans and woolen cloth, salt, a barrel of lard, another that held china dishes packed in straw. Hidden under the trader's cargo was an eight-foot-long, ten-by-twelve-inch freshly milled mountain hemlock railroad tie.

The trader was dead, stripped naked and tossed off a hillside. He was nearly as tall as the Wrecker, and his clothes fit the Wrecker reasonably well. A hole bored the length of the squared timber was stuffed with dynamite.

The Wrecker followed a buggy road that likely had started out as an Indian trail long before the railroad was built and a mule-deer track before then. While steep and narrow, the road unerringly found the gentlest slopes in a land that was harsh. Most of the remote settlements it touched upon were abandoned. Those that weren't, he avoided. Their hardscrabble residents might recognize the wagon and wonder what had happened to its owner.

Here and there, the road crossed the new railroad, offering an opportunity to drive the wagon onto the tracks. But every time he neared the cutoff line, he saw patrols, police riding horseback and police pumping handcars. His plan was to drive his wagon along the tracks at night to the edge of a deep canyon, where he would replace an in-place crosstie with his explosive one. But as afternoon waned and the slopes darkened, he was forced to admit that his plan would not succeed.

Isaac Bell's hand was obvious in the precautions, and the Wrecker cursed yet again the killers he had hired in Rawlins who had botched the job. But all his cursing and all his regretting would not change the fact that Bell's patrols meant that he could not risk driving the wagon on the tracks. The railroad cut was narrow. Much of it consisted of sheer rock on one side and a steep drop on the other. If he ran into a patrol, there was no place to hide a wagon, and, in most places, no way to drive it off the tracks at all.

The hemlock crosstie weighed two hundred pounds. The spike

puller he needed to remove an existing tie weighed twenty. The puller could double as a crowbar to dig out the ballast, but he couldn't drive spikes with it, so he still needed a hammer and that weighed another twelve pounds. He was strong. He could lift two hundred thirty pounds. He could lift the hemlock tie with the hammer and puller lashed to it and hoist it to his shoulder. But how many miles could he carry it?

Unloading the tie from the wagon, it felt even heavier than he had imagined. Thank God it hadn't been creosoted in coal-tar distillates. The wood would have absorbed another thirty pounds of the dark liquid.

The Wrecker leaned the tie against a telegraph pole and roped the spike puller and hammer to it. Then he drove the trader's wagon behind some trees a short distance from the tracks. He shot both mules with his derringer, pressing the muzzle to their skulls to muffle the reports in case a patrol was nearby. He hurried back to the tracks, crouched and tilted the massive weight onto his shoulder. Then he straightened his legs and started walking.

The rough wood dug through his coat, and he regretted not taking a blanket from the wagon to cushion his shoulder. The pain started as a dull ache. It sharpened quickly, biting deep. It cut into the muscle of his shoulder and ground against the bone. After only half a mile, it burned like fire. Should he put it down, run back to the wagon, and get a blanket? But then Bell's patrols could find it lying by the rails.

The Wrecker's legs were tired already. His knees began to shake. But his shaking knees and the awful pain in his shoulder were soon forgotten as the weight compressed the bones in his spine, squeezing nerves. The nerves radiated a burning sensation into his legs, shooting sharp pains through his thighs and calves. He wondered if he put the tie down and stopped to rest whether he could lift it again. While he debated the risk, the decision was made for him.

He had carried the tie for a mile when he saw a creamy glow in the sky up ahead. It brightened quickly. A locomotive headlamp, he realized, coming fast. Already he could hear it over the sound of his labored breathing. He had to get off the tracks. There were trees close by. Feeling his way in the dark, he descended the slope of the roadbed and careened through them. The headlamp threw crazy beams and shadows. He pushed in deeper, then knelt down carefully, tipping the massive crosstie down until its end rested on the ground.

The relief of having the weight off him was an almost overwhelming pleasure. He leaned the other end of the tie against a tree. Then he sagged to the ground and stretched out on the pine needles to rest. The locomotive grew louder and roared past, drawing a train that rattled with the peculiar higher pitch of empty cars. It passed too quickly. Too soon, he had to stand up, tip the crushing weight onto his shoulder, and struggle up the slope to the rails.

The heel of his boot caught on the head of the rail as he tried to step between the tracks. He felt himself pitching forward, falling face-first. He fought to regain his balance. But before he could get his feet under him in the headlong rush, the weight pushed him down. He twisted frantically to get out from under the tie. But the weight was too massive to escape entirely. A sledgehammer blow crushed his arm, and he cried out in pain.

Facedown on the roadbed, he wrenched his arm out from under the tie, knelt as if in prayer, heaved it onto his aching shoulder, stood up, and pressed on. He tried to count his steps but kept losing track. He had five miles to go. But he had no idea how far he had staggered. He started counting ties. His heart sank. There were almost three thousand ties for every mile of track. After a hundred, he thought he would die. After five hundred, he was almost destroyed by the realization that five hundred ties was no more than a fifth of a mile.

His mind began to scatter. He imagined carrying the tie all the way to Tunnel 13. Through the stone mountain all the way to the Cascade Canyon Bridge.

I'm the "Hero Engineer"!

Giddy-headed laughter dissolved into a sob of pain. He felt himself drifting out of control. He had to shift his thoughts away from the pain and the fear that he could not continue.

He drove his mind toward his early rote training in mathematics and engineering. Structure—the physics that made a bridge stand or fall. Struts. Ties. Foundation piers. Cantilever arms. Anchor arms. Live loads. Dead loads.

The laws of physics ruled how to distribute weight. The laws of physics said he could not carry the crosstie another foot. He drove that madness from his mind and concentrated instead on fencing moves, the light, airy motion of a sword. "Attack," he said aloud. "Beat. Lunge. Parry. Riposte. Feint. Double feint." On he plodded, the weight pounding his bones to jelly. *Attack. Beat. Lunge. Parry.* German intruded. Suddenly, he was mumbling the engineering terms from his student days. Then shouting the language of Heidelberg when he learned to kill. *"Angriff. Battutaangriff. Ausfall, Parade. Doppelfinte."* He imagined someone humming in his ear. Attack: *Angriff.* Beat: *Battutaangriff.* Lunge: *Ausfall.* Parry: *Parade.* Double feint: *Doppelfinte.* Someone he could not see was humming a tuneless ditty. It grew shrill. Now he heard it right behind him. He whirled around, the weight of the crosstie nearly spinning him off his feet. Harsh acetylene light blazed on the tracks. It was a police patrol pumping along on an almost silent handcar.

A sheer rock wall pressed against the right-of-way on his left. To his right, the mountain dropped sharply. He sensed more than saw a steep drop. The feathery tops of small trees piercing the dark indicated it could be as much as twenty feet down. He had no choice. The handcar was almost on top of him. He dropped the tie over the edge and jumped after it.

He heard the tie hit a tree and snap the trunk. Then he smashed into a springy tree, knocking the wind out of him.

The humming dropped in tone. The handcar was slowing down.

To his horror, they stopped. He could hear men talking fifteen feet above his head and saw beams of flashlights and lanterns. They dismounted. He could hear their boots crunching on the ballast as they strode the rail bed, shining their lights. A man shouted. Abruptly as they had appeared, they left. The handcar creaked into motion and hummed away, leaving him fifteen feet down the steep embankment in the dark.

Moving cautiously, hunched over on the slope, digging his boots in, he felt in the dark for the crosstie. He smelled pine pitch and traced the odor to the broken tree. Several feet down, he bumped into the square end of the tie. He felt for his tools. Still tied on. He looked up the slope. The rim of the rail bed towered above him.

How would he climb up it carrying the tie?

He tipped it on one end, worked his shoulder under it, and struggled to stand.

Every mile he had come so far, every escape, meant nothing. This was the real test: to climb back up the embankment. It was only twenty feet, but each foot could have been a mile. The combination of the weight he was carrying and the distance he had come and the steepness of the embankment seemed insurmountable.

As his strength failed, he saw his dreams of wealth and power fading before his eyes. He slipped and fell, then struggled to his feet again. If only he had killed Isaac Bell. He began to realize that he was battling Bell more than the tie, more than the cutoff, more than the Southern Pacific.

The nightmare of Bell stopping him gave him the strength to rise. Inch by inch, foot by foot. Attack: *Angriff.* Beat: *Battutaangriff.* Lunge: *Ausfall.* Parry: *Parade.* Double feint: *Doppelfinte.* Twice he fell. Twice he got up. He reached to the top and staggered on. If he lived to be ninety, he would never forget that gut-wrenching climb.

The pounding of his heart was growing louder and louder, so loud that he eventually realized it couldn't be his heart. A locomotive? He stopped dead in the middle of the tracks, stunned and dismayed. Not another patrol. Thunder? Lightning flickered. He was hearing the rumble of thunder. Cold rain began to fall. He had lost his hat. Rainwater streamed down his face.

The Wrecker laughed.

The rain would drench the patrols, chase them indoors. He laughed deliriously. Rain instead of snow. The rivers were rising, but the tracks would not blocked by snow. Osgood Hennessy must be delighted. So much for the experts predicting an early winter. The railroad president had given up on the meteorologists and had actually paid an Indian medicine man to predict the weather, and he told Hennessy that the snows would come late this year. Rain instead of snow meant more time to complete the cutoff.

The Wrecker steadied the tie on his shoulder, and spoke aloud. *"Never."*

A huge bolt of lightning lit everything stark white.

The tracks curved sharply, clinging to the narrow cut. Below was a dizzying view of a rampaging river at the bottom of a deep canyon. This was the spot. The Wrecker dropped the hemlock tie, loosened the ropes that held his tools, and pried up the spikes on both sides of an existing tie and set them carefully aside. Then he scrabbled at the crushed rock with the spike puller, loosening the sharp stones. He raked them out from under the tie and spread them carefully so they didn't roll down the embankment.

When he had dug the ballast away, he used the puller as a lever to work the tie out from under the rails. Then he shoved his hemlock tie with the dynamite in it into the space and began scooping back the stone ballast, packing it under the tie. Last, he hammered in the eight spikes. With the tie securely under the rails and the ballast carefully spread, he attached the trigger, a nail wedged under the rail into a hole drilled in the tie.

The nail rested in the wood an inch above a fulminate-mercury detonator. He had calculated carefully, driving a hundred nails to measure the force, so that a patrol walking the ties or a handcar rolling on the rails would not press the nail deeply enough to detonate the explosive. Only the full weight of a locomotive could trigger the detonator.

One last brutal task remained. He tied his tools to the crosstie he had removed, tipped it onto his shoulder, and rose on shaking legs. He staggered a quarter mile from the trap he had laid and heaved tie and tools down the cliff where no patrol could see it.

He was reeling with exhaustion, but his heart set with icy resolve.

He had crippled the cutoff with dynamite, collision, and fire.

He had shaken the mighty Southern Pacific by derailing the Coast Line Limited.

So what if Bell had twisted his New York attack to Hennessy's advantage?

The Wrecker raised his face to the storming sky and let the rain cleanse him. Thunder pealed.

"It is mine!" he roared back. "Tonight I earned it."

He would win this final round.

Not one man on the work train would survive to finish Tunnel 13.

·31·

A THOUSAND MEN MILLED ABOUT THE CUTOFF CONSTRUCTION camp at dawn. Twenty cars of wooden benches stood empty behind a locomotive venting excess steam. The men stood in the rain, preferring the cold and wet to shelter on the work train.

"Stubborn bastards!" Hennessy raged, watching from his private car. "Wire the Governor, Lillian. This is insurrection."

Lillian Hennessy placed her fingers on the telegraph key. Before she tapped, she said to Isaac Bell, "Is there nothing else you can do?"

In Bell's opinion, the men bunched in the rain did not look stubborn. They looked afraid. And they looked embarrassed to be afraid, which said a lot for their courage. The Wrecker had erased innocent lives by dynamite, train wreck, collision, and fire. Death and injury had attended attack after attack. Men had died in derailments, the tunnel collapse, the ditched Coast Line Limited, the runaway railcar, and the terrible explosion in New Jersey.

"The patrols have inspected every inch of rail," he answered Lillian. "I don't know what I can do that they haven't done already. Short of riding on the cowcatcher to check it myself . . ."

The detective spun on his heel, strode from Hennessy's car, crossed the rail yard at a rapid pace, and shouldered through the crowd. He climbed the ladder on the back of the work train's tender, nimbly crossed the heaped coal, and jumped on the roof of the locomotive's cab. From the vantage of the pulsing machine, he could see sullen track layers and hard-rock miners spread from one end of the yards to the other. They fell silent. A thousand faces were rising toward the incongruous sight of a man in a white suit standing on the locomotive.

Bell had once heard William Jennings Bryan address a crowd at the Atlanta Exposition. Standing in front near Bryan, he had been struck by how slowly the famous orator spoke. The reason, Bryan told him at a later meeting, was that words bunched up as they moved through the air. When they reached the back of the crowd, they arrived at a normal cadence.

Bell now raised his hands. He brought his voice up from deep within. He spoke slowly, very slowly. But every word was a challenge thrown in their faces.

"I will stand watch."

Bell reached slowly into this coat.

"This locomotive will steam slowly to the railhead."

Slowly, he drew his Browning pistol.

"I will stand on the cowcatcher on the front of this locomotive."

He pointed the pistol at the sky.

"I will fire this pistol to signal the engineer to stop the train the instant I see danger."

He squeezed the trigger. A shot echoed off the roundhouse and shops.

"The engineer will hear this shot."

He fired again.

"He will stop the train."

Bell held the weapon pointed at the sky and continued speaking slowly.

"I will not say that any man unwilling to ride behind me is the lowest coward in the Cascade Mountains."

Another shot echoed.

"But I will say this . . . Any man unwilling to ride should go back to where he came from and live in the care of his *mother*."

Laughter rumbled from one end of the yard to the other. There was a tentative surge of movement toward the train. For a second, he thought he had convinced them. But an angry voice bawled, "You ever work on a track gang?" And another voice: "How the hell will *you* know if something's wrong?" Then a big man with a beefy red face and hot blue eyes clambered up the tender's ladder and stalked across the coal to where Bell stood atop the locomotive's cab. "I'm Malone. Track boss."

"What do you want, Malone?"

"So you're going to stand on the *cowcatcher*, are you? You don't even know enough to call the *engine pilot* by its proper name, and *you're* going to spot what's wrong on the rails before it blows you to kingdom come? Cowcatcher, for the love of God . . . But I'll give you one thing: you got guts."

The foreman thrust a callused hand at Bell.

"Put 'er there! I'll ride with you."

The two men shook hands for all to see. Then Malone raised his voice, which carried like a steamship horn.

"Any man here says Mike Malone won't know trouble when he sees it?"

None did.

"Any of youse wants to live with his mother?"

With a roar of laughter and a thousand cheers, the workmen jumped aboard the train and crowded into the wooden benches.

Bell and Malone climbed down and mounted the wedge-shaped pilot. There was room to stand on either side, hanging into a rail just under the locomotive's headlamp. The engineer, conductor, and fire-man came up front for orders.

"How fast you want to go?" the engineer asked.

"Ask the expert," said Bell.

"Keep her under ten miles a hour," said Malone.

"Ten?" the engineer protested. "It'll take two hours to get to the tunnel."

"You prefer a shortcut over a cliff?"

The train crew trooped back to the cab.

Malone said, "Keep that pistol handy, mister." Then he grinned at Bell. "Just remember, if we hit a mine or jump a loose rail, we'll be the first to experience the consequences."

"The thought had occurred to me," Bell said drily. "But, fact is, I've had every foot of this line scoured for the past two days. Hand-car, on foot, horse patrol."

"We'll see," said Malone, grin fading.

"Would you like these?" asked Bell, offering his Carl Zeiss binoculars.

"No thanks," said Malone. "I've been inspecting track with these eyes for twenty years. Today's not the day to learn something new."

Bell slung the binoculars strap over his head so he could drop the glasses and draw his pistol to fire a warning shot.

"Twenty years? You're the man to tell me, Malone. What should I look for?"

"Missing spikes that hold the rails to the ties. Missing fishplates that join the rails. Breaks in the rails. Signs of digging in the bal-last in case the bastard mined it. The roadbed's newly laid. It should look smooth, no dips, no humps. Look for loose rock on the ties. And whenever we round a bend in the road, look extra hard 'cause the saboteur knows that around the bend is where the engineer will never see it in time to stop."

Bell raised the binoculars to his eyes. He was acutely aware that he had persuaded the thousand men behind him to risk their lives. As Malone had observed, he and Bell, riding in front, would take the brunt of an attack. But only at first. A derailment would tumble them all to their deaths.

THE TRACKS HUGGED THE EDGE OF THE MOUNTAIN ON A NARROW cut. To the left rose sheer rock, scarred by drills and dynamite. To the right was air. The drop-off varied from mere yards to a quarter of a mile. Where canyon floors were visible from the tracks, Bell saw treetops, fallen boulders, and raging rivers swollen by the rain.

He scanned the tracks a hundred feet ahead. His binoculars had modern Porro prisms that intensified the light. He could see the offset spike heads clearly, eight driven into each tie. The chocolate-brown squared timbers flowed under him with numbing regularity.

"How many ties per mile?" he asked Malone.

"Two thousand seven hundred," answered the foreman. "Give or take."

Brown tie after brown tie after brown tie. Eight spikes in each. Each spike securely embedded in the wood. Fishplates holding each joint, half hidden by the bulge of the rail. The ballast, sharp-edged crushed stone, glistened in the rain. Bell watched for dips in the smooth surface. He watched for loose stone. He watched for loose bolts, missing spikes, breaks in the gleaming rails.

"*Stop!*" shouted Malone.

Bell triggered his Browning. The sharp crack of the gunshot resounded off the rock wall and echoed across the canyons. But the engine kept rolling.

"*Fire!*" Malone shouted. "*Again!*"

Bell was already squeezing the trigger. The drop was steep along this bend in the road, the canyon floor below littered with boulders. As Bell's second shot rang out, the brake shoes struck with a bang and a hiss, and the locomotive slid to a halt on screeching wheels. Bell hit the ground running. Malone was right behind him.

"There!" said Malone.

Twenty feet ahead of the train, they stopped and stared at an almost imperceptible bulge in the ballast. Whereas the freshly laid crushed stone presented a smooth, flat incline from the ties to the edge of the cliff, here was a gentle bump that rose a few inches higher.

"Don't get too close!" Malone warned. "Looks like they've been digging here. See how it didn't settle like the original?"

Bell walked straight to the bulge and stepped onto it.

"Look out!"

"The Wrecker," said Bell, "would make absolutely certain that nothing less than the weight of a locomotive would detonate a mine."

"You seem mighty sure of that."

"I am," said Bell. "He's too smart to waste his powder on a handcar."

He knelt down on a tie and looked closely. He passed his hand over the crushed stone.

"But what I don't see are any signs of recent digging. These stones have been sitting awhile. See the coal dust undisturbed?"

Malone stepped closer reluctantly. Then he knelt beside Bell, scratching his head. He ran his fingers over the coal dust crusting in the rain. He picked up some chunks of ballast and examined them. Abruptly, he rose.

"Shoddy work, not explosives," he said. "I know exactly who

was in charge of laying this section and he is going to hear from me. Sorry, Mr. Bell. False alarm."

"Better safe than sorry."

By then, the train crew had disembarked. Behind them, fifty workmen gawked, and others were piling off the cars.

"Everyone back on the train!" Malone roared.

Bell took the engineer aside.

"Why didn't you stop?"

"You caught me by surprise. Took me a moment to act."

"Stay alert!" Bell retorted coldly. "You've got men's lives in your hands."

They got everyone back on the train and rolling again.

The ties slid by. Squared timber after squared timber. Eight spikes, four on each rail. Fishplates securing the rails. Sharp-edged crushed ballast glistened in the wet. Bell watched for more bumps in the flat surface, disturbed stone, missing bolts, absent spikes, cracks in the rails. Tie after tie after tie.

For seventeen miles, the train trundled slowly. Bell began to hope against hope that his precautions had paid off. The patrols and constant inspections had ensured the line was safe. Only three miles to go and then the men could return to work, boring the vital Tunnel 13.

Suddenly, as they rounded a sharp curve that rimmed the deepest canyon on the route, something unusual caught Bell's eye. He couldn't pinpoint what it was at first. For an instant, it barely penetrated.

"Malone!" he said in a whipcrack voice, "Look! What's wrong?"

The red-faced man beside him leaned forward, squinted, his face a mask of concentration.

"I don't see nothing."

Bell raked the tracks with his binoculars. Bracing his feet on the pilot, he held the glasses with one hand and drew his pistol with the other.

The ballast was smooth. No spikes were missing. The ties . . .

In seventeen miles, the work train had crossed fifty thousand ties. Each of the fifty thousand was a chocolate-brown color, the wood darkened by preservatives absorbed in creosoting. Now, only a few yards ahead of the locomotive, Bell saw a wooden tie that was colored yellowish white—the shade of freshly milled mountain hemlock that had not been creosoted.

Bell fired his pistol again and again as fast as he could pull the trigger.

"*Stop!*"

The engineer slammed on the brakes. Wheels locked. Steel screeched on steel. The heavy locomotive slid along on the massive force of its momentum. The weight of twenty cars shoved behind it.

Bell and Malone leaped off the pilot and ran ahead of the skidding locomotive.

"What is it?" the track foreman shouted.

"That tie," Bell pointed.

"God Almighty!" roared Malone.

The two men turned as one and raised powerful arms as if to stop the train with their bare hands.

33

THE ENGINEER THREW HIS JOHNSON BAR INTO REVERSE.

Eight ponderous drive wheels spun backward, showering sparks and slivers from the rails. For a moment, it looked as if two strong men were actually stopping a Consolidation locomotive. And when it did grind to a stop with a ground-shaking shudder, Isaac Bell looked down and saw his boots planted firmly on the suspect crosstie.

The tip of the pilot was hanging over it. The leading wheels of the engine truck had come within two yards of it.

"Back her up," ordered Malone. "Softly!"

GENTLY SCRAPING AWAY THE ballast from either end, Bell discovered upon close inspection that the suspect tie had a round wooden plug like a whiskey barrel bung. It was the diameter of a silver dollar and almost indistinguishable from the timber's end grain.

"Move everyone farther back," he told Malone. "He packed the tie with dynamite."

The triggering device was a nail positioned to set off a detonator. There was enough dynamite to blow rails out from under the locomotive, which would have tumbled off the cut and dragged the whole train down the side of the mountain. Instead, Bell was able to wire back to Osgood Hennessy that the Van Dorn Detective Agency had won another victory over the Wrecker.

Hennessy moved his special train to the head of the line, where the miners and trackmen who had arrived safely were hard at work boring through the last hundred feet of Tunnel 13.

EARLY NEXT MORNING, OSGOOD HENNESSY called Bell onto his private car. Lillian and Mrs. Comden offered coffee. Hennessy was grinning ear to ear. "We're about to hole through. We always do a ceremony on the long tunnels where I clear the last stone. This time, the hands sent a delegation demanding that you take the last poke for what you did yesterday. It's a big honor, I'd accept it if I were you."

Bell walked into the tunnel with Hennessy, hugging the wall when they had to step off the tracks to let a locomotive pass with debris-filled dump cars. For hundreds of yards, the sides and arched ceiling were already finished with masonry shoring. Near the end, a temporary web of timbers shored up the ceiling. In the final yards, the miners worked under a shield of cast iron and timber that protected them from falling rock.

The chattering drills stopped as Bell and the railroad president approached. Miners cleared the crumbling stone with sledges and shovels, then stepped back from the wall that remained.

A towering hard-rock miner with long apish arms and a gap-toothed grin handed Bell a sixteen-pound sledgehammer.

"Ever swing one of these before?"

"Driving tent pegs for the circus."

"You'll do fine." The miner leaned in and whispered, "See that chalk mark? Smack her there. We always set it to come down for the ceremony . . . Gangway, boys! Give the man room."

"Are you sure you don't want to do this?" Bell asked Hennessy.

Hennessy stepped back. "I've dug plenty of tunnels in my day. You earned this one."

Bell whipped the heavy sledge over his shoulder and swung hard at the chalk mark. Cracks spread, and a gleam of light showed in the wall. He swung again. The miners cheered as the rock collapsed and daylight poured in.

Bell stepped into the jagged opening and saw the Cascade Canyon Bridge glittering in the sunlight. The long, layered latticework of steel spanned the deep gorge of the Cascade River on two tall, slim towers set on massive stone piers. Floating high above the watery mists and foam, the most important bridge on the cutoff line looked almost complete. Crossties were already laid on it in anticipation of steel rails arriving through the tunnel.

Bell saw that it was heavily guarded. Railroad police stood every fifty feet. A sentry house stood at either end and one at each pier. As Bell watched, a cloud passed over the sun, and the shadow turned the silvery girders black.

"What do you think, son?" Hennessy asked proudly.

"She's a beauty."

How would the Wrecker strike?

In the shadow of the bridge nestled the town of Cascade, established where the original lowland railroad from the desert terminated at the foot of the mountains. He could see the elegant 1870s Cascade Lodge, long a draw for intrepid tourists willing to brave the long, slow climb on endless switchbacks up the foothills. From that railhead, Hennessy had built a temporary freight line with even more switchbacks to lift materials to the bridge construction site. Almost impossibly steep, it was a jagged series of sharp climbs and hairpin turns that had been nicknamed by the railroad workers the Snake Line. The grade was so heavy that a string of freight cars Bell saw ascending were pulled by three smoke-billowing locomotives, with four pusher engines helping from behind. The Snake Line locomotives had done their job. From now on, materials would arrive on the cutoff line.

The Wrecker wouldn't hit the Snake Line, its job was done. He wouldn't hit the town. He would hit the bridge itself. Destroying the long truss-and-pier bridge would set back the cutoff project by years.

"What the deuce is that?" asked Hennessy. He pointed at a column of dust racing up a switchback buggy road from the town below.

Isaac Bell's face opened in a broad grin of appreciation. "*That* is the Thomas Flyer automobile you and I were talking about. Model 35, four cylinders, sixty horsepower. Look at him go!"

The bright yellow motor car topped the switchback, bounced over the rocky shelf, and skidded to a halt twenty feet away from where Bell and Hennessy stood in the mouth of the tunnel. The canvas top was down and folded back, and the only one in it was the driver, a tall man clad in boot-length duster, hat, and goggles. He jumped from behind the wooden steering wheel and strode toward them.

"Congratulations!" he called, whipping off his goggles with a dramatic flourish.

"What the hell are you doing here?" asked Hennessy. "Isn't Congress in session?"

"Celebrating your cutoff hole through," said Charles Kincaid. "I happened to be meeting with some very important California gentlemen at the Cascade Lodge. I told my hosts they would have to wait while I drove up to shake your hand."

Kincaid seized Hennessy's hand and pumped it heartily.

"Congratulations, sir. Magnificent achievement. Nothing can stop you now."

THE BRIDGE

Bell Saves the Cascade Bridge

34

RED-FACED, FIERY-EYED SOUTHERN PACIFIC TRACK BOSS MIKE Malone stalked from the mouth of Tunnel 13 trailed by handlers gripping heavy lengths of rail in their tongs and a locomotive behind them belching smoke and steam. "Somebody move that automobile before it gets squashed," he bawled.

Charles Kincaid ran to rescue his Thomas Flyer.

Isaac Bell asked Osgood Hennessy, "Are you surprised to find the Senator waiting here?"

"I'm never surprised by men hoping for my daughter's inheritance," Hennessy answered over the clatter of Malone's track gangs spreading roadbed stone ballast in front of the engine and laying down crossties.

Senator Kincaid came running back.

"Mr. Hennessy, the most important businessmen and bankers of California wish to throw a banquet for you in the Cascade Lodge."

"I've got no time for banquets before I lay track across that bridge and build my staging yards on the other side."

"Can't you come down after dark?"

Mike Malone barreled up.

"Senator, if it wouldn't be too much trouble would you please move that goddamned automobile before I have my boys throw it off the cliff?"

"I just moved it."

"It's still in our way."

"Move it," growled Hennessy. "We're building a railroad here."

Bell watched Kincaid hurry off to move his car again, and said to Hennessy, "I'd like to see what they're up to at that banquet."

"What the hell for?"

"It is a strange coincidence that Kincaid is here today."

"I told you, he's hanging around my daughter."

"The Wrecker has inside knowledge of the Southern Pacific. How does he know about your plans?"

"I told you that too. Some busybody put two and two together. Or some fool blabbed."

"Either way, the Wrecker is no stranger to your circle."

"All right," said Hennessy. "I can stand a banquet if you can." He raised his voice over the din to shout. "Kincaid! Tell your friends if the invitation still holds in three days, I'll take it."

The Senator professed astonishment. "Surely you won't be across and set up in only three days."

"Heads will roll if I'm not."

The shrunken old man snapped his fingers. Engineers rushed to his side, unfurling blueprints. Surveyors were right behind, propping transits on their shoulders, trailed by chainmen with red-and-white ranging rods.

Isaac Bell intercepted Kincaid as he climbed into his car.

"Funny coincidence that your meeting is here, of all places."

"Not at all. I want Hennessy on my side. As the California gentlemen were willing to rent an entire lodge to persuade me to run for president, I figured it might as well be one near him."

"Still playing hard to get?" asked Bell, recalling their conversation at the *Follies*.

"Harder than ever. The moment you say yes to their sort, they think they own you."

"Do you want the job?"

In answer, Charles Kincaid slipped a big hand under the lapel of his coat and flipped it over. A campaign button that had been hidden by the cloth read KINCAID FOR PRESIDENT.

"Mum's the word."

"When will you turn your button out?"

"I'm planing to surprise Mr. Hennessy at his banquet. They want you to come too, seeing as how you're the man who saved the line from the Wrecker."

None of this rang true to the detective.

"I'm looking forward to it," Bell said.

The Wrecker pretended not to notice Bell's probing gaze. He knew his presidential ruse would not fool the Van Dorn detective much longer. But he stood his ground, allowing his eyes to rove curiously over the gleaming bridge as if he hadn't a care in the world.

"That broad plateau on the far side of the gorge," he remarked casually, "seems the likely spot for Hennessy to build his head-of-the-line staging yards." There were times, he thought proudly, he really should have been an actor.

"Do you regret leaving engineering?" Bell asked.

"I would if I didn't enjoy politics so much." Kincaid laughed. He let his smile fade as he pretended to reflect soberly. "I might feel differently if I had been as brilliant an engineer as Mr. Mowery who built this bridge. Look at that structure! The grace, the strength. He was a star. Still is, despite his years. I was never more than a capable journeyman."

Bell was staring.

Kincaid smiled. "You're looking at me strangely. That's because you're still a young man, Mr. Bell. Wait until forty overtakes you. You'll learn your limitations and find other lines at which you might do better."

"Such as running for president?" Bell asked lightly.

"Exactly!"

Kincaid laughed, slapped the detective's rock-hard arm, and vaulted into his Thomas Flyer. He engaged the motor, which he had left running, and started down the mountain without looking back. Any hint that he was concerned would only fuel the detective's imagination.

In fact, he was exultant.

Osgood Hennessy was charging forward at full steam, obliviously putting his head in a noose. The faster the cutoff crossed the bridge, the sooner Osgood would hang. For if new staging yards at the front end of the construction represented Hennessy's head and his torso was the Southern Pacific Railroad empire, then the Cascade Canyon Bridge was his neck.

35

Isaac Bell planted men in every work gang to watch for sabotage.

Hennessy had told him that holing through was just the beginning. He intended to build as far across the bridge as he could before the first snow. Even the most cowardly Wall Street banker, the railroader boasted, would be assured by the proof that the Southern Pacific was primed to continue cutoff construction when it melted in the spring.

Bell directed horse patrols to guard the route that the railroad was surveying deep into the mountains. Then he asked Jethro Watt to take personal command of his railroad police. They walked the bridge and agreed to beef up the contingents guarding the piers below and the span above. Then they inspected the surrounding area on horseback, the giant Watt mounted on an enormous animal named Thunderbolt who kept trying to gnaw the police chief's leg. Watt subdued the animal by swatting its head, but any judge of horseflesh knew that Thunderbolt was merely biding his time.

By nightfall that first day of frenzied activity, carpenters had erected temporary shoring in Tunnel 13 and a timber rock shed around its freshly hewn portal. Masons were following close behind with stonework. And track gangs had laid rail from the tunnel to the edge of the gorge.

Osgood Hennessy's red train streamed through the tunnel, pushing a string of heavily laden materials cars ahead of it and up to the closely guarded bridge. Track gangs unloaded rails and work continued by electric light. Ties supplied by a timber operation upstream in the mountains were already laid on the bridge. Spike mauls rang through the night. When the rails were secured, Hennessy's locomotive pushed the heavy materials cars onto the span.

A thousand railroaders held their breath.

The only sounds were mechanical, the chuff of the locomotive, the dynamo powering the lights, and the grinding of cast iron on steel. As the lead car, heaped with rails, edged forward, all eyes shifted to Franklin Mowery. The elderly bridge builder was watching closely.

Isaac Bell overheard Eric, Mowery's bespectacled assistant, boast, "Mr. Mowery was the same cool as a cucumber when he finished Mr. Hennessy's Lucin Cutoff across the Great Salt Lake."

"But," said a grizzled surveyor, peering into the deep gorge, "that one was a lot nearer the water."

Mowery leaned nonchalantly on his walking stick. No emotion showed on his round face, no worry rippled his sweeping jawline, or twitched his Vandyke beard. He had a cold, smokeless pipe firmly clamped in his broad, good-humored mouth.

Bell watched Mowery's pipe. When the materials car reached the far side without mishap and the workmen greeted it with a cheer, Mowery removed his pipe from his mouth and picked splinters of crushed stem from his teeth.

"Caught me," he grinned at Bell. "Bridges are strange critters, highly unpredictable."

They double-tracked the bridge by noon.

In a long burst of action, they laid dozens of sidings. Soon, the remote plateau had been transformed into a combination railroad yard and construction staging arena. Hennessy's red special steamed across the gorge and parked on an elevated sidetrack from which the president of the Southern Pacific could oversee the entire operation. A steady stream of materials trains began crossing the bridge. Telegraph wires followed, transmitting the good news back to Wall Street.

Hennessy's telegrapher handed Bell a wad of encoded messages.

No telegraph operator on the continent had been more closely scrutinized than J. J. Meadows had been by the Van Dorn Agency. "Honest as the day is long and beholden to no man," was the verdict. But with the memory still fresh of the Wrecker's renegade telegraphers shooting it out with Texas Walt Hatfield, Bell was taking no chances. All his Van Dorn correspondence was encrypted. He locked the door to his private stateroom, two cars back on the special, and decoded them.

These were the first results of the background reports Bell had ordered to ferret out the spy in the railroad president's inner circle. Nothing in the record of the Southern Pacific's head engineer suggested he was less than respectable. He was loyal to the Southern Pacific, loyal to Osgood Hennessy, and loyal to the high standards of his profession.

The same was said for Franklin Mowery. The bridge builder's life was an open book studded with professional accomplishment. His many charitable deeds included serving as a director of a Methodist orphanage.

Lillian Hennessy had been arrested a surprising number of times for such a young and privileged woman, but only while demonstrating for the right to vote. The charges had always been dismissed. Testament, Bell assumed, to overzealous policing or the power of a doting father who happened to be president of the nation's biggest railroad.

Of the two bankers Hennessy had named who might have deduced his plans, one had been convicted of fraud, the other named as a correspondent in a divorce. One of the attorneys had been disbarred in Illinois, another had amassed a fortune in railroad stock by buying with foreknowledge of the railroads' intentions. On closer examination, the Van Dorn investigators reported, both bankers had transgressed in their youth, while the disbarred attorney had subsequently been readmitted. But the holder of the fortune, Erastus Charney, drew Bell's interest, as he was clearly a man who traded on the power of knowing ahead of time which way the wind blew. Bell wired to dig deep into Charney's affairs.

Bell was not surprised that the lively Mrs. Comden had lived a colorful life even before she became consort to the railroad magnate. A child piano prodigy, she'd made her concert debut with the New York Philharmonic at age fourteen, performing Chopin's Concerto for Piano and Orchestra No. 2 in F Minor—"a bear to play at any age," noted the Van Dorn operative. She had toured the United States and Europe, where she stayed to study in Leipzig. She had married a wealthy physician connected at the German court, who'd then divorced her when she ran off with a highborn officer of the First Guards Cavalry Brigade. They had lived together in Berlin until the officer's scandalized family intervened. Emma then married a struggling portrait painter named Comden, only to be widowed within the year. Penniless, her concert-playing days behind her, the Widow Comden had landed in New York, drifted to New Orleans and San Francisco, and answered a newspaper ad to tutor Lillian Hennessy. Her nomadic ways continued on the luxurious special employed by the ever-moving Hennessy. On the rare occasions that the irascible Osgood appeared socially, the lovely Mrs. Comden was at his side. And woe, noted the Van Dorn operative, to the fortunes of the politician, banker, or industrialist whose wife dared snub her.

Charles Kincaid's life had been far less colorful than Preston

Whiteway's newspapers led readers to believe. He had studied engineering briefly at West Point, switched to civil engineering at the University of West Virginia, done postgraduate work in civil engineering at the Technische Hochschule of Munich, and hired on with a German firm building the Baghdad Railway. The facts behind his "Hero Engineer" moniker were questionable. That Turkish revolutionaries had frightened American nurses and missionaries tending to Armenian refugees was likely. The Whiteway newspaper accounts of Kincaid's role in their rescue were, the Van Dorn operative noted acerbically, "less so."

Bell fired back two more queries: "Why did Kincaid leave West Point?" and "Who is Eric Soares?"

Franklin Mowery's assistant was always at his side. Whatever special knowledge of Hennessy's affairs that the bridge builder knew, young Eric would know, too.

Speaking of young assistants, what was taking James Dashwood so long to catch up with the blacksmith who had fashioned the hook that derailed the Coast Line Special? Isaac Bell reread Dashwood's meticulously detailed reports. Then he wired the apprentice care of the Los Angeles office.

BLACKSMITH STOPPED DRINKING.

INQUIRE TEMPERANCE MEETINGS.

ISAAC BELL RECEIVED A report from the Kansas City office that Eric Soares was an orphan whom Franklin Mowery had sponsored through Cornell University and had taken on as his assistant. Soares was by some accounts a talented engineer, by others an upstart riding the coattails of a famously generous man.

Bell reflected upon the fact that Mowery did not have the physical stamina or agility to do fieldwork without help. Eric would perform duties that required physical activity, such as inspecting work done on the bridge. He telegraphed Kansas City to keep digging.

"Private wire, Mr. Bell."

"Thank you, Mr. Meadows."

Bell took the telegram to his stateroom, hoping it was from Marion. It was, and he exclaimed with pleasure when he read:

DO NOT—REPEAT NOT—WISH TO JOIN PRESTON
WHITEWAY CASCADE LODGE FOR PICTURE WORLD
NEWSREELS. BUT ARE YOU STILL THERE? IF SO, WHAT
DO YOU WISH?

Bell called on Lillian Hennessy. His schemes to extricate himself from the girl's infatuation and rescue Archie Abbott from his mother seemed to be working. Since his return from New York, most of their conversations veered toward the subject of Abbott, and she tended now to treat Bell as an adored big brother or older cousin. After they spoke, he wired Marion back.

COME! BE HENNESSY'S GUEST ABOARD SPECIAL.

While Bell pursued his investigation, and kept honing his efforts to protect the Cascade Canyon Bridge, the railroad forged ahead. Two days after the cutoff had crossed the canyon, the staging area on the far plateau had room and track to accommodate the endless strings of freight cars arriving with steel rail, spikes, ballast, and coal. A creosoting plant arrived in parts. It was assembled alongside the stockpiled crossties and was soon belching noxious black smoke as raw wood entered one end and floated out the other steeped in preservative.

Wagons that had delivered the ties down twisted mountain trails from the remote East Oregon Lumber Company now carried planks and beams. An entire trainload of carpenters hammered together tin-roofed roundhouses for the locomotives, powerhouses to shelter dynamos for electricity, blacksmith shops, kitchens, bunkhouses for the track gangs, stables for the mules and horses.

Holed through the last tunnel, connected to the bridge and linked by it to strategically positioned staging yards, Hennessy could now bring in men and material directly from California. The task of guarding the four-hundred-mile route as well as the bridge fell to Van Dorn detectives and Southern Pacific railway police. Isaac Bell urged Joseph Van Dorn to borrow U.S. Army troops to assist their thinly spread force.

EIGHT MILES UPSTREAM FROM the Cascade Canyon Bridge, the East Oregon Lumber Company's forest rang from dawn to dark with the incessant bite of double-bladed axes. Modern high-lead winches snaked logs from the steepest slopes. "Steam donkeys," powerful stationary steam engines, turned drums of wire rope that hauled logs to the mill on a corduroy skid road. Tie after tie was sawn and squared and sent down the terrible roads by wagon. When work stopped at night, the exhausted lumberjacks could hear the distant moan of locomotive whistles, a reminder even as they slept that the railroad craved more timber.

The miles between the bridge and the camp felt more like eighty than eight to the teamsters who delivered lumber to the cutoff staging yard. So rugged were the mountain roads that Gene Garret, the ambitious, greedy manager of the sawmill, was grateful for the Panic that had brought hard times. If the economy had been booming, the mill would be short of hands. The mule skinners would seek jobs elsewhere rather than climb the mountains for another load. And the lumberjacks who had shot the rapids down the river in dugout canoes to celebrate payday Saturday nights would not walk eight miles back to work on Sunday.

An enormous artificial lake was filling beside the remote lumber camp. Muddy water crept daily up the sides of a natural bowl that was formed where three mountain slopes converged at the Cascade River. The fourth side was a rough dam built of tumbled stones and logs. It towered fifty feet above the original masonry constructed years before for a millrace to power the saws. Now power came from the steam donkeys that the new owners of East Oregon Lumber had delivered in pieces by oxcart. The original millpond had vanished under the ever-deepening lake. The mule barns and the bunk- and cookhouses had been moved twice to escape the rising water.

The Wrecker was proud of that dam.

He had designed it on the principle of a beaver dam, which controlled water flow without stopping it entirely. His design employed giant tree trunks instead of sticks, man-size boulders instead of mud. The trick was to impound enough of the river flow to fill the lake while letting sufficient through so that downstream it appeared normal. If the river seemed a little lower than usual for late autumn as it tumbled through the town of Cascade, few residents took notice. And because the Cascade Canyon Bridge was newly built, there were no ancient high-water marks to compare to the river rushing by the stone piers.

Manager Garret would never question the purpose of the lake nor the enormous investment in an operation too remote to deliver enough timber to earn it back. The Wrecker's shell corporation, which had secretly purchased the timber operation, paid the sawmill manager a fat bonus for every board and crosstie delivered to the railroad. All Garret cared about was squeezing as much work as humanly possible out of his lumberjacks before winter snows shut them down.

The lake kept rising as autumn rains swelled the countless streams and creeks that fed the river. With bitter humor, the Wrecker named it Lake Lillian for the headstrong girl who spurned him. He calculated that more than a million tons of water filled the deep gorge already. Lake Lillian was a million-ton insurance policy in case the flaws he had built into the Cascade Canyon Bridge didn't cause it to collapse on its own.

He turned his horse and rode up the trail for a mile to a log cabin nestled in a clearing by a spring. Firewood was stacked nearby beneath a canvas lean-to. Smoke rose from a mud-and-stick chimney. A single window overlooked the road. Rifle slits on all four sides of the cabin commanded a 360-degree field of fire.

Philip Dow stepped out the door. He was a compact, self-possessed man in his forties, clean-shaven, with a thick head of curly black hair. Originally from Chicago, he was dressed incongruously for his cabin in a dark suit and derby.

His sharp eyes and impassive face could belong to a veteran cop, or an Army sniper, or an assassin. He was the latter, with a ten-thousand-dollar dead-or-alive reward on his head posted by the Mine Owners' Association. Through sixteen years of bitter Coeur d'Alene strikes, Philip Dow had murdered, in his own words, "plutocrats, aristocrats, and all the other rats."

A cool head, a talent for leadership, and a rigid code of personal honor that set loyalty above all made Dow a rare exception to Charles Kincaid's rule that no accomplice survived who had seen his face much less knew his true identity. Kincaid had offered shelter when the murder of Governor Steunenberg had made the northern Idaho panhandle too hot for Dow to stick around. The deadly master of sap, knife, gun, and explosive was safe in his cabin in the Wrecker's lumber camp, touchingly grateful and absolutely loyal.

"Isaac Bell is coming down to the lodge for the banquet tonight. I've worked up a scheme for an ambush."

"Van Dorn dicks don't kill easy," Dow replied. It was a statement of fact, not a complaint.

"Are any of your boys up to pulling it off?"

Dow's "boys" were a bunch of hard-bitten lumberjacks he had

whipped into a powerful gang. Many were on the run from the law, hence the appeal of East Oregon Lumber's remote site. Most would rather commit murder for money than break their backs cutting timber. Charles Kincaid never dealt with them directly—none knew his connection—but, under Dow's command, they extended the Wrecker's reach, whether to set up an attack on the railroad or terrorize his paid but at times tentative accomplices. He had dispatched a pair to kill the Santa Monica blacksmith who had seen his face. But the blacksmith had disappeared and the lumberjacks fled. Thinly treed, sun-drenched southern California was not safe for brawny, handlebar-mustachioed, wool-clad woodsmen with prices on their heads.

"I'll do it myself," Dow said.

"His woman is coming," the Wrecker told him. "In theory, he'll be distracted. That should make it easier for them to catch Bell off balance."

"I'll still do it myself, Senator. It's the least I can do you."

"I appreciate your kindness, Philip," said Kincaid, aware that Dow's code required a certain archaic formality of expression.

"What does Bell look like? I've heard about him but never set eyes on him."

"Isaac Bell is about my height . . . Actually, a hair taller. A build like mine, though perhaps a little leaner. Stern face, like you've seen on lawmen. Yellow hair and mustache. And, of course, he'll be wearing fancy clothes for the banquet. Here, I'll show you the scheme. The woman is staying on Hennessy's train. The time to do it is late, after they come back from the banquet. Hennessy has trouble sleeping. He always invites his guests for a nightcap . . ."

They went into the cabin, which Dow kept spotless. On the oilcloth-covered table, the Wrecker spread a chart that depicted the layout of Hennessy's special.

"Working back from the locomotive and tender, N1 is Hennessy's own car, as is N2. Next is the baggage car, with a passage through it. The stateroom cars, Car 3 and Car 4, are behind it, then the diner, Pullman sleepers, lounge. The baggage car is the divider. No one goes forward of it without an invitation. Bell's fiancee will be in Car 4, Stateroom 4, the rearmost. Bell is in Car 4, Stateroom 1. She will go to bed first. He will linger for appearances."

"Why?"

"They're not married yet."

Philip Dow looked baffled.

"Am I missing something here?"

"Same as a weekend in the country except it's a train," Kincaid explained. "An agreeable host arranges bedrooms to serve the guests' liaisons so no one has to tiptoe too far down the hall. Everyone knows, of course, but it's not 'public knowledge,' if you understand my meaning."

Dow shrugged as if to say it was more important to kill aristocrats than understand them.

"Bell will enter Car 4 from the head end, walking back from Hennessy's parlor. He will pass to the rear and knock on her door. As she opens it to let him enter, you will emerge from this alcove—the porter's station. I recommend your sap since it is quiet, but, of course, I leave such details to you."

Philip Dow traced the route with a manicured finger, thinking it through. To the extent that he could feel affection for anyone, he liked the Senator. He would never forget that the man had gone to bat for him when anybody else would have turned him in for the reward. Plus, Kincaid knew how things worked. It was a pretty good scheme, clean and simple. Although the woman could be trouble. With the hangman waiting for him in Idaho, he could not afford to get caught. He would have to kill her too before she screamed.

The sap made sense. Guns, of course, were noisy, while the slightest mistake with a knife could set off loud howling. Besides, from what he could remember of his bloody lifelong rampage, he had killed more enemies with a sap than guns, knives, and explosives combined. The concentrated weight of loosely bagged lead shot shaped itself to a man's temple so tightly that it usually shattered bone and always blew out brains.

"Let me ask you something, Senator."

"What?"

"You're out to destroy Osgood Hennessy, aren't you?"

Kincaid looked away so that Dow could not see in Kincaid's eyes that Dow was only an instant from having his skull smashed in with the poker on the hearth.

"Why do you ask?" Kincaid asked.

"I could kill him for you."

"Oh." Kincaid smiled. Dow was only trying to help. "Thank you, Philip. But I prefer to keep him alive."

"Revenge," Dow nodded. "You want him to know what you're doing to him."

"Correct," the Wrecker lied. Revenge was for fools. Even for a thousand insults, revenge was not worth the trouble. Osgood Hennessy's untimely death would throw all his plans into a cocked hat. Lillian, heir to his fortune, was only twenty. Hennessy's bankers would bribe a probate judge to appoint a guardian to protect their interests. J. P. Morgan himself would seize that opportunity to control the Southern Pacific by making Lillian Hennessy his ward. None of this would serve Charles Kincaid's scheme to be first among the "favored few."

Philip Dow had turned his attention back to the chart. He foresaw another problem. "What if the porter is in his station?"

"He's not likely to be at that hour. If he is, how you deal with him is up to you."

Philip Dow shook his head. "I don't kill workingmen. Unless I have no choice."

The Wrecker looked at him, inquiringly. "He's only a porter. It's not like he's white."

Dow stood back, expression darkening, eyes hard as anthracite. "The worst job on the train is the best job their people can get. Everyone is the Pullman porter's boss. That makes him workingman enough for me."

The Wrecker had never met a unionist who welcomed blacks to the labor movement. He hurried to assuage the angry assassin. "Here, take this."

He gave Dow a six-pointed sterling silver star.

"If in your judgment, Philip, you would be safe merely ordering the porter off the train, show him this."

Dow hefted the badge in his hand and read the inscription.

"Captain of the Southern Pacific Railway police?" He smiled, clearly relieved that he would not have to kill the porter. "The poor porter won't stop running until he hits Sacramento."

Marion Morgan arrived from San Francisco with only an hour to spare before Preston Whiteway's banquet for Osgood Hennessy. Lillian Hennessy welcomed her aboard the special and took her to her stateroom in Car 4. She offered to stay to help Marion with her gown, but it was soon apparent to Isaac Bell's fiancée that the beautiful young heiress's main purpose was to ask questions about Archie Abbott.

Isaac Bell had already ridden down to the town to inspect the guardhouses protecting the piers of the Cascade Canyon Bridge. He spoke sternly to the guard captain, reminding him for the third time that sentries should change position at irregular intervals so that an attacker could never predict what he was going to run up against. Satisfied for the moment, he hurried to the Cascade Lodge.

It was a vast log-and-timber building decorated with stuffed game, Navaho rugs, rustic furniture that was more comfortable than it looked, and gas lamps with Louis Comfort Tiffany shades. A band was warming up with "There'll Be a Hot Time in the Old Town Tonight" as he removed the linen duster he had worn over a midnight-blue single-breasted tuxedo. Moments later, Osgood Hennessy arrived with Mrs. Comden, Lillian, Franklin Mowery, and Marion.

Isaac thought Marion looked stunning in her low-cut red gown. If he had never seen her before in his life, he would have walked right up to her and asked her to marry him. Her green eyes sparkled. She had her blond hair swept high on her head and her decolletage artfully screened by the ruby necklace he had given her for her birthday. She had removed the bandage that had covered the cut on her cheek from the flying glass. A touch of rouge made it invisible to any eye but his.

"Welcome to Cascade Canyon, Miss Morgan," he smiled, greeting her formally since there were too many people around to sweep her into his arms. "I have never seen you more beautiful."

"I am so happy to see you," she said, smiling back.

Preston Whiteway, trailed closely by waiters bearing champagne and looking flushed like he'd had a few already, bustled up to greet them. "Hello, Marion." He smoothed his blond waves. "You look great . . . Oh, hello there, Bell. How's that Locomobile running?"

"Like a top."

"If you ever want to sell—"

"I don't."

"Well, enjoy your dinner. Marion, I've seated you between me and Senator Kincaid. We'll have a lot of business to talk about."

Osgood Hennessy muttered, "I'll deal with this," went directly to the head table, and coolly switched all the place cards.

"Father," Lillian protested. "It is uncouth to change place cards."

"If they want to honor me, they can start by seating me between the two best-looking women in the room who aren't my daughter. I've put you by Kincaid, Lillian. It's dark work, but someone has to do it. Bell, I moved you between Whiteway and Miss Morgan so he'll stop staring down her dress. O.K., let's eat!"

NO SOONER HAD PHILIP DOW set foot in the enormous Cascade Canyon yards than a railway cop stopped him. "Where you going, mister?"

Dow turned cold eyes on the cinder dick and flashed the sterling silver star.

The cinder dick practically fell over himself backing away.

"Sorry, Captain. I forgot I'd seen you before."

"Better safe than sorry," said Dow, doubly glad to have the badge. Any cop who'd seen him before had a sharp memory for wanted posters.

"Anything I can do to help, Captain?"

"Yeah. Keep it under your hat 'til morning. What's your name, Officer?"

"McKinney, sir. Darren McKinney."

"You'll be on the right side of my report, McKinney. I barely put my foot on the property before you spotted me. Good work."

"Thank you, Captain."

"Continue your rounds."

"Yes, sir."

Sauntering briskly, relying on his suit and derby to look like an official who belonged among the tank engines shuttling strings of gondolas, Dow crossed track after track. At the head end, Osgood Hennessy's special glowed gold and red just beyond the harsh glare of the bridge lights. The president of the railroad's special was parked on a raised siding with a view of the entire yards.

BELL DANCED WITH MARION between courses.

"When are you going to let me teach you that slow Boston Waltz?"

"Not when they're playing 'There'll Be a Hot Time in the Old Town Tonight.'"

As Preston Whiteway wandered over to cut in, a sharp glance from the Van Dorn detective changed his mind and he returned to the floor with Mrs. Comden.

Dessert was Baked Alaska, a cake-and-ice-cream concoction wrapped in meringue. Guests who had never been east of the Mississippi swore it was the equal of any served in New York City's famous Delmonico's Restaurant.

New York City reminded Lillian Hennessy of Archie Abbott.

"That's quite a smile you're wearing," Charles Kincaid said, interrupting her thoughts.

"I was anticipating your speech," she snapped.

Bell overheard and gave her a private grin.

Lillian noticed that Isaac had been unusually quiet and serious despite the company of his beautiful fiancée. Nearly as quiet as the anxious-looking Franklin Mowery. Something was really worrying him. She reached past Kincaid to give the poor old man a pat on his hand. He nodded distractedly. Then Preston Whiteway tapped a spoon on a glass and the double row of plump red faces rimming the long table turned in anticipation.

"Gentlemen. And ladies"—the newspaper publisher bowed to Emma Comden, Lillian Hennessy, and Marion Morgan, the only women in the lodge—"I am honored you could join me in saluting the great builders of the Southern Pacific Railroad. As they forge ever onward toward their final goal, let them know that our prayers go with them and let us hope that our fervent admiration will spur them on. Builders make America great, and we are honored to be in the presence of the boldest builders in the West."

Shouts of "Hear! Hear!" echoed to the rafters. The Californians rose as one, clapping loudly. Osgood Hennessy nodded his thanks.

"Just as we applaud these men who build with their hands and their hearts, so do we entreat another man in this splendid banquet hall to build the future of our great nation with his leadership and wisdom. I refer, of course, to our good friend Senator Charles Kincaid, whom I believe just might make an announcement that will gladden the heart of every man and woman in this room. Senator Kincaid."

Kincaid rose, smiling, acknowledging applause. He hooked his thumbs to his lapels as the clapping died down. He gazed at the admiring faces. He turned and smiled at Lillian Hennessy. He looked Osgood Hennessy in the face. Then he turned his attention to the elk and grizzly bear heads jutting from the log walls.

"I have come here at the invitation of the most accomplished businessmen in California and Oregon. Men who have worked long and hard to develop this great land. Indeed, this rustic setting reminds us that our manifest destiny in the American West is to tame nature for the prosperity of the entire United States. Timber, mining, crops, and cattle, all served by the great railroads. Now these gentlemen have asked me to lead them toward new accomplishments to benefit our great nation and protect her from her enemies . . . They have been very persuasive."

He looked out over the tables.

Bell noticed that he possessed the politician's gift for seeming to look at each and every person. Suddenly, Kincaid turned his lapel inside out, revealing the red-and-white KINCAID FOR PRESIDENT button he had shown Bell.

"I am persuaded!" he said, his handsome face wreathed in smiles. "You've talked me into it. I will serve my country as you gentlemen see fit."

"President?" Osgood Hennessy asked Bell, as the room erupted in applause and the band played loudly.

"Sounds that way, sir."

"Of the United States?"

Preston Whiteway called out, "That's right, Mr. Hennessy. We gentlemen of California pledge our considerable support to Senator Charles Kincaid, the 'Hero Engineer.'"

"Well, I'll be damned."

"Surprised me, too!" shouted a wealthy redwoods lumberman from Marin County. "He fought us tooth and nail. Practically had to hog-tie him before he agreed."

Preston Whiteway acknowledged the laughter, then said, "I believe that Senator Kincaid has a few more words on the subject."

"Just a few," said Kincaid. "I'll be glad to go down in history as the president who gave the shortest speeches." He acknowledged their laughter, then grew sober. "As you say, I was honored but hesitant when you first broached the possibility. But the horrific events two weeks ago in New Jersey and New York City persuaded me that every public servant must rise to the defend the American people from the Yellow Peril. That dastardly explosion was detonated by a Chinaman. The streets of the city were littered with broken windows. As I went to the aid of the stricken, I will never forget the sounds of the ambulance tires crunching the glass. A sound I will never forget . . ."

Isaac Bell listened closely as Kincaid went on in that vein. Did Kincaid believe what he was saying? Or was his warning about the Yellow Peril the kind of political claptrap his supporters expected? Bell glanced at Marion. A mischievous light was igniting her eyes. She felt his gaze on her and looked down, biting her lip. Lillian leaned behind her father to whisper to her, and Bell saw both women cover their mouths to stifle laughs. He was happy, but not surprised, that they had taken a liking to each other.

". . . The Yellow Peril we face, the tidal waves of immigrating Chinamen taking American jobs, frightening American women, was suddenly driven home that terrible night in New York City. That dastardly Chinaman exploded tons of dynamite in a busy rail yard near a crowded city for his own unfathomable reasons that no white man could ever begin to understand . . ."

IN THE SHADOW OF a string of freight cars, Philip Dow watched the lighted windows of the railroad president's special. Senator Kincaid had given him the dining schedule for the employees who lived on the train. He waited until the diner crew had served the guests. Then, while they were eating their own suppers with the porters and the white train crew ate in the baggage car, he climbed aboard the front end of Car 3. He checked the layout in Car 3 and Car 4 and traced escape routes through the train and off each.

Car 4's porter station was a small closet with a curtain for a door. It was crammed with clean towels and napkins, cold and hang-over cures, a shoe-shine kit, and a spirit stove to heat water. Dow unscrewed a lightbulb to cast shadow on the short length of corridor along which he would dart to Marion Morgan's Stateroom 4. Then he rehearsed.

He practiced watching the corridor through the porter's curtain, tracing the route Isaac Bell would take from the front of the car toward the rear. Then he practiced stepping silently into the corridor and swinging his sap. Restricted by the confines of the narrow space, he swept it underhanded. The momentum of running the three steps, combined with a long reach that started well behind, would accelerate the heavy pouch of lead shot with deadly force into Isaac Bell's temple.

ISAAC BELL PRESSED FINGERS to his temple.

"Headache?" Marion murmured.

"Just hoping this 'short speech' will be over soon," he whispered back.

"Anarchy?" shouted Charles Kincaid, building steam. "Emperor worship? Who knows how the Chinaman thinks? Hatred of the white man. Or deranged by smoking opium, his favorite vice . . ."

His supporters leaped up, applauding.

Preston Whiteway, red-nosed on good wine, bellowed in Osgood Hennessy's ear, "Didn't the Senator nail the Yellow Peril threat square on the head?"

"We built the transcontinental railroad with John Chinaman," Hennessy retorted. "That makes him good enough for me."

Franklin Mowery stood up from the table and glanced at Whiteway, muttering, "Next time your train glides through the Donner Summit, cast your eye on their stonework."

Whiteway, deaf to dissent, grinned at Marion. "I'll wager that old Isaac here applauds Senator Kincaid's understanding of the threat, since he's the hotshot detective who stopped that opium-maddened Chinaman in his tracks."

Bell thought that Whiteway's grins at Marion were getting dangerously close to leers. Dangerous for Whiteway, that is.

"The motivation appears to have been money," Bell replied sternly. Dodging Marion's kick under the table, he added, "We have no evidence that the man who paid him smoked anything stronger than tobacco."

Mowery gathered up his walking stick and limped toward the porch.

Bell hurried to hold the door for him, as his young assistant had not been invited to the banquet. Mowery tottered across the covered porch and leaned on the railing that overlooked the river.

Bell watched curiously. The engineer had been acting strangely all day. Now he was staring at the bridge piers, which were lighted by the electric arc lamps. The old man seemed mesmerized.

Bell joined him at the railing.

"Quite a sight from down here?"

"What? Yes, yes, of course."

"Is something the matter, sir? Are you not feeling well?"

"Water's rising," said Mowery.

"It's been raining a lot. In fact, I think it's starting up again now."

"The rain only makes it worse."

"Beg your pardon, sir?"

"For thousands of years, the river has descended from the mountains at a steep gradient," Mowery answered as if lecturing from a textbook. "At such a gradient, countless tons of debris tumble in the water. Abrasive materials—earth, sand, gravel, rocks. They grind the riverbed deeper and wider. In doing so, they dredge up more debris. Where the river's gradient decreases, she deposits this material. Crossing flats like the one this town's built on, the river spreads out and meanders. Her channels interweave like braid. Then they bunch up here in the gorge, laying down tons and tons of sediment. God alone knows how much lies between here and bedrock."

Suddenly, he looked Bell full in the face. His own features reflected skull-like in the harsh electric light.

"The Bible tells us a foolish man builds his house on sand. But it doesn't tell us what to do when we have no choice but to build on sand."

"I suppose that's why we need engineers." Bell smiled encouragingly, sensing that the engineer was trying tell him something that he was afraid to voice.

Mowery chuckled but did not smile. "You hit that nail on the head, son. That's why we *trust* engineers."

The door opened behind them.

"We're heading back up to the train," Marion called. "Mr. Hennessy is tired."

They thanked their hosts and said their good-byes. Charles Kincaid came with them, giving Franklin Mowery an arm to lean on.

Isaac took Marion's hand as they walked through the rain to the foot of the steep freight line.

She whispered, "I am going to plead weariness from my long journey and slip off to bed."

"Not too weary, I hope, for a knock on your door?"

"If you don't, I'll knock on yours."

They boarded the Snake Line passenger car in which they had arrived. Three engines in front and two in back huffed them slowly up the steep switchbacks to the plateau where Hennessy's special was parked on its siding, windows glowing in welcome.

"Come on in, gents," Hennessy ordered. "Brandy and cigars."

"I thought you were tired," said Lillian.

"Tired of businessmen blathering," Hennessy shot back. "Ladies, there's champagne for you in the diner while the gents have a smoke."

"You're not getting rid of me," said Lillian.

Mrs. Comden stayed too, quietly needlepointing in a corner chair.

Marion Morgan said good night and headed back to her stateroom.

Isaac Bell, waiting a decent interval for propriety's sake, continued to observe Kincaid closely.

PHILIP DOW LOOKED OUT the curtain when he heard someone enter the stateroom car from the front vestibule. He glimpsed a beautiful woman walking toward the porter's station. She wore a red gown and a full necklace of red rubies. Such displays of wealth usually raised a visceral anger in the union man. But he was taken by her happy smile. Women as beautiful as she, with her straw-blond hair, long, graceful neck, narrow waist, and coral-sea green eyes always smiled like they were congratulating themselves on their looks. This one was different. She smiled with happiness.

He hoped she would not stop at Marion Morgan's door. He

dreaded having to kill such a lovely creature. But she did stop and enter Stateroom 4. He had never killed a woman. He didn't want to start now. Particularly this one. But he was not eager to meet the hangman either.

Quickly, he revised his plan of attack. Instead of waiting for her to open the door when Isaac Bell knocked, he would strike the instant that Bell raised his hand to knock. Bell would not be as distracted as he would be a moment later, stepping into her arms. The detective would be more alert to defending himself, but that was the price Dow was willing to pay for not killing her. He shoved his revolver in his belt so he could grab it quickly if Bell managed to dodge the sap. A gunshot would complicate escape, but he would pay that price too not to kill the woman. Unless she gave him no choice.

37

ISAAC BELL WATCHED SENATOR KINCAID'S MOUTH WRINKLE with distaste as Lillian Hennessy demonstrated that she was a modern woman. Not only did she refuse to leave the gentlemen to their cigars, she lighted a cigarette herself, telling her father, "If President Roosevelt's daughter can smoke, so can I."

Hennessy was no less annoyed than the Senator. "I will not have that grandstanding, opportunistic, self-promoting blowhard's name uttered in my railcar."

"You should count yourself lucky that I only smoke. Alice Roosevelt is also known to appear at White House parties wrapped in a python."

Mrs. Comden looked up from her needlepoint. "Osgood, may I presume that you will not permit snakes in your railcar?"

"If Roosevelt's for snakes, I'm agin' 'em."

Senator Kincaid laughed heartily.

Bell had already observed that the Senator assumed his KINCAID FOR PRESIDENT button had raised his stature in Hennessy's eyes. He also noticed that Hennessy appeared to be recalculating the Senator's potential.

"Tell me, Kincaid," the railroad president asked in all seriousness, "what *would* you do if you were elected president?"

"Learn on the job," Kincaid answered boldly. "Just like you learned railroading."

Mrs. Comden spoke up, again. "Mr. Hennessy did not *learn* railroading. He *teaches* it."

"I stand corrected." Kincaid smiled stiffly.

"Mr. Hennessy is *empirizing* the railroads of America."

Hennessy shushed her with a smile. "Mrs. Comden has a way with words. She studied in Europe, you know."

"You're too kind, Osgood. I studied in Leipzig, but only music." She stuffed her needlepoint into a satin-lined bag. Then she rose from her corner chair, saying, "Please don't stand, gentlemen," and left the parlor.

They sat awhile, puffing cigars, sipping brandy.

"Well, I think I'll turn in," said Isaac Bell.

Kincaid said, "Before you go, do tell us how your hunt for the so-called Wrecker is going."

"Damned well!" Hennessy answered for him. "Bell's stopped the murdering radical at every turn."

Bell rapped his chair arm with his knuckles. "Knock wood, sir. We've caught some lucky breaks."

"If you've stopped him," said Kincaid, "then your job is done."

"My job is done when he hangs. He is a murderer. And he threatens the livelihood of thousands. How many men did you say you employ, Mr. Hennessy?"

"A hundred thousand."

"Mr. Hennessy is modest," said Kincaid. "Factoring in all the lines in which he holds controlling interests, he employs over one million hands."

Bell glanced at Hennessy. The railroad president did not dispute the enormous claim. Bell was struck with admiration. Even engrossed in the titanic effort to build the cutoff, the old man continued to extend his empire.

"Until you do hang him," Kincaid asked, "what do you think he intends next?"

Bell smiled a smile that did not warm his eyes. He was reminded of the last time he'd jousted with Kincaid, trading table talk over their game of draw poker. "Your guess is as good as mine, Senator."

Kincaid smiled back as coolly. "I would have thought that a detective's guess is better than mine."

"Let's hear it."

"*My* guess is, he'll take a crack at the Cascade Canyon Bridge."

"That's why it's heavily guarded," said Hennessy. "He'd need an army to get near it."

"Why would you guess that he would attack the bridge?" asked Bell.

"Any fool can see that the saboteur, whoever he is—anarchist, foreigner, or striker—knows how to guarantee the greatest damage. Clearly, he's a brilliant engineer."

"That thought has crossed several minds," Bell said drily.

"You're missing a bet, Mr. Bell. Look for a civil engineer."

"A man like yourself?"

"Not me. As I told you the other day, I was trained and able but never brilliant."

"What makes a brilliant engineer, Senator?"

"Good question, Bell. Best put to Mr. Mowery, who is one."

Mowery, ordinarily talkative, had been very quiet ever since Bell had spoken with him in the shadow of the bridge. He waved Kincaid off with an impatient gesture.

Kincaid turned to Hennessy. "Even better put to a railroad president. What makes a brilliant engineer, Mr. Hennessy?"

"Railroad engineering is nothing more than managing grade and water. The flatter your roadbed, the faster your train."

"And water?"

"Water will do its damnedest to wash out your roadbed if you don't divert it."

Bell said, "I put the question to you, Senator. What makes a brilliant engineer?"

"Stealth," Kincaid replied.

"Stealth?" echoed Hennessy, shooting a baffled look at Bell. "What in blazes are you talking about, Kincaid?"

"Concealment. Secrecy. Cunning." Kincaid smiled. "Every project demands compromise. Strength versus weight. Speed versus cost. What an engineer grasps in one fist, he surrenders with the other. A *brilliant* engineer hides compromise. You will never see it in his work. Take Mr. Mowery's bridge. To my journeyman's eye, his compromises are invisible. It simply soars."

"Nonsense," rumbled Franklin Mowery. "It's only mathematics."

Bell said to Mowery, "But you yourself told me about engineering compromises just the other day at the Diamond Canyon Loop wreck. What do you think, sir? Is the Wrecker a brilliant engineer?"

Mowery brushed the point of his beard distractedly. "The Wrecker has shown knowledge of geology, explosives, and the roadbed, not to mention the habits of locomotives. If he's not an engineer, he's missed his calling."

Emma Comden returned, bundled to her chin in a fur coat. The collar framed her pretty face. A matching fur cap was perched jauntily on her hair, and her dark eyes sparkled.

"Come, Osgood. Let's stroll along the siding."

"What the heck for?"

"To look at the stars."

"Stars? It's raining."

"The storm has passed. The sky is brilliant."

"It's too cold," Hennessy complained. "Besides, I have telegraphs to wire as soon as Lillian stubs out that damned cigarette and gets her notepad. Kincaid, take Mrs. Comden for a walk, would you? Good man."

"Of course. It will be my pleasure, as always." Kincaid found his coat and offered Mrs. Comden his arm as they started down the steps to the roadbed.

Bell stood up, chafing to get to Marion. "Well, I'll leave you to your work, sir. I'm going to turn in."

"Sit with me a moment . . . Lillian, would you excuse us?"

She looked puzzled but didn't argue and retreated toward her stateroom in *Nancy No. 2*.

"Drink?"

"I've had enough, thank you, sir."

"That is a fine woman you've tied onto."

"Thank you, sir. I feel I am very lucky." And hoping, he thought to himself, to demonstrate how lucky he felt very soon.

"Reminds me of my wife—and she was a gal to reckon with . . . What do you know about your friend Abbott?"

Bell looked at him, surprised. "Archie and I have been friends since college."

"What's he like?"

"I must inquire why you ask. He's my friend."

"I understand my daughter showed an interest in him."

"Did she tell you that?"

"No. I learned it from another source."

Bell thought a moment. Mrs. Comden had not been in New York but had stayed in the West with Hennessy. "Since you inquire about my friend, I have to ask you who told you that."

"Kincaid. Who do you suppose? He was with her in New York when she met Abbott. Please understand, Bell, I am fully aware that he would say anything to undermine any rival for her hand . . . Which he will get over my dead body."

"Lillian's too, I imagine," said Bell, which drew a smile.

"Although," Hennessy went on, "I must admit that this president talk is a new wrinkle. I may have underestimated Kincaid . . ." He shook his head in amazement. "I've always said I'd rather have a baboon in the White House than Theodore Roosevelt. We should be careful what we wish for. But at least Kincaid would be *my* baboon."

Bell asked, "If you would accept a baboon in the White House, provided he was your baboon, would you take him as a son-in-law?"

Hennessy dodged that question, saying only, "I'm asking about your friend Abbott because when I have to weigh suitors, I want to know my options."

"All right, sir. Now I understand. I will tell you what I know. Archie Abbott—Archibald Angell Abbott IV—is an excellent detective, a master of disguise, a handy fellow with his fists, a deft hand with a knife, deadly with a firearm, and a loyal friend."

"A man to ride the river with?" Hennessy asked with a smile.

"Without reservation."

"And his circumstances? Is he as poor as Kincaid claims?"

"He lives on his detective salary," said Bell. "His family lost everything in the Panic of '93. His mother stays with her brother-in-law's family. Before that, they were reasonably well-off, as the old New York families were in those days, with a good house in the right neighborhood."

Hennessy looked at Bell, sharply. "Could he be a gold digger?"

"Twice he walked away from wealthy young ladies whose mothers would be thrilled to marry them into as illustrious a family as the Abbotts. One was the only child of a man who owned a steamship line, another the daughter of a textile magnate. He could have had either for the asking. In both cases, their fathers made it clear they would take him into the business or, if he preferred not to work, simply put him on an allowance."

The old man stared hard at him. Bell held his eye easily.

Hennessy finally said, "I appreciate your candor, Bell. I won't be around forever, and I'm pretty much the only family she has. I want to see her set before anything happens to me."

Bell stood up. "Lillian could do a lot worse than Archie Abbott."

"She could also do worse than First Lady of the United States of America."

"She is a very capable young woman," Bell said neutrally. "She'll deal with any hand dealt her."

"I don't want her to have to."

"Of course you don't. What father would? Now, let me ask *you* something, sir."

"Shoot."

Bell sat back down. As much as he wanted to join Marion, there was a question troubling him that had to be answered.

"Do you really believe that Senator Kincaid has a chance for the nomination?"

CHARLES KINCAID AND EMMA COMDEN had walked in silence past the special's insistently sighing steam engine, past the train yards and into the night, beyond the glare of the electric lights. Where the ballast laid for new rail ended, they stepped down to the newly cleared forest floor that had been brushed out for the right-of-way.

The stars were vivid in the thin mountain air. The Milky Way flooded the dark like a white river. Mrs. Comden spoke German. Her voice was muffled by the fur of her collar.

"Be careful you don't twist the devil's tail too hard."

Kincaid responded in English. His German, honed by ten years studying engineering in Germany and working for the German companies building the Baghdad Railway, was as good as hers, but the last thing he needed was someone to report he had been overheard conversing in a foreign tongue with Osgood Hennessy's mistress.

"We will beat them," he said, "long before they figure out who we are or what we want."

"But every way you turn, Isaac Bell thwarts you."

"Bell has no idea of what I have planned next," Kincaid said scornfully. "I am so close, Emma. My bankers in Berlin are poised to strike the instant that I bankrupt the Southern Pacific Company. My secret holding companies will buy it for pennies, and I will seize controlling interests in every railroad in America. Thanks to Osgood Hennessy's 'empirizing.' No one can stop me."

"Isaac Bell is no fool. Neither is Osgood."

"Worthy opponents," Kincaid agreed, "but always several steps behind." And, in the case of Bell, he thought but did not say, unlikely to survive the night if Philip Dow was his usual deadly self.

"I must warn you that Franklin Mowery is growing suspicious about his bridge."

"Too late to do anything about it."

"It seems to me that you are growing reckless. So reckless that they will catch you."

Kincaid gazed up at the stars, and murmured, "They can't. I have my secret weapons."

"What secret weapons are those?"

"You for one, Emma. You to tell me everything they're up to."

"And what do I have?" she asked.

"Anything money can buy when we have won."

"What if I want something—or *someone*—money can't buy."

Kincaid laughed again. "I'll be in great demand. You'll have to get in line."

"In line . . . ?" Emma Comden raised her sensual face to the starlight. Her eyes shone darkly. "What is your other secret weapon?"

"That's a secret," said Kincaid.

In the unlikely event Bell somehow survived the attack and got lucky enough to thwart him again, he could not risk telling even her about "Lake Lillian."

"You would keep secrets from me?" she asked.

"Don't sound hurt. You know that you are the only one I have ever given the power to betray me."

He saw no profit in mentioning Philip Dow. Just as he would never tell Dow about his affair with Emma, which had started years before she became the railroad president's mistress.

A bitter smile parted her lips. "I have never known a worse man than you, Charles. But I would never betray you."

Kincaid looked around again to make sure absolutely sure no one could see them. Then he snaked an arm inside her coat and drew her close. He was not at all surprised when she didn't resist. Nor was he surprised that she had removed every stitch of her clothing before she put her fur on.

"And what have we here?" he asked, his voice thickening with desire.

"The front of the line," said Mrs. Comden.

·38·

"When it comes to politics," Osgood Hennessy snorted in answer to Isaac Bell's question, "I'll believe anything that happens."

Isaac Bell said, "I'm serious, sir. Do you believe that Kincaid is making an earnest run for the office of president?"

"Politicians can delude themselves into anything that suits their fancy. Could he get elected? I suppose. Voters do the damnedest things. Thank God, women don't vote. He'd get elected on his pretty-boy looks alone."

"But could he get nominated?" Bell pressed.

"That's the real issue."

"He's got Preston Whiteway behind him. Whiteway must think there's a chance."

"That rabble-rouser will stop at nothing to sell newspapers. Don't forget, win or lose, Kincaid for President still makes for a story right up to the last night of the convention."

Bell named several of the California businessmen in Whiteway's group. "Do they really believe they could bull Kincaid past the party regulars?"

Osgood Hennessy chuckled cynically. "Successful businessmen

believe they succeed because they're intelligent. Fact is, most businessmen are birdbrains except for that one small thing each was clever at in order to make money. But I don't understand why they wouldn't be perfectly happy with William Howard Taft. Surely they know that if they split the party, they would hand the election to the Democrats and William Jennings Bryan, that populist fiend. Hell, maybe they're just soaking up a free holiday at Whiteway's expense."

"Maybe," said Bell.

"Why do you ask?" said Hennessy, probing him with shrewd eyes.

Bell probed back. "It doesn't feel right."

"You wouldn't by any chance be undermining your friend's rival for my daughter's hand?"

Bell stood up. "I'm not sly. Nor furtive. I'll tell you here and now, to your face, that your daughter deserves better than Charles Kincaid. Good night, sir."

"Wait," said Hennessy. "Wait . . . Wait . . . I apologize. That was uncalled for and obviously not true. You're a straight shooter. I do apologize. Sit down. Keep an old man company for a moment. Emma will be back from her walk any minute."

CHARLES KINCAID SAW EMMA COMDEN to the door of the double stateroom she shared with Osgood Hennessy. They heard Bell and Hennessy still talking in the parlor at the front of the car.

"Thank you for walking me to see the stars, Senator."

"A pleasure as always. Good night, Mrs. Comden."

They shook hands chastely. Then Kincaid headed to his own stateroom several cars back in the special. His knees were shaking, the usual effect Emma Comden had on him, his head still reeling, and he had unlocked his door and closed it behind him before he realized that someone was sitting in the easy chair. Dow? Escaping pursuit? Never. By the killer's strict code, he would shoot himself in the head before he would risk betraying a friend. Kincaid pulled his derringer from his pocket and turned up the light.

Eric Soares said, "Surprise, Senator."

"How did you get in here?" Kincaid asked the engineer.

"Jimmied the lock," he answered nonchalantly.

"What the dickens for?"

Soares removed his wire-rimmed glasses and made a show of polishing them with his handkerchief. Finally, he put them back on, smoothed the tips of his handlebar mustache, and answered, "Blackmail."

"Blackmail?" Kincaid echoed, thinking furiously.

As Senator Kincaid, he knew that Eric Soares was engineer Franklin Mowery's assistant. Only as the Wrecker did he know that Soares falsified inspection reports to Mowery about the state of the stone piers supporting the Cascade Canyon Bridge.

He pressed the derringer to the young engineer's head. Soares didn't flinch.

"You can't shoot me in your own stateroom. Which is mighty fancy compared to my miserable little upper Pullman berth. It's even posher than Mr. Mowery's."

"I *can* shoot you and *will*," Kincaid said coldly. "It was dark. I didn't realize it was poor Mr. Soares startling me. I thought it was a radical assassin and defended myself."

"That might satisfy the law. But shooting an orphan who is practically the adopted son of the most famous bridge builder on the continent will not exactly boost your presidential hopes."

Kincaid pocketed his gun, poured himself a brandy from the crystal decanter provided by the Southern Pacific Railroad, and sipped it while leaning on the paneled wall and staring down at the intruder. He was greatly relieved. Soares, like everyone else, believed his Kincaid for President sham. That probably meant Soares did not know that he was the Wrecker. But what did he know that he thought was worth blackmail?

"I'd like a drink, too."

Kincaid ignored the request. While it might be helpful to get him intoxicated, it would be more helpful to remind the little weasel of his place.

"You're absolutely right about my political aspirations," he said. "So let's stop playing games. You've broken in here for a purpose. What is it? What do you want?"

"I told you. Money."

"Why would I give you money? For what?"

"Don't be dense, Senator. For not revealing that you hold a controlling interest in the Union Pier and Caisson Company of St. Louis, Missouri."

The Wrecker concealed his astonishment, but only just. He felt the legs knocked out from under him, and this time he couldn't blame Emma Comden.

"What gave you that idea?" he asked.

"I got curious about who was paying me to lie about the piers. Reckoned sabotaging the biggest bridge in the West ought to be worth a few bucks more if I knew who my bribes came from. So I went to my old bunkie from the orphanage. He took up banking when I took up engineering. He explored a maze of holding companies. The maze turned into a jungle, but my old bunkie is really good. He finally traced them back to you. You bought enough shares secretly, a controlling interest, in the company building the piers for the Cascade Canyon Bridge."

It had to happen sometime, Kincaid thought bleakly. But it never occurred to him that disaster would come at him like a bad joke: tripped up by an orphan whom a kindhearted bridge builder took under his wing.

Kincaid surveyed his options. Kill Soares, if not tonight, tomorrow or the next day. Wring the name of his confederate out of him before he died and kill bunkie, too. Unfortunately, he needed Eric Soares, to continue concealing the truth about the piers. Mowery would immediately replace him if he disappeared. Upon close inspection, and a thorough review of Eric's doctored reports, any competent engineer who took over his position would see that the piers were not strong enough to support the bridge when the river rose.

Soares said, "You're working for the Wrecker just like me."

"I suppose I should be grateful that you're not accusing me of being the Wrecker himself."

"Don't make me laugh. You've got too big a future as a senator. Even president, if I don't turn you in."

Home free, thought Kincaid. *In the clear.*

"How much do you want?"

"Triple what your Union Pier and Caisson Company pays me to look the other way."

Kincaid reached for his wallet. "I think I can arrange that," he said, not at all surprised by how small Soares's dreams were.

ISAAC BELL FINALLY TORE himself loose from Osgood Hennessy and hurried back to the stateroom cars. As he passed through Hennessy's *Nancy No. 2* car, Lillian Hennessy lurched out of her stateroom and blocked the way with a bottle of Mumm. She had changed out of her gown into a clinging robe and had removed her pearl-and-diamond choker, revealing the smooth skin of her throat. Her hair was down, draping her shoulders, and her pale blue eyes were warm. The bottle was dripping from the ice bucket, the foil torn off. But the wire muzzle still held the cork firmly in place.

"I eavesdropped," she whispered. "Thank you for saying what you did about Archie."

"I only told the truth."

She thrust the bottle into Bell's hand.

"For Marion. Tell her, Sweet dreams."

Bell leaned down and kissed her cheek.

"Good night."

He paused in the baggage car and spoke with the sleepy telegrapher. No urgent telegrams. He pulled open the rear baggage car door and crossed the vestibule, reaching for the door to the first car of staterooms. A smile lit his face. He felt like a kid. His mouth was dry just thinking of Marion. Good thing they had Lillian's champagne.

He pushed through the door into the side corridor that was lined with night-blackened windows on the right side and the polished-walnut stateroom doors on the left. A man was hurrying along the far end of the corridor. There was something furtive in his movement, and Bell paused to observe him. Small to medium build, wearing a black sack suit. Dark hair. As the man turned the slight jog to exit into the vestibule, Bell glimpsed his pencil-thin handlebar mustache and wire-rimmed glasses.

Eric Soares, Mowery's assistant, apparently just leaving the old man's stateroom and heading back to his berth in the Pullman cars. Thinking that the hour was awfully late for a meeting, particularly after the old man had been up late at the long banquet, Bell gave Soares plenty of time to pass through the next car rather than get delayed by a conversation.

Finally, Bell walked the length of Car 3, pushed into its rear vestibule, and crossed the coupling into the vestibule of Car 4.

PHILIP DOW HEARD SOMEONE coming, pressed deeper into the porter's closet, and peered through a crack in the curtain. His ears told him it was not Isaac Bell, but a smaller man, unless the detective was exceptionally light on his feet. He did not slow as he passed the curtain, but hurried along as if passing through the stateroom car on his way farther back in the train. Dow's ears were accurate. A slim man in a black suit whisked past Marion Morgan's stateroom and pushed through the rear door that led to the Pullman cars.

A minute later, he heard heavier footfalls. He waited until the man passed before he parted the curtain. Sure enough. Taller than Kincaid, a yellow-haired man in fancy duds from the banquet was making a beeline for Marion Morgan's door. He was carrying a bottle of champagne and humming a tune, "There'll Be a Hot Time in the Old Town Tonight."

Dow heard the words of the song's Chicago version in his head as he ran silently, swinging the sap:

Old Mrs. Leary left the lantern in the shed
and when the cow kicked it over,
she winked her eye and said
it'll be a hot time, in the old town, tonight!
FIRE FIRE FIRE!

Before Philip Dow reached his victim, the stateroom flew open. The woman must have been standing there, gripping the knob, listening for Bell. Bell waved the champagne bottle. Her eager smile went out like a light and her eyes flashed angrily.

"Preston! What are you—"

"Look out!" a voice roared behind Dow.

The man whose skull Dow was about to crush with his sap whirled around, and Dow saw no yellow mustache above the mouth that dropped open in drunk confusion. The champagne bottle he raised instinctively deflected Dow's blow. The heavy sap whizzed a quarter inch from Marion Morgan's face and smashed into the stateroom door, denting the hard walnut.

No yellow mustache! thought Dow. It wasn't Isaac Bell. That put Bell behind him; it was he who had shouted the warning. Dow shoved past the cringing drunk he had almost killed to use him for a shield.

Dow saw the detective running at him full steam. He jerked his revolver from his waistband. Bell was a third of the way down the eighty-foot corridor, drawing a Browning No. 2 semiautomatic pistol from his tuxedo with liquid ease. Dow whipped up his heavy .45, willing to bet that a Van Dorn operative who favored a light Browning could hit a gnat in the eye at twenty paces.

Isaac Bell saw a man whose features he remembered from a Mine Owners' Association wanted poster. Philip Dow, assassin. Preston Whiteway lurched into Bell's way. Bell held his fire. "Down!" he shouted.

Dow pulled his trigger as fast as he could. He couldn't miss. Bell filled the narrow corridor like a locomotive speeding through a single-tracked tunnel.

"Marion, don't!" Bell cried.

Dow felt the beautiful woman in the red dress grab his arm with both hands.

His first shot hit the champagne bottle the detective was carrying, and it exploded in a foamy spray of green glass. His second shot hit the detective. His third shot plowed into the floor. He jerked his arm free and aimed his revolver in the woman's face.

Isaac Bell felt a sledgehammer blow as the assassin's bullet tore through his forearm. He switched the Browning to his left hand and looked for a clear shot. Marion had the good sense to step back into the stateroom. But Preston Whiteway was still flailing about the corridor, blocking his shot. As Bell saw the man who had shot him turn his weapon into Marion's stateroom, he squeezed his trigger.

Philip Dow heard an explosion in his head. For a second, he thought he had taken a bullet and somehow survived. Then he realized that Bell had shot his ear off. He felt a tug on his arm as Bell's second shot scored. His fingers opened involuntarily, and the revolver flew from his hand. Dow shoved the drunk at Bell before the detective could fire again, and ran the few feet to the vestibule door behind him, flung it open, and jumped off the train.

A cinder dick was running toward the sound of gunfire. Dow wasted no time thinking. His sap was still in his right hand. He smashed the cop between the eyes and bolted for the dark.

Bell got as far as the bottom step from the vestibule before the pain in his arm knocked him to his knees. Railroad police were running toward the Hennessy special. "There!" Bell pointed with his pistol. "One man. Medium height. Dark suit and derby. He dropped his gun. Probably has another."

The cops stormed off, blowing whistles for assistance. Bell stumbled up the steps just as Marion came down. "Are you all right?" they chorused.

"I'm fine," she said, and shouted to a conductor running up, "Get a doctor!"

She helped Bell into the car. Preston Whiteway was leaning on her door, blocking it.

"Say, what's going on?" he asked.

"Preston!" said Marion Morgan. "Get out of our way before I pick up that gun and shoot you."

The newspaper publisher shambled off, scratching his head. Marion helped Bell into her stateroom and onto the bed.

"Towels," muttered Bell. "Before I make a mess of your sheets."

"How badly hurt are you, Isaac?"

"I think I'm O.K. He only got my arm, thanks to you."

By the time the doctor came from the Southern Pacific's hospital car, the railroad police had reported to Bell that the man who had shot him had disappeared in the dark.

"Keep looking," Bell said. "I'm pretty sure I winged him. In fact, I think I shot his ear off."

"You sure did! We found a chunk of it. And a trail of blood right to the edge of the lights. But not enough to kill him, unfortunately."

"Find him! His name is Philip Dow. There's ten thousand dollars on his head. I want to know if he is working for the Wrecker."

The Southern Pacific Company doctor was a rough-and-ready sort used to the puncture and crush wounds encountered in railroad building. Bell was relieved that he was singularly unimpressed by the bloody furrow that Dow's .45 caliber slug had plowed through his flesh and muscle. The doctor washed it thoroughly with water. Then he held up a bottle of carbolic acid. "This is going to hurt."

"Blood poisoning will hurt more," Bell said, gritting his teeth. There was cloth in the wound. "Pour it on."

After the doctor dosed it with the fiery disinfectant, he dressed it. "You may want to rest it in a sling for a couple of days. But the bone's all right. Bet it hurts like the blazes."

"Yes," Bell said, grinning at Marion, who looked a bit pale. "Now that you mention it."

"Don't worry, I'll take care of that."

The doctor took a hypodermic needle from his leather bag and started to draw a clear fluid into the barrel.

"What's that?" asked Bell.

"Morphine hydrochloride. You won't feel a thing."

"No thanks, Doc. I need a clear head."

"Suit yourself," said the doctor. "I'll change that dressing tomorrow. Good night. Good night, ma'am."

Marion shut the door behind him.

"*Clear head?* Isaac, you've been shot. You're white as a ghost. The pain must be awful. Can't you take the rest of the night off?"

"I intend to," said Bell, reaching for her with his good arm. "That's why I want a clear head."

"Father, dear father,
come home with me now,"

sang the Ventura County Temperance Glee Club, sixty voices strong.

James Dashwood craned his neck, hoping to spot slope-shouldered blacksmith Jim Higgins, who had run when he showed him the sketch of the Wrecker. Isaac Bell was betting that Higgins had taken the abstinence pledge at a temperance meeting. This meeting, in the beet-farming town of Oxnard, filled a tent big enough to hold a circus.

Dashwood had attended six such meetings already, enough to know the ropes. Nimbly, he dodged the smiling mothers who nudged their daughters in his direction. Men were outnumbered by women whenever the pledge of abstinence was sought. Few were young as he, or as clean and neatly turned out. More typical was the prospector sitting next to him, in a patched coat and floppy hat, who looked like he'd come to get out of the rain.

The singers finally finished. Ushers rigged a powerful acetylene-lit magic lantern. Its long lens shined a circle of light on a screen on the other side of the tent. All eyes watched the circle. Some sort of show was about to commence.

The next speaker was a fiery Methodist.

"The rank and file of the red-nosed corps scorn us as Utopians!" he thundered. "But to proclaim that there ought to be no place in the world for intoxicating drink does not make us Utopians. We are not conducting a dangerous experiment. Practicing personal abstinence is no new thing. The *danger* comes with trying to live *with* drink."

He gestured toward the magic lantern.

"With the aid of a powerful microscope and this magic lantern, I will now demonstrate that to imbibe distilled spirit is to drink poison. When you drink intoxicating liquor, you poison your mind. You poison your family. You poison your own body. Watch the screen, ladies and gentlemen. Under the enlarging powers of this microscope, I place this glass of pure natural water drawn from the well of the church down the road and project it on the screen."

Greatly magnified, the well water was alive with swimming microbes.

He held up an eyedropper, inserted it down the neck of a bottle of Squirrel whiskey, and drew brown liquid into it.

"I now place a single drop of whiskey in the water. Only one, single drop."

The magnified drop of whiskey struck like mud fouling a pond. A brown cloud spread through the water. Microbes fled, swimming frantically toward the edges of the glass. But there was no escape. Writhing, shriveling, they fell still and died. The prospector seated beside Dashwood shuddered.

"Look at all them slimy varmints," he said. "Last time I'll drink water that don't have whiskey in it."

Dashwood spied a big man in a dark coat near the front of the gathering and hurried after him.

"Who will come forward," the speaker called. "Who will sign the certificate of abstinence and pledge never to drink?"

When he got closer, Dashwood saw that the man in the dark coat was not Jim Higgins. But by then Dashwood was within reach of the speaker's assistants, comely young ladies, who descended upon him flourishing Waterman fountain pens and blank certificates.

"TWO MORE WIRES, MR. BELL," said J. J. Meadows. "How's the arm this morning?"

"Tip-top."

The first wire addressed Bell's question about Senator Charles Kincaid's early departure from the Military Academy at West Point. Van Dorn's Washington, D.C., office, which had informal access to United States Army records, reported that Kincaid had withdrawn voluntarily to pursue his studies at the University of West Virginia. They had unearthed no hint of impropriety and no record of dismissal. The operative ventured the opinion that the quality of civil engineering schools had risen above that of the military, which was, before the Civil War, the only learning ground for engineers.

Bell was more intrigued by the second message, which contained new information about Franklin Mowery's assistant, Eric Soares. Deeper digging revealed that Soares had run away from the Kansas City orphanage that Mowery supported. Soares had surfaced after a couple of years in a reform school. Mowery had taken personal responsibility for him, hired tutors to fill the gaps in his schooling, and then put him through engineering college at Cornell. Which explained, Bell thought, the uncle-and-favorite-nephew relationship they shared.

Bell called on the old man in the afternoon, when Soares was down at the river conducting his daily inspection of the work on the bridge piers. Mowery's office was a converted stateroom on Hennessy's special. He was surprised to see Bell.

"I thought you'd be in the hospital. You're not even wearing a sling."

"The sling hurt more than no sling."

"Did they catch the fellow who shot you?"

"Not yet . . . Mr. Mowery, may I ask you a few questions?"

"Go ahead."

"I'm sure that you can imagine how wide-ranging our investigation is. So please forgive me if I appear to get personal."

"Shoot, Mr. Bell. We're on the same side. I'm building it. You're making sure that criminal doesn't knock it down."

"I am concerned about your assistant's past," Bell said bluntly.

Mowery put his pipe in his mouth and glared.

"When I chose to help Eric, the boy was fifteen years old and had been living in the street. Well-meaning folks told me he would pick my pocket and knock me on the head. I told them what I'll tell you: I don't believe in the existence of a criminal class."

"I agree there is no such thing as a criminal class," said Bell. "But I am familiar with a criminal *type*."

"Eric earned his degree," Mowery retorted. "The times I pulled wires to get him a job, he never disappointed. The folks at Union Pier and Caisson are pleased with his work. In fact, they have already asked him to stay on with their firm after this job is finished. I would say by now the young man is over the hump, wouldn't you?"

"I suppose you'll miss him if he stays with Union Pier and Caisson . . ."

"I wish him well in his career. As for me, I'm going back to my rockin' chair. I'm too old to keep Hennessy's pace. Did him a favor. Glad I did. We built a fine bridge. Osgood Hennessy. Me. And Eric Soares."

"Funny thing, though," said Bell. "I heard Jethro Watt, the chief of the railway police, repeat an old saying, recently: 'Nothing is impossible for the Southern Pacific.'"

"Truer words were never spoken, which is why working for the Southern Pacific is a younger man's game."

"Jethro said it meant that the railroad does it all. Builds its own engines and rolling stock and tunnels. And bridges."

"Famous for it."

"So why did they hire Union Pier and Caisson to sink the piers for your bridge?"

"River-pier work is a specialized field. Especially when you have tricky conditions like we found here. Union is the best in the business. Cut their teeth on the Mississippi. If you can build piers that stand up to the Mississippi River, you can build them anywhere."

"Did you recommend hiring the firm?"

Mowery hesitated.

"Now that you mention it," he finally said, "that is not precisely true. I was originally inclined to let our company do the job. But it was suggested to me that Union might be the wiser course because the geology here proved to be complicated . . . as I mentioned to you last night. We encountered challenging conditions on the Cascade River bottom, to say the least. Even more shifting than you'd expect in these mountains."

"Did Eric recommend Union?"

"Of course. I had sent him ahead to conduct the survey. He knew the river bed and he knew Union. Why are you asking all this?"

The tall detective looked the elderly engineer in the eye. "You appeared troubled in Mr. Hennessy's car last night after the banquet. Earlier, when we were down at the lodge, you were staring long and hard at the bridge piers."

Mowery looked away. "You don't miss much, do you, Mr. Bell? . . . I didn't like the way the water flowed around them. I could not pin down why—still can't—but it just looked different than it should."

"You have an instinct that something is wrong?"

"Perhaps," Mowery admitted reluctantly.

"Maybe you're like me that way."

"How so?"

"When I'm short on facts, I have to go on instinct. For instance, the fellow who shot me last night could have been a robber who followed Preston Whiteway onto this train intending to knock him on the head and take his wallet. I believe I recognized him as a known assassin. But I have no hard facts to say he wasn't looking to make easy money. Whiteway was visibly intoxicated and therefore defenseless, and he was dressed like a wealthy gentleman likely to be carrying a big roll in his pocket. Since the 'robber' escaped, those are my only facts. But my instinct suggests that he was sent to kill me and mistook Whiteway for me. Sometimes, instinct helps put two and two together . . ."

This time, when Mowery tried to look away, Bell held him with the full force of his compelling gaze.

"It sounds," Mowery muttered, "like you want to blame Eric for something."

"Yes, it does," said Bell.

He sat down, still holding the old man's gaze.

Mowery started to protest, "Son . . ."

A wintery light in Bell's blue eyes made him reconsider. The detective was no man's son but his own father's.

"Mr. Bell . . ."

Bell spoke in cool, measured tones. "It is curious that when I remarked that we need engineers, you countered that we need to *trust* engineers. And when I observed that you seemed troubled by the piers, you replied that I sounded as if I want to blame Eric."

"I believe I had better have a talk with Osgood Hennessy. Excuse me, Mr. Bell."

"I'll join you."

"No," Mowery said. "An engineering talk. Not a detective talk. Facts, not instincts."

"I'll walk you to his car."

"Suit yourself."

Mowery grabbed his walking stick and heaved himself painfully to his feet. Bell held the door and led the way up the side corridor, helping Mowery through the vestibule doors between the cars. Hennessy was in his paneled office. Mrs. Comden was with him, reading in her corner chair.

Bell blocked the door for an instant.

"Where is Soares now?" he asked Mowery.

41

ONE HOUR LATER IN ST. LOUIS, A TELEGRAM ARRIVED AT THE basement hovel of an anarchist who had fled Italy and changed his name to Francis Rizzo. Rizzo closed the door on the Western Union messenger boy's face before he opened the envelope. A single word was typed on the buff-colored form:

"Now."

Rizzo threw on his hat and coat, caught a streetcar to a neighborhood where no one knew him, purchased a quart tin of kerosene, and boarded another streetcar, which carried him toward the Mississippi River. He got off and walked quickly through a warehouse district until he found a saloon in the shadow of the levee. He ordered a beer and ate a sausage at the free-lunch counter, eyes locked on the swinging doors. The instant that warehouse workers and carters barreled in, marking the end of the business day, Rizzo left the saloon and hurried along dark streets to the offices of the Union Pier & Caisson Company.

A clerk was locking up, the last man out. Rizzo watched from across the street until he was sure the offices were empty. Then, on a route plotted months earlier, he entered an alley that led to a narrow passage between the back of the building and the levee standing between it and the river. He tugged a loose board, pulled out a short crowbar he had stashed behind it, and pried open a window. He climbed in, found the central wooden staircase that led to the top of the three-story building, climbed it, and opened several windows. Then he pierced the kerosene tin with his pocketknife and started back down the stairs, splashing the volatile liquid on the steps. At the bottom, he lit a match, touched it to the kerosene, and watched the flames leap up the dry wood. He waited until he was sure that the wood itself had caught fire. Then he slipped back out the window and left it open to feed the draft.

ISAAC BELL RODE THE slow Snake Line switchback train down to the town of Cascade. Eric Soares had told Franklin Mowery that he might work late, as he often did. As usual, he would take his supper in the town, then would bunk down in one of the guard shacks beside the piers and start work early in the morning rather than waste time riding the train back up to the top.

When Bell got to the guard shacks, the detective discovered that the supposedly hardworking Soares had quit early.

No one knew where he had gone.

DOWN THE RIVER FROM the original town of Cascade, a shanty-and-tent city called Hell's Bottom had sprung up. It owed its existence to the ironworkers, masons, and caisson miners who'd built the Cascade Canyon Bridge, the railroaders who'd laid the steep Snake Line from the town and its lowland railhead up to the bridge, and the lumberjacks and teamsters who had revived the old East Oregon Lumber Company back in the mountains.

Eric Soares headed for Hell's Bottom, feeling flush. In fact, he thought, with the cash in his pocket that the Senator had forked over as the first of many payments, he was sure to be the richest man in the boomtown tonight. He was also in love, which his hard-knocks youth had demonstrated was about as half-witted as a man could get. Particularly falling in love with a whore. Half-witted or not, he visited her every night he could get away from Old Man Mowery. Now, thanks to the Senator, he could afford to keep her for himself all night long.

There were three grades of brothels in Hell's Bottom.

The roughest serviced the lumberjacks and mule skinners. The men risked their lives to get there Saturday nights by shooting the rapids down the rocky river in "Hell's Bottom Flyers," dugout canoes made by hollowing logs with axes and fire.

The women of the next-roughest brothels serviced the railroad gangs, who arrived via the Snake Line. Track layers descended on Saturday night. Trainmen, brakemen, conductors, and locomotive engineers working railroad schedules swaggered in night and day swinging their red lanterns.

There was only one top-grade establishment. Gabriel's was comparatively genteel, particularly by western boomtown standards, and more expensive than a laboring man could dream of affording. Its customers were the upstanding business owners and professionals of Cascade, wealthy tourists staying at the famous lodge, and the higher-paid senior engineers, lawyers, and managers who worked for the railroad.

Madame Gabriel greeted Eric Soares like the regular he had become.

"I would like Joanna," he told her.

"Engaged, sir."

"I'll wait."

"She's gonna be a while," she said.

He felt a foolish stab of jealousy. Foolish, sure, he thought. But the feeling was as real as the sudden angry pounding of his heart that made it difficult to breathe.

"There's a new girl you might enjoy."

"I'll wait for Joanna."

If provoked, Madame Gabriel had the coldest eyes he had ever seen on a woman. They grew icy now, and despite his broad experience of the world for one so young Eric felt something akin to fear. He looked away, afraid of provoking her further.

She surprised him with a warm smile. "Tell you what, sir. The new girl is yours on the house if you can look me in the face after and tell me she wasn't worth top dollar. In fact, I'll even give you your money back if you can honestly tell me she isn't better than Joanna. How can you lose?"

How could he lose?

Madame Gabriel's bouncer walked him to a door in the back of the sprawling house, knocked for him, and threw it open. Eric stepped into a room glowing with pink lantern light. The bouncer closed the door behind him. Two men dressed like lumberjacks closed in from both sides.

A gun barrel materialized out of a blur of motion. It whizzed past the hand he raised too late to stop it and smacked his skull. He felt his legs collapse under him as if his bones had turned to jelly. He tried to yell. They yanked a rough sack over his head, tied his wrists behind him. He tried to kick them. They smashed him in the groin. While he was gasping, paralyzed with pain, they tied his ankles, picked him up, and carried him out of the building. He felt himself slung over a saddle, felt his hands and feet looped under the horse. He yelled through the sack. They hit his head again, and he lost consciousness.

He awoke as they untied his hands and feet, jerked his arms behind his back, and tied his hands again. They removed the sack and shined a light in his eyes. The two men were hulking shadows behind the light. He smelled water and heard it running. They were in some sort of cellar with water in it. Like a mill, he thought, with a stream racing through. The lumberjacks leaned in from the shadows.

"What is the name of your old bunkie from the orphanage?"

"Go to hell," said Eric Soares.

They grabbed his feet, jerked him into the air upside down, and lowered his head into the ice-cold stream. He was so startled, he didn't have time to take a deep breath. He ran out of air, struggling frantically. He struggled so hard, his glasses unhooked from his ears. He couldn't stop himself from breathing in. Water filled his nose and mouth. They lifted him out of the water and held him, still upside down, with his face inches from the stream.

"The name of your bunkie from the orphanage."

"Why do you . . ." he started to ask, even though he knew exactly why.

He had misread the Senator. Kincaid had turned out to be no patsy.

The lumberjacks dropped him headfirst in the water again. He had had time to suck in air, and he held it as long as he could. Arching his back, he tried to rise out of the water. They pushed him in deeper and held him until he had to breathe in. Water filled his nose and mouth. He struggled, but his strength was failing, and his whole body gradually went limp. They pulled him up. Coughing and gasping, he vomited water and finally sucked in air. As he caught his breath, he could hear them speaking. He began to realize they had pulled him out so they could ask again.

"The name of your bunkie from the orphanage."

"Paul," he gasped.

"Last name?"

"What are you going—"

"Last name?"

He hesitated. After lights-out in the orphanage, he and Paul had stood back-to-back, fighting off anyone who tried to attack them. He felt their hands tighten around his ankles. "No!" he screamed, but he was already underwater again, raw throat and nose burning, vision fading to pink, then to black. When they finally pulled him out, he yelled, *"Paul Samuels! Paul Samuels! Paul Samuels!"*

"Where does he live?"

"Denver," Soares gasped.

"Where does he work?"

"Bank."

"What bank?"

"First Silver. What are you going to do to him?"

"We already done him. Just wanted to make sure we got the right bunkie."

They lowered Eric Soares's face into the stream again and he knew it was for the last time.

THEY SEARCHED THE PULLMANS, but no one could find Franklin Mowery's assistant. Isaac Bell dispatched railroad police to search Cascade and the boomtown downriver called Hell's Bottom. But he doubted they would find him. A foreman had vanished too, along with several Union Pier & Caisson laborers.

Bell went to Osgood Hennessy. "You better inspect the bridge piers," he said, grimly. "That's what he worked on."

"Franklin Mowery's already down there," Hennessy replied. "He's wired Union Pier all morning. No reply yet."

"I doubt he'll get one."

Bell wired Van Dorn's St. Louis office. The answer came back immediately. The headquarters of the Union Pier & Caisson Company had burned to the ground.

"What time?" Bell wired back.

The return wire was a testament to the Wrecker's inside information. Adjusting for the difference between Pacific and Central time zones, the first alarm for the fire had been turned in less than two hours after Bell had confronted Franklin Mowery with his suspicions about Eric Soares.

Bell had seen Emma Comden with Hennessy when Mowery reported his concerns about the piers. But within minutes, Hennessy had summoned a dozen cutoff engineers to access the potential for disaster that Mowery feared. So Emma was not the only one aware. Still, Bell had to wonder whether the beautiful woman was playing the old man for a fool.

Bell went looking for Mowery and found him in one of the guard shacks protecting the piers. There were tears in the old man's eyes. He had blueprints spread out on the table where the railroad cops ate supper and a folder of reports filed by Eric Soares.

"False," he said, thumbing through the pages. "False. False. False. False . . . The piers are unstable. A flood of water will cause them to collapse."

Bell found it hard to believe. From where he stood in the guard shack, the massive stone piers supporting the airy towers that held the bridge truss looked solid as fortresses.

But Mowery nodded bleakly out the window at a barge tied alongside the nearest pier. Tenders lifted a diver out of the water and unhinged his faceplate. Bell recognized the new Mark V helmet. That the company spared no expense was yet another indication of the importance of the bridge.

"What do you mean?" Bell asked.

Mowery fumbled for a pencil and drew a sketch of the pier standing in the water. At the foot of the pier, he scratched the pencil point through the paper.

"We call it scour. The effect of scour occurs when the water scoops a hole in the riverbed immediately upstream of the pier. All of a sudden, the footing is not supported. It will plunge into this hole or crack under the unequal forces . . . We have built our house on sand."

42

Isaac Bell walked across the Cascade Canyon Bridge.

The span was dead silent. All train traffic had been stopped. The only sounds Bell could hear were the click of his boot heels and the echo of the rapids far below. No one knew how unstable the bridge was yet, but the engineers all agreed it was only a matter of time and water flow before it fell. When he reached the midpoint between the lips of the gorge, he stared down at the river tumbling against the flawed piers.

He was staggered by the Wrecker's audacity.

Bell had wracked his brain to predict how the Wrecker would attack the bridge. He had guarded every approach, guarded the piers themselves, and watched the work gangs with an eagle eye. It had never occurred to him that the criminal had already attacked it, two full years ago, *before* they started building the bridge.

Bell had stopped him in New York City. He had stopped him on the rails. He had stopped him all the way through Tunnel 13 right up to the bridge. But here, under this bridge, the Wrecker had proved his mettle with a devastating long-term counterthrust in case all else failed.

Bell shook his head partly in anger and partly in grim admiration for his enemy's skills. The Wrecker was despicable, a merciless killer, but he was formidable. This sort of planning and execution went far beyond even the New York dynamite attack.

All that Isaac Bell could say in his own defense was that when the Cascade Canyon Bridge fell into the gorge, at least it would not come as a surprise. He had uncovered the plot before the catastrophe. No train loaded with innocent workmen would fall with it. But though no people would die, it was still a catastrophe. The cutoff, the vast project he had vowed to protect, was as good as dead.

He sensed someone walking toward him and knew who it was even before he smelled her perfume.

"My darling," he called without turning his bleak gaze from the water, "I'm up against a mastermind."

"A 'Napoleon of crime'?" Marion Morgan asked.

"That's what Archie calls him. And he's right."

"Napoleon had to pay his soldiers."

"I know," Bell said bleakly. "Think like a banker. That hasn't gotten me very far."

"There is something else to remember," said Marion. "Napoleon may have been a mastermind, but in the end he lost."

Bell turned around to look at her. Half expecting a sympathetic smile, he saw instead a big grin filled with hope and belief. She was incredibly beautiful, her eyes alight, her hair shining as if she had bathed in sunlight. He could not help but smile back at her. Suddenly, his smile exploded into a grin as broad at hers.

"What is it?" she asked.

"Thank you for reminding me that Napoleon lost."

She had set his mind churning again. He scooped her exuberantly into his arms, winced from the lingering pain of Philip Dow's bullet to his right arm, and shifted her smoothly into his unscathed left.

"Once again I have to leave you right after you arrive. But this time it's your fault because you really made me think."

"Where are you going?"

"I'm going back to New York to interrogate every banker in the railroad business. If there's an answer to the riddle of *why* he is attacking this railroad, it will come from Wall Street."

"Isaac?" Marion took his hand, "Why don't you go to Boston?"

"The biggest banks are in New York. Hennessy and Joe Van Dorn can pull strings. I'll start with J. P. Morgan and work my way down."

"The American States Bank is in Boston."

"No."

"Isaac, why not ask your father? He is vastly experienced in finance. When I worked in banking, he was a legend."

Bell shook his head. "I've told you that my father was not happy that I became a detective. In truth, he was heartbroken. Men who are legends hope their sons will continue building on the foundations that they laid. *I do not regret going my own way.* But I have no right to ask him to forgive me."

Bell hurried to Osgood Hennessy's private car to ask him to make arrangements in New York. He found him in a gloomy state of worry and defeat. Franklin Mowery was with him. Both men appeared shattered. And they seemed to reinforce each other's pessimism.

"Ninety percent of my cutoff is on the far side of the bridge," the railroad president mourned. "All in place for the final push. Track, coal, ties, creosote plant, roundhouse, locomotives, machine shops. All on the wrong side of a bridge that won't hold a wheelbarrow. I'm whipped."

Even the normally cheerful Mrs. Comden seemed defeated. Still, she tried to buck him up, saying sympathetically, "Perhaps it is time to let Nature take her course. Winter is coming. You can start fresh next year. Start over in the spring."

"I'll be dead by spring."

Lillian Hennessy's eyes flashed angrily. She exchanged a grim look with Isaac Bell. Then she sat down at the telegraph table and perched her fingers on the key.

"Father," she said, "I better wire the Sacramento shop."

"Sacramento?" Hennessy asked distractedly. "What for?"

"They've finished fabricating truss rods for the Cascade Canyon Bridge. So they have time to build a pair of rocking chairs."

"Rocking chairs? What the devil for?"

"For retirement. For two of the sorriest geezers I ever saw in my life. Let's build a porch on the roundhouse you can rock on."

"Now, hold on, Lillian."

"You're giving up, just like the Wrecker wants."

Hennessy turned to Mowery and asked him, with little hope in his voice, "Is there any chance of shoring up those piers?"

"Winter's closing in," Mowery muttered. "We've got Pacific storms bearing down on us, water's already rising."

"Mr. Mowery?" Lillian purred through clenched teeth. "What color would you like your rocking chair painted?"

"You don't understand, little lady!"

"I understand the difference between giving up and fighting back."

Mowery stared at the carpet.

"Answer my father!" Lillian demanded. "Is there any chance of shoring those piers before they collapse?"

Mowery blinked. He tugged a sail-sized handkerchief from his pocket and dabbed his eyes.

"We could try building flow deflectors," he said.

"How?"

"Spur dikes off the bank. Harden the bank with riprap. And riprap upstream and downstream of the piers. The same riprapping that double-crossing little bas— was supposed to install properly. We might try collar plates, I suppose." He picked up a pencil and halfheartedly drew a sketch of flow deflectors steering the river currents around the piers.

"But that's only short-term," Hennessy countered gloomily. "'Til the first flood. What about long-term?"

"Long-term, we would somehow have to try to extend the depth of the pier footings. Straight to bedrock, if we can locate it. But at least below the depth of streambed scour."

"But the piers are already in place," groaned Hennessy.

"I know." Mowery looked over at Lillian. "You see, Miss Lillian, we'd have to sink all new caissons for the sandhogs to excavate"—he drew a picture showing the base of the piers surrounded by watertight chambers in which men could work beneath the river—"but before we could even start sinking caissons we'd have to erect coffer dams, temporary protection around the piers to keep the river out, here and here. See? We haven't the time."

He dropped the pencil and reached for his walking stick.

Before Mowery could stand, Bell leaned over him and put his finger firmly on the sketch.

"These coffer dams look like those collar plates. Could coffer dams deflect flow?"

"Of course!" Mowery snapped. "But the point—"

The old engineer's voice trailed off midsentence. He stared. Then his eyes began to gleam. He pushed his walking stick aside and snapped up a pencil.

Isaac Bell shoved a fresh sheet of paper toward him.

Mowery scribbled frantically.

"Look here, Osgood! To the devil with short-term. We'll build the caissons straight off. Shape their coffer dams to function as flow deflectors, too. Better than collar plates, when you think about it."

"How long?" asked Hennessy.

"At least two weeks, round-the-clock, to put the coffer dams in place. Maybe three."

"Weather's getting worse."

"I'll need every hand you can spare."

"I've got a thousand in the yard with nothing to do."

"We'll riprap here and here, harden the bank."

"Just pray we don't get a flood."

"Extend this spur deflector . . ."

Neither the bridge builder nor the railroad president noticed when Isaac Bell and Lillian Hennessy retreated silently from what had blossomed into a full-fledged engineering conference.

"Nice work, Lillian," Bell said. "You stirred them up."

"I realized I had better insure my financial future if I'm going to be courted by a penniless detective."

"Would you like that?"

"I think I would, Isaac."

"More than a candidate for president."

"Something tells me it would be more exciting."

"In that case, I've got good news for you: I've wired Archie to come take over for me."

"Archie's coming here?" She seized Bell's hands in hers. "Oh, Isaac, thank you. That's wonderful."

Bell's golden mustache fanned open with his first carefree smile since they discovered the catastrophe of the sabotaged piers.

"You must promise not to distract him too much. We still haven't caught the Wrecker."

"But if Archie is taking over here, where are you going?"

"Wall Street."

43

Isaac Bell raced across the continent in four and a half days. He took limited flyers when he could and chartered specials when the trains ran slow. He made the final eighteen-hour dash on the Broadway Limited, proudly named for the broad, four-tracked roadbed between Chicago and New York.

On the ferry to Manhattan, he saw how quickly Jersey City and the railroads were repairing the damage from the Wrecker's dynamite explosion. The station roof was already replaced, and a new pier was rising where less than three weeks ago he had seen the blackened stumps of pilings submerged by the tide. The wrecked ships were gone, and while many windows were still covered with raw boards many more gleamed with new glass. The sight filled him with hope at first, reminding him that back in the Oregon Cascades Hennessy and Mowery were driving round-the-clock work gangs to save the Cascade Canyon Bridge. But, he admitted soberly, their task was vastly more difficult, if not downright impossible. The bridge's very foundations were sabotaged. And the Wrecker was still at large, determined to wreak more damage.

Bell disembarked at Liberty Street and walked quickly to nearby

Wall Street. On the corner of Broad stood the white marble head-quarters of J. P. Morgan & Company.

"Isaac Bell to see Mr. Morgan."

"Do you have an appointment?"

Bell opened his gold watch. "Mr. Joseph Van Dorn arranged our meeting for ten this morning. Your clock is slow."

"Oh yes, of course, Mr. Bell. Sadly, however, Mr. Morgan had an abrupt change of plans. He is on the boat to England."

"Who did he leave in his place?"

"Well, no one can take his place, but there is a gentleman who might be able to help you. Mr. Brooks."

A messenger boy led Bell into the bowels of the building. He sat for nearly an hour in Brooks's waiting room, which offered a view of a nickel-clad, steel-barred vault guarded by two armed men. He passed the time by working out the details of two foolproof robberies, a day job and a night job. Finally, he was ushered into Brooks's office.

Brooks was short, compact, and curt. He greeted Bell irritably, without apology for keeping him waiting.

"Your meeting with Mr. Morgan was arranged without my knowledge. I've been instructed to answer your queries. I am a very busy man, and I cannot imagine what information I can impart to a detective."

"I have one simple question," said Bell. "Who would gain if the Southern Pacific Railroad Company went bankrupt?"

Brooks's eyes gleamed with predatory interest.

"Do you have information to support that inference?"

"I infer nothing," Bell retorted sternly before inadvertently inject-ing a fresh element into the endless battle to consolidate the railroads, and undermining Hennessy's reputation in the marketplace. "I am asking who would gain *if* that event were to occur?"

"Let me get this straight, Detective. You have no information that Osgood Hennessy is in a weakened position?"

"Absolutely none."

The interest slid out of Brooks's eyes.

"Of course not," he said sullenly. "Hennessy has been impregnable for thirty years."

"If he were not—"

"If! If! If! Banking is not a business of *ifs*, Mr."—he pretended to glance at Bell's card as if to jog his memory—"Bell. Banking is a business of facts. Bankers do not speculate. Bankers act upon certainties. Hennessy speculates. Hennessy blunders ahead."

"And yet," Bell said mildly, "you say that Hennessy is impregnable."

"He is crafty."

Bell saw he was wasting his time. Closemouthed, and angling for profit, bankers like this one would give nothing to a stranger.

Brooks stood up abruptly. He stared down his nose at Bell, and said, "Frankly, I don't understand why Mr. Morgan would waste his time answering a detective's questions. I suppose it is another example of his overly kind nature."

"Mr. Morgan is not kind," Bell said, containing his anger as he rose to his full height. "Mr. Morgan is intelligent. He knows that he can learn valuable information by listening to another man's questions. Which is why Mr. Morgan is your boss and you are his flunky."

"Well! How dare—"

"Good day!"

Bell stalked out of J. P. Morgan's building and across the street to his next meeting.

Half an hour later, he stalked out of that one, too, and if another banker had rubbed him the wrong way at that exact moment, he would have punched him in the mouth or simply shot him with his derringer. The thought provoked a rueful grin, and he stopped in the middle of the crowded sidewalk to consider if it would even be worth it to keep his next appointment.

"You look perplexed."

Standing before him—gazing up with a warm, impish smile—
was a handsome, dark-haired man in his early forties. He wore an
expensive coat with a fur collar and on his head a yarmulka—a small,
round disk of a velvet hat that bespoke the Hebrew faith.

"I *am* perplexed," said Bell. "Who are you, sir?"

"I am Andrew Rubenoff." He thrust out his hand. "And you are
Isaac Bell."

Astonished, Bell asked, "How did you know?"

"Sheer coincidence. Not coincidence that I recognize you. Just
coincidence that I saw you standing here. Looking perplexed."

"How did you recognize me?"

"Your photograph."

Bell made a point of avoiding photographers. As he had reminded
Marion, a detective had no use for a famous face.

Rubenoff smiled his understanding. "Not to worry. I have only
seen your photograph on your father's desk."

"Ah. You've done business with my father."

Rubenoff waggled his hand in a yes-and-no gesture. "On occa-
sion, we consult."

"You're a banker?"

"So I am told," he said. "In truth, when I arrived from Russia, I
was not impressed by New York's Lower East Side, so I took a train
across the country. In San Francisco, I opened a saloon. Eventually,
I met a pretty girl whose father owned a bank, and the rest is a very
pleasant history."

"Would you have time to join me at lunch?" said Isaac Bell. "I
need to talk to a banker."

"I am already spoken for lunch. But we can have tea in my offices."

Rubenoff's offices were around the corner on Rector Street, which
the police had blocked off so a grand piano could be hoisted safely
from an electric GMC moving van up to the fifth story, where a window had been removed. The open window belonged to Rubenoff,

who ignored the commotion as he ushered Bell in. Through the gaping hole in his wall poured first a cold Hudson River wind, then the swaying black piano accompanied by the shouts of the movers. A matronly secretary brought tea in tall glasses.

Bell explained his mission.

"So," said Rubenoff. "It's not at all a coincidence. You would have found me eventually after others showed you the door. That I recognized you saves time and trouble."

"I'm grateful for your help," said Bell. "I got nowhere at Morgan. The boss was away."

"Bankers are clannish," said Rubenoff. "They band together, even though they dislike and distrust one another. The elegant bankers of Boston dislike the brash New Yorkers. The Protestants distrust the German Jews. The German Jews dislike Russian Jews like me. Dislike and distrust make the world go round. But enough philosophy. What precisely do you want to know?"

"Everyone agrees that Osgood Hennessy is impregnable. Is he?"

"Ask your father."

"I beg your pardon, sir."

"You heard me," he said sternly. "Don't ignore the finest advice you could get in New York City. Ask your father. Give him my regards. And that is all you will hear from Andrew Rubenoff on the subject. I don't know if Hennessy is impregnable. Up until last year, I would have known, but I have gotten out of railroads. I put my money into automobiles and moving pictures. Good day, Isaac."

He stood up and went to the piano. "I will play you out."

Bell did not want to travel to Boston to ask his father. He wanted his answers here and now from Rubenoff, whom he suspected knew more than he admitted. He said, "The movers just left. Don't you need to tune it first?"

In answer, Rubenoff's hands flew at the keys, and four chords boomed in perfect harmony.

"Mr. Mason and Mr. Hamlin build pianos you can ride over Niagara Falls before you have to tune them . . . Your father, young Isaac. Go talk to your father."

Bell caught the subway to Grand Central Terminal, wired his father that he was coming, and boarded the New England Railroad's famous "White Train" flyer. He remembered it well from his student days, riding it down to New Haven. They had called the gleaming express the Ghost Train.

Six hours later, he disembarked at Boston's new South Station, a gigantic, pink-hued stone temple to railroad power. He took an elevator five stories to the station's top floor and checked in with Van Dorn's Boston office. His father had wired back: "I hope you can stay with me." By the time he made his way to his father's Greek Revival town house on Louisburg Square, it was after nine.

Padraic Riley, the elderly butler who had managed the Bell home since before Isaac was born, opened the polished front door. They greeted each other warmly.

"Your father is at table," said Riley. "He thought you might enjoy a late supper."

"I'm famished," Bell admitted. "How is he?"

"Very much himself," said Riley, discreet as ever.

Bell paused in the drawing room.

"Wish me luck," he muttered to his mother's portrait. Then he squared his shoulders and went through to the dining room, where the tall, spare figure of his father unfolded storklike from his chair at the head of the table.

They searched each other's faces.

Riley, hovering at the door, held his breath. Ebenezer Bell, he thought with a twinge of envy, seemed ageless. His hair had gone gray, of course, but he had kept it all, unlike him. And his Civil War veteran's beard was nearly white. But he still possessed the lean frame and erect stance of the Union Army officer who had fought the bloody conflict four decades ago.

In the butler's opinion, the man that his master's son had grown into should make any father proud. Isaac's steady blue-eyed gaze mirrored his father's, tinged with the violet bequeathed by his mother. So much alike, thought Riley. Maybe too much alike.

"How can I help you, Isaac?" Ebenezer asked stiffly.

"I'm not sure why Andrew Rubenoff sent me here," Isaac replied just as stiffly.

Riley shifted his attention to the older man. If there was to be reconciliation, it was up to Ebenezer to make it stick. But all he said was a terse, "Rubenoff is a family man."

"I don't understand."

"He was doing me a kindness . . . It's in his nature."

"Thank you for inviting me to stay the night," Isaac replied.

"You are welcome here," the father said. And then, to Riley's great relief, Ebenezer rose gallantly to the opportunity his son had presented him by agreeing to stay, which he had not in times past. In fact, thought the butler, the stern old Protestant sounded almost effusive. "You look well, son. I believe that your work agrees with you."

Both men extended their hands.

"Dinner," said Riley, "is served."

OVER A WELSH RAREBIT and a cold poached salmon, Isaac Bell's father confirmed what Marion suggested and he suspected. "Railroad magnates are not as all-powerful as they appear. They control their lines by wielding small minority interests of stock. But if their bankers lose faith, if investors demand their money, they find themselves suddenly on a lee shore." A smile twitched Ebenezer Bell's lips. "Forgive my mixing shipping metaphors, but they get in trouble when they must raise capital to prevent rivals from taking them over just as their stock plummets. The New England Railroad you rode here today is about to be swallowed whole by the New York, New Haven and Hartford. And not a moment too soon—little wonder the NE is known as the 'Narrow Escape.' Point is, the New England suddenly has no say in the matter."

"I know that," Bell protested. "But Osgood Hennessy has gobbled up every railroad that ever crossed his path. He is too intelligent and too well established to be overstretched. He admits that he will run out of credit for the Cascades expansion if the Wrecker stalls it. That would be a terrible loss, but he claims that he has plenty of credit to operate the rest of his lines."

"Consider how many lines Hennessy has combined, how many more he is allied with . . ."

"Exactly. He owns the mightiest combine in the country."

"Or a house of cards."

"But everyone agrees that Osgood Hennessy is secure. Morgan's man used the word *impregnable.*"

"Not according to my sources." Ebenezer Bell smiled.

In that moment, Isaac Bell saw his father in a different light. He knew, of course, that as a young officer Ebenezer had distinguished himself in U.S. Army intelligence. He had the medals to prove it. But a strange idea stuck Isaac. It was one that he had never thought of before. Had his father too once longed to be more than a banker?

"Father. Are you saying that if the Wrecker were in a position to buy, if the Southern Pacific Company tottered under the weight of its failed Cascades expansion, he could end up owning it?"

"Not *only* the Southern Pacific, Isaac."

44

"Every railroad in the country," said Isaac Bell.

Complete understanding dawned at last.

The Wrecker's crimes were driven by a purpose as bold as they were evil.

"At last," said Isaac, "I know what he wants. His motive makes twisted sense. He is too ambitious for anything less. Monstrous crimes to serve a mastermind's dream. But how could he enjoy his victory? The instant he seizes the railroads, we will hunt him mercilessly from one end of the continent to the other."

"On the contrary," said Ebenezer Bell, "he will enjoy his victory in private splendor."

"How?"

"He has shielded himself from being identified, much less investigated. Who do you hunt? In what country? A criminal as resourceful as you've described would model his 'retirement,' shall we say, on the European munitions dealers. Or the opium cartels. I know of speculators and profiteers and stock frauds who have plied their illegal trade unmolested for thirty years."

"How?" Isaac demanded, though he was beginning to get the picture.

"If I were the Wrecker," Ebenezer answered, "I would go abroad. I would establish a maze of foreign holding companies shielded by corrupt governments. My shell corporations would bribe the authorities to turn a blind eye. A war minister, a treasury secretary. The European chancelleries are infamous."

"And in America," Isaac said quietly, "a member of the United States Senate."

"The corporations bribe senators. Why wouldn't a criminal? Do you have a senator in mind?"

"Charles Kincaid."

"Hennessy's man. Although I must say that I've always thought of Kincaid as even more of a buffoon than most who sit in that august chamber."

"So he seems. But I have had a terrible suspicion about him for quite a while now. What you suggest would explain why. He could be the Wrecker's agent."

"With unfettered access to government officials anxious to please. And not only the Wrecker's agent in the United States but also the Wrecker's spy inside Hennessy's inner circle. That would be diabolical, wouldn't it, son?"

"Effective!" said Isaac. "If the Wrecker has shown himself to be anything more than cold-bloodedly ruthless, it is effective . . . But there is one problem with this theory: Charles Kincaid appears to be angling to be nominated for the presidency."

"You don't say!"

"Preston Whiteway is backing a run. It's hard to imagine a politician who wants to be president risking getting caught taking bribes from a murderer."

Ebenezer Bell said quietly, "He would not be the first politician sufficiently arrogant to convince himself no one can catch him."

Padraic Riley interrupted to say that he had laid out brandy and coffee in the library and would be going to bed if nothing else was required. He turned on his heel and disappeared before anything was.

He had also left a coal fire glowing in the grate. While Ebenezer Bell splashed generous dollops of brandy in two coffee cups, Isaac Bell stared into the flames, thinking hard. It could have been Kincaid who hired the prizefighters to kill him in Rawlins.

"I bumped into Kenny Bloom on the Overland Limited," he said.

"How is the scamp?"

"About sixty pounds plumper than your average scamp and richer than ever. Father, how would the Wrecker raise the capital to buy the Southern Pacific?"

Ebenezer answered without hesitation. "From the richest bankers in the world."

"Morgan?"

"No. As I understand it, Morgan is stretched tight. He couldn't touch Hennessy's roads. Nor could Vanderbilt or Harriman or Hill, even if they combined. Does Van Dorn have offices overseas?"

"We have reciprocal arrangements with foreign investigators."

"Look to Europe. The only bankers rich enough are in London and Berlin."

"You keep referring to Europe."

"You've described a criminal who needs to raise extraordinary amounts of capital in strictest secrecy. Where could he turn to but Europe for his money? And it's where he will hide in the end. I recommend you use Van Dorn's European connections to run down his bankers. In the meantime, I'll try to help by beating what bushes I can."

"Thank you, Father." Isaac clasped his hand. "You've brought this case to life."

"Where are you going?"

Isaac was striding toward the hall. "Back to the cutoff as fast as I can. He'll keep attacking until Hennessy topples."

"But there'll be no fast trains this late."

"I'll charter a special to Albany and join a Chicago flyer."

His father hurried with him to the door, helped him into his coat, and stood in the foyer as his son dashed into the night.

"When I can return," Isaac called over his shoulder, "there's someone I want you to meet."

"I'm looking forward to making Miss Morgan's acquaintance."

Bell stopped short. Was that the flicker of the gas lamps or a twinkle in his father's eye?

"You know? You've heard?"

"My sources are unanimous: 'Your son,' they tell me, 'is a lucky man.'"

ANOTHER LATE-AUTUMN PACIFIC STORM was blowing hard while James Dashwood attended his twelfth temperance meeting. This one took place in a chilly Santa Barbara hall rented from the Elks. Rain lashed the windows, wind whipped the trees and spattered wet leaves on the glass. But the speaker was inspired and the audience enthusiastic, expecting salty passion from the gnarly, red-faced "Captain" Willy Abrams, Cape Horn clippermaster, shipwreck survivor, and reformed drunkard.

"That alcohol is not nutritious . . ." Captain Willy thundered. "That it awakens a general and unhealthy physical excitement. . . That it hardens the tissues of the brain . . . is proven by every scientific analysis. Ask any ship's officer what makes mutineers. His answer? *Alcohol*. Ask a police officer what makes criminals. His answer? *Alcohol*. Ask the prison warden. *Alcohol*. And think of the expense! How many loaves of bread could grace the kitchen table with the money spent upon intoxicating liquors? How many snug homes could that money build? Why, that money could even pay off the entire National Debt!"

Dashwood paused, momentarily distracted from scanning the men in the audience. Of the many temperance orators he had heard on his search for blacksmith Jim Higgins, Captain Willy Abrams was the first to promise relief of the National Debt.

When it was over and Dashwood saw no one in the dwindling crowd who resembled the blacksmith, he approached the dais.

"One more?" asked Captain Willy, who was packing up his notes. "Always time for one more pledge."

"I've already pledged," said Dashwood, flourishing a Total Abstinence Declaration registered four days earlier by the Ventura chapter of the Woman's Christian Temperance Union. He had ten more in his suitcase, along with the train-wrecking hook fashioned from an anchor and a stack of the lumberjack's sketches.

"I'm looking for a friend, whom I hope has taken the pledge but might have stumbled. He's disappeared, and I fear the worst. A tall, strapping fellow, a blacksmith named Jim Higgins."

"Blacksmith? Big man. Sloped shoulders. Dark hair? Sad and weary eyes."

"You've seen him?"

"Seen him? You bet I've seen him. Thanks to me, the poor devil's mended his ways. In the extreme."

"How do you mean?"

"Instead of taking the pledge never to drink alcohol again, he's pledged to give up everything a man could ever want."

"I don't follow you, Captain Willy."

The speaker looked around, confirmed there were no women within earshot, and dropped a wrinkled lid over a bloodshot eye. "Gave up drink, gave up worldly possessions, even gave up girls. Now, I truly believe, brother, that drinking and drunkenness are inseparable evils. Our Savior Jesus Himself could not keep His customers sober if He ran a saloon. But never let it be said that Captain Willy advocates abandoning *all* earthly pleasures."

"What did Jim Higgins do?"

"Last I heard, he became a monk."

"A monk?"

"Joined a monastery, that's what he's done."

James Dashwood whipped out his notebook.

"Which order?"

"Not sure about that. Order of Saint Somebody or other. I had never heard of them before. Not one of the regulars, sort of an offshoot . . . like you find in these parts."

"Where?"

"Up the coast a ways. Understand they have a heck of a spread."

"What town?"

"Somewhere north of Morro Bay, I believe."

"In the hills or by the sea?" Dashwood pressed.

"Both, I heard. Heck of a spread."

IT HAD BEEN FORTY years since the first transatlantic telegraph cable annihilated time and space. By 1907, more than a dozen stretched under the ocean between Ireland and Newfoundland. The latest could transmit a hundred twenty words per minute. As Isaac Bell rocketed west, a notable share of the cable's capacity was taken up by the Van Dorn Detective Agency gathering information on the Wrecker's European bankers.

Cablegrams poured aboard at every crew change and water stop. By the time he reached Buffalo in his chartered Atlantic 4-4-2—a high-wheeled racer born for the lakeshore water-level route—Bell had a suitcase full of paper. Van Dorn agents and research contractors joined him along the way, specialists in banking, and French and German translators. There were general reports, at first, on the European financing of railroads in China, South America, Africa, and Asia Minor. Then, as the agency's contacts dug deeper, the reports grew more specific, with repeated references to Schane & Simon Company, a little-known German investment house.

Bell picked up a Pullman sleeper in Toledo for his growing staff and replaced the 4-4-2 with a more powerful Baldwin 4-6-0. He added a dining car in Chicago so the investigators could spread their work out on the tables as they sped through Illinois and Iowa.

They crossed Kansas, switching locomotives to the new, highly efficient Baldwin balanced compound Atlantics for speeding up the light but relentless grade of the Great Plains. They picked up wires at every stop. The diner's tables were buried under their yellow paper. Isaac Bell's operatives, accountants, and auditors named their special train the Van Dorn Express.

The Rocky Mountains came into view, blue as the sky, then hardening out of the mist into three distinct snowcapped ranges. The railroad's Mountain Division superintendents, eager to help, wheeled out their best Prairie-type engines, with Vauclain compound cylinders, to suit the grade. So far on the cross-country run, a total of eighteen locomotives and fifteen crews had driven the Van Dorn Express at speeds that surpassed the previous year's record time of fifty hours from Chicago.

Bell saw a pattern swirling around Schane & Simon, which was based in Berlin. Years ago, it had forged close ties with the German government through the powerful chancellor Otto von Bismarck. These ties had grown stronger under the current ruler, Kaiser Wilhelm. Van Dorn's sources reported that the banking house appeared to have channeled government money to the builders of the Baghdad Railway secretly to maintain the fiction that Germany was not building the railroad to a Persian Gulf port to challenge British, French, and Russian interests in the Near East.

"Senator Charles Kincaid's employer, I recall," said one of the translators, who had served with the Department of State before Joseph Van Dorn lured him away.

"In his 'Hero Engineer' days."

Bell wired Sacramento to look for transactions between Schane & Simon and members of Osgood Hennessy's inner circle.

Charles Kincaid, of course, had remained foremost in Isaac Bell's mind ever since his father had explained that foreign holding companies and their secret owner would be shielded by corrupt government officials. Surely, a U.S. senator could do much to promote the Wrecker's interests and guard his secrets. But what motive would drive Kincaid to risk his already lucrative political career? Money? Much more than he got from Southern Pacific Railroad stock. Anger at Hennessy for not encouraging Lillian to marry him? Or was courting her a ruse, an excuse to hang around Hennessy's ever-rolling headquarters?

But how did spying for the Wrecker jibe with his presidential aspirations? Or was he encouraging Preston Whiteway to launch the campaign merely to provide a smoke screen? Had Charles Kincaid surrendered political dreams to concentrate on accumulating an immense fortune in bribes? Or, as Bell's father suggested, was he so arrogant as to believe he could get away with both?

EBENEZER BELL'S DEFINITION OF "beating the bushes" was broad and enterprising. The president of the American States Bank had started out querying trusted friends and associates in Boston, New York, and Washington, D.C., by telephone, telegraph, and private messenger. Learning what he could through lofty connections, he then delved deep into the middle of the country, paying particular attention to St. Louis, home of the burned-out Union Pier & Caisson Company. In the West, information he gathered canvassing the top bankers of San Francisco, Denver, and Portland led him to call in favors from smaller banks in California and Oregon.

A request from the patrician Boston banker prompted a private meeting in Eureka, a deepwater port serving the redwood timber industry two hundred twenty-five miles north of San Francisco. Stanley Perrone, the rough-and-ready president of the Northwest Coast Bank of Eureka, dropped by the office of up-and-coming lumberman A. J. Gottfried. Gottfried had borrowed heavily from Perrone's bank to modernize the Humboldt Bay Lumber Company. His office overlooked his timber pier, which jutted into the rain-lashed harbor.

Gottfried pulled a bottle of good bourbon from his desk, and the men sipped whiskey for a while, chatting about the weather. That it was turning from awful to worse could be predicted by the sight of a red steam launch chugging purposefully between the moored and anchored lumber schooners.

"Son of a gun. Looks like we're getting hit again."

The red launch was piloted by the special messenger from the U.S. Weather Bureau who delivered forecasts of violent storms to the captains of vessels in the harbor.

The banker got down to business. "As I recall, A.J., you bought Humboldt Bay Lumber with the proceeds of the sale of your timber operation in eastern Oregon."

The lumberman, intending to make hay out of this unexpected visit from his banker, answered, "That's exactly how it happened. Though *I* recall that you made it easier by promising to help me replace the old equipment."

"A.J., who bought your East Oregon Lumber Company?"

"A feller with more money than sense," Gottfried admitted cheerfully. "I had despaired of ever unloading it 'til he came along. It was just too expensive to snake the timber down off those mountains.

Not like here, where I can load lumber schooners right at my own wharf. Provided, of course, the ship don't founder trying to get into the harbor."

Perrone nodded impatiently. Everyone knew that the entrance into Humboldt Bay deserved its title "Graveyard of the Pacific." Pea-soup fog, pounding breakers that dissolved into spindrift, and a thick haze of smoke from the lumber mills made finding the channel an exercise that turned sea captains' hair white. "I understand," he said pointedly, "you're considering adding a sash and door factory to your business."

"If I can raise the means," Gottfried answered, hoping he had heard right. "This Panic isn't making it any easier to borrow money."

The banker looked the lumberman in the eye, and said, "I suspect that favored borrowers will get a sympathetic ear despite the Panic. Who bought your East Oregon business?"

"Can't tell you everything about him. As you can imagine, I wasn't looking that particular gift horse in the mouth. Soon as we shook on the deal, I was gone from that place so fast you could hear me whiz."

He drained his glass and poured another, and topped off the banker's glass, which hadn't gone down as far.

"What *do* you know about the purchaser of the East Oregon Lumber Company?" Perrone pressed.

"For one thing, he had plenty of cash."

"Where'd he draw his check from?"

"Well, that was interesting. I would have thought San Francisco or Portland. But his check was on a New York bank. I was a little suspicious, but it cleared lickety-split."

"Was the fellow from New York?"

"Might've been. Sure didn't know much about the lumber business. Now that you mention it, it occurs to me he was buying it for somebody else."

The banker nodded, encouraging the lumberman to continue talking. Ebenezer Bell had made it clear that he didn't expect the whole story from any one source. But every bit helped. And the powerful American States president had also made it clear that he would be grateful for every nugget Perrone could wire him.

· 45 ·

THE VAN DORN EXPRESS PAUSED IN DENVER'S UNION DEPOT just long enough for a Van Dorn agent in bowler hat and checkerboard suit to swagger aboard bearing fresh reports from London and Berlin. "Howdy, Isaac. Long time no see."

"Sit there, Roscoe. Go through these Schane and Simon Company records with a fine-tooth comb. Have your queries ready to wire at the next stop."

A lawyer who connected in Salt Lake City brought more on Schane & Simon. The foundation of the German bank's power was an investment network that backed modernization projects throughout the Ottoman Empire. But as far back as the nineties, they had begun doing business in North and South America.

The Van Dorn Express was racing across the Great Salt Desert when Roscoe, who had boarded in Denver, hit pay dirt in the heaps of cablegrams about Schane & Simon.

"Isaac! Who's Erastus Charney?"

"Railroad attorney. Got rich on Southern Pacific stock. Seemed to know more than he should about when to buy and when to sell."

"Well, he sure as heck sold something to Schane and Simon. Look at these deposits with Charney's stockbroker."

Bell wired Sacramento from Wendover, while the train quickly watered and coaled for the climb into Nevada, instructing them to follow up on Roscoe's discovery. But he feared it was too little too late. If Simon & Shane did bankroll the Wrecker, then the evidence was clear that Charney had been bribed to pass information about Hennessy's plans to the saboteur. Unfortunately, the fact that the crooked railroad attorney was still alive suggested that his link to the murderous Wrecker was circuitous, and Charney would know nothing about him. But at least they would take another of the Wrecker's accomplices out of action.

Two hours later, the train was pulling out of Elko, Nevada, when a plump accountant sprinted for the last car. Thirty pounds overweight and a decade past his sprinting years, Jason Adler tripped. One soft pink hand was already clinging to the vestibule rail, the other gripping a fat satchel. As the train dragged him along the platform, he held on with all his might, coolly calculating that he was now flying too fast to let go without suffering grievous injury. An alert conductor rushed to the vestibule. He sank both hands into the folds of the accountant's coat. Too late, he realized that the weight of the falling man was dragging both of them off the train.

Burly Van Dorn detectives sprang to their aid.

The accountant ended up on the vestibule floor, clutching his satchel to his chest.

"I have important information for Mr. Isaac Bell," he said.

Bell had just fallen asleep for the first time in twenty-four hours when they tugged open the curtain to his Pullman berth. He was wide awake instantly, eyes glittering with ferocious concentration. The operative apologized for waking him and introduced an overweight man clutching a briefcase to a suit that looked like he'd been turning somersaults in a coal yard.

"This is Mr. Adler, Mr. Bell."

"Hello, Mr. Adler, who are you?"

"I am an accountant employed by American States Bank."

Bell swung his feet off the bunk. "You work for my father."

"Yes, sir," Adler said proudly. "Mr. Bell specifically asked for me to take on this audit."

"What have you got?"

"We have uncovered the name of the secret owner of the Union Pier and Caisson Company of St. Louis."

"Go on!"

"We should talk in private, Mr. Bell."

"These are Van Dorn agents. You can say your piece here."

Adler clutched his briefcase closer. "I apologize to you gentlemen, and to you Mr. Bell, but I am under strict orders from my boss, Mr. Ebenezer Bell, president of the American States Bank, to speak to you and only you."

"Excuse us," said Bell. The detectives left. "Who owns Union Pier?" he demanded.

"A shell corporation established by a Berlin investment house."

"Schane and Simon."

"Yes, sir. You are well informed."

"We're getting there. But who owns the shell corporation?"

Adler lowered his voice to a whisper. "It is wholly controlled by Senator Charles Kincaid."

"You're sure?"

Adler hesitated only a second. "Not beyond all doubt, but reasonably sure Senator Kincaid is their client. Schane and Simon supplied the money. But there are numerous indications that they did it on his behalf."

"That implies that the Wrecker is well connected in Germany."

Adler answered, "That was your father's conclusion, too."

Bell wasted no time congratulating himself on the discovery that

Kincaid likely served the Wrecker just as he had suspected. He ordered an immediate investigation of every outside contractor hired by the Southern Pacific Company to work on the Cascades Cutoff. And he wired a warning to Archie Abbott to keep a close eye on the Senator.

"TELEGRAPH, MR. ABBOTT."

"Thank you, Mr. Meadows."

Archie Abbott broke into a broad grin when he decoded the message from Isaac Bell. He combed his red hair in the reflection of a railcar window and straightened his snappy bow tie. Then he marched straight to Osgood Hennessy's private office with a fine excuse to call on Miss Lillian, who was wearing a ruby velvet blouse with a fitted waist, an intriguing row of pearl buttons down the front, and a riveting flow of fabric over her hips.

The Old Man was not in a friendly mood this morning. "What do you want, Abbott?"

Lillian was watching closely, gauging how Archie handled her father. She would not be disappointed. Archie had no trouble with fathers. Mothers were his weakness.

"I want you to tell me everything you know about outside contractors working on the cutoff," Abbott said.

"We already know about Union Pier and Caisson," Hennessy replied heavily. "Otherwise, several down in Cascade. Purveyors, hotels, laundries. Why do you ask?"

"Isaac doesn't want a repeat of the pier problem and neither do I. We're checking into all the outside contractors. Do I understand correctly that a contractor was hired by the Southern Pacific to supply crossties for the cutoff?"

"Of course. When we started building the cutoff, I arranged to stockpile crossties on this side of the Canyon Bridge so we'd be ready to jump as soon as we crossed."

"Where is the mill?"

"About eight miles up the mountain. New owners modernized the old water mill."

"Did they supply ties as promised?"

"Pretty much. It's slow snaking timber down from there, but, by and large, it's worked out. I gave them a long head start, and the creosoting plant has more than it can handle."

"Is the plant an outside contractor, too?"

"No. It's ours. We just knock it down and move it up the line where we need it."

"Why didn't you establish your own sawmill as you've done in the past?"

"Because the bridge was far ahead of the rest of the road. These folks were already up and running. It seemed the fastest way to get the job done. That's all I can tell you."

"By the way, have you seen Senator Kincaid today?"

"Not since yesterday. If you're that interested in the timber operation, why don't you ride up there and have a look?"

"That's exactly where I'm headed."

Lillian jumped up. "I'll ride with you!"

"No!" chorused Archie Abbott and Osgood Hennessy.

Her father pounded the table for emphasis. Archie offered a heart-grabbing smile and an apology.

"I wish you could ride with me, Lillian," he said, "but Van Dorn policy . . ."

"I know. I've heard it already. You don't bring friends to gunfights."

46

James Dashwood located St. Swithun's Monastery from a clue dropped by the Women's Christian Temperance Union orator Captain Willy Abrams: "A heck of a spread."

Its boundaries encompassed thirteen thousand acres that sprawled from the foothills of the Santa Lucia Mountains to the bluffs that reared over the Pacific Ocean. A muddy road miles from the nearest town led through iron gates onto an undulating plateau planted in orchards of fruit trees, nut trees, and vineyards. The chapel was a spare, modern building with simple Art Nouveau stained-glass windows. Low stone buildings of similar design housed the monks. They ignored James when he asked to see a recent arrival, a blacksmith named Jim Higgins.

Man after man in swaying robes walked past him as if he did not exist. Monks harvesting grapes and picking nuts just kept working no matter what he said. Finally, one took pity, picked up a stick, and wrote in the mud VOW OF SILENCE.

Dashwood took the stick and wrote BLACKSMITH?

The monk pointed at a cluster of barns and corrals opposite the dormitories. Dashwood headed there, heard the distinctive clank of a hammer on iron, and quickened his pace. Rounding a barn, he saw a thin column of smoke rising through the branches of a chestnut tree. Higgins was bent over a forge, pounding a horseshoe on the horn of his anvil.

He wore a brown robe under his leather apron. His head was bare to the cold drizzle. The robe made him look even bigger than Dashwood remembered. In one powerful hand, he gripped a massive hammer, and in the other long tongs that held red-hot iron. When he looked up and saw Dashwood in his city clothes carrying a suitcase, Dashwood had to suppress the strong impulse to flee.

Higgins stared long and hard at Dashwood.

Dashwood said, "I hope you haven't taken vows of silence like the others."

"I'm just a novice. How did you find me?"

"When I heard you stopped drinking, I went to temperance meetings."

Higgins gave a snort that was half laugh, half angry growl. "Figured the last place the Van Dorns would find me would be in a monastery."

"You were scared by the sketch I showed you."

Higgins raised the hot horseshoe in his tongs. "Guess I figured wrong . . ."

"You recognized him, didn't you?"

Higgins threw the horseshoe into a bucket of water. "Your name is James, ain't it?"

"Yes. We're both Jims."

"No, you're a James, I'm a Jim . . ." He leaned his tongs against the anvil and stood his hammer beside it. "Come on, James. I'll show you around."

Jim Higgins lumbered off toward the bluff. James Dashwood followed him. He caught up and walked beside Higgins until they had to stop at the bluff's crumbling edge. The Pacific Ocean spread as far as they could see, gray and forbidding under a lowering sky. Dashwood looked down, and his guts clenched. Hundreds of feet below them, the ocean thundered on a rocky beach, hurling up spray. Had Higgins lured him to this lonely precipice to throw him to his death?

"I have known for some time that I was going to Hell," the blacksmith intoned gravely. "That's why I stopped drinking whiskey. But it didn't help. Stopped beer. Still going to Hell." He turned to James Dashwood with burning eyes. "You turned me inside out when you came along. Scared me into running. Scared me into hiding."

James Dashwood wondered what he should say. What would Isaac Bell do under these circumstances? Try to clamp handcuffs around his thick wrists? Or let him talk?

"Bunch of big shots started this monastery," Higgins was saying. "Lot of these monks are rich men who gave up everything to live the simple life. You know what one of them told me?"

"No."

"Told me that I'm blacksmithing exactly like they did in the Bible, except I burn mineral coal in my forge instead of charcoal. They say that working like folks in the Bible is good for our souls."

He turned his back on the cliff and fixed his gaze on the fields and meadows. The drizzle strengthening into rain shrouded the vineyards and the fruit trees.

"I figured I was safe here," he said.

He stared for a long time before he spoke again.

"What I didn't figure was liking it here. I like working outdoors under a tree instead of cooped up with trucks and automobiles stinking up the air. I like being with weather. I like watching storms . . ." He whirled around to face the Pacific, which was checkered with dark squalls. To the southwest, the sky was turning black as coal. "See there?" he asked Dashwood, pointing to the blackness.

Dashwood saw a grim, cold ocean, a crumbling precipice at his feet, and rocks far below.

"Look, James. Don't you see it coming?"

It struck the apprentice detective that the blacksmith had gone crazy long before the train wreck. "See what, Jim?"

"The storm." The blacksmith's eyes were burning. "Mostly, they angle in from the northwest, a monk told me, down from the northern Pacific where it's cold. This one's coming from the south where it's warm. From the south brings more rain . . . You know what?"

"What?" Dashwood asked, hope fading.

"There's a monk here whose daddy owns a Marconi wireless telegraph. Do you know that right now, four hundred miles at sea, there's a ship telegraphing to the Weather Bureau what the weather is out there!" He fell silent, contemplating that discovery.

It was a chance to prime the pump, and James seized it. "They got the idea from Ben Franklin."

"Huh?"

"I learned it in high school. Benjamin Franklin noticed that storms are moving formations, that you can track where they're going."

The blacksmith looked intrigued. "He did?"

"So when Samuel Morse invented the telegraph, it made it possible to send warnings to folks in the storm's path. Like you say, Jim, now Marconi's wireless telegraph lets ships send radiotelegraph storm warnings from way out in the ocean."

"So the Weather Bureau's known about that one for quite some time now? Isn't that something?"

Dashwood reckoned that the weather had taken them about as far as they could go.

"How did I scare you?" he asked.

"That picture you showed me."

"This?" Dashwood took the sketch without the mustache from his suitcase.

The blacksmith turned away. "That's who wrecked the Coast Line Limited," he said softly. "Except you got his ears too big."

Dashwood rejoiced. He was closing in. He reached into his bag. Isaac Bell had wired him to get in touch with a pair of Southern Pacific cinder dicks named Tom Griggs and Ed Bottomley. Griggs and Bottomley had taken Dashwood out, got him drunk and into the arms of a redhead at their favorite brothel. Then they'd taken him to breakfast and given him the hook that had derailed the Coast Line Limited. He pulled the heavy cast iron out of his bag. "Did you make this hook?"

The blacksmith eyed it morosely. "You know I did."

"Why didn't you say anything?"

"Because they'd blame me for killing those poor people."

"What was his name?"

"Never said his name."

"If you didn't know his name, why did you run?"

The blacksmith hung his head. Tears welled in his eyes and rolled down his red cheeks.

Dashwood had no idea what to do next, but he did sense that it would be a mistake to speak. He turned his attention to the ocean in an effort to remain silent, hoping the man would resume his confession. The weeping blacksmith took Dashwood's silence as condemnation.

"I didn't mean no harm. I didn't mean to hurt nobody. But who would they believe, me or him?"

"Why wouldn't they believe you?"

"I'm just a blacksmith. He's a big shot. Who would you believe?"

"What kind of big shot?"

"Who would you believe? A drunken smithy or a senator?"

"A senator?" Dashwood echoed in utter despair. All his work, all his chasing, all his running down the blacksmith had led him to a lunatic.

"He always hugged the dark," Higgins whispered, brushing at his tears. "In the alley behind the stable. But the boys opened the door and the light fell on his face."

Dashwood remembered the alley. He remembered the door. He could imagine the light. He wanted to believe the blacksmith. And yet he couldn't.

"Where had you seen that senator before?"

"Newspaper."

"A good likeness?"

"Like you standing there beside me," Higgins answered, and Dashwood decided that the man believed every word as strongly as he blamed himself for the wreck of the Coast Line Limited. But belief did not necessarily make him sane. "The man I saw looked just like that big-shot senator. It couldn't've been him. But if it was—if it was him—I knew I was in a terrible fix. Big trouble. Trouble I deserved. By the work of this hand."

Weeping harder, chest heaving, he held up a meaty paw wet with his tears.

"By the work of this hand, those people died. The engineer. The fireman. That union feller. That little boy . . ."

A gust of wind whipped Higgins's monk's robe, and he looked down at the crashing waves as if they offered peace. Dashwood dared not breathe, certain that one wrong word, a simple "Which senator?" would cause Jim Higgins to jump off the cliff.

OSGOOD HENNESSY WAS READING the riot act to his lawyers, having finished excoriating his bankers for bad news on Wall Street, when the meeting was interrupted by a short, amiable-looking fellow wearing a string tie, a vest, a creamy-white Stetson, and an old-fashioned single-action .44 on his hip.

"Excuse me, gents. Sorry to interrupt."

The railroad attorneys looked up, their faces blossoming with hope. Any interruption that derailed their angry president was a gift from Heaven.

"How'd you get past my conductor?" Hennessy demanded.

"I informed your conductor—and the gentleman detective with the shotgun—that I am United States Marshal Chris Danis. I have a message from Mr. Isaac Bell for Mr. Erastus Charney. Is Mr. Charney here by any chance?"

"That's me," said the plump and jowly Charney. "What's the message?"

"You're under arrest."

THE WINCHESTER RIFLE SLUG that had nearly blown the renegade telegrapher Ross Parker off his horse had shredded his right biceps and riddled the muscle with bone splinters. Doc said he was lucky it hadn't shattered his humerus instead of just chipping it. Parker wasn't feeling lucky. Two and a half weeks after the Van Dorn detective with the Texas drawl had shot him and killed two of his best men, it still hurt so bad that the act of lifting his arm to turn the key in his post office box made his head swim.

It hurt more to reach into the box to extract the Wrecker's letter. It even hurt to slit the envelope with his gravity knife. Cursing the private dick who had shot him, Parker had to steady himself on a counter as he removed the luggage ticket he had been hoping to find.

The daily Weather Bureau postcard with the forecast stamped on it sat on the counter in a metal frame. The rural mail carrier had delivered one every day to the widow's farm outside of town where he had been recuperating. The forecast today was the same as yesterday and same as the day before: more wind, more rain. Yet another reason to get out of Sacramento while the getting was good.

Parker took the luggage ticket around the corner to the railroad station and claimed the gripsack the Wrecker had left there. He found the usual wads of twenty-dollar bills inside, along with a map of northern California and Oregon showing where the wires should be cut and a terse note: "Start now."

If the Wrecker thought Ross Parker was going to climb telegraph poles with his arm half blown off and two of his gang shot dead, the saboteur had another think coming. Parker's plans for this bag of money did not include working for it. He practically galloped across the station to line up at the ticket window.

A big man shoved ahead of him. With his vest, knit cap, checked shirt, dungarees, walrus mustache, and hobnailed boots, he looked like a lumberjack. Smelled like one too, reeking of dried sweat and wet wool. All he was missing was a double-bladed ax slung over one shoulder. Ax or no ax, he was too big to argue with, Parker conceded, particularly with a bum arm. A bigger fellow, smelling the same, got on line behind him.

The lumberjack bought three tickets to Redding and paused nearby to count his change. Parker bought a ticket to Chicago. He checked the clock. Plenty of time for lunch and a snort. He left the station and went looking for a saloon. Suddenly, the lumberjacks who'd been on the ticket line fell in on either side of him.

"Chicago?"

"What?"

"Mr. Parker, you can't take the train to Chicago."

"How do you know my name?"

"Folks are counting on you right here."

Ross Parker thought fast. These two must have been watching the luggage room. Which meant the Wrecker, whoever the hell he was, was several jumps ahead of him.

"I got hurt," he said. "Shot. I can't climb a pole."

"We'll climb for you."

"Are you a lineman?"

"How tall's a telegraph pole?"

"Sixteen feet."

"Mister, we're high riggers. We top spar trees two hundred feet off the ground and stay up there for lunch."

"It's more than climbing. Can you splice wire?"

"You'll learn us how."

"Well, I don't know. It takes some doing."

"Don't matter. We'll be doing more cutting than splicing anyhow."

"You have to splice, too," said Parker. "Snipping wires isn't enough if you want to shut the system and keep it shut. You have to hide your cuts so the repair gang don't see where the line is broken."

"If you can't learn us how to splice," the lumberjack said conversationally, "we'll kill you."

Ross Parker resigned himself to his fate.

"When do you want to start?"

"Like it says on your map. Now."

·47·

HOUR AFTER HOUR, ISAAC BELL'S VAN DORN EXPRESS POUNDED up the steep approach to the Donner Pass. Cresting the summit at last, locomotive, tender, diner, and Pullman thundered between the stonework known as the "Chinese Walls" and roared through Summit Tunnel. Then it raced down the Sierra Nevada.

Gaining speed with every sloping mile, it topped a hundred five miles per hour. Even with another coal and water stop, Bell reckoned that at this rate they'd make Sacramento in an hour.

He wired ahead when the special stopped at Soda Springs. To save time changing locomotives, he asked the Sacramento superintendent to have a fresh engine standing by to race him north to the Cascade Canyon Bridge.

Bell kept making the rounds of his auditors, lawyers, detectives, and researchers, speaking repeatedly with every man on the train. They were closing in on the puzzle of which European bankers were paying for the Wrecker's rampage. But how much closer was he to the Wrecker himself?

Ever since his father's accountant had confirmed Charles Kincaid's role as the Wrecker's agent and spy, Bell had been mentally replaying the draw hand when he'd bluffed Kincaid on the Overland Limited. He recalled that he had bluffed the steel magnate James Congdon out of the hand first. That Kincaid had folded too had been more of a surprise. It was a smart fold. It had been the act of a calculating player, a player brave enough to cut his losses but a more cautious player than he had been all night. More cunning.

A strange phrase started churning in Bell's mind: *I am thinking the unthinkable.*

ASTRIDE A CHESTNUT HORSE on a trail that overlooked his East Oregon Lumber Company, the Wrecker watched everything turn his way. The rains were arriving in earnest now. After many setbacks, his luck had changed. Snowstorms were sweeping the mountains to the north. Portland and Spokane were blizzard bound. But here fell rain, flooding the freshets, streams, and creeks that fed the Cascade River. "Lake Lillian" was topping its makeshift dam.

It was raining too hard to cut timber. East Oregon Lumber's steam donkeys stood silent. The high-lead yarding lines, wire ropes that snaked logs to the mill, swayed idly in the wind. The greedy manager paced sullenly in his office. Mules dozed in the stables. Oxen huddled with their backs to the rain. Teamsters and lumberjacks sprawled in their bunkhouses, drunk on bootleg.

A Hell's Bottom Flyer dugout canoe lay on the riverbank below the dam filled with rainwater. No work, no pay. Saloons rarely offered credit with winter coming on. Women never did.

The Wrecker turned his horse up the trail and rode the steep mile to Philip Dow's cabin.

Dow did not come out to greet him. The Wrecker tied the horse under the lean-to, slung a saddlebag over his shoulder, and knocked on the door. Dow opened the door immediately. He had been watching through a rifle slit.

His eyes were feverish. The skin around the bandage that covered the remains of his ear was inflamed. Repeated douses of carbolic acid and raw whiskey were barely keeping infection at bay. But it was more than infection taking its toll, the Wrecker suspected. Dow's failure to kill Isaac Bell and the subsequent shootout with the detective had left the assassin dangerously unbalanced.

"Powder, fuse, and detonators," the Wrecker said, putting the bag down in the corner farthest from the fireplace. "Watertight. How is your hearing?"

"I can hear fine on this side."

"Can you hear that locomotive whistle?" A Consolidation was blowing faintly nine miles down in the cutoff yards.

Dow cocked his good ear. "Now that you mention it . . ."

"You ought to have one of your boys up here with you so he can hear my signal to blow the dam."

"I'll leave the door open. I'm not deaf. I'll hear it."

The Wrecker did not argue the point. He needed to keep Dow in a loyal, cooperative frame of mind, and it was clear that in his current state a hulking, evil-smelling lumberjack inside his neat-as-a-pin cabin would provoke him to kill the man.

"Don't worry about it," he said. "I'll tie down two whistles at once. You'll hear them fine."

The sound of simultaneously doubled locomotive whistles would fly up the mountain louder than winged banshees shrieking, "Blow Lake Lillian's dam!"

"How are you going to manage that?"

"Do you believe that every trainman in those yards works for Osgood Hennessy?" the Wrecker asked enigmatically. "I'll have two locomotives parked unattended at the edge of the yards. By the time anyone investigates why they're blowing their whistles, you'll have lit your fuse."

Dow smiled. He liked that.

"You're everywhere, aren't you?" he said.

"Everywhere I have to be," said the Wrecker.

Dow opened the saddlebag and inspected the explosives with a practiced eye.

"Blasting gelatin," he said approvingly. "You know your business."

The dam was soaking wet. Water would exude the nitroglycerine out of common dynamite. The Wrecker had brought gelignite, which would stand up to water. The detonators and the fuse passed muster too, liberally dipped in wax.

The Wrecker said, "I wouldn't set the charge before noon tomorrow to be absolutely sure to keep the detonator dry."

The ordinarily polite Dow revealed how tightly he was strung by snapping, "I know how to blow a dam."

The Wrecker rode back down to the lake. Some logs had floated to the spillway, further impeding the flow. Excellent, he thought. By tomorrow afternoon, Lake Lillian would be even bigger. Suddenly, he leaned forward in his saddle, every nerve alert.

Down in the camp, a horseman was riding up the wagon trail from the Cascade Canyon Bridge. Eight miles of muddy ruts did not invite a casual ride even if it weren't pouring rain. The man on that horse had come looking specifically for the East Oregon Lumber Company.

A Stetson covered his hair, a pale yellow slicker his torso and the rifle in its scabbard. But the Wrecker had a fair notion who it was. His first sight of him had been across Hammerstein's Jardin de Paris theater seated next to Isaac Bell. Neither hat, slicker, nor the fact that he was astride a horse could conceal his shoulders-back, head-high, New York actor's bearing that cried out *Look at me!*

A hungry smile twisted the Wrecker's face as he pondered how to make use of this unexpected visit.

"Detective Archibald Angell Abbott IV," he said aloud, "come a-calling . . ."

• • •

ARCHIBALD ANGELL ABBOTT IV liked nothing about the East Oregon Lumber Company. From the muddy eight-mile climb to the steam donkeys standing still and mute to the glum lumberjacks watching him from their bunkhouses, he saw nothing that made any economic sense. Even if he had never seen a timber operation—and he had, in fact, seen plenty in deep-woods Maine and the Adirondacks while visiting Angell and Abbott family summer camps with his mother—he could tell that this remote and rugged site could not harvest enough timber to pay for all the new machinery much less make a profit.

He rode past the office and the bunkhouses.

No one even bothered to open a door to offer shelter from the rain.

He liked the lake even less. The ramshackle dam looked ready to burst. Water was leaking out top to bottom and pouring over the spillway in torrents. What was it doing here? He urged his horse up a steep trail for a closer look. The trail brought him to the top of the dam and a view of the lake. It was enormous, much bigger than it had to be. There was no race to channel the water. Besides, the modern circular saw blades he had seen down in the mill were powered by steam.

Abbott saw movement farther up the muddy trail. A horseman was coming down it at a dangerously fast trot. His flapping rain slicker was tucked to one side, exposing his rifle. Company cop on patrol, Abbott assumed.

Abbott leaned on the pommel of his saddle, rainwater dripping from his hat, and rolled a cigarette with the deft fingers of one hand. It was an old cowhand trick he had learned from Texas Walt Hatfield that suited his saddle-tramp disguise. He had just managed to get it smouldering with a damp match when he realized that the horseman descending on him was none other than Senator Charles Kincaid.

Well, well, well . . . The very man Isaac said to watch.

Abbott tossed his smoke in a puddle.

"Kincaid. What are you doing here?"

"I could ask you the same."

"I'm doing my job. What are you doing?"

"I got curious about this operation."

"So was Isaac Bell. Asked me to have a look."

"What do you think?"

"You've seen more of it than me from up there." Abbott nodded up the trail. "What do *you* think?"

"Strikes me as a thoroughly modernized operation," answered the Wrecker as he weighed methods of killing Abbott. "All it's lacking is a cable-draw works to snake timber down to the railhead."

The heavy report of the Wrecker's rifle would bring men running from the bunkhouse. So would the crack of the revolver he was carrying in his shoulder holster. Pressing the barrels of his pocketed derringer to the detective's skull would muffle the sound. But to get close enough to do that, he would have to expose himself to a seasoned fighter, and Abbott looked thoroughly capable of killing him. So he had to use his telescoping sword. But it might tangle in his slicker. Best to get off their horses first, and farther away from the bunkhouses.

He was about to say that he had seen something up on the lake that Abbott would find interesting when he heard a woman call out. The Wrecker and Abbott turned toward the trail that entered into the skid road.

"Well, I'll be darned," Abbott said, smiling, and he raised his voice to call back, "Does your father know you're here?"

"What do you think?"

Lillian Hennessy was mounted comfortably on the enormous Thunderbolt, the only horse in the company stables big enough to carry Jethro Watt. She touched her heels to Thunderbolt's ribs, and the monster cantered amiably toward Abbott and Kincaid.

The young heiress's cheeks were pinkened by the cold rain. Her eyes were an even paler shade of blue in the gray light. An alluring wisp of flaxen hair had escaped from her brimmed hat. If there was a more agreeable sight in Oregon at that moment, neither man could imagine it. Each produced his best smile.

"Charles, what are you doing here?"

"Whatever I'm doing here, I'm not disobeying my father."

But she had already turned to Abbott with a smile. "Did you find the gunfight you were looking for?"

"Not yet," he answered seriously. "I'm got to speak with the manager. Please wait for me. I'd rather you didn't ride back alone."

"She won't be alone," said Kincaid. "I'd ride her back."

"That's exactly what I meant," said Abbott. "I'll be back shortly, Lillian."

He rode to the frame building that looked like an office, dismounted, and knocked on the door. A gaunt, hard-eyed man who looked to be in his late thirties opened it.

"What?"

"Archie Abbott. Van Dorn Agency. Have you a moment for a few questions?"

"No."

Abbott stopped the door with his boot. "My client is the railroad. Seeing as how they're your only customer, do you want me to complain?"

"Why didn't you say so? Come in."

The manager's name was Gene Garret, and Abbott found it hard to believe that he was not aware that there was no way the operation could be turning a profit. When Abbott pressed, pointing out the expense that had gone into the operation, Garret snapped, "The owners pay me a good wage, plus a bonus for delivery. That says to me they're making a profit and then some."

Archie poked his head into the millhouse, looked over the machinery, and then joined Lillian and Kincaid, who were standing silently under the canvas lean-to with their horses. It was a slow ride down the awful road to the staging yards.

Abbott took Lillian's horse to the stables so she could slip back onto her train undetected by her father. Then he went to telegraph a report to Isaac Bell, recommending that Van Dorn auditors delve deeply into the owners of East Oregon Lumber and reporting that he had discovered Kincaid on their property and would be keeping a close eye on him.

"I'll send it the second the line's repaired," promised J. J. Meadows. "Wires just went dead as a doornail. Poles must have toppled from the rain."

JAMES DASHWOOD LEAPED FROM the Southern Pacific Railroad ferry at Oakland Mole. White weather-warning flags with black centers were snapping in the stiff breeze blowing off San Francisco Bay. White with black centers forecast a sudden drop in temperature.

He ran full speed for the connecting train to Sacramento desperate to intercept Isaac Bell at that junction. His train was already rolling from the platform. He ran after it, jumped aboard at the last possible second, and stood on the rear vestibule catching his breath. As the train cleared the terminal building, he saw the white flags being hauled down. Up their staffs shot red flags with black centers. Just like the blacksmith predicted.

Storm warnings.

48

Isaac Bell wasted no time in Sacramento. In response to his wire, the railroad had its newest Pacific 4-6-2 ready to hitch on—steam up, watered, and coaled. Minutes after it pulled in from the east, the Van Dorn Express was rolling north.

Bell directed new arrivals to the diner, where the work was being done. He lingered on the rear platform, brow furrowed, as the train crept out of the yards. That strange phrase kept churning in his mind: *I am thinking the unthinkable.* Over and over and over.

Had Charles Kincaid acted the fool earlier in the poker game? Had Kincaid allowed him to win the enormous pot to distract him? No doubt it was Kincaid who had jumped off the train in Rawlins to hire the prizefighters to kill him. And it had probably been Kincaid, acting on the Wrecker's behalf, who had alerted Philip Dow to ambush him on Osgood Hennessy's special when his guard was down.

He recalled again Kincaid pretending to admire Hennessy for taking enormous risks. He had deliberately undermined his benefactor's standing with the bankers. Which made him a very efficient agent for the Wrecker. A very devious spy.

But what if the famous United States senator was *not* the Wrecker's corrupt agent? Not his spy?

"I am," Bell said out loud, "thinking the unthinkable."

The train was picking up speed.

"Mr. Bell! Mr. Bell!"

He looked back at the frantic shouting.

A familiar figure lugging a suitcase was sprinting through the maze of rails, jumping switches, and dodging locomotives.

"Stop the train!" Bell ordered, yanking open the door so the conductor could hear him.

Locomotive, tender, dining car, and Pullman sleeper ground to a stop. Bell grasped the outstretched hand which was wet with rain and perspiration and pulled James Dashwood into the vestibule.

"I found the blacksmith."

"Why didn't you wire?"

"I couldn't, Mr. Bell. You'd think I was a lunatic. I had to report face-to-face."

A fierce glance from Bell sent the conductor quickly retreating inside the car, leaving them alone on the platform.

"Did he recognize the sketch?"

"He admits he was drunk the night he made the hook for the Wrecker. But he thinks that the man he saw might have been a very important personage. So important, I can't believe it. That's why I have to report face-to-face."

Isaac slapped Dashwood's shoulder and shook his hand. "Thank you, James. You have made thinkable the unthinkable. Senator Charles Kincaid is the Wrecker."

49

"How did you know?" James Dashwood gasped.

The moment Isaac Bell said it, he knew it was true. Senator Charles Kincaid was not the Wrecker's spy. Kincaid was the Wrecker himself.

Charles Kincaid raced from attack to attack on a senator's railway pass. ("Oh, he gets around, sir," said the conductor on the Overland Express. "You know those officeholders, always on the go.")

Charles Kincaid had penetrated Hennessy's inner circle. (Hanging around pretending to court Lillian Hennessy. Toadying to her father. Recruiting intimate functionaries like Erastus Charney.)

Charles Kincaid was a civil engineer who know how to extract the most damage from every attack. ("Look for an engineer," he had taunted.)

"How did you know?"

The crestfallen expression on the boy's face prompted Bell to answer kindly.

"James, I could never have said it aloud if you hadn't told me what you learned. Well done. Mr. Van Dorn will hear about you . . .

Conductor! Back the train to the dispatcher's office. I want his telegraph."

The dispatcher's office occupied a wooden building in the middle of the busy train yard. The floor shook as switch engines shuttled trains past with only inches of clearance. Bell dictated a telegram to Archie Abbott at the Cascade Canyon Bridge: "ARREST SENATOR CHARLES KINCAID."

The telegrapher's eyes popped wide.

"Keep writing! 'KINCAID IS THE WRECKER.'

"*Keep writing!* 'TAKE EVERY PRECAUTION. DO NOT FORGET—REPEAT—DO NOT FORGET—HE GOT THE DROP ON WISH CLARKE AND WEBER AND FIELDS.'

"Send it!"

The telegrapher's key started clicking faster than a belt-fed Vickers. But he got no further than the word ARREST. His hand froze on the dash knob.

"What are you waiting for?"

"The wire's gone dead."

· 50 ·

"WE'VE BEEN HAVING TROUBLE ALL DAY."

"Wire Dunsmuir!" said Bell. He had posted Van Dorn operatives at that railroad center. He would order them to commandeer a loco-motive north to tell Archie to arrest the Wrecker.

The telegrapher tried, with no success. "Dead to Dunsmuir."

"Wire Redding." Texas Walt Hatfield was watching Redding.

"Sorry, Mr. Bell. It appears all lines are dead from here in Sacra-mento north."

"Find a way around it."

Bell knew that multiple telegraph lines connected Sacramento to the rest of the country. Commercial networks linked large towns and cities. The second system was the railroad's private network for transmitting train orders.

"I'll get right on it."

With Bell at his shoulder, the telegrapher polled train-order sta-tions in the region, trying to gauge the extent of the system's failure.

The anxious dispatcher hovered, explaining, "North of Weed, Western Union lines follow the old Siskiyou route to Portland. The new Cascades Cutoff has only the railroad wires."

"They've been deluged by rain," said the telegrapher, still waiting for responses. "Ground gets soft, poles fall."

Bell paced the floor.

All wires down?

Not due to weather, he was certain.

This was the Wrecker's work. Kincaid was taking no chances that Bell would figure out who he was. He had isolated the Cascades Cutoff railhead for a final assault on the bridge to bring the cutoff to a standstill and bankrupt the Southern Pacific. He would attack the reinforcement effort while the piers were still vulnerable.

"Avalanches of mud, too," said the dispatcher. "And there's more rain coming."

Desperate to placate the grim-faced, furiously pacing detective, the dispatcher snatched the morning papers off his desk. The *Sacramento Union* reported rivers twenty feet above the low-water mark and numerous washouts already. Preston Whiteway's *San Francisco Inquirer* ballyhooed the "Storms of the Century" with a luridly embellished illustration of the Weather Bureau map that showed a series of Pacific storms hot on the heels of the first.

" 'The floods could be the most serious in Oregon's history,' " the dispatcher read aloud. " 'Railroad tracks in the valleys are underwater and may be washed away.' "

Bell kept pacing. A freight trundled by, rattling windows in their wooden frames. Clouds enveloped the building as Bell's locomotive, parked alongside, was forced to let off steam she had built to speed him to the Cascade Canyon Bridge.

"The wires are open to San Francisco and Los Angeles," reported the telegrapher, confirming Bell's worst fear. The Wrecker—Kincaid—was concentrating on the Cascades route.

"Loop around through San Francisco or from Los Angeles up to Portland and then down from there."

But the Wrecker's telegraph saboteurs had thought about that, too.

Not only was all telegraph dead from Sacramento to the north, lines from farther north—from Dunsmuir, Weed, and Klamath Falls—were down, too. Charles Kincaid had completely isolated the cutoff railhead at the Cascade Canyon Bridge.

Bell whirled toward a commotion at the door. Jason Adler, the American States Bank auditor, burst in.

"Mr. Bell. Mr. Bell. I've just gone through the telegrams we picked up when we arrived here. We've found a company he controls through the Schane and Simon Company. They bought East Oregon Lumber, which has a contract with the Southern Pacific Railroad to supply crossties and lumber to the cutoff."

"Where?" Bell asked with a sinking heart. But the name said it all.

"Above the Canyon Bridge on the Cascade River. That's the same bridge his Union Pier and Caisson—"

"Clear the track!" Bell commanded the Sacramento dispatcher in a voice that rang like steel.

"But materials and work trains have priority on the cutoff, sir."

"My train has authority straight through to the Cascade Canyon Bridge," Bell shot back.

"But with the lines dead, we can't clear the track."

"We will clear the track as we go!"

"I protest," said the dispatcher. "This is a breach of all safety procedures."

Bell hurried out to the train, shouting orders.

"Uncouple the Pullman. Accountants, lawyers, translators, and auditors: stay here. Keep digging until we know *everything* Kincaid planned. We don't want any more surprises blowing up in our faces. Armed operatives, get on the train!"

Brakemen scrambled. When they had uncoupled the extra car, Bell saw James Dashwood standing forlornly in the Pullman's vestibule.

"What are you waiting for, James? Get on the train."

"I don't have a gun."

"*What?*"

"You said 'armed operatives,' Mr. Bell. Van Dorn apprentices are only allowed to carry handcuffs."

Guffawing detectives exchanged incredulous looks.

Hadn't anyone told the kid that that was the first rule you broke?

Bell raised his voice. "Boys, meet James Dashwood, former apprentice with the San Francisco office. He's just been promoted for uncovering a key clue that exposed Senator Charles Kincaid as the Wrecker. Can anyone lend him a firearm?"

Fists plunged into coats, hats, waistbands, and boots. An arsenal of automatics, revolvers, derringers, and pocket pistols flashed in the rainy light. Eddie Edwards got to Dashwood first and thrust a nickel-plated six-gun into his hand.

"Here you go, Dash. It's double-action. Just keep squeezing the trigger. Reload when it stops making noise."

"*Get on the train!*"

Bell climbed up into the Pacific's cab.

"We're cleared through to Cascade Canyon," he told the engineer.

"How they gonna know we're coming with the telegraph dead?"

"Good question. Stop at the roundhouse."

Bell ran inside the dark and smoky cavern, where twenty locomotives were undergoing noisy repairs on the giant turntable. The Southern Pacific rail cops standing guard led him to the black and greasy foreman.

"Heard all about you, Mr. Bell," the foreman shouted over the din of steel and iron. "What can I do for you?"

"How long will it take you to pull the headlamps off two of these locomotives and attach them to mine?"

"One hour."

Bell pulled out a stack of double-eagle gold coins. "Make it fifteen minutes and these are yours."

"Keep your money, Mr. Bell. It's on the house."

Fourteen minutes later, the Van Dorn Express accelerated out of Sacramento with a triangle of headlights blazing like a comet.

"Now they'll see us coming!" Bell told the engineer.

He tossed the fireman his scoop.

"Shovel on coal."

THE PACIFIC STORM THAT Jim Higgins had shown James Dashwood slammed into the mountain range that rimmed the coasts of northern California and southern Oregon and drenched the Siskiyous with eight inches of rain. Then it leaped the Coast Range as if lightened of its watery burden. Instead, it rained harder. The storm lumbered inland, deluging the narrow valleys of the Klamath River. The detectives aboard the Van Dorn Express saw logjams damming rivers, steel bridges swept away, and farmers in tall rubber boots trying to rescue stranded livestock from flooded fields.

Moving from southwest to northeast, the storm battered the eastern Cascades. The effect on the line leading to the cutoff threatened catastrophe. Streams and creeks jumped their banks. Rivers rose. Most ominously, rain-soaked hillsides began to move.

Dunsmuir's Sacramento Street looked from the racing train like another brown river. People were paddling down it in canoes, dodging floating wooden sidewalks that the floodwaters had ripped from the buildings. In Weed, whole houses were afloat. On the run to Klamath Falls, farms looked like lakes, and Klamath Lake itself was as storm-tossed as an ocean. A lake steamer, torn loose from its mooring, was pressed by the current against a railroad trestle. Bell's train squeezed by and kept going.

A landslide stopped them north of the lake.

A hundred feet of rail was buried under knee-deep mud and stone. Track gangs had come out from Chiloquin to clear it. The telegraph, they reported, had been dead when they left. No one knew how long it would take to repair. Bell sent the brakeman up a pole to tap into the wire. Still dead. At his command, the detectives piled down from the train in the driving rain and pitched in with shovels. They were moving again in a hour, the blistered, soaking-wet, mud-splattered men in a dangerous mood.

As night fell, they saw refugees from flooded farms huddled around bonfires.

Bell spotted a fleet of handcars parked on a siding when they stopped to water the locomotive in the Chiloquin yards. He ordered a lightweight three-wheeler, like the hand-pumped and pedaled track-inspection vehicle the Wrecker had stolen to derail the Coast Line Limited, tied onto his engine pilot. If the worst happened, if his train was stopped by another slide, they could carry it past the buried track and keep going.

A train dispatcher's apprentice came running after them as they started out of the yards, piping in a thin voice that the telegraph wire had opened up from Sacramento. Bell learned that Southern Pacific linemen had encountered three separate acts of sabotage where cut wires were concealed with artful splicing. Proof, he told his operatives, that the Wrecker was swinging into action, isolating the head of the Cascades Cutoff for a final attack.

The second message through the repaired line was a wind-velocity warning from the U.S. Weather Bureau's San Francisco forecast district. High winds meant more storms and more rain. Right behind that warning came reports that another storm had careened off the Pacific Ocean at Eureka. Eureka's streets were flooded, a steamer had foundered in the approach to Humboldt Bay, and lumber schooners were adrift in the harbor.

It snowed in the north. Railroad traffic was at a standstill. Portland was paralyzed and cut off from Seattle, Tacoma, and Spokane. But the temperatures remained milder farther south, where heavy rains prevailed. On inland rivers, loggers drowned attempting to break up logjams that threatened to flood entire towns. The fast-moving new storm was already rampaging through the Klamath Mountains, catching up and combining with rear elements of the storm inundating the cutoff. The Portland forecast district's eight p.m. forty-eight-hour forecast predicted more snow in the north and more rain in the south.

Bell tried again to telegraph Archie Abbott. The wires were still dead north of Chiloquin. The only way to communicate with the Cascade Canyon Bridge was to steam there on the Van Dorn Express.

The special pounded northward, triple headlights blazing. But it was forced repeatedly to slow when startled southbound train crews saw it coming, hit their brakes, and backed up onto the nearest siding many miles back. Only after the southbound freight was safely sidetracked could the Van Dorn Express surge ahead again.

Isaac Bell stayed all night in the locomotive cab. He spelled the fireman scooping coal into the firebox, but he was really there to encourage the frightened engineer to keep driving hard. They made it through the night without a collision. When a grim, gray dawn finally lit the stormy mountains, they were speeding along a narrow cut. A slope rose steeply to the left of the tracks and dropped sheer to the right.

James Dashwood came slipping and stumbling across the tender, balancing a pot of hot coffee. Bell portioned it out to the train crew before he took a grateful sip. When he looked up to thank Dashwood, he saw the newly promoted detective had fixed his gaze in wide-eyed horror on the mountainside.

Bell heard a deep growl, a low-pitched noise louder than the locomotive, that seemed to rumble from the depths of the earth. The rails shook beneath the heavy engine. A cliff detached from the side of the mountain.

"Hit your throttle!"

An entire forest of western hemlocks was sliding toward the tracks.

THE FOREST HURTLED DOWN THE STEEP MOUNTAIN ON A landslide of mud and tumbling boulders. Astonishingly, the sliding trees remained standing upright as the mass of ground they grew in bore down on the Van Dorn Express.

"Hit your throttle!"

The engineer panicked.

Instead of throttling the big Pacific to outrun the juggernaut of timber, mud, and rock, he tried to stop the train, hauling back his Johnson bar and slamming on his air brakes. With only one light-weight diner car behind the tender, the locomotive slowed abruptly. Bell, Dashwood, and the fireman were thrown against the firewall.

Bell scrambled to his feet and faced the rumbling mountain. "Ahead!" he shouted, wresting the throttle from the engineer. "Full ahead!"

The engineer recovered his nerve and jammed the Johnson bar forward. Bell shoved the throttle. The big engine leaped as if stampeding for its life. But the landslide picked up speed, the mass of towering trees still moving as one. Wider than the train was long, it tore down the mountain like an ocean liner launched sideways.

Bell felt a blast of wind so powerful it actually rocked the speed-ing locomotive. The airburst that the landslide pushed ahead of it was wet and cold. It chilled the hot cab as if the coal fire raging under its boiler had been extinguished.

Then the hurtling mass began to break apart. As it crumbled, it spread out wider.

The trees on the edges of the hurtling forest pitched forward, thrusting at the train like gigantic lances. Stones shoved ahead of the main mass bounced on the tracks and clattered against the locomo-tive. A boulder as big as an anvil burst through the cab's side window and smashed the fireman and the engineer to the floor.

Dashwood jumped to help the bloodied men. Bell yanked him back. A second boulder tore like a cannon ball through the space his head had just occupied. Massive stones rocked the locomotive, thun-dered against the tender and shattered windows in the passenger car, showering detectives with broken glass.

The landslide split in two. Half tore ahead of the locomotive. Accelerating, it angled toward the tracks like a runaway train racing the Van Dorn Express to a junction where only one of them could pass. It was a race that Bell's train could not win. A boiling torrent of rocks and mud buried the tracks ahead of the engine.

The larger half of the landslide impaled the passenger car with tree trunks. A boulder bigger than a barn crashed into the tender and swept it off the tracks. The heavy tender, which rode between the locomotive and the passenger car, started to drag both with it. Its coupler held tight to the locomotive, pulling its rear truck off the rails. The rails spread under the enormous forces, dumping the loco-motive's drive wheels onto the ties. The hundred-ton engine leaned toward the ravine and, still lurching ahead, began to tip over. Then her pilot wheels ran into the rocks heaped up by the landslide. She reared up onto them and stopped suddenly. The violent stop broke the coupling to the tender and the tender tumbled into the ravine.

Bell looked back, searching for the car carrying his detectives.

Shattered telegraph poles dangled from their wires. Two hundred yards of track were buried in mud, rock, and crushed timber. Had the coupling to the passenger car snapped, too? Or had the tender dragged it into the ravine with it? Where the detectives' car had been was a jagged mound of trees. Bell rubbed the rain from his eyes and stared harder, hoping against hope. Then he saw it. It was still on the road, shattered wreckage held in place by fallen trees thrust through its windows like knitting needles in a hank of yarn.

Bell cupped his hands to shout across the debris-strewn gouge in the mountain that had been railroad tracks. "Eddie! Are you O.K.?"

Bell cocked his ears for an answer. All he could hear was a river tumbling through the ravine and steam hissing from the wrecked engine. He called again and again. Through the rain, he thought he saw a familiar flash of white hair. Eddie Edwards waved one arm. The other hung limp at this side.

"Busted up," Eddie shouted back. "None dead!"

"I'm going ahead. I'll send a doctor on the wreck train. *James. Quick!*"

The boy was white as a sheet. His eyes were round with shock.

"Handcar. Move. Now!"

Bell led the way out of the leaning cab to the front of the precariously balanced engine. The handcar was intact. They untied it from the pilot and carried it, slipping and stumbling over fifty feet of rock that had tumbled onto the rails. Minutes later, Bell was pumping the handles and pedals with all his strength.

Fifteen miles up the line, they came upon a freight train waiting on a siding. Bell ordered the locomotive unhitched, and they drove it backward the last ten miles to Tunnel 13. They thundered through the tunnel. The engineer slowed her as they emerged into the yard, which was crowded with material trains that had been barred from crossing the weakened bridge. Bell was surprised to see a heavy coal train parked on the bridge itself. The black cargo heaped on fifty hopper cars glistened in the rain.

"I thought the bridge can't bear weight. Did they fix it already?"

"Lord, no," replied the engineer. "They've got a thousand hands down at the piers, working round the clock, but it's touch-and-go. A week's more work, and the river's rising."

"What's that coal train doing there?"

"The bridge started shaking. They're trying to stabilize it with down pressure."

Bell could see that the main staging yard on the far side of the bridge was also packed with trains. Empties, with no way back to the California shops and depots. Having all hands working at the piers explained the eerie sense of a deserted encampment.

"Where's the dispatch office?"

"They set up a temporary one on this side. In that yellow caboose."

Bell jumped down from the locomotive and ran to the caboose, Dashwood right behind him. The dispatcher was reading a week-old newspaper. The telegrapher was dozing at his silent key.

"Where is Senator Kincaid?"

"Most every one's down at the town," said the dispatcher.

The telegrapher opened his eyes. "Last I saw, he was heading for the Old Man's special. But I wouldn't go there, if I was you. Hennessy's hoppin' mad. Somebody sent him four trains of coal instead of the traprock they need to riprap the piers."

"Round up a doctor and a wreck train. There're men hurt at a landslide fifteen miles down the line. Come on, Dash!"

They ran across the bridge, past the parked coal train. Bell saw ripples in the rain puddles. The weakened structure was trembling despite the weight of the coal train. A glance over the side showed that the Cascade River had risen many feet in the nine days since he left for New York. He could see hundreds of workmen ganged on the banks, guiding barges with long ropes, dumping rock in the water, trying to divert the flood, while hundreds more swarmed over new coffer dams and caissons being sunk around the piers.

"Have you participated in many arrests?" Bell asked Dashwood as they neared the special on its raised siding. Train and yard crews were changing shifts. A row of white yardmen's lanterns and signal flags were lined up beside Hennessy's locomotive, the lanterns glowing in the murky light.

"Yes, sir. Mr. Bronson let me come along when they captured 'Samson' Scudder."

Bell hid a smile. The ironically named Samson Scudder, a prolific second-story man who weighed ninety pounds dripping wet, was known as the sweetest-natured crook in San Francisco.

"This one's poison," he warned soberly. "Stick close and do exactly what I say."

"Should I draw my firearm?"

"Not on the train. There'll be people around. Stand by with your handcuffs."

Bell strode alongside Hennessy's special and up the steps to *Nancy No. 1*. The detective he had assigned to guard the car since Philip Dow's attack was covering the vestibule with a sawed-off.

"Senator Kincaid aboard?"

Osgood Hennessy stuck his head out the door. "You just missed him, Bell. What's going on?"

"Which way did he go?"

"I don't know. But he parked that Thomas Flyer up the line."

"He's the Wrecker."

"The devil, you say."

Bell turned to the Van Dorn detective. "If he comes back, arrest him. If he gives you any trouble, shoot first or he'll kill you."

"Yes, sir!"

"Send word to Archie Abbott. Railway cops to guard the bridge and the town in case Kincaid doubles back. Van Dorns, follow me. Dash! Grab a flag and a couple of lanterns."

Dashwood picked up a signal flag, which was rolled tightly around its wooden staff, and two yardman's lanterns and ran after Bell.

"Give me one!" Bell said, explaining, "If we look like we're railroad men, it will buy us a few seconds to get closer."

From the vantage of the raised siding, Bell scanned the ranks of still trains and the narrow walkways between the sidings. He had less than six hours of daylight to catch up with Kincaid. He looked toward the bridge. Then he looked toward the end of the line where new construction had ceased when they learned the bridge had been sabotaged. The road was brushed out, cleared of trees and shrubs, well past the point it crossed the mud road to East Oregon Lumber.

He could not see Kincaid's Thomas Flyer from where he stood. Had Kincaid already reached his car and driven away? Then, on the edge of the deserted yards, he saw a man emerge from between two strings of empty freight cars. He was walking briskly toward a pair of locomotives that were parked side by side where the tracks ended.

"There he is!"

THE WRECKER WAS HURRYING TOWARD THE LOCOMOTIVES TO
signal Philip Dow to blow the dam when he heard their boots pounding behind him.

He looked back. Two brakemen were running fast, signaling with
white train-yard lanterns. A skinny youth and a tall, rangy man, wide
of shoulder and narrow in the waist. But where was the locomotive
they were guiding with their lights? The pair he was hurrying toward
were sidetracked, with only enough steam up to keep them warm.

The tall one wore a broad-brimmed hat instead of a railroader's
cap. *Isaac Bell*. Running after him was a boy who looked like he should
still be in high school.

Kincaid had to make a instant decision. Why was Bell prowling
the yards pretending to be a brakeman? Assume the best, that Bell
still had not tumbled to his identity? Or walk toward them, wave
hello, and pull his derringer and shoot them both and hope no one
saw? The second he reached for his gun, he knew he had made a
mistake wasting time to think about it.

Bell's hand flickered in a blur of motion, and Charles Kincaid found himself staring down the barrel of a Browning pistol held in a rock-steady grip.

"Don't point that pistol at me, Bell. What the devil do you think you're doing?"

"Charles Kincaid," Bell answered in a clear, steady voice, "you are wanted by the law for murder and sabotage."

"Wanted by the *law*? Are you serious?"

"Remove your derringer from your left pocket and drop it on the ground."

"We'll see about this," huffed Kincaid. His every mannerism bespoke the aggrieved United States senator put upon by a fool.

"Remove your derringer from your left pocket and drop it on the ground before I blow a hole in your arm."

Kincaid shrugged, as if humoring a madman. "All right." Moving very slowly, he reached for his derringer.

"Careful," said Bell. "Hold the weapon between your thumb and forefinger."

The only eyes Charles Kincaid had ever seen so cold were in a mirror.

He lifted the derringer from his pocket between his thumb and forefinger and crouched as if to place it gently on the ground. "You realize, of course, that a private detective cannot arrest a member of the United States Senate."

"I'll leave the formalities to a U.S. marshal . . . or the county coroner, if your hand moves any closer to the knife in your boot."

"What the devil—"

"Drop your derringer!" Bell commanded. *"Do not go for your knife!"*

Very slowly, Kincaid opened his hand. The gun fell from his fingers.

"Turn around."

Moving as if in a trance, Kincaid slowly turned away from the grim detective.

"Clasp your hands behind your back."

Slowly, Kincaid placed his hands behind his back. Every sinew was poised. If Bell was going to make a mistake, he would make it now. Behind him, Kincaid heard the words he was praying to hear.

"Your handcuffs, Dash."

He heard the steel clink. He let the first cuff snap around his wrist. Only as he felt the cold metal of the second cuff brush his skin did he whirl into motion, turning to get behind the youth and clamp his arm around his throat.

A fist smashed into the bridge of his nose. Kincaid flew backward.

Knocked on his back, stunned by the punch, he looked up. Young Dashwood was still standing to one side, watching with an excited grin on his face and a shiny revolver in his hand. But it was Isaac Bell who was looming over him, triumphantly. Bell, who had knocked him down with a single punch.

"Did you really think I would let a new man within ten feet of the murderer who killed Wish Clarke, Wally Kisley, and Mack Fulton?"

"Who?"

"Three of the finest detectives I've had the privilege to work with. On your feet!"

Kincaid got up slowly. "Only three? Don't you count Archie Abbott?"

The blood drained from Bell's face, and, in that instant of total shock, the Wrecker struck.

53

THE WRECKER MOVED WITH INHUMAN SPEED. INSTEAD OF attacking Isaac Bell, he rushed James Dashwood. He ducked under the boy's pistol, got behind him, and slid his arm around his throat.

"Is it all right now if I reach for my boot?" the Wrecker asked mockingly.

He had already pulled his knife.

He pressed the razor-sharp blade to Dashwood's throat and sliced a line in the skin. Blood trickled.

"Table's turned, Bell. Drop your gun or I'll cut his head off."

Isaac Bell dropped his Browning on the ground.

"You too, sonny. Drop it!"

Only when Bell said, "Do what he says, Dash," did the revolver clatter on the wet ballast.

"Unlock this handcuff."

"Do what he says," said Bell. Dashwood worked the key out of his pocket and fumbled it into the cuff on the wrist that was crushing his windpipe. The cuffs clattered on the ballast. There was silence, but for the huffing of a single switch engine somewhere, until Bell asked, "Where is Archie Abbott?"

"The derringer in your hat, Bell."

Bell removed his two-shot pistol from his hat and dropped it beside his Browning.

"Where is Archie Abbott?"

"The knife in your boot."

"I don't have one."

"The Rawlins coroner reports a prizefighter died with a throwing knife in his throat," said the Wrecker. "I presume you purchased a replacement."

He cut Dashwood again, and a second trickle of blood merged with the first.

Bell lifted out his throwing knife and placed it on the ground.

"Where is Archie Abbott?"

"Archie Abbott? Last I saw, he was mooning over Lillian Hennessy. That's right, Bell. I tricked you. Took advantage of your terrible penchant for caring."

Kincaid let go of Dashwood and slammed an elbow into the boy's jaw, knocking him senseless. He gave his knife a peculiar flick of his wrist. A rapier-thin sword blade flew at Bell's face.

BELL DODGED THE THRUST that had killed his friends.

Kincaid lunged like lightning and thrust again. Bell dove forward, hit the crushed stone, tucked his long legs and rolled. Kincaid's sword whipped through space he had occupied a second earlier. Bell rolled again, reaching for the double-action revolver Eddie Edwards had given James Dashwood.

As Bell extended his hand, he saw steel gleam as Kincaid got to it first. The needle-sharp tip of his telescoping sword hovered over the gun. "Try to pick it up," he dared Bell.

Bell slid sideways, grabbed the brakeman's signal flag that James had dropped, and rolled to his feet. Then he advanced in a fluid motion, holding the flagstaff in the *en garde* position.

Kincaid laughed. "You're brought a stick to a swordfight, Mr. Bell. Always one step behind. Will you never learn?"

Bell held the tightly rolled cloth end and thrust the wooden staff. Kincaid parried.

Bell responded with a sharp beat, striking the thin metal just below the tip of Kincaid's weapon. The blow exposed him to a lightning thrust, an opportunity Kincaid did not waste. His sword pierced Bell's coat and tore a burning crease along his ribs. Falling back, Bell delivered another sharp beat with the flagstaff.

Kincaid thrust. Bell avoided it and beat hard for a third time.

Kincaid lunged. Bell whirled, sweeping him past him like a toreador. And as Kincaid spun around swiftly to attack again, Bell delivered another hard beat that bent the front half of his sword.

"Compromise, Kincaid. Every engineering decision involves a compromise. Remember? What you grasp in one fist you surrender with the other? The ability to conceal your telescoping sword weakened it."

Kincaid threw the ruined sword at Bell and drew a revolver from his coat. The barrel tipped up as he cocked it. Bell lunged, executing another sharp beat. This one rapped the tender skin stretched tightly across the back of Kincaid's hand. Kincaid cried out in pain and dropped the gun. Instantly, he attacked, swinging his fists.

Bell raised his own fists, and said derisively, "Could it be that the deadly swordsman and brilliant engineer neglected the manly art of defense? That's the clumsiest fisticuffs I've seen since Rawlins. Were you too busy plotting murder to learn how to box?"

He hit the Wrecker twice, a hard one-two that bloodied his nose and rocked him back on his heels. Holding the clear advantage, Bell moved in to finish him off and cuff his hands. His roundhouse right landed square on target. The punch would have knocked most men flat. The Wrecker shrugged it off, and Bell realized to a degree he never had before that the Wrecker was extraordinarily different, less a man and more an evil monster that had climbed fully born out of a volcano.

He regarded Bell with a look of sheer hatred. "You will never stop me."

Switching tactics with astonishing agility, he snatched up a signal lantern, swung it high. Bell stepped nimbly aside. The Wrecker brought it low, smashing its glass against a rail. Kerosene spilled, and the lantern ignited in a ball of liquid fire, which the Wrecker hurled on the still form of James Dashwood.

54

A WAVE OF FIRE BROKE OVER DASHWOOD. FLAME SPLASHED his trousers, his coat, and his hat. Smoke spewed the stench of burning hair.

The Wrecker laughed triumphantly.

"You choose, Bell. Save the boy or try to catch me."

He ran toward the locomotives parked at the edge of the siding.

Isaac Bell had no choice. He tore off his coat and waded into the smoke.

The fire burned most fiercely on Dashwood's chest, but the first priority was to save his eyes. Bell wrapped his coat around the boy's head to smother the flames, then threw his body over the fire on the boy's chest and legs. Dashwood woke up screaming. What Bell thought were cries of pain and fear muffled by his coat turned out to be frantic apologizing. "I'm sorry, Mr. Bell, I'm sorry I let him get the drop on me."

"Can you stand up?"

Face black with soot, half his hair singed to a greasy mat, blood streaming down his throat, Dashwood jumped to his feet. "I'm O.K., sir, I'm sorry—"

"Find Archie Abbott. Tell him to round up the Van Dorns and follow me up the mountain."

Bell scooped his knife, his derringer, and his Browning from the ballast. Kincaid's derringer lay nearby, and he pocketed it, too.

"Kincaid owns East Oregon Lumber. If there's a back way out, the killer knows it. Tell Archie on the jump!"

A sudden shriek of a locomotive whistle snapped Bell's head around.

Kincaid had climbed into the cab of the nearest engine. He was holding the whistle cord and attempting to tie down the braided loop.

Bell raised his Browning, aimed carefully, and fired. The distance was great, even for such an accurate weapon. A bullet whanged off steel. The Wrecker coolly finished tying the cord and started to jump through the open door of the cab. Bell fired again through the open window, intending to pin him down until he got there. Kincaid jumped anyway and hit the ground running.

The whistle stopped abruptly. Kincaid looked back, his face a mask of dismay.

In the sudden silence, Bell realized his shot had missed Kincaid but by chance had severed the whistle cord. Kincaid started to turn back to the locomotives. Bell fired again. The whistle was important, a signal of some sort. So important that Kincaid was running back to the locomotives in the face of pistol fire. Bell triggered another shot.

Kincaid's hat flew in the air, ripped from his head by Bell's lead slug. He turned away and ran behind a tender. The square bulk of the coal-and-water carrier blocked Bell's field of fire. He ran toward the tender as fast as he could. Rounding it, he saw the Wrecker, far ahead of him, jump from the end of the ballast roadbed. When Bell reached the end of the roadbed, he glimpsed the Wrecker running down the middle of the brushed-out line. He made an elusive target, weaving and jinking, flickering through the shadows of the trees that crowded the path, disappearing as the bed curved with the slope of the mountain.

Bell jumped from the ballast to the cleared forest floor and charged after him.

Rounding the turn in the brushed-out roadbed, he saw in the distance, down a long straightaway, a flash of yellow—Kincaid's Model 35 Thomas Flyer—and then a flicker of Kincaid running up to it.

Kincaid reached under the red leather driver's seat, pulled out a long-barreled revolver, and coolly fired three shots in rapid succession. Bell dove for cover, the slugs whistling around him. Scrambling behind a tree, he snapped off another shot. Kincaid was in front of the car, trying to start his motor, bracing himself with his left hand on one of the headlights and turning the starter crank with his right.

Bell fired again. It came close. Kincaid ducked but kept cranking. That was six shots. He had one shot left before he had to replace the magazine.

The motor caught. Bell heard a ragged chugging as, one by one, the four gigantic cylinders boomed to life. Kincaid leaped behind the steering wheel. Bell was close enough now to see the fenders fluttering from the cold motor running rough. But the car was built high in the back and the canvas top was up, its small rear window covered over with three spare tires that hung from the top. All he could see of Kincaid was his hand when he reached out to grip the side-mounted gearshifter. Too hard a shot to waste his last bullet on.

The rattling, chugging noise dropped in pitch. The motor was engaging the drive chain. Bell put on a burst of speed, heedless of the rough ground. The Thomas started moving. Blue smoke trailed it. The rattling chug sound sharpened to a hollow, authoritative snap as it accelerated up the cleared right-of-way. Fast as a man. Now fast as a horse.

Bell ran after the yellow car. He had one shot left in the Browning's magazine, no clear view of Kincaid, who was hidden by the canvas top and the tires on back, and no time to reload. Bell was running like the wind, but the Thomas Flyer was pulling away.

Ahead of the Thomas, the clearing suddenly widened where the Southern Pacific right-of-way crossed the East Oregon Lumber Company's muddy trail. The Thomas swerved off the brushed-out bed onto the lumber trail and slowed as its wheels spun in soft mud and deep wagon ruts. Its engine was howling with effort, its tires flinging earth and water, its exhaust pipe spewing smoke.

Bell drew within feet of the Thomas and jumped.

He grabbed for the rearmost spare tire with his free hand and clamped his powerful fingers inside its rubber rim. With Bell's weight on back increasing the traction of its rear wheels, the Thomas picked up speed.

Boots dragging in the mud, Bell grabbed hold with both hands to work his way forward. Swinging his feet for momentum, he reached to the right side of a trunk mounted on the rear leaf springs and caught hold of a leather strap, which he used to pull himself alongside and onto the rear fender. The wheel's twelve mud-crusted spokes blurred under him. The fender sagged under his weight, rubbing the tire. The screech of metal on rubber alerted Kincaid to his presence.

Kincaid instantly slammed on the brake to throw Bell off. Bell went with the maneuver, letting his momentum carry him forward and closer to Kincaid. He reached for the shifting levers, missed, but grabbed a brass tube that delivered oil to the chain drive. Kincaid swung a monkey wrench at Bell's hand. Bell let go and fell. As he did, he gripped a utility box bolted to the running board.

Now he was partly ahead of the rear wheel, which threatened to roll over him. The chain, just inside the wheel, whizzed inches from his face. He yanked his automatic out of his coat, reached in front of the wheel, and jammed the muzzle under the upper half of the chain.

The chain jammed the gun into the teeth of the sprocket. The automobile jerked hard and skidded on locked wheels.

Kincaid disengaged the clutch. The chain jumped. Bell's gun went flying, and the car surged ahead. Steering with his left hand, Kincaid swung the wrench. It grazed Bell's hat. Bell clutched the utility box with his right arm, kept his left hooked over the fender, and pulled his throwing knife from his right boot. Kincaid swung the wrench.

Forced to let go before Kincaid shattered bone, Bell jabbed his knife into the sidewall of Kincaid's tire. The racing wheel ripped the knife out of Bell's hand, and he fell to the road.

The Thomas Flyer's exhaust sounded a hollow snap as it picked up speed, crested the slope, and disappeared around a hairpin turn. Bell rolled to his feet, covered in mud, and ran back searching the ruts for his gun. He found his hat first and then the automatic, stripped it, blew off the mud, reassembled it, and exchanged magazines for a fully loaded one. He now had one slug chambered and six on call. Then he discarded his coat, which was heavy with mud, and started running up the timber road after the Wrecker.

Hoofs rumbled behind him.

Archie Abbott rounded the bend, leading a posse of ten Van Dorn detectives on horseback with Winchester rifles jutting from their saddle scabbards. Archie gave him the horse they brought for him. Bell started to mount. The horse tried to bite his leg.

"Lillian Hennessy didn't have any trouble riding him," said Abbott.

Bell flexed his powerful left arm to draw Thunderbolt's head down and spoke sternly into his pointed ear. "Thunderbolt. We have work to do." The animal let Bell on board, and poured himself over the rough ground, pulling ahead of the pack.

After two miles, Bell saw a gleam of yellow through the trees.

The Thomas was stopped in the middle of the road. The right

rear tire was half off the wheel and rim cut. Bell's knife, still sticking out of it, had done it in. Kincaid's footprints headed straight up the road. Bell ordered one man to stay behind, replace the tire, and bring the car along.

At the end of three more hard-slogging miles up the mountain, with less than a mile to go to the East Oregon Lumber Company's camp, the horses were tiring. Even the eighteen-hand monster under Bell was breathing hard. But he and Thunderbolt were still in the lead when they ran into the Wrecker's ambush.

Flame lanced from the dark trees. Winchester rifles boomed. A rain of lead exploded through the air. A heavy slug fanned Bell's face. Another plucked his sleeve. He heard a man cry out and a horse go down behind him. The Van Dorns dove for cover, dragging their own long guns from their scabbards. Dodging the flailing hooves of frightened animals, the detectives scattered off the road. Bell stayed on his horse, firing repeatedly in the direction of the attack, his Winchester's ejection lever a blur of motion. When his men had finally found safety in the trees, he jumped down and took up a position behind a thick hemlock.

"How many?" called Abbott.

In answer came a second fusillade of high-powered slugs crackling through the brush.

"Sounds like six or seven," Bell answered. He reloaded his rifle. The Wrecker had chosen well. Slugs were pouring down from high above. His gunmen could see the Van Dorns, but, to see back, the Van Dorns had to expose their heads to gunfire.

There was only one way to deal with it.

"Archie?" Bell called. "Ready?"

"Ready."

"Boys?"

"Ready, Isaac," came the chorus.

Bell waited a full minute.

"Now!"

The Van Dorns charged.

THE WRECKER KEPT A cool head. Nothing about the Van Dorn Detective Agency surprised him anymore. Nor was their bravery in doubt. So he was already half expecting their concentrated, disciplined counterattack. Philip Dow kept a cool head too, firing only when he could see a target flitting through the trees, clearly a man most alive when he was in battle. But Dow's lumberjacks were thugs accustomed to fighting two on one. Quicker with fists or ax handles than rifles, they panicked in the face of ten guns coming up the hill spitting fire like the devil's brigade.

The Wrecker felt them waver. Seconds later, they broke and ran, some actually dropping their rifles, stampeding through the forest for higher ground as if, in their panicked state, they thought hiding would save them. Nearby, Dow kept firing. Not that there was much to hit among the targets dodging tree to tree, but ever closer.

"Fall back," the Wrecker ordered quietly. "Why shoot them when we can drown them?"

Isaac Bell had ruined his plan to signal Dow by locomotive whistles. If Dow had even heard the bare few seconds of a single locomotive whistle, which was all the noise he had produced before Bell started shooting, the assassin had failed to understand the go-ahead to blow up the dam that held Lake Lillian.

The two men retreated from the ambush site, loping up the same mule deer trail that Dow had led his men down from the lumber camp. When they got to the camp, lumberjacks and mule skinners who weren't part of Dow's gang were peering down the road at the sound of gunfire. Seeing the Wrecker and Dow emerge from the trees, rifles in hand, they wisely retreated into their bunkhouses, leaving questions to those who were fools enough to ask armed men.

"Philip," said the Wrecker. "I'm counting on you to blow the dam."

"Consider it done."

"They won't go easy on you."

"They'll have to catch me first," said Dow. He offered his hand.

The Wrecker took it gravely, imparting a sense of ceremony. He was not one bit emotionally moved but he was relieved. Whatever strange codes the assassin lived by, Dow would detonate the explosives if it took the last breath in his body.

"I'll cover you," he told Dow. "Give me your rifle. I'll hold them off as long as I've got ammunition."

He would make his final escape when the flood swept the Cascade Canyon Bridge into the gorge. If his luck held, he would be the last man across it.

· 55 ·

ABBOTT SCRAMBLED ALONGSIDE BELL WHEN THE WRECKER'S
gang stopped shooting.

"Isaac, he's got a huge lake up there impounded behind a dam.
I'm thinking if he were to blow it, he'd flood the bridge."

Bell sent four detectives to track the fleeing gunmen through
the woods. He settled three wounded men as best he could
beside the road and made sure that at least one could defend them
in case the attackers came back. There were two dead horses in the
road. The rest had bolted. Bell started running up the rutted track,
with Abbott and Dashwood hot on his heels.

"That's the camp ahead," called Abbott.

Just as the road opened up at the lumber camp, withering rifle fire
sent them diving behind trees.

"It's a diversion," said Bell. "So he can blow the dam."

They emptied their Winchesters in the direction of the
attack. The shooting stopped, and they pressed on, drawing their
sidearms.

• • •

CROUCHED AT THE BASE of the log dam, soaked by the spray of the water tumbling fifty feet to the river beside him, Philip Dow knew his life was over when the Winchesters stopped booming. Kincaid had held off the detectives as long as he could.

The killer had no regrets.

He'd stayed loyal to his principles. And he'd relieved the world of a fair number of plutocrats, aristocrats, and other rats. But he knew when it was time to call it quits. All he had to do to end with honor was to finish this one last job. Blow the dam before the Van Dorns killed him. Or caught him alive, which would be worse than dying. Except first, before he lit the fuse and took the Big Jump, he wanted to send a few more rats ahead of him.

Three of them charged out of the woods, pistols in hand. They would mob him the instant he attacked. This was a bomb job, and, fortunately, he had ample bomb makings already laid in the dam. He pulled a bundle of six sticks of gelignite from its nest between two logs. Then he snipped off a short length from the fuse and carefully removed one of detonators.

The detectives spotted him. He heard their shouts faintly over the roar of the water. They came running, slipping and sliding on the wet logs of the skid. He had only seconds. With fingers as steady as sculpted stone, he attached the short fuse to the detonator and jammed the detonator inside the gelignite bundle. He blocked the spray with his body, took a dry match and striker from their corked bottle, and touched the flame to the fuse. Then he held the six sticks behind his back and walked rapidly toward the detectives.

"Drop your gun!" they shouted.

Dow raised his empty hand to the sky.

"Show your hand!"

They drew beads on him. He kept walking. The range was still long for pistols.

Isaac Bell fired his Browning and hit Dow in the shoulder.

So concentrated was Dow's mind on getting close to the detectives, he barely felt the light-caliber, underpowered slug. He did not stop, but turned that shoulder toward them and swung the explosives behind him, straightening his arm to catapult the bomb high and far. One of the detectives sprinted ahead of the others, raising a large, shiny revolver. It was big enough to stop him. If a running man could possibly hit a target at that distance.

"Get back, Dash!" Bell shouted. "He's got something."

Dow wound up to hurl the gelignite. The man Bell called Dash stopped dead and thrust his gun forward. He took deliberate aim. Then he made a fist with his empty hand and crossed his chest, which shielded his heart and lungs and steadied his weapon. Dow braced for the bullet. Dash was a man who knew how to shoot.

The heavy slug hit Dow squarely, staggering him before he could hurl the bomb. Everything within Dow's range of vision stood still. The only sound was the roar of the water cascading over the dam. He remembered that he hadn't yet lit the fuse to the charge that would blow the dam. The only fuse he'd lit was the one burning toward the gelignite in his hand. How could he call it quits if he didn't finish the job?

His legs and arms felt like wood. But he summoned all his strength to turn his back to the guns and shamble toward the dam.

"Dash! Get out of the way!"

They saw immediately what Dow was doing. All three opened fire. He took a slug in his shoulder and another in his back. One in the back of his leg, and he started to go down. But those that hit him propelled him forward. He fell against the dam. He was hunched over the gelignite, pressing it with his chest to the wet logs, when he saw the flame jump from the fuse to the detonator. With a microsecond left to live, he knew he had finished the job and taken a squad of Van Dorn rats with him.

ISAAC BELL SEIZED JAMES DASHWOOD BY THE SCRUFF OF HIS
neck and threw him to Archie Abbott, who caught him on the run
and whirled him farther up the riverbank like a lateral pass. He was
reaching for Bell's hand when the bomb exploded. Twenty paces, less
than a hundred feet, separated them from the blast. The shock wave
crossed that distance in an instant, and the two friends saw a kaleidoscope of spinning trees as it slammed them off their feet and threw
them after Dashwood. Ears ringing, they scrambled higher up the
slope in an attempt as desperate as it was hopeless to escape the wall
of water that they knew would burst through the exploded dam.

WHEN THE WRECKER HEARD the explosion, he knew that something had gone wrong. It was not loud enough. Not all the gelignite
had detonated. He paused in his flight at a spot in the road where he
could see the river down below in the canyon and watched anxiously
for the moving wall of water the fallen dam would release. The river
was rising, the water was definitely higher, but it was not what he

expected, and he feared the worst. The partial explosion had only damaged the dam, not destroyed it.

Hoping it had at least killed many detectives, he started back down the road, confident that eventually the dam would collapse and send a flood smashing into the bridge, whether it took minutes or hours. Suddenly, he heard the sound of a motorcar—his Thomas Flyer—coming up the road.

His face lit darkly with a pleased smile. The Van Dorns must have repaired the flat tire. Kind of them. Pistol in one hand, knife in the other, he quickly chose a spot where particularly deep ruts would force the car to slow.

"It's a miracle," said Abbott.

"A brief miracle," Bell answered.

A torrent of water as big around as an ox was blasting through the hole the assassin's bomb had blown in the log-and-boulder dam. But the bomb Philip Dow had tried to kill them with hadn't detonated the rest of the charge, and the dam had held. At least for the moment.

Bell surveyed the damage, trying to calculate how long the dam would last. A cataract was pouring over the top, and jets of water were blasting like fire hoses through cracks in the face.

Abbott said, "Dash, how'd you learn to shoot like that?"

"My mother wouldn't let me join the Van Dorns until she taught me."

"Your *mother*—"

"She rode with Buffalo Bill's Wild West Show when she was young."

Bell said, "You can tell your mother you saved our bacon. And maybe the bridge. Hopefully, that coal train will hold it . . . What's the matter, Archie?"

Abbott looked suddenly alarmed. "But that was Kincaid's idea."

"What idea?"

"To stabilize the bridge with down pressure. Kincaid said they did it once in Turkey. Seemed to work."

"Kincaid has never done a thing in his life without purpose," said Bell.

"But Mowery and the other engineers wouldn't have allowed it if the weight of the train wouldn't help. I'd guess he knew the jig was up when he saw me ride up here. So he acted helpful to throw off suspicion."

"I've got to get down there right now."

"The horses scattered," said Abbott. "But there are mules in the stables."

Bell looked around for a better way. Mules trained to pull lumber carts would never ride them to the bridge in time to undo whatever the Wrecker had set in motion with the coal train.

His eye fell on a dugout canoe on the riverbank. The water had already risen to it and was tugging at the front end. "We'll take the Hell's Bottom Flyer!"

"What?"

"The dugout canoe. We'll ride it to the bridge."

They manhandled the heavy, hollowed-out log on its side to spill out the rainwater.

"On the jump! Grab those paddles!"

They pushed the canoe into the river and held it alongside the bank. Bell climbed in front, ahead of the crosspiece the lumberjacks had stiffened it with, and readied his paddle. "Get in!"

"Hold your horses, Isaac," Abbott cautioned. "This is insane. We'll drown."

"Amorous lumberjacks have survived the run for years. Get in."

"When that dam lets loose, it'll sweep a tidal wave down the river that will wash over this canoe like a matchstick."

Bell looked back at the dam. The torrent that gushed from the hole that Dow had blown in the bottom was tearing at the edges.

"That hole's getting larger," said Abbott. "See the logs above it sagging?"

"He's right," said Dash. "It could collapse any minute."

"You're both right," Bell said. "I can't risk your lives. Catch up when you can."

"Isaac!"

Bell shoved off from the bank. Abbott lunged to grab the back of the canoe. The current jerked it into the middle of the narrow torrent.

"I'll meet you down there!" Bell called, paddling furiously to keep the current from smashing him into a rock. "Enjoy the mules."

The speed took him by surprise. The raging current drove the canoe faster than any horse and most automobiles. Hurtling along at this rate, he would be under the Cascade Canyon Bridge in twenty minutes.

If he didn't drown.

The banks were steep, the river narrow and studded with boulders. Fallen trees jutted into it. He overtook whole cut trunks floating along almost entirely submerged. The little canoe rode up on one of them, and he started to overturn in a flash. He threw his weight the other way to right it. Then a tree that had been ripped from the bank by the flood rolled ponderously beside him, splaying the air with giant roots that reached for the canoe like tentacles. He fended them off with the paddle, then dug deep in the water, trying to outrun the flailing monster. A root whipped him in the face and nearly threw him out of the canoe.

Paddling for his life, he pulled ahead of the rolling tree, dodged another boulder, slid between two more, and banged over a flat rock hidden under the surface. Then the canyon walls closed in, and deep water tore between them in a long, relatively straight run of several miles. This was better, and Bell began to think he might make it to the bridge intact.

He looked back repeatedly. No sign that the dam had burst.

The straight run ended in a series of sharp bends. The bends caused whirlpools that spun the canoe in circles that one man, in the front of the canoe, could not control. Bell concentrated instead on keeping the canoe upright and fending off rocks that were suddenly jumping out of nowhere. Floating out of the third bend backward, he looked over his shoulder to see where he was going. The canyon walls had spread wider apart, and the water had climbed onto a shallow bank that produced rock-strewn rapids. The current thrust him at the rapids. He paddled with all his strength to straighten out the canoe and head toward the deeper water of the original bed.

But as soon as he had righted himself, he heard an ominous mutter that grew swiftly to a loud rumble. It sounded like a wall of water was rampaging after him. He looked behind him, expecting the worst. But the river was no wilder than before, which was wild enough. The dam, miles behind, was apparently still holding. But the rumble grew louder. Suddenly, Bell realized that the sound echoing off the steep canyon walls came from around the bend *ahead* of him.

The current sluiced him through the bend in the river.

He caught a glimpse of ropes tied to the trees on the bank. Then his eyes were riveted on what appeared to be a line across the river. But it was not a line. It was the clear break in the water where the river disappeared over a waterfall.

The lumberjacks must have tied the ropes to hold when they climbed out of their canoes to carry them around the falls. Portage was not an option for Isaac Bell. The current had already accelerated and was throwing his canoe at the falls at thirty miles per hour.

The rains saved him. At low water, he would be dead, smashed to splinters on the rocks. The high water shortened the fall and cushioned his landing.

He was still afloat, still flying along high and dry, when suddenly he was bearing down on an island-sized boulder that split the river in half. He dug in his paddle to steer around it. The stream rejoined on the other side of the boulder in a violent leap of spray and foam that battered the canoe on both sides.

Then, against the darkening sky, he saw the airy arch and crisp straight line of the Cascade Canyon Bridge joining the two sides of the gorge. It was strange that the clearest description of its simple beauty was from the Wrecker himself: it soared. It was hard to believe that any structure so large could look so light or span such a long distance. The coal train parked in the middle of it was fifty cars long and yet there were empty stretches of track in front and in back of it.

But the Wrecker who so artfully described the Cascade Canyon Bridge was the man who would destroy it. Surely the Wrecker knew a secret about the coal train that would gain him control of every major railroad in the country. Every act that Bell had seen him commit, every crime the Wrecker had perpetrated, every innocent he had killed, told him that Charles Kincaid had tricked the Southern Pacific Company into parking that coal train on the bridge for a reason that would serve his monstrous ambition and vicious dreams.

Moments later, Isaac Bell saw the lights of the town clustered along the bank under the bridge. He tried to paddle to shore, but it proved futile. The heavy canoe was firmly in the grip of the river. He raced by the outskirts of the town, and as the river narrowed and accelerated he saw electric lights blazing on the piers and on the coffer dams and caissons built around them. A thousand men and a hundred machines were teamed to shore up the flow deflectors with tons of rock and raise the sides of the coffer dams with massive timbers to keep above the rising water.

The river was sweeping Bell's canoe between the piers. No one noticed him coming, for the canoe looked little different than the many dark logs racing low in the water. Just as he thought he would be swept under the bridge and into the night, the canyon walls narrowed the river. Currents leaped crazily.

The canoe was hurled sideways toward the pier farthest from town. It jumped over a tongue of stone jetty, spun wildly, and crashed against the wooden coffer dam. Fifty exhausted carpenters spiking planks to the timber frame looked up blearily as Bell stepped briskly from the canoe and marched across the gangplank that connected the coffer dam to the stone pier it surrounded.

"Good evening, gentlemen," Bell said, not pausing to answer cries of "Who?" and "Where?"

He spied a steel ladder affixed to the stone and started up it rapidly, calling an urgent warning down to the men below. "There's a flood crest coming down the river any minute. Build higher, and be ready to run for it."

Sixty feet above the water, the stone stopped and the steel began. The pillar consisted of a square framework bolstered with triangles of girders, and it too had ladders. For painting, he presumed. From where he was standing on the top stones, the pillar looked to be as tall as the Singer Building he had seen in New York City, which Abbott once had boasted was six hundred feet tall. Hoping that this was a case of a confusing perspective, Bell reached for the bottom rung.

He felt the bridge trembling the instant he touched the ladder. It seemed to be shaking harder than when he'd run across it hours earlier. But not much harder. Was the coal train having the promised effect? Was it stabilizing the bridge? Baffled by the Wrecker's intentions, Bell climbed faster.

His wounded forearm where Dow had shot him was beginning to throb. He was less concerned by the pain, which was growing sharper, than by what it meant. He had a long way to go to the top of the bridge and needed all four limbs in working order. The higher he climbed, the shakier the bridge felt.

How much worse would it shake without the added weight?

He smelled smoke as he neared the top, which seemed odd since there were no trains running on the bridge. At last, the ladder topped out on a catwalk that traversed the steel arch and led to a shorter ladder to the deck. He hauled himself up the last few rungs and swung his legs onto the deck, where he found himself in the narrow space between the coal train and the open edge. His head was reeling with the effort, and he leaned over to rest, bracing himself with his hand on the gondola.

He jerked his hand back with a startled shout of pain.

The steel side of the gondola was hot—so hot it burned his skin.

Bell ran to the next gondola and touched it tentatively. It was hot, too. And now he smelled the smoke again, and he realized in a flash the diabolic trick the Wrecker had pulled. So-called down pressure was stabilizing the bridge as he had promised. But the vibrations from the water pounding the weakened piers were shaking the bridge. In turn, the bridge was shaking the train, which was shaking the coal. Deep inside fifty coal cars, thousands of pieces of coal were rubbing against each other and creating friction. Friction made heat, like a frontiersman rubbing two sticks to start a fire.

Even as Bell realized the perverted genius of Kincaid's scheme, the coal ignited. A dozen small sparks became a hundred flames. Soon, a thousand fires would mushroom through the coal. The entire train was smouldering on the middle of the bridge. Any second, the wooden crossties under the train would catch fire.

He had to move the train off the bridge.

The staging yard was jammed with stranded trains and locomotives. But with no work to do, none of the engines had steam up. Bell spotted the big black Baldwin attached to Hennessy's special. It always had steam up, to heat and light the Pullmans and the private cars and to be ready to move at the railroad president's whim.

Bell ran to it. Every brakeman and yardman he saw he ordered to throw switches to direct the Old Man's locomotive to the bridge. Hennessy himself, looking frail in shirtsleeves, was standing next to the Baldwin. He was breathing hard and leaning on a fireman's scoop.

"Where's your train crew?" Bell asked.

"I was keeping up steam before they were born. Sent every hand below to work on the coffer dams. Just had to catch my breath. Something's wrong. What do I smell? Is that fire on the bridge?"

"The coal has ignited. Uncouple your engine. I'll pull the train off."

With Hennessy directing brake- and yardmen, who ran around throwing switches, Bell drove the Baldwin off the special, ran it forward, then backed it onto the bridge. Partway across, he coupled onto the lead coal gondola, while every man still in the yard worked to switch a path of rails to an isolated siding where the burning train could be safely moved.

Bell shoved the Johnson bar forward and notched the throttle ahead, feeding steam to the pistons. This was the hard part. He had spent enough time in the cab to know how to drive locomotives, but driving and pulling fifty heavy gondolas were two different propositions. The wheels spun, the train did not move. He remembered the sand valve, which spread sand under the wheels to improve adhesion, and found its lever. Smoke was billowing from the gondolas now, and he saw flames start to shoot up. He reached for the throttle to try again.

Suddenly, the Wrecker spoke through the side window.

"With what will you replace the weight?" he asked mockingly. "More coal?"

57

"BALLAST WOULD HOLD THE BRIDGE, BUT SOMEHOW SIGNALS GOT crossed. Hennessy ordered track ballast. He kept getting coal. I wonder how that happened."

The Wrecker swung into the cab through the open back and whipped a knife from his boot.

Suspecting a backup weapon identical to the sword he had ruined, Bell swiftly drew his Browning and pulled the trigger. But the automatic had suffered one too many douses of mud and water. It jammed. He heard the Wrecker's knife click. The telescoping blade flew out and struck him before he could move in the confined space.

It was no flesh wound, but a terrible thrust below Bell's shoulder. Stunned, wondering if the sword had punctured his lung, Bell reached under his jacket. He felt warm blood on his hand. He couldn't focus his eyes. The Wrecker was standing over him, and Bell was surprised to discover that he had collapsed to the footplate.

58

CHARLES KINCAID DREW HIS SWORD BACK TO RUN ISAAC BELL through his heart.

"I was not unaware of my weapon's weakness," he said. "It wasn't made to stand up to a beat. So I always carry an extra."

"So do I," said Bell. He tugged from an inside pocket Kincaid's own derringer, which he had picked up from the tracks earlier. It was slippery with his blood, sliding in his hand. The shock of the wound was making him see double, fading in and out of awareness. He gathered his spirit, focused like a headlight on Kincaid's broad chest, and fired.

Kincaid stepped back with a look of disbelief. He dropped his sword. Rage twisted his handsome features as he fell backward off the locomotive to the tracks.

Bell tried to stand. He was having difficulty getting his legs under him. From far below, beneath the bridge, he heard cries of alarm. A steam whistle on a barge crane set up a desperate scream. He dragged himself to the back of the cab. From there, he saw what was terrifying the men working on the piers. Upstream, the Wrecker's dam had broken at last. The flood crest was on the march.

An angry white wave, tall as a house and studded with cut logs and whole trees, filled the river from shore to shore. Shouting men struggled to move the electric dynamos above the flood. A barge overturned. The work lights went dark.

Bell grabbed onto the Johnson bar and fought to regain his feet.

The bridge was shaking the locomotive. Flames were shooting skyward from the coal cars. If he moved the burning train, he would save the bridge from the fire. But even dead on the tracks, the Wrecker would have his way. If Bell moved the train, he would remove the stabilizing weight, and the bridge would collapse from the scouring floodwater. If he didn't move the train, the bridge would burn. Already he smelled burning creosote as the crossties under the train began to smoulder.

The only solution was a compromise.

Bell reversed the Johnson bar, notched open the throttle, and backed the train to the edge of the bridge. Holding tight to handrails, he climbed down painfully. A yard foreman came running, casting fear-filled eyes on the burning train. "We're opening switches, mister, so you can move her onto a siding out of the way."

"No, I need tools. Get me a crowbar and a spike puller."

"We gotta shunt her aside before she sets off the whole yard."

"Leave the train right here," Bell ordered calmly. "I will need it in a moment. Now, please get me those tools."

The foreman ran off and returned in a moment. Bell took the spike puller and the heavy crowbar and shambled across the bridge as fast as the hole in his chest would let him. On the way, he passed the Wrecker's still form huddled between the rails. The train had passed clean over him but not mauled his body. Bell kept going almost to the far side. There he crouched down and began prying spikes out of the fishplates that held the rails on the upstream side of the bridge.

He could feel the bridge shaking violently now that the train was off it. A glance below showed the Cascade Canyon River raging like an ocean in a hurricane. Mind reeling from a lack of oxygen and lost blood, he felt himself getting giddy as he desperately pried up spike after spike.

Who's the Wrecker now? he thought. The tables were turned. Isaac Bell, chief investigator for the Van Dorn Detective Agency, was battling with every ounce of his failing strength to derail a train.

It was getting harder to breathe, and he could see a bubble of blood rising and falling from the wound in his chest. If Kincaid's sword had punctured his chest cavity and he didn't get help soon, air would fill it and collapse his lung. But he had to free an entire length of rail first.

THE WRECKER WAS NOT as grievously wounded as Bell, but he was equally determined. He had regained consciousness as Bell shambled past with a spike puller. Now, ignoring a bullet lodged between two ribs, he was running, doubled over, as fast as he could toward the coal train. The detective's spike puller told him all he had to know. Bell meant to derail the burning train into the river to divert floodwater from the weakened piers.

He reached the locomotive, dragged himself up to the cab, and shoveled several scoops of coal into the firebox.

"Hey, what are you doing?" shouted a trainman, climbing the ladder to the cab. "Mr. Bell said to leave the train here."

Kincaid drew the long-barreled revolver he had taken from his Thomas Flyer and shot the man. Then he set the locomotive steaming ahead with a sure hand on the throttle and sand valve. The drive wheels bit smoothly, the couplers unslacked, and the locomotive drew the coal cars onto the bridge. The Wrecker saw the probing white beam of the headlight fall on Isaac Bell, who was struggling to loosen the rail.

• • •

THE HEAVY COAL TRAIN dampened the vibrations shaking the bridge. Feeling the difference, Bell looked up into the blinding beam of a locomotive headlamp and knew instantly that his derringer shot had not killed Charles Kincaid.

The locomotive was bearing down on him. He felt its wheels grinding the rails. Now he saw Kincaid thrust his head from the cab window, his face a mask of hatred. His mouth spread in a ghastly grin of triumph, and Bell heard the steam huff harder as the Wrecker opened the throttle.

Bell ripped the final spike out of its crosstie. Then he hurled his weight against the crowbar, battling with fading strength to shift the loosened rail before Kincaid ran him over.

Bell felt the front truck wheels roll onto his rail. The weight of the engine was holding it down. Summoning his last strength, he moved it the vital "one inch between here and eternity."

The locomotive slipped off the rails and slammed onto the ties. Bell saw the Wrecker with his hand on the throttle, saw his triumph turn to despair as he realized that he was about to drag the burning train off the bridge and down to the river.

As Bell turned and ran, the V-shaped engine pilot on the front of the locomotive struck him. Like a fly swatted by a giant, he tumbled ahead of the locomotive and over the edge of the deck before catching himself on a girder. Wedged in the steelwork, Isaac Bell watched the locomotive crash over the side. It was a long, long way down, and for a moment the entire train seemed suspended in the air.

The locomotive and the string of cars thundered into the river with a splash that deluged the banks. Stream and smoke billowed. Even submerged, the fire continued to glow cherry red in the gondolas. But the cars were heaped in a tight string across the riverbed like the closely bunched islands of a barrier beach that protected the mainland from the power of the ocean. Floodwater tumbled over and around them, its force dissipated, its impact diminished.

The Cascade Canyon Bridge stopped shaking. The fallen train had diverted the flood. And as Isaac Bell passed in and out of consciousness, he saw the electric work lights blaze to life again as bargeloads of railroad men swarmed back into the caissons to buttress the piers.

59

BRAVING A BLIZZARD, CROWDS GATHERED BEFORE A GRAYSTONE mansion at Thirty-seventh Street and Park Avenue to watch the guests arrive at *the* wedding of 1908's winter season: the union of a son of Old New York and the daughter of a shirtsleeve railroad titan. Those observing a handsome couple crossing the snowy sidewalk to mount the steps of the mansion assumed that the tall, impeccably dressed gentleman with the golden mustache was gripping the arm of the beautiful woman at his side so she would not slip on the ice. The opposite was true, but no one heard Isaac Bell say to Marion Morgan, "Who needs a walking stick when he has a strong woman to lean on?"

"A detective recovering from a punctured lung . . ."

"Only slightly. Never would have made it, otherwise."

". . . nearly bleeding to death, infection, and pneumonia, is who."

"If that cameraman takes my picture, I'll shoot him."

"Don't worry. I told him that *Picture World* would fire him and throw his family in the street if he points it anywhere near you. Do you have the ring?"

"In my vest pocket."

"Hold tight, darling, here come the steps."

They made it, Bell pale with effort. Butlers and footmen ushered them inside. Marion gasped at the flowers arrayed through the foyer and up the grand staircase. "Sweet peas, roses, and cherry blossoms! Where did they get them?"

"Anywhere it's spring beside the father of the bride's railroad tracks."

The father of the bride hurried up to greet them. Osgood Hennessy was dressed in a pearl-gray morning coat with a rose boutonniere. Bell thought he looked a little lost without Mrs. Comden at his side and grateful for a friendly face. "Marion, I'm so glad you came all the way from San Francisco. And you, Isaac, up already and full of go."

"A wedding without the best man would be like a hanging without the rope."

Marion asked if the bride-to-be was nervous.

"Lillian nervous? She's got seventeen bridesmaids from all those fancy schools she got kicked out of and ice water in her veins." Hennessy beamed proudly. "Besides, there has never been a more beautiful bride in New York. Wait 'til you see her." He turned his head to favor J. P. Morgan with a chilly nod.

Bell whispered to Marion, "That record will fall if we decide to marry in New York."

"What was that?" said Hennessy, sending Morgan off with a perfunctory slap on the shoulder.

"I was just saying, I should check in with the groom. May I leave Marion in your care, Mr. Hennessy?"

"A pleasure," said Hennessy. "Come along, my dear. The butler told me we're supposed to wait till after the vows to drink champagne, but I know where it's kept."

"Could I see Lillian first?"

Hennessy pointed the way upstairs. A knock at her door elicited squeals and giggles inside. Three girls escorted her to Lillian's dressing table, where more girls hovered. Marion had to smile at how her extra years seemed to awe them.

Lillian jumped up and hugged her. "Is this too much rouge?"

"Yes."

"Are you sure?"

"You're heading toward a bridal suite, not a bordello."

Lillian's school friends convulsed with laughter, and she told them, "Go away."

They sat alone a moment. Marion said, "You look so happy."

"I am. But I'm a little nervous about . . . you know, tonight . . . after."

Marion took her hand. "Archie is one of those rare men who truly love women. He will be everything you could desire."

"Are you sure?"

"I know the type."

BELL FOUND ARCHIE ABBOTT in a gilded reception room with his mother, a handsome woman with an erect carriage and a noble bearing whom Bell had known since college. She kissed his cheek and inquired after his father. When she glided off, stately as an ocean liner, to greet a relative, Bell remarked that she seemed pleased with his choice of bride.

"I thank the Old Man for that. Hennessy charmed the dickens out of her. She thinks this mansion is extravagant, of course, but she said to me, 'Mr. Hennessy is so marvelously rough-hewn. Like an old chestnut beam.' And that was *before* he announced he's building us a house on Sixty-fourth Street with a private apartment for Mother."

"In that case, may I offer double congratulations."

"Triple, while you're at it. Every banker in New York sent a wedding gift . . . Good Lord, look who came in from the great outdoors."

Texas Walt Hatfield, longhorn lean and windburned as cactus, swaggered across the room, flicking city men from his path like ciga-rette ash. He took in the gilded ceiling, the oil paintings on the walls, and the carpet beneath his boots. "Congratulations, Archie. You struck pay dirt. Howdy, Isaac. You're still looking mighty peaked."

"Best-man nerves."

Hatfield glanced around at the elite of New York society. "I swear, Hennessy's butler looked at me like a rattlesnake at a picnic."

"What did you do to him?"

"Said I'd scalp him if he didn't head me toward you. We gotta talk, Isaac."

Bell stepped close and lowered his voice. "Did you find the body?"

Texas Walt shook his head. "Searched high and low. Found a shoulder holster that was probably his. And a boot with a knife sheath. But no body. The boys think coyotes et it."

"I don't believe that," said Bell.

"Neither do I. Critters always leave something, if only an arm or a foot. But our hound dogs turned up nothing . . . It's been three months . . ."

Bell did not reply. When a smile warmed his face, it was because he saw Marion across the room.

"Everything's deep in snow . . ." Texas Walt continued.

Bell remained silent.

". . . I promised the boys I'd ask. When do we stop hunting?"

Bell laid one big hand on Texas Walt's shoulder and the other on Archie's, looked each man in the eye, and said what they expected to hear. "Never."

UNFINISHED BUSINESS

Bugatti at the Train Station

Isᴀᴀᴄ Bᴇʟʟ ғᴀsᴛᴇɴᴇᴅ ʜɪs ᴄʟɪᴍʙɪɴɢ sᴋɪɴs ᴛᴏ ʜɪs sᴋɪs ᴏɴᴇ ʟᴀsᴛ time and dragged his sled up a steep slope that was raked by wind-blown snow and slick with ice. At the top stood Kincaid's castle. Before he reached it, he stopped to peer at a halo of electric light several hundred yards away that marked the checkpoint of armored vehicles where German soldiers guarded the road that led to the main gate.

He saw no sign that they weren't huddling from the storm and resumed his climb, veering toward the back of the castle. The loom-ing structure was a testament to Kincaid's resourcefulness. Even in defeat, he had managed to salvage enough to live in comfort. Towers flanked the ends of a great hall. Lights where the guards and servants lived shone at the bottom of the far tower. A single window lit in the near tower marked Kincaid's private quarters.

Bell stopped in the drifts beside the ancient walls and caught his breath.

He took a grappling hook from the sled, twirled out a length of knotted rope, and threw it high. The iron grapnel was wrapped in rubber and bit quietly onto the stone. Using the knots for handholds, he pulled himself up to the edge. It was littered with broken glass. He cleared an area with his sleeve, pulling the glass toward him so it fell silently outside the wall. Then he pulled himself over the top, retrieved the knotted rope, lowered it inside the wall, and climbed down into the courtyard. The lighted window was on the second floor of the five-story tower.

He worked his way to the thick outer door and unbolted it, leaving one bolt engaged so the door wouldn't swing in the wind. Then he crossed the courtyard to a small door in the bottom of the tower. Its lock was modern, but Van Dorn's spies had ascertained the maker, allowing Bell to practice picking it until he could do it blindfolded.

He had no illusions about an easy arrest. They had almost caught Charles Kincaid eighteen years ago, but he had slipped loose in the chaos that wracked Europe at the end of the World War. They had come close, again, during the Russian civil war, but not close enough. Kincaid had made friends on both sides.

As recently as 1929, Bell thought he had Kincaid cornered in Shanghai, until he escaped by coming as close as any criminal had yet to killing Texas Walt. He had no reason to believe that the Wrecker was any less resourceful five years later, or any less deadly, despite the fact that he was now in his late sixties. Evil men, Joe Van Dorn had warned with the grimmest of smiles, don't age because they never worry about others.

The lock tumbled open. Bell pushed the door on oiled hinges. Silent as a tomb. He slipped inside, closed it. A dim paraffin lamp illuminated a curving stairway that led to cellars and a dungeon below and the Wrecker's apartments above. A thick rope hung down the center as a handhold to climb the steep and narrow steps. Bell did not touch it. Stretching from the roof to the dungeon, any movement would make it slap the stone noisily.

He drew his pistol and started up.

Light shone under the door that led to the Wrecker's apartment.

Suddenly, he smelled soap, and he whirled toward motion that he sensed behind him. A heavyset man in servant's garb and a pistol in a flap holster at his waist had materialized from the dark. Bell struck with lightning swiftness, burying the barrel of his pistol in the German's throat, stifling his cry, and knocking him senseless with a fist to the head. Quickly, he dragged the man down the hall, tried a door, found it open, dragged him inside. He slashed drapery cords with his knife, tied the man hand and foot, and used a knotted cord as a gag.

He had to hurry. The guard would be missed.

He checked the hall outside Kincaid's door and found it empty and silent. The door was heavy, the knob large. Bell had learned that Kincaid did not lock it, trusting to the walls, the outer door, his guards, and the German solders who blocked the road.

Bell pressed his ear to the door. He heard music, faintly. A Beethoven sonata. Likely on the phonograph, as it was doubtful the radio penetrated these mountains. All the better to muffle the sound of opening the door. He turned the knob. It was not locked. He pushed the door open and stepped inside a room that was warm and softly lit.

A fire flickered and candles and oil lamps cast light on bookcases, carpets, and a handsome coffered ceiling. A wing chair faced the fire with its back to the door. Bell eased the door shut to avoid alerting the Wrecker with a draft. He stood in silence while his eyes adjusted to the light. The music was playing elsewhere, behind a door.

Isaac Bell spoke in a voice that filled the room.

"Charles Kincaid, I arrest you for murder."

The Wrecker sprang from the wing chair.

He was still powerfully built but looked his full sixty-nine years. Standing slightly stooped and wearing a velvet smoking jacket and eye-glasses, Kincaid might have passed for a retired banker or even a university professor were it not for the scars from his miraculous escape from the Cascade Canyon. A shattered cheekbone flattened the left side of his once-handsome face. His left arm ended abruptly just below his elbow. His expression mirrored his scars. His eyes were bitter, his mouth twisted with disappointment. But the sight of Isaac Bell seemed to invigorate him, and his manner turned mocking and scornful.

"You can't arrest me. This is Germany."

"You'll stand trial in the United States."

"Are your ears failing with age?" Kincaid mocked. "Listen closely. As a loyal friend of the new government, I enjoy the full protection of the state."

Bell pulled handcuffs from his ski jacket. "It would be easier for me to kill you than bring you in alive. So keep in mind what happened to your nose last time you tried to pull a fast one while I put the cuffs on you. Turn around."

Covering Kincaid with his pistol, he clamped one cuff around his whole wrist and the other tightly above the elbow of his maimed arm. He confirmed that Kincaid could not slip it over the protruding joint.

The sound of the cuff locking seemed to paralyze Charles Kincaid. Voice anguished, gaze dull, he asked Isaac Bell, "How did you do this to me? The German Geheime Staatspolizei intercept everyone that comes within twenty miles of my castle."

"That's why I came alone. The back way."

Kincaid groaned as he abandoned all hope.

Bell looked his prisoner in the eye. "You will pay for your crimes."

The music stopped abruptly, and Bell realized that it had not been a phonograph but an actual piano. He heard a door open and a rustle of silk, and Emma Comden glided into the apartment in a stylish, bias-cut dress that appeared sculpted to her curves. Like Kincaid, her face revealed the years, but minus the scars and the bitter rage that ravished his. Her lines of age, her wrinkles and her crow's-feet, traveled the route of smiles and laughter. Though tonight her dark eyes were somber.

"Hello, Isaac. I always knew we'd see you one day."

Bell was taken aback. He had always liked her, before he knew she had been Kincaid's accomplice. It was impossible to separate the spying she had done for the Wrecker from the men he had murdered. He said coldly, "Emma, fortunately for you I have room for only one or you'd be coming with me, too."

She said, "Rest easy, Isaac. You will punish me by taking him from me. And I will suffer for my crime in a way that only you could understand."

"What do you mean?"

"As you love your Marion, I love him . . . May I say good-bye?"

Bell stepped back.

She stood on tiptoe to kiss Kincaid's flattened cheek. As she did, she slid a small pocket pistol toward Kincaid's cuffed hand.

Bell said, "Emma, I will shoot you both if you pass him that gun. Drop it!"

She froze. But instead of dropping the gun or pointing it at him, she jerked the trigger. The shot was muffled by Kincaid's body. He went down hard, landing on his back.

"Emma!" he gasped. "Damn you, what's going on?"

"I cannot bear to think of you dying in prison or executed in the electric chair."

"How could you betray me?"

Emma Comden tried to say more, and when she could not she turned beseechingly to Isaac Bell.

"She hasn't betrayed you," Bell answered bleakly. "She's given you a gift you don't deserve."

Kincaid's eyes closed. He died with a whisper on his lips.

"What did he say?" asked Bell.

"He said, 'I deserve everything I want.' That was his worst belief and his greatest strength."

"He's still coming with me."

"The Van Dorns never give up until they get their man?" she asked bitterly. "Alive or dead?"

"Never."

Emma sank to her knees, sobbing over Kincaid's body. Despite himself, Bell was moved. He asked, "Will you be all right here?"

"I will survive," she said. "I always do."

Emma Comden retreated to her piano and began to play a sad, slow rag. As Bell knelt to hoist Kincaid's body onto his shoulder, he recognized a melancholy improvisation on a song she had played long ago on a special in the Oakland Terminal, Adaline Shepherd's "Pickles and Peppers."

Bell carried the Wrecker's body down the stairs and out the tower door and into the snow. Across the courtyard, he opened the single bolt he had left in place, pushed through the massive gate and along the wall to where he had left the sled. He strapped it into the canvas litter, put on his skis, and started down the mountain.

It was a somewhat easier run than the long, brutal slog across the valley, three miles of steep but regular slopes. And though the snow fell thicker than ever, navigation was a simple matter of going downhill. But, as Hans had warned him, the slope tilted suddenly much more sharply for the last thousand yards to the village. Tiring, starting to lose control of his legs, he fell. He got up, righted the sled, and got close enough to see the railroad station lights before he fell again. Back on his skis, the sled upright, he descended the last two hundred yards without incident and stopped behind a shed a short way from the station.

"*Halt!*"

A man was watching from the doorway. Bell recognized the trench coat and high officer's visor cap of the Geheime Staatspolizei.

"You look straight out of vaudeville."

"I'll take that as a compliment," said Archie Abbott. "And I'll take our friend to the baggage car." He wheeled a wood coffin from the shed. "Do we have to worry about him having enough air to breathe?"

"No."

They heaved Kincaid, still wrapped in the litter, into it and screwed the lid shut.

"Train on time?"

"It takes more than a blizzard to delay a German railroad. Got your ticket? I'll see you at the border."

A halo of snow whirled by a rotary plow in front of the train sparkled in the locomotive's headlight as it steamed into the station. Bell boarded, showed his ticket. Only when he sank gratefully into a plush seat in a warm first-class compartment did he realize how cold and weary he was and how much he ached.

Yet he reveled in a powerful sense of joy and accomplishment. The Wrecker was finished, run to ground for his crimes. Charles Kincaid would kill no more. Bell asked himself whether Emma Comden was sufficiently punished for helping him by spying on Osgood Hennessy. Had he let her go scot-free? The answer was no. She would never be free until she escaped the prison of her heart. And that, Isaac Bell knew better than most men, would never happen.

An hour later, the train slowed at Mittenwald. The conductors came through loudly warning passengers to have their papers ready for inspection.

"I came for the skiing," said Bell, when asked by the border guard.

"What is this 'luggage' in the baggage car?"

"An old friend crashed into a tree. I was asked to accompany his body home."

"Show me!"

Soldiers armed with Karabiner 98b rifles snapped to attention in the corridor and trailed closely as Bell followed the border guard to the baggage car. Archie Abbott was sitting on the coffin. He was smoking a Sturm cigarette, a nice touch Bell admired, as the Sturm brand was owned by the Nazi Party.

Abbott did not bother to stand for the border guard. Gray eyes cold, face a mask of disdain, he barked in flawless, curt German, "The victim was a friend of the Reich."

The guard clicked heels, saluted, returned Bell's papers, and shooed away the riflemen. Bell stayed in the baggage car. Half an hour later, they got off at Innsbruck. Austrian porters loaded the coffin into a hearse that was waiting on the station platform, accompanied by an embassy limousine. Both vehicles flew American flags.

An assistant chargé d'affaires shook hands with Bell. "His excellency, the Ambassador, sends his regrets that he couldn't greet you personally. Hard to get around these days. Old football injuries, you know."

"And half a ton of blubber," muttered Abbott. President Franklin Delano Roosevelt, grappling with the Great Depression, had defanged the obstacle of Preston Whiteway's reactionary newspapers by appointing Marion's old boss Ambassador to Austria.

Bell laid his hand on the coffin. "Tell Ambassador Whiteway that the Van Dorn Detective Agency appreciates his help and give him my personal thanks . . . Wait one moment!"

Bell took a delivery label from deep inside his jacket, licked the back, and glued it on the coffin. It read:

VAN DORN DETECTIVE AGENCY

CHICAGO

ATTENTION: ALOYSIUS CLARKE, WALLY SISLEY,

MACK FULTON

• • •

IT WAS A RAW, cold morning in Paris when Isaac Bell disembarked from his train at the Gare de l'Est. As he waved for a taxi, he paused to admire an elegant blue-and-black Bugatti Type 41 Royale. Touted as the world's most expensive car, it was beyond any doubt as graceful as it was majestic.

The Bugatti swept silently to the curb in front of Bell. The uniformed chauffeur jumped from his open cockpit.

"Bonjour, Monsieur Bell."

"Bonjour," said Bell, wondering, Now what? and regretting he had left the German automatic in his bag.

The chauffeur opened the door to the luxurious passenger compartment.

Marion Morgan Bell patted the seat beside her. "I thought you'd like a ride."

Bell got in and kissed her warmly.

"How did it go?" she asked.

"It's done," he said. "By now, Joe Van Dorn has his body on a cruiser in the Mediterranean. In two weeks, it'll be in the States."

"Congratulations," Marion said. She knew that he would tell her all when he was ready. "I am so happy to see you."

Bell said, "I'm so happy to see you, too. But you shouldn't have gotten up so early."

"Well, I'm not entirely up." She opened the top of her coat to reveal a red silk nightgown. "I thought you'd want breakfast."

The car pulled swiftly into the traffic. Bell took Marion's hand. "May I ask you something?"

"Anything." She pressed his hand to her cheek.

"Where did you get this Bugatti Royale?"

"Oh, this. I was having a nightcap in the hotel bar last night and

the sweetest Frenchman tried to pick me up. One thing led to another, and he insisted we use his car while we're in Paris."

Isaac Bell looked at the woman he had loved for nearly thirty
years. "'Sweetest Frenchman' is not a phrase to assure a husband.
Why do you suppose this old gentleman was so generous with his
automobile?"

"He's not old. Quite a bit younger than you are. Though hardly in
such good condition, I might add."

"Glad to hear it. I still want to know how you charmed him into
giving you his car."

"He was a hopeless romantic. The dear boy actually got tears in
his eyes when I told him why I couldn't go with him."

Isaac Bell nodded. He waited until he could trust his voice. "Of
course. You told him, 'My heart is spoken for.'"

Marion kissed him on the lips. "Is that a tear in your eye?"